SCHATTENGEIST

A Gothic Romance

Book Two of
THE WITCH AND THE RINGMASTER
Duology

RICHELLE MANTEUFEL

Contents

Reader's Note — VI

Epigraph — VII

1. A Haunting Woman — 1

2. A Haunted Man — 4

3. At the Masquerade — 13

4. When the Portrait Cried — 23

5. Kheima Part 1 — 31

6. Vincenzo Estate — 35

7. To Tame a Ghost — 45

8. Power at Great Cost — 55

9. Kheima Part 2 — 64

10. It Wasn't Loneliness — 67

11. In the Vampyre Garden — 74

12. Sweet Nothings — 81

13. Kheima Part 3 — 88

14. Make Me a Warlock! — 89

15. No More Masks   96

16. Ghost, Witch, and Sovereign   105

17. To Court a Ghost   115

18. A Waltz in Witching Hours   124

19. This Paranormal Fever   133

20. Kheima Part 4   141

21. A Wager It Is!   147

22. The Dragon Prepares   156

23. The Demon Descends   162

24. Master Vincenzo's Madness   171

25. The Gilded Noodle   178

26. Kheima Part 5   184

27. Come With Me!   188

28. Research   196

29. Kheima Part 6   206

30. Enlightened Spring   208

31. The Manna of Hope   218

32. Kheima Part 7   227

33. Burning Summer   231

34. Storming Fall   242

35. Kheima Part 8   251

36. Looming Winter   254

37. What Madness is Love   263

38. Kheima Part 9   270

39. The Witch's Duel   274

40. Kheima Part 10   281

41. Valley of the Shadow   289

42. House Vincenzo Part 1   296

43. A Dragon's Promise   300

44. House Vincenzo Part 2   305

45. Breaking Kheima   309

46. Breaking Demons   317

47. House Vincenzo Part 3   325

48. Mine   333

49. Lady Vincenzo   336

50. No More Secrets   342

51. First Yule of Many   347

Twenty Years Later   353

52. Autumn Comes to Kheima   354

The End   359

Acknowledgements   360

Also by Richelle Manteufel   362

READER'S NOTE

This title's prequel *Waldgeist: A Gothic Tragedy* presents the witch Yasmin's POV and takes place a decade prior. *Schattengeist: A Gothic Romance* is written with dual POV, although the ringmaster's perspective is prominent.

Schattengeist features several references to the main characters' history and life events in Waldgeist. It is the author's strong recommendation that all readers finish Waldgeist before reading this novel.

Please enjoy Manteufel's Victorian Gothic later-in-life romance.

Love born in autumn gales is no less sweet than passion wrought in spring. It is, however, far more fierce.

R. M.

Frédéric Chopin Étude Op. 25, No. 11 "Winter Wind"

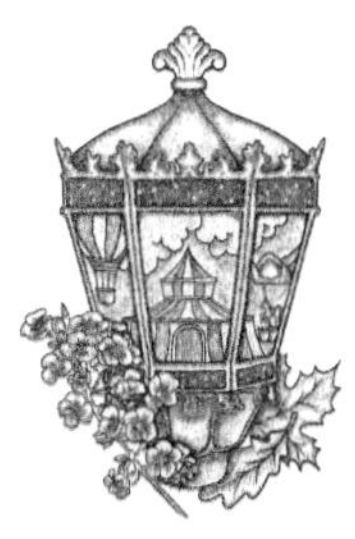

1

A HAUNTING WOMAN

Narrator

A PIERCING GASP BROKE the silence, but the specter would not yield.

She advanced. One long, bare, vein-lined foot, then the other. The hungry silver discs of her irises mirrored moonlight, swallowing up her minuscule pupils. A translucent veiling covered her head in mourning swaths.

Ripples of curled hair clad the victim's neck, nestled in a high velvet collar. The ghost's dark lips parted in a sigh. Her sorrow seized the frightened woman's heart and tugged upon its fragile strings. That first moment, she did not fear the frigid specter. She felt only sorrow. Pity. *This woman died of love,* she thought, her face paling beneath the specter's silver gaze. *She picked up her cross and carried it to the bitter end.*

The haunt's melting sadness hardened into something deadly. The victim shrieked. She scrambled back, clawing the dirt. The stern face of a tombstone halted her frantic retreat. "Please! I have a family! God above, preserve me!" Her fingers fluttered the sign of the cross as prayer after prayer dropped like lead from her lips.

And still, the ghost advanced. Her shrunken pupils clapped onto her victim. *I've sacrificed everything. My true love. My soul. To relent would be foolish weakness,* the ghost mouthed soundlessly.

A chilling melody followed the specter's white heels. It clung to her as a looming shadow, inevitable darkness unfolding from her wake. Coils of pale-blue light whispered from her gown. Distant children's voices lifted in song,

> "Mothers, let thy children know,
> Wounded is the sun.
> Fathers, tend thy fields of woe,
> Spring shall ne'er come."

All glory, laud, and honor to Anmut, the Queen of Kheima: Winter Evermore, the Tearspring of Eve, Ebonwood Sorceress at His Right Hand.

All glory, laud, and honor to Rothadamas: First Prince of Eden, the Ebonwood Dirge, Guardian of the Flaming Sword, and Keeper of the Knowledge of Evil.

The specter lifted one languid hand. Snowflakes drifted from her fingertips. Incantations poured from her lips—dark wine from a cursed chalice. They anointed the sobbing woman, turning her flesh white as salt, her eyes sunken and gray. As she stilled, collapsing in a heap of velvet and satin bows, she faded away.

The ghost-witch turned and floated back to the gates, humming. Her fingers twitched until she raised them to her mouth and bit them to make them still. The wild shimmer in her eyes dulled but slightly; her driving hunger was not satisfied.

The Thinning of the Veil drew near. *I must be ready,* she thought. Whatever the cost, she would be ready.

Winds of impending autumn summoned leaves from the cemetery loam. They rattled in harsh condemnation of the hunting ghost. Rushing at her face, they would fain have battered it, but there was no flesh to batter. Only a beam of winter moonlight breathing the shape of a lovelorn witch, beautiful and bitter, radiating a passionate restraint that barely contained her power.

Lightning in a cracked bottle.

2

A Haunted Man

Sergio

"I loved Erbanhue. I loved him with a strength of adoration that frightened me."

Clapping the well-worn diary shut, I abandoned it on my nightstand to pace the room.

Moonlight streaked the windowpanes. The night wind sang through the trees, rocking them to and fro. The dim tendrils of my gothic garden tapped the sides of the mansion, as if requesting entry. I paced the echoing bedchamber—through my morning room, through the paneled hall, and from thence to my office. Stopping at the massive window to fumble with the curtain's tassel ties, I threw the drapes open wide. Unfastening the latch, I hurled the window ajar, too.

I needed air.

Now, you must understand, Sergio Vincenzo is no imbecile. Nor was I a naïve, young whippersnapper at forty-one revolutions 'round the sun. I saw it in her eyes more times than I could tally: I knew Yasmin Lange had loved me. That caustic, callous witch strove to mask her worshipful devotion, but her intentions fell short of her object with laughable prevalence. Hard and sharp as nails in most situations, her quick-witted mind was rendered soft and malleable once the tempest of love capsized it.

Yasmin Lange.

Once that dark veil was torn from my eyes, I remembered her in all her sterling glory. She was not pretty—at least not by common standards—but she was fascinating. Her soft, ash-blonde hair reflected starlight. How stunning she would be standing here now, absorbing the night-wing glow, coiling her bruised fingers around a blue rose, enchanted to seduce and captivate my soul.

A charming notion, but I did not have a soul for her to capture... it had been stolen by something else. Something that had claimed her soul, too. Despite this profound handicap, she had loved me.

Despite it all—poverty, cruelty, demonic possession—Yasmin had loved me.

How *could* a woman bereft of her soul manage to love? I could not do it, even when I tried to. Yasmin bound her heart close beneath a wreath of thorns, yet loved in spite of herself. She knew what hopeless love would cost her, and for a long time, she was unwilling to pay the price. In the end, she relinquished her silent vow never to love and paid the price in full.

How did Yasmin succeed where I had failed? And why had she loved *me*, in God's almighty name?

Muttering bitter reproofs, I clasped my hands behind my back. I had used her. Bruised her. Treated her so harshly. I'd plagued her heart out with impolitic cruelty. I'd lavished my attention on other women just to poke the sleeping beauty tucked deep within the wells of her silver-gray eyes—eyes that had only flashed to life when envy or intellectual stimulation woke them. I'd liked few things better than kindling that fire in her stern expression. It was akin to working a subtle, very particular magic. Magic that only I had the power to wield.

Then the Witch would rise to form a wall around the shifting sea of the beauty's emotions, calling Yasmin back into her fortress. An impenetrable domain of dark-humored solitude that no one was permitted to visit, much less abide in.

No one but the Ringmaster.

And where was the ringmaster now? That potent, vengeful, fiery fellow whom Yasmin so tenderly nicknamed *the Dragon?* Ah! Well, the reflection before me displayed him still, though Sergio Erbanhue Vincenzo might be more advanced in years, with softer lines about his broad form and crow's feet flexing in time to his "cattish grin." And just last evening at supper, my sweet Lillias was kind enough to point out a string of silvery hairs sprouting at her dear father's temples, and she *laughed.*

At the thought of my beloved daughter, I crossed back to the bedroom and snatched up the diary again. After Yasmin's rushed funeral, Aislinn found me musing at the gravestone and handed this journal to me without a single word. Several months passed before I could bring myself to read it, for I knew with absolute certainty that Yasmin the Piquant would *not* paint a flattering portrait of me, preferring to devote every stroke to the truth, refusing to omit a single fault. Despite my preening confidence, I was well aware that I was chock-full of faults.

Her diary revealed more than I dared to dream. Her profound depth, her *spirit* itself, drove me to distraction with such intensity. It was a wonder she didn't run stark, raving mad! The first time I read her book through,

I wept like a child. For it was Yasmin Lange and no other who rescued my darling Lillias from the mouth of a demon. And it was Yasmin Lange who had rescued *me*, a damned warlock, from the same.

What wouldn't I give to catch her by her languid hands and tell her, with that seething draconian force that she so loved, what her sacrifice meant to me? What wouldn't I give to erase my cold, roguish kiss from her lips with a kiss bearing all my awakened passion? What *wouldn't* I give...

For I considered all I had achieved to be hers, from the foundations of House Vincenzo itself to the fortune settled upon my estate, all earned from a decade of success with my thriving Fair of Phantoms. A Fair that Yasmin's influence on me had inspired.

No longer the Fair's ringmaster, but still its owner, my precious Fair of Phantoms flourished like the tended flora of a hothouse. Lillias Vincenzo should inherit a small fortune. Well-groomed, self-important lads rode in from miles around seeking to court my daughter. (I frequently envisioned beating them away with my cane, a contemplation as relieving to my feelings as it was amusing.)

Yes, my Lillias and I were happy, free, and flourishing, but in eternal debt to Yasmin Lange. That realization haunted me like a ghost. *What wouldn't I give?*

"Papa?"

I jolted out of reverie, donning a cheerful grin. "My lady!"

Lillias grimaced at me. Her pert brown curls glistened "good morning" in merry daylight. The tinkle of cutlery rattled from the tea tray as the maid placed it on the table. "You're seldom grim-faced, Papa," Lillias reprimanded me. "And you're always reminding me that we must live every day with joyful purpose, as we are not guaranteed tomorrow. Must I remind you of your own admonishments?"

"You needn't remind me, Lady Goose," I snorted, seizing the knife and dashing a vulgar portion of butter over my bread. "I was merely considering whether I ought to have the attic cleared out. It's a musty mess, and I couldn't find a young elephant standing in it if I put it there myself."

Lillias chuckled, a smile dressing her charmingly freckled face. Her cinnamon eyes shone with affection. Eighteen years had softened her mischievous grins into the coy charm of maturity, but I loved my little woman all the more for it. "Papa, I've been meaning to speak with you regarding your sober demeanor of late. It's not like you. I know you must feel lonesome by and by, since I'm often absent." She slyly scooped an extra portion of sugar into her tea, as if I wouldn't notice, seated directly across from her. "I fear I've grown popular thanks to that coming-out ball you insisted I endure."

With a boisterous laugh, I flicked my napkin at her. "*Endure?* What provoking nonsense dost thou utter, Lillykins? You adored that party, and you well know it!"

"I did, I did!" Lillias grasped her beige napkin to assault me in return. "I knew that would wake you up a little. Anyway," she retrieved her napkin and tucked it back into her lap, "you used to visit the surrounding estates often, and go hunting with the gentlemen of our acquaintance. You were the life of the ballroom at every seasonal party. Why don't you go out more and amuse yourself, as you used to?"

I shrugged. Swooping for a scone, I lathered it with clotted cream and jam. *Ah, the English certainly know how to eat.* Sailing from America had been no picnic, but the victuals alone were worth it. "Common company

bores me of late. We say the same dull things around the same dull people."
I crammed a voracious bite into my mouth, chasing it down with a swig
of coffee, which I still preferred over tea. "'Tis far better to spend my free
time improving the estate." Leaning closer to the window, I considered the
statues in the Oak Park and the fountain I had ordered for the Vampyre
Garden—the gothic garden of my dreams brought to life. It thrilled me
every bit as much as House Vincenzo itself, another fever dream ascending
from the bowels of pure fancy, glittering with circus-scene stained glass
and dragons for grotesques. One of the staircases shifted depending on
the time of day. Cherrywood paneling gleamed from the walls, flooring,
furnishings, and beamed ceilings, allowing for globes and sconces of red,
blue, green, or purple to cast weird shadows into candlelit corners. Color
and gloom reigned alike, contrasting in a breathtaking, maddening dance.

As one might surmise, the town thought me off my rocker.

Lillias sighed, clinking her teaspoon against her cup with the air of a
weary saint. "You ought to leave improving the estate to *me*, infuriating
man! I am the lady of the house. It should be my delightful task and my
honor to look after the house and delegate, as is only proper. *Do* let me
have the keys, Father."

I sighed, rolling my eyes at the maid. "Well, Eloise? What say you? Shall
the king bow out of his throne and relinquish the crown to his heir?"

"If that would please you, sir." Eloise murmured with a blush. She
usually blushed when I addressed her, as did half the female staff.

"Ha! So pristinely polite; so utterly useless! See what I mean, Lillykins?"
I swept my mustache clean and tossed my napkin over Eloise's shoulder.
Accustomed to my abrupt playfulness, she caught it without comment or
a smidgen of surprise crossing her face. "Proper society says such a lot," I
recommenced, "but for all their lingual graces, they blow naught but hot

air in one's ears and expect one to respond in kind. Blarg! Humph! Let me clear the lawns instead. I'll enjoy it more."

"Oh, dear." Lillias rose from the table, straightening her lace sleeves and shaking her glossy head. "For years, I have feared the day when my sweet, jolly Papa would become a sour, grumpy Scrooge. And now the day has come."

Lillias swept across the polished dining room to me. She stood behind me and passed her arms around my neck, blessing my bearded cheek with a kiss. "What have you there?" she asked.

"What have I where?"

Reaching down, her dark curls tickled my neck as she withdrew a small, worn book peeping from my coat pocket. Yasmin's journal. My face caught flames; I didn't remember bringing it down. "You're reading this again?" she questioned, her nimble fingers caressing the tattered cover. Leaning forward, her inquisitive eyes sought mine. I avoided her perceptive gaze. "She was a good writer," I mumbled.

"No wonder you're feeling blue." Lillias kissed me again. "Papa dearest, you've done whatever you could to honor Yasmin's memory. You started a charity in her name, you toast to her memory on her birthday every year, and you ordered that beautiful monument to her in our garden. She will not be forgotten—you have ensured it. Please, don't dwell on the sorrows of the past."

She proceeded to walk away from me, still in possession of Yasmin's book. An unaccountable, unavoidable impulse launched me from my dining chair and after my daughter, recapturing the purloined diary and securing it in my pocket. "Oh no, you don't. This is mine." I turned away from Lillias's anxious expression.

A cold set of fingers brushed the back of my hand, currently shielding the book. They tried to pry the diary loose. "Don't, Lillias!" I snapped.

"Don't *what,* Papa?"

I looked at her. Lillias stood by the cupboard; she hadn't stirred an inch. She was not near enough to touch me. I grunted, rubbing my hand, which yet retained that brief, ice-cold impression. "Never mind. I have work to do. Don't disturb me unless it's urgent."

"Very well, Papa." Two tiny creases formed on her forehead as she stared at me.

Office-bound, I stormed through the grand room and up the main staircase. I tried not to think about that strange winter-born touch; surely I had imagined it.

Lillias was right. I was letting this diary haunt my head. Yasmin was gone, and with her, that tormented plane of ghastlings, ghouls, spirit-children, and demon-spawn. *What have we to do with them now?*

And the hideous irony of Yasmin's sacrifice? The most tragic truth of all?

If she hadn't been so supernaturally stubborn—if she had only accepted her love for me much sooner, and thus been goaded to action against Rothadamas from the beginning—she might not have needed to buy our freedom with her life. In the end, 'twas her own apathy that destroyed her. She did not lift a finger against her curse until it was too late.

I hated it.

The truth tasted so bitter that I yearned to harden my heart against her. It would be far easier on my conscience to simply blame her and move on with my life. My rich, comfortable, easy life, with my charming daughter.

Alas, it was beyond my power to achieve. Heaven above knew I retained rough mannerisms aplenty. But now, these sore qualities lay buried in the shadowed alcoves of my heart, rather than basking in its pulsing center. Yasmin's witchery had removed my heart of stone and replaced it with a heart of flesh. And I missed her.

By the gods! I missed her more than I'd ever guessed possible. I wanted her to tease me and call me vain, and challenge my superstitious fancy, and admire my theatrical tastes. Only after she was taken from me did I fully treasure her stimulating presence.

3

AT THE MASQUERADE

Sergio

AFTER OBSERVING, DIRECTING, AND delegating, I hoisted my cantankerous self outside to meditate by Yasmin's monument.

Following her death, I ordered an angelic statue carven in her likeness and clutching a stained-glass lantern. The lantern's multihued light embraced a poem carved directly opposite. My sterling witch loved poetry, but she couldn't compose it to save her life. She'd tried once or twice on our evening walks over the circus grounds, and they were so lamentable that I laughed openly—yet she appreciated them with the passion of a seasoned scholar. Such a hearty, smooth-sailing naiveté suited her to perfection. It fitted her just as well as her silver, silk dress and the five-pointed star she took to wearing in her last days. A gift from Aislinn, if memory served me well.

A beautiful woman, Aislinn Bláthnaid, I mused as I stood before the monument, arms crossed. *I daresay the most beautiful woman of any I ever knew. But I never trusted her any further than she could be tossed.*

I'd trusted Yasmin. I sorely missed her candor. She never flattered me or told me pretty lies. One reason I took to shunning ballrooms was the flagrant lies—the worst of them flaunted from the ruddy lips of widows who panted after my American fortune, exotic appearance, and mysterious history.

I could only pray that the rumor I'd started might serve me well. *The Lord of House Vincenzo is a hapless spendthrift and a shameless drunk.* The best rumors bear an element of the truth. I *did* enjoy spending my fortune on anything and everything that pleased me, and I *had* been a drunk once.

Chuckling at the sordid memory, I rubbed my bearded chin. I could afford to laugh at my past now. Yasmin's monument flickered beneath the shifting light of a coming storm. "Well, Yassy. Did you think to amuse yourself by startling my senses after a decade of tranquility? Did you think you'd see me squirm, shiver, and shout? Try again! Your haunting performance is as tremulous as your singing voice."

Silence. The wind answered me, whistling autumnal tunes in my ears, but nothing else stirred. I shifted my weight. I lashed her stone twin with sardonic smiles. "Come, Anmut." My voice dropped lower. "Come out and play with your Dragon."

Nothing.

I straightened and left the Oak Park, striding to the fountain in the Vampyre Garden. I was far from done with teasing her, but I wouldn't risk the staff or Lillias catching me talking to statues. Leaning against the puckered basin, I tugged at the ends of my mustache and stared at my aging reflection in the ripples. The figure of a gaping vampyre woman leered above me, bent as if scooping the dark water into her fanged mouth. Last year, I instructed my butler to dye the water red, just to amuse me. The maids were not amused.

Would Yasmin still think me handsome? I couldn't help but wonder. I used to catch her staring at me with such raw, pensive emotion that I was obliged to compile a menacing statement or two to bring her back down to earth. She'd have harmed herself up there on the high rope if she divided her attention like that. And I couldn't abandon my post in the ring; I had my own work to do. An intolerable distraction, that Yasmin Lange, both to herself and to me. Both in life, and now in death.

"Sergio."

A melting ice-drop of a whisper. A snowflake's touch of breath. *Her* voice itself, resounding in my ear.

Unclenching my fingers from the basin, I drew in a breath, slowing my pounding heart. I tucked my hands in my pockets, donning a mask of impenetrable sangfroid. I had not one sovereign inkling of the condition of her spirit; she might be here to curse me. "That you, witchling?"

"Wherever I am... Whatever I become..."

Breathy and decidedly paranormal. Yet denial was out of the question. It was she. I could never imagine such a thrilling echo. I couldn't invent the breath of a winter banshee wafting against my earlobe, as if she stood there at my elbow where she'd often liked to be. Something about having her at my side gave me profound satisfaction, too. Her poise drew forth my confidence. I might conquer the world so long as the Witch Anmut blessed the endeavor.

However, I never dared to tell her so. She'd have become even more enamored with me. I'd feared she might lose her sanity. A crucial part of her had been broken, and the fracture let in things that shouldn't have been there. Things the common world would never notice, Yasmin tended diligently in her heart.

And unless *I* was losing my sanity…

She still loved me. Her spirit sounded depressed, not enraged. It fell to me, then, to be rather firm with her once more. Besides, she liked it.

"Yasmin." Extracting my hands from my pockets, I held them up in a supplicating gesture. "Appear before me now. I know you're here, but I need to *see* you to scold you properly. I need your caustic, plain little face, and your cold eyes dashing curses at me. Show me where and what you are! No matter what manner of creature *He* turned you into, I am not afraid."

Though I waited for quite some time, alternating between coaxing and threatening declarations, she either *could not* or *would not* appear. Not another word did that ghostly voice utter. Huffing, I whirled on my heel and stomped back to the mansion. I'd never permitted her to lead me by the nose before she died, and I'd be hanged if I let her take the posthumous reins.

What *did* I see in her, after all? Why invite her to haunt me? A plain, peppery, boney Germaness who only allowed me to order her about because she wanted to imitate me. "Obsession is not love," I proclaimed aloud. Her diary itself would agree with the sentiment.

And yet, my chest ached when I thought of it. Of *her.* Her diary continued to appear in my possession no matter how many times I locked it away. Her obsession haunted me, and re-reading her book was my sole alleviation.

"Papa, no! Wear the red one."

Groaning, I removed my black waistcoat to sling it above the wardrobe door. "I'm not a ringmaster anymore, Lady Goose. I don't care to dress like one."

"Don't be silly, Papa! It's not as if 'ringmaster' is stitched anywhere on your clothes. Just think of it as a nice bold waistcoat with stunning embroidery, which is precisely what it is."

"I've gained weight, Lillykins. It won't fit."

"Yes, it will. Stop making excuses like a fretting child." Lillias slipped between the oversized wardrobe doors and emerged with my "glory days" vest, securing it over my shoulders and buttoning it for me. I'd worn it to perform at my last show with the Fair of Phantoms. "You look so handsome in red. It's the perfect contrast to your blue eye, and it brings out the touch of ruby-red shimmering in your mahogany eye."

I chuckled. "Well, thank'ee. Thou flatterest me, Lillias."

My daughter paused from smoothing the awkward bow at my neck. She regarded me thoughtfully. "Yasmin used to say that very phrase."

One brow scaled my forehead. "You remember that?"

"Of course." Lillias's gentle smile put me at ease. "That's the phrase she employed to shield herself from any compliment ever fired in her direction, no matter how small or elegantly worded it was. She craved attention, yet hated open praise. What a walking contradiction she was! It's no wonder that she died a spinster, poor thing. If *I* were a man, I wouldn't have had the slightest notion how to handle her."

I "humphed" and batted her hands aside to finish the final touches myself. Lillias pursed her lips as she handed me my dragon-themed mask. Her next words grazed my ears so softly, I could barely make them out. "Did you love her, Papa?"

My mouth dropped open. "Love?" I managed to echo. My voice cracked on the impossible word, and I coughed, thumping a palm against my chest to alleviate the sudden tightness in my lungs.

"There's no shame in it if you did. By your own admission, she was fascinating, and certainly the most talented woman in your circus. You still talk about how smart she was."

I untied the bow again, retying it with forced haste. "We were friends. Nothing more."

"But did you *want* more?"

"... No."

Lillias accepted my response without complaint. Donning our masks, we departed my dressing room to the landing, descending the staircase to meet the carriage outside. Sullenly, I reasoned within myself: *No. I did not want more back then. It was simply not attainable, as long as she hid herself within the fortified castle of her mind and kept pointing her barbed spears at all intruders.*

But now, at long last privy to Yasmin's most intimate thoughts... I struggled with a yearning planted far, far too late in the season of frost.

The Gardeners were holding a masquerade ball.

It was a marvelous October evening. The setting sun flashed orange against the bronze leaves and lanterns decking the Samhain halls. Despite its brilliance, I longed for my mansion, but I pushed the childish yearning firmly aside. Lillias was right to be worried about me. I used to bask in these events, delighting my acquaintances with my practiced storytelling and exciting former life. I should bathe in the glow of the regal society that accepted me despite my vague bloodline, not shrink from it. Indeed, the sheer privilege of being a rich, handsome bachelor was not lost upon me... until recent months when Yasmin's journal outshone everything else, until the very ballrooms were full of shadows in comparison.

Glancing around the Gardener estate, I chuckled at the pagan influence of the ornamentation. Yassy's friendship with Aislinn had given her a strong admiration for such frills. I caught the feverish malady from Yasmin, and thus elevated my Fair of Phantoms with paganism's highly satisfactory imaginative touch. Yasmin had harbored the taste of a true artist... she just never knew what to do with it. I wondered how she would have turned out with a proper education. *Ah, the realms of possibility.*

Snapping back to the present moment, I realized I'd been staring stupidly at Lord Gardener for a full five minutes, not contributing a single statement of value to his soliloquy. I'd also downed a third cup of punch without noticing what it tasted like. Not a whit daunted, that fine fellow blathered on in his dull, preachy fashion. "Onward Christian Soldiers" darted suddenly into my head, and I barely restrained a smirk. *Conversation with His Lordship is much like marching to war, indeed.* Once upon a time, I'd relished opinionated sparring with my fellow mansion lords. But my heart persisted in waging war with my head, pulling Yasmin into the focus of my mind's eye. It was terribly distracting.

I looked for Lillias. Her (woefully overpriced) golden slippers soared over the marble floor as she twirled in the arms of a brainless sop. I entertained a growl. *Well, I shall have to give in one of these days, and it would be cruel to rob her of innocent diversion.* For the moment, I indulged in brief but intense glaring.

Once I managed to escape said battle of wits with our host, I flirted with a wealthy, unattached widow or two before sauntering outside to clear my mind.

Yasmin Lange. Try what I might, I couldn't get her out of my head. I might well prove my own rumor tonight and render myself gloriously drunk. Perhaps that would do the trick?

Memory roiled within my skull, battering my brain like a ship lost at sea. I gripped the balcony rails as I thought of the May Day festival when we danced. The night before, I'd given into the temptation to kiss her, starved for the results of such a brazen experiment. I'd expected her to scream and slap my face. She did not. Her coolness surprised me, but I refused to drop my own level-headed mask, just as she never for an instant removed hers. The experiment resulted in a stalemate.

And yet, her pupils had *devoured* me. They'd flexed so wide and black, I'd felt absorbed by them. I thought they would expand into starving monsters and swallow me whole. If I were a different sort of man, I might have taken to my heels and avoided her ever after. That was something else I'd never admitted aloud, and certainly never to her—that sometimes she was terrifying.

Perhaps I was drowning in this intolerable melancholy because Yasmin's soul had somehow enmeshed itself with mine. She'd tucked herself into my spiritual being as comfortably and naturally as a child winding a favorite blanket around her shoulders. Despite the holes, tears, and imperfect stitching, little Yassy was perfectly content to keep her shabby old blanket. Even in death, she would not be parted from it.

Was it fear? Did she think if she discarded it, she would never find another? A newer one? One that would keep her warm, serve her better than the faulty patchwork?

As I pondered, my gaze fixed upon a dark, sturdy tree below the balcony. It was already bare, but the red, orange, and yellow coils of autumnal vines crept over its trunk, reaching for the branches that bent and swayed. It struck me strange, how *lively* that tree looked despite the lack of wind.

A shadow lurked behind the lantern-lit tree.

The flutter of a silvery train caught my eye. I squinted against the lantern's glare. The tall, boney shape of a woman in translucent blueish-white peeped from behind her natural safeguard.

She wore a veil over her face. Despite this impediment, her silver eyes flashed from behind its meager folds like two hungry stars seeking for planets to devour. Her long, bare hands gripped the bark of the tree with such vehemence that I discerned gashes in the trunk, even from up in the balcony.

I was leaning against the railing. I started up with a sharp breath. If there had been a centimeter of doubt, the wild waves of ash-blonde hair negated any chance of misidentification. There was only one woman I'd known with hair like that—ghostly before she was even a ghost. "Yasmin!" I yelled.

Warm with the Gardener's famous punch, my excitement displaced my astonishment. In my heart of hearts, I knew she'd been there all the while. Trying to reach me. I yanked off my top hat and waved it at her, thrilled as a schoolboy. "Yasmin, you God-forsaken relic of a decade-absent witch! Don't lurk; you know I cannot abide lurking. Come up here with me and see the masquerade!"

She did not answer. Melancholy woe stirred in her hungry eyes. It stung my conscience. *That unfortunate woman.* What had she suffered? What was she *yet* suffering, while I pranced about my blasted manor like a pompous king?

The spirit of Yasmin gradually absorbed the fact that *I could see her.* Shock, longing, and resentful wrath flashed across her thinly-veiled face.

I was so glad to see those silvery eyes, I didn't consider what state of mind their owner might be entertaining. I frowned, leaning over the railings again to observe her better. Pity would not be appreciated, I knew. Directness would be best, as frank and honest as if she were yet alive. "Yasmin? You've shown yourself at last, so you must have come to spend a little time with your Dragon. Won't you come up?" I removed my mask, just in case she wasn't *certain* it was me—although the rarity of my mismatched irises ought to have placated her.

I had no intention to beg. I'm unfamiliar with bowing and scraping. However, I was coming dangerously close to it, for the specter would not budge. The eerie light from her eyes continued to flash and froth like storm clouds. Yes. She knew me; that much was certain.

"Yassy." I tried one last time, stepping back and holding my arms open wide. "Come to me. I'm not afraid. You know that."

At last, her pale arms fell from the tree trunk to her sides. With a piercing, otherworldly cry, the spirit flew to me. Flew *through* me.

A shuddering gasp seized my throat. Ten long years of wrath, ruin, ice, and thorns. Of torture, of blood, of enslaving children and stealing the souls of countless innocents. Of gathering more proxies for the forest demon and aiding Him in His demented creations. A thousand wretched sensations nearly rent my soul in two. I clutched at my chest, my heart flailing against it. And I knew.

This was not Yasmin. Not as I remembered her. This was a ghost-witch. Forlorn, enraged, and dehumanized, a mere fragment of the woman I once knew. The shadow of her spirit. *Ein verfluchter Schattengeist.*[1]

"What has that demon done to you?" I whispered.

---

1. A cursed shadow spirit.

4

WHEN THE PORTRAIT CRIED

Sergio

IN THE CIRCUS, I sought the comfort of long walks over the grounds while smoking my pipe. Now retired, I practiced the same rambling in the mansion or on the grounds of the estate. I found perpetual motion calming, even if I achieved nothing meaningful beyond physical exercise.

The hallways of the third floor suited my wandering habit nicely. My heavy boots summoned moans from the creaking floorboards, stirred drafts through listless corners, and confronted leering shadows from the various candelabrum. I might pace at my leisure with no fear of getting in anyone's way—not that the lord of the mansion had to think about such things. It's a precious odd thing, you know, growing up two steps away from poverty, then suddenly refitting a manor to your own tastes, hiring staff, and not having to pander to anyone else's comfort or convenience.

As I awaited the mansion's reconstruction, I managed to locate the likenesses of some of my relatives and submit them to local painters. The result: The third hallway lined with the regal glowering of deceased relatives, so respectfully framed and lighted that nothing more could be desired in a handsome English homestead. I couldn't be *absolutely* freakish in my decorating, I supposed; there had to be some traditional touches somewhere. Sergio Vincenzo had to look like he cared, even if he didn't... sometimes.

Truthfully, I regarded these portraits with the utmost indifference. I'd never known any of them well and had hardly spoken face-to-face with one-third of them. But family was still family, even when we liked them best in oil paintings.

To digress, I was "minding my beeswax," trudging along and staining the hall with the incense of tobacco smog, when the torches framing my portraits flickered and went out.

Indecent of them.

I walked to the nearest one to hold my hand near it, expecting to detect a draft. Something I had missed when I reviewed the original hall.

A woman's low, persistent sob trickled from behind the walls. I flinched. Across from me, the largest portrait (a scowling likeness of my father) had the preternatural audacity to water up at the eyes and *leak tears*. From what few memories I retained of my father, the concept of him crying was mirth-inducing... Or would have been, if the hairs on the back of my neck weren't raised. I took a step closer, then a step back again, unsure whether to touch the portrait or not, to make certain those tears were real.

Quite disturbing, to be sure. Yet it was thrilling, too. My face flushed from the excitement of it. *A haunting!* My own circus mansion, possessed by spooks. *Delightful!*

The sun was not yet down. Bronze light penetrated the window and fell upon the portrait. I blinked, and the patch of light hitting my father's stolid right hand suddenly formed the shape of a lantern.

A man's voice, the voice of my father perhaps, sternly commanded: *"You must light the lantern!"*

Once I blinked again, the lantern was gone. Father's voice had stilled. "Fascinating," I murmured. I finally pawed the portrait, but the tears had dried up. Not a trace of the supernatural remained. "Ho-hum." Ghosts scared me not one whit. Had I not been plagued by a witch for several years? What were *ghosts,* then? If Yasmin didn't frighten me, I doubted the imprints of spirits could score that admirable objective themselves.

Considering the lantern-shaped light, I frowned. I knew from reading Yasmin's journal that she was prone to hallucinations—at least, she thought she was. Did I now suffer the same malady? Was it catching? I prayed not. It would be too bad for poor Lillias, on the cusp of courtship and wedlock, to be stuck at home tending her mad father.

Turning on my heel, I marched back down the hallway. Again, the withering whimper of a woman crying tickled my ears. Yasmin (were it indeed her) sounded desperate—lost—at her wit's end. It was the despairing yet enraged cry of someone who had made every conscionable effort to accomplish *something*, and had been met with failure at every turn.

A wave of sympathy smote my heart. "I hear you, spirit. Please tell me why you're crying. What have you to say?" I ventured, spreading my hands open wide to indicate friendly salutations.

The sobbing ceased, but nothing showed and nothing stirred. A chilly, ominous silence descended. My hands fell back to my sides. "Well, I'll wait. But *do* show yourself to me the moment you find it convenient. House Vincenzo could use a bit of stirring up, and a ghost would be just the thing."

So declaring, I pocketed my hands and strode away, whistling.

Afterward, every lantern I could possibly contemplate arrested my attention. But there was one I found particularly suggestive, or rather a section of them.

The grounds at House Vincenzo boasted of specific artistry—a tailored vision that only a ringmaster from a Fair of Phantoms might think to display. Nearest the house was the Vampyre Garden. Only the darkest and most forbidding plants in black, purple, burgundy, and dark green were permitted to grow in tangled flower beds and up wrought-iron fences. It was meant to look a tad chaotic, so the gardeners were instructed to pull weeds but otherwise let it do what it wanted to. I had no use for anything *tame.*

Beyond the garden, oak trees provided the main attraction with stepping-stones leading my park wanderers from one weathered trunk to the next. Hence, its obvious title, the Oak Park. Before six of the largest trees, I ordered six statues, each wielding a stained-glass lantern.

Every statue held a precise meaning for me. The first was carven in the image of a tiger with the lantern handle clenched between its carnivorous teeth. Vainavi, of course. Anyone who followed my circus career knew that

I loved her as fervently as I loved my own flesh and blood. She passed on after a long and celebrated life, and to be frank, I've yet to get over it.

The second, a carousel horse with the lantern planted between its front hooves. The *Phantom Horses* yet lived, but the carousel's rotation creaked and cranked in the most appalling way (or so I'd heard). I had contemplated retiring the horses to the Oak Park, but the expense required to ferry them over would be nothing short of an outrage. I wasn't certain I wanted it *that* much. I *had* coveted Yasmin's old caravan that much... although I secreted it in the back of the Park, loath to stir up curious comments. I didn't want anyone else to touch it.

Anyhow, once the carousel broke down entirely, perhaps I'd send for the lead horse. It would look wonderful in the foyer.

The third: a stern dragon with a flaming-red orb tucked in its maw. "What vanity!" you say. Yes, a vain piece, but stunning nonetheless. Since my youth, I'd harbored an insatiable fascination with fire.

The fourth: a graceful dancer clothed in a long, flowing skirt. Inspired by my prize contortionist and dancer extraordinaire, Arusi. I often pondered what became of her. She had quit my Fair one day with neither a word of explanation nor farewell, and no one had laid eyes on her since. I trusted she was well; her talent and training could take her anywhere she wanted to go.

The fifth: a curly-haired child holding a clutch of flowers in her little hands, with a small yellow lantern hanging beneath them. My own Lillias, naturally. I paused at this statue to sigh over bygone days, as a good parent should. There were a few cloudy, blurry years in the circus that, for some reason, were very difficult to recall with clarity... regardless, my sweet girl had been blessed with a happy childhood.

And the sixth statue, last but far from least. The angel bearing the most ornate lantern of all. This one boasted rich colors and rosy portrayals of circus tents, wild creatures, forest gambols, and crystal orbs. This statue served as Yasmin's monument, although the likeness was unfortunately not quite to satisfaction. I endeavored again and again to obtain a portrait of my sterling witch, only to at last arrive at the conclusion that she'd never had one made. What *were* her parents thinking? According to Yassy's journal, they were good people. Yet children ever idealize their parents; I could not trust her filial affections implicitly.

Still, of the two monuments resurrected in Yasmin's honor—the angel and the poem opposite—I believed she would like the angel best. There was a sort of serene irony about it. Yasmin had not been guilty of angelic qualities while she'd lived, but death had touched her waxen forehead with its crowning glory, and sacrifice ripened the richness of her closed heart until it blossomed wide. Both to myself and to Lillias, Yasmin Lange was an angel.

On dim evenings beset with clouds and angel tears *drip-dripping* from the sky, down the mighty oaks, and lending a delicate shimmer to the angel statue, some artistic impulse drew me into the Oak Park and forced me to stay until the shower ended. I had more plans for it yet, but even in its fledgling state, my Park thrilled something buried deep in my layers of soul. It was the art of simple elegance, I ventured, left to thrive in freedom. Precious few manor lords had the sense to employ simplicity, preferring to cull every millimeter of their estate until it resembled meticulously combed, stiff pomade hair.

The next night, I stood at the angel monument, ruminating on when the portrait had cried. Yellow, orange, and purple light slanted through the lantern (my butler lit all six of them at dusk, no matter rain or shine). I stared at the ornate circus imagery. *What a park for a haunter's playground! Yasmin, won't you come?*

It was nothing, really, just a whim springing up from a lonesome, dark night. Yet the frigid breath that blew over me and sent a shudder through my bones made me wonder if I'd summoned her. Air caught in my throat, and I stared more fixedly than ever at the angel, waiting to see it blink. To beckon me. To come to life.

I was beginning to feel foolish when I swore I felt a soft, cold hand slip into mine. I was no ninny, but I jumped, rubbing my hand against my side. "Is that you, witchling?" I asked aloud, attempting to soothe my galloping heartbeat with the sound of my own voice. "Don't tease a fellow. Come out and greet me properly, as a lady should. You showed yourself once before—why not again?"

Her crisp, laughing echo rippled from deep in memory's cove: *Circus performers are not ladies!*

"Right, right. Forgive me." Still speaking aloud, solely for my own benefit, I grinned and headed back into the house, flexing and rubbing my shocked hand. It buzzed as though a flash of winter lightning had seized it and turned my blood.

I was either a haunted man, or I was going mad. Perhaps both. Either way, I continued to ensure that the Park lanterns were lit every single night, rain or shine.

5

KHEIMA PART I

Yasmin

IN THE PAST, IT had cost me many agonizing minutes of prayer and supplication to enter Kheima. No more. The demon's realm was just as much my own as it was *His*.

I waved my hand in a careless motion. My surroundings collapsed and reformed to expose the winter forest. Pale-blue snowflakes rode chariots of mournful wind. In the center of the black-ice woods rose the immense Twisted Tree, the throne of my fallen master, Rothadamas. The throne's guard, the Creature of Many Eyes—formed by moonstones—approached me with a mien of affectionate reverence. But I had no patience for it; I turned it away. I wished to speak with *Him*.

Rothadamas sensed that I sought His presence. He melted into view in a soft white glimmer, morphing from His ebony hunting form into His angelic aspect. Oversized wings laden with precious gemstones dragged along the frozen ground. I drifted to His side, dropping a quick curtsy. We exchanged telepathic words in rapid German.

"Greetings, Anmut. Where hast thou been?"

Unflinching, I stared into His azure eyes and stark white pupils. The forest demon preferred clear, precise communication. *"My diary. I need it back."*

"Ah. I presume your Dragon has it? Otherwise, thou wouldst not be so enraged."

"I am not angry."

A low growl rattled from His white throat. I hardened my gaze. Knowing my place and my power, I would not be intimidated. *"I am aware that it seems such a small matter to you, I might as well be reporting upon the weather... which has not changed since the Garden faced God's wrath, leaving it a frozen forest. But I left my book to Aislinn, and why she handed it to him, I cannot venture to guess."*

That was a lie. I *could* guess. It must have been pity. Aislinn had loved me, and she wanted the ringmaster to know the love he had scorned, once I was far beyond his reach. That charming Celtic witch sought to be my vengeance. My brows knitted together in a frown. *I don't need pity. If she knew how influential I've become since my death, she'd know that I pity* her.

As I pitied all the living.

I severed the morbid flow of my thoughts, vexed with myself for letting Rothadamas hear more of them than I'd intended to expose. Indeed, our wretched minds were intertwined as one. Lies were worse than useless. I couldn't hide anything from Him.

"Am I correct in supposing that you wish to go and fetch it yourself?" Rothadamas hummed, static annoyance thick in His psychic tone. *"You might send one of the children on your behalf. 'Tis beneath thee to waste thine energy on such a paltry errand, Anmut."*

My focus wandered to the impassive slate of His face, where His mouth slanted across it like a fine crack in marble. Handsome, yet alien and ice-cold. Residual pulses of static tensed in my specter-skull. *"I proved my unshakable loyalty to You over no less than a decade,"* I reminded Him. *"I have tested my strength, and I know I can manifest my spirit to walk the Earth in secrecy, seen only by the mortals I choose. The children will not be as subtle, as cautious, as I shall be."*

I paused, pruning away inconvenient emotions, gathering my thoughts so I only communicated the essentials. *"You have graciously allowed me autonomy in recent years, but for this, I prefer to have direct permission. I shall accomplish no other task beyond that which I have described: regaining my journal."*

And my dignity.

Scathing, annoying, disruptive Erbanhue! You haven't changed. Yet, it makes me love you just as much as I ever have. Why did I lose my black heart to a scoundrel, just as the storybook damsels always did? I openly scorned them in my youth. Yet there I was, committing the same dreadful blunder: loving someone who, by most accounts, did not deserve it.

"We can't help who we love," Rothadamas purred. I cursed myself. This telepathic connection He and I shared would be the Second Death of me. To my relief, He looked amused instead of angry. I'd caught Him on a good day. *"Since your journal means so much to you, my charming immortal, then you may go."* The Demongod's lifted cadence dropped. *"But return soon. I have an errand for you in mine brother's realm that cannot wait for long."*

"Master." I bowed my head and left without delay.

Sergio Erbanhue Vincenzo, if you utter one teasing word regarding my personal, private contemplations, I swear to Rothadamas that you shan't live to see another day.

Despite my snapping rage, beneath the scarlet leaves of wrath there bloomed a blush-pink petal—an aftergrowth of passionate desire. I longed to hear my ringmaster's voice again. If I could hear but *one* word... How my dead heart would rejoice! Even if it raised the monster called Limerence from its slumber, a fleeting moment of happiness would be mine, and no other's.

6

Vincenzo Estate

Sergio

I woke in a cold sweat.

Many were the dreams I'd suffered of the fate of Yasmin Lange; sore were the emotions battling for dominance. Wiping my weary face, I staggered from the curtain-closed bed and trudged to the balcony doors, flinging them open wide.

The light trickle of rain refreshed me. Trees moaned and flailed in the rising wind. I leaned against the railing to force a calming breath or two.

House Vincenzo bore a modest title for so grand a home. My reasoning came from a place of subconscious disbelief—I struggled to absorb the fact that it was *mine*—six stories high with elegant railing, trim, balusters, and spiked gable tops and gable ends. Ivy stained by autumn's kiss curled over ebony siding. Stained-glass lanterns matched the windows, casting their fae glow upon the covered porch. Enduring and masterful, but with the artistic touch of finer circus imagery so dear to my covetous soul. *Is that mine?* I asked myself almost every time I entered House Vincenzo.

"Is that… is that mine?" Yasmin asked, pointing at the caravan with a shaking hand. My heart warmed in my chest as I gazed at her wide-eyed wonder. Had I bought her a castle by the sea, her bafflement could not have been greater.

One glance around her dirty little cottage, and I knew I could give her something better. So, I picked a fight with Janet.

Blows and botheration! I'd just managed to banish Yasmin's memory to the back of my brain, and there she was again. I was still scolding myself when the lantern behind me flickered and went out.

I sighed but didn't think much of it. It was a windy night. However, this incident was followed by the soft shuffle of bare feet approaching me from behind.

Turning, I expected to see Eloise or Brandon, my butler. Beholding neither person—and indeed, no one at all—my baffled gaze strayed to the wet footprints on the floorboards. One at a time, new ones were birthed beneath my very eyes, marching steadily toward me. But no one was there.

I see. Another haunt commences. An amused grin lifted my lips. Nevertheless, that delicate imprint with its long, slender toes and the high arch of a ballet dancer struck me familiar. And well they should! I knew them from the time they were fourteen years treading this earth. I'd seen them wrapped in nothing but dirty rags, or scrambling precariously across the high rope, or tucked in the showy material of aerialist slippers. I saw them dance in silken stockings one fair May Day; I perceived their waxen owner as she dipped them in wild streams, rinsing the blood and the many bruises, massaging their callouses with sober patience.

Yes, I knew those feet. They were most welcome. *Still, I must be cautious.* Yasmin Lange made no ordinary spook, and House Vincenzo was no ordinary haunter's mansion, with its bizarre themes and shifting staircase. I'd amused myself by adding all manner of trap doors, secret hallways, and a couple passages leading to nothing but an extravagant piece of art. If you toyed with the grandfather clock enough, you'd unlock the hidden door to the speakeasy. Yasmin was not used to mansions at all, let alone mine; she might get lost.

And she was... not really human.

It fell upon me to call her humanness forth from the icy dark of Kheima, where it waited, buried and slumbering deep. Did she even know where she was, or who? Did she truly remember me, or was her spirit drawn to mine like a blind moth to a flame? According to Yasmin's written word, I was once a warlock (though unaware of it for many years). Then was it not possible that I retained charismatic powers over my former protégé? I never planned for her to become my disciple, but Fate shaped her for the role and would not countenance refusal.

What an awkward situation. She didn't just haunt *me*, you see. We haunted each other in equal measure. Put *that* in your pipe and smoke it, Catherine Crowe[1]!

As had become my habit, I opened my hands to her. "Yasmin, thou chilly gray witchling! Have you come to inspect the house? Rather precocious of you to do so without asking my leave, by-the-by. But since I owe you my life, I won't protest. Can you touch me, spirit?"

Ignoring me (or so it seemed), Yasmin's footprints skirted 'round my circumference and darted to my nightstand. A translucent blueish-silver hand slipped from the ether. Snatching up the diary, the hand vanished,

---

1. A famous paranormal investigator who wrote about hauntings and mysterious phenomena in her book *The Night-Side of Nature* (1848).

and the defrosting footprints turned upon their ghostly heels as if to leave. Her journal coasted in midair.

"No, you don't!" I crowed. With one swift stride and a persistent tug, I had the precious book back in my possession. "So, you came to rob me of the one volume I treasure most." I chuckled, delighted by the opportunity to rouse her. Irritation would do the trick, if anything would; no tender kisses for the Fair of Phantoms witch. "What tender memories you've recorded of your Dragon! I wouldn't part from them for all the money in the world, Yassy."

Yasmin's spiritual face flashed from the dark, a splice of lightning. Her bright eyes had tiny pupils, sharp as specks of ice. Dark lips parted in a short, plaintive shriek, painful to my ears. She either *would not* or *could not* speak, but I read it from her countenance as plain as day: *"Give me back my diary."*

I shook my head at her and smiled.

Despite my outward composure, I realized I was risking much. An angry ghost-witch was loosed upon me in my own house. And for what purpose? It was feasible that the forest demon sought to recapture my soul, binding me to Kheima again and ever after. In which case, I should run and not look back.

That being said, I'd never tamed a ghost before. The prospect filled me with preemptive glee... all the more so since the ghost was Yasmin. *No, there shall be no running,* I decided right then and there.

Assuming a humble expression, I knelt at the edge of the ornate carpeting and held out my hand again. "Yasmin. We are friends; let us be friendly."

For a long time, nothing happened. I felt the breath of her ice-cold presence upon my face, but little else. Finally, a hesitant, long-fingered hand brushed against mine. I swallowed a gasp from the winter shock seizing my frame. It was like a December gale wrought in the shape of a woman's hand and breathing against my skin, but I knew by its touch that her invisible hand was quietly surrendered to mine.

As I straightened, the shape of her hand bloomed forth. Its pale-blue glow grew upward and outward, flushing her entire body out of the ether. Yasmin's shadow spirit stood before me, gazing into my face with ethereal maleficence.

She was terrifying. Her eyes, hideously intense and stripped of nearly all human emotion, pierced mine from behind her transparent veil. Her dark lips were coarse and chapped. Shadowed wells pooled beneath her eyes. And below the slender curves of her emaciated neck, her upper chest bore the scar of Rothadamas. A frail circle with an *X* through it.

Grief churned like a frothing cauldron, threatening to boil over and ruin our first real moment together. A sardonic remark rose from the chaos of my mind: *"Well, at least you were never a beauty to begin with."* I wanted to tease her, but I forced it back. That was ugly possessed-Erbanhue thinking, and it needed to be purged. It would not do to provoke her in earnest. I hoped to soothe her instead, to see if I could raise a smile from beyond the grave. "At long last, you've come to me," I murmured, soft and solicitous. "Now I can speak the words that have weighed on my heart for a decade, Yasmin Lange."

Her spectral attire floated as if tossed by waves. The bodice was old-fashioned, cut low to expose her ample décolletage. (I quickly directed my pupils elsewhere.) Her long hair, loose and wild, drifted around her delicate face in silver serpentine motions. Paranormal power lurked in her strange eyes. I swore I sensed it crawling over my skin, looking for a break in it. Sniffing for my blood. Searching for a point of entry.

Anyone who fears being confronted by a witch ought to pray that they never face a *ghost-witch*. It set my own teeth on edge, and I was no coward.

Inwardly, I sneered at my nerves and bled them dry. *Courage, man!* "I was not kind to you, Yassy." I trusted that using her nickname might recall her to more pleasant days. "I wounded you with my insolent disregard; I only considered my own comfort, my own success. Even in the single capacity of your employer, this was unacceptable. And later on, when we became friends, I never apologized to you for the abominable way I'd behaved. I had been possessed by *Him* at the time, but that was no excuse, since you never treated me as I treated you. You were kind to me when I did nothing to deserve it. You looked after me and kept me company. Thank you, Yasmin, and I'm sorry. So damnably sorry."

I had no idea if my sincerity reached her. She stood motionless, her lips pinched tightly together, and didn't drop one word.

The silence rattled my hardened nerves. So, I prattled on, "You tended to me when I was ill, even when I drank myself into oblivion like the careless fool I was. And when you noticed me pacing the grounds late at night for lack of sleep, plagued with anxiety over how to raise my troupe from obscurity, you walked with me and wouldn't leave my side until I went to bed. We'd watch the sun rise together, talking about anything we liked. You distracted me from my worries with sarcastic yet earnest cheer; you amused me with your rapid wit. You advised me with a keen wisdom far beyond your years. And for all this, I repaid you with envy and scorn..."

I paused, brows creasing thoughtfully as I debated whether to proceed. To risk a full confession that might anger her. *Might as well. In for a penny, in for a pound.* "My demon-led self schemed to rise above you, to crush you beneath my boot and serve at the demon's right hand myself." I instinctively moved to lift her veil, to impress my own humanity into the reflections of her inhuman gaze. But my fingers passed through the veil. "Can you forgive me, Yassy?" I pleaded.

Her lips parted as if to speak.

I eagerly leaned forward. To again hear that plaintive voice with its stern German accent would delight me almost beyond reason. Instead of cherished words, she gave only another sigh.

"Can't you speak?" I asked.

The spirit bowed her head, indicating a sober negative.

I sighed, too, but at least she understood me. "No fear, Yassy. I shall remedy that in due time. For now, come! I'll show you the house. Won't you keep me company through the night, just as you used to?"

A hesitant nod. The *suggestion* of a smile from the depths of those unsettling eyes. Or did I imagine it?

Nevertheless, my broad chest swelled with joy. I stamped through my private rooms first, describing how I'd elected to decorate each, proudly displaying my personal library secreted near the winding staircase. Next, I trudged through the many bedrooms and washrooms of the third floor (tiptoeing past Lillias's suite), then to the billiard room, armory, tearoom, circus memorabilia, etc. comprising the second floor, and from thence to the opulent grand room, living rooms, dining hall, kitchen, wine pantry, breakfast room, and drawing rooms of the vast main floor.

I skimmed over the hidden speakeasy for the time being. *Yasmin was not overly fond of spirits*, I recalled with an internal guffaw at my pun. *Let's not risk ghost quips just yet.*

Specter Yasmin drifted at my elbow, silent as the grave that birthed her, wide eyes fastened on my face. A pale-blue snowflake drifted from her fluttering sleeve and melted against the heat of my arm. A childlike sort of amazement emanated from her incomprehensible mien. As if she couldn't really believe it was me.

"What do you think of your aged Dragon, then?" I questioned her, flexing my tattooed arms and grinning. "Do you approve of my lengthy locks?" I wore my black-mahogany tresses past my shoulders, gathered in a black, braided ring. "And the glints of gray at my temples, and in my beard? Am I not a distinguished-looking old gentleman?"

Again, no reply but that of her fixed expression. My imagination furnished the words: *You were always handsome, sir.*

I nodded gravely. "Just so! You'll be further pleased to know that my servants find me an amicable master, thanks to your success at purging the Kheiman dark." I beamed into her waxen face. "Just you wait and see, you witch! I'll render you the same service. And you'll surely stay with me, for House Vincenzo suits you better than any other estate on Earth. You must evaluate all the rooms and tell me which you like best. Name it, and it is yours." I stopped, uttering a short bark of a laugh; I was still a tad nervous. "Or point it out, then. Until you can speak."

At last, her attention flickered away from me and to the wall opposite, losing all prior focus. I felt she was seeing past me into the distant future.

Back in our circus days, Yasmin's emotional state was a mystery to everyone else—including herself—but no mystery to me. However, it was difficult to comprehend her in her present form. Not unlike a star, she floated in an atmosphere of frigid, lifeless serenity, brilliant but deathly to embrace. The ghost-witch seemed an unsolvable enigma, as she fondly believed herself to be when she was only a witch. *Che meraviglia!*[2] I liked it, though. I admired people who were challenging to read.

"I seem to recall that you like the color blue," I said, casting her one of my sidelong glances with a minuscule climb of the brow. "Would you like the blue bedchamber? Lillias calls it the Ocean Room."

Upon hearing my daughter's name, Yasmin's quicksilver eyes flashed back to me and latched onto my pupils, seizing hold and digging deep. "Yes,

---

2. How wonderful!

Yassy, you cured her of His curse, too. She's very well." I crossed my arms. "You'll be wanting to see her for yourself, eh? I've no objection as long as you swear to be discreet and not show yourself. I won't have you giving my daughter nightmares. In fact, 'twould be best if you promise *never* to reveal your presence. Once she's obliged to believe in ghosts, she may never sleep again."

Another small, hesitant nod.

At least I can tell whether she comprehends me or not. An irrepressible smile possessed my face. To tame a ghost! How to go about it, precisely? Delicious question! My blood quickened in my veins at the prospect. It would be better fun than planning gardens, that much was clear. I rubbed my hands together, anticipation firing through every limb. *Perhaps I'll write a book. Better take notes.*

Where should I begin? Surely the answer was taking one step at a time, and step one would be to crack open the box currently holding her speech captive. I just needed the key.

Was she afraid to speak to me? Was her spectral voice a curse to the ears, an ungodly shriek beyond mortals' ability to withstand without immediate descent into madness? I hadn't considered that. Yasmin was capable of shyness, especially around me. It might have returned in full force.

Theory the second: Having spent a decade in Kheima with no one to converse with besides a forest demon, she might have *forgotten* how to speak.

As if to confirm my theory, Yasmin's spirit exhaled another low sigh. A cloud of depressed turmoil hung about her translucent form like a cape. I suffered an impulse to slip my arm around her frail shoulders and hug her close; this, of course, I could not do.

A sudden memory granted me inspiration. I proceeded to hum "My Lady's Galleon," a song I'd dreamed up myself with Yassy's hungry, steely little optics in mind... not that I'd ever humored her with that knowledge. I'd simply sung it within her auditory range, allowing her to draw whatever meaning from it she entertained. She'd dubbed me "wily Erbanhue" for good reason, you see.

It had the desired impact, both then and now. The cloud of sadness lightened, and her spirit tilted its head in my direction with a *teeny* smile lifting the corners of her scarred lips.

She remembers.

Ah, music! The cure to many human ills—spirit ills, too, I judged it safe to say.

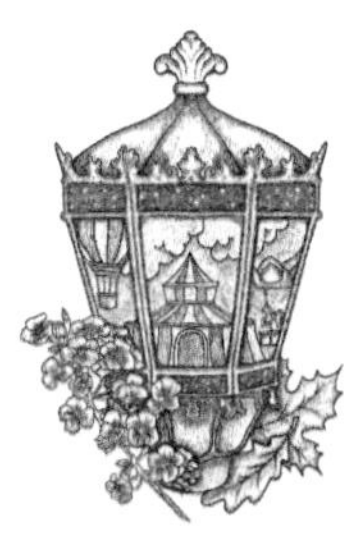

7

TO TAME A GHOST

Sergio

AFTER A FORTNIGHT ELAPSED with a ghost upon the premises, I came to the conclusion that ghostly Yasmin was a thing of beauty and a joy forever. If you didn't mind vacillating fits of mood, that is, born from causes known solely to herself. I remained indulgent with her, for I well imagined the evils Rothadamas had forced her to orchestrate on His behalf.

Most evenings, my blank-faced little Schattengeist appeared the instant the shadows lengthened in the grand room, darkening the face of the chiming grandfather clock. She'd flit about the premises in search of me, then latch herself onto my elbow and stay there as if affixed with hide glue. It annoyed me exceedingly, at first. I was used to complete and utter freedom, for Lillias had her own affairs to attend to—visitors to entertain in the drawing rooms, parties to plan, dresses to order, etc.—and we both liked to come and go with no interference.

Now, there was someone overseeing my every move. Even when I entered the washroom, I wasn't entirely sure she'd left me. She maintained the irritating ability to melt into the ether whenever she didn't wish to be perceived. Sometimes I *felt* her sulking and staring from afar, just far enough to avoid a scolding, refusing to allow me out of her frigid sight.

The first time I removed my jacket, waistcoat, and shirt in bathing preparations, I checked in the mirror several times, wary of her peeping from the shadowed alcove. Suddenly aware of her rudeness, she jolted away, white cheeks flushed and eyes as wide as I'd ever seen them. I laughed—I couldn't help it. "'Callous, changeful, and hasty creature,' I believe you once termed me," I called after her. "Why not take a look in the mirror sometime and see that very description echoed in your own praise? Oh, Yasmin, my little soul twin; how I missed thee!"

I sang as I gathered the implements to trim my beard. Of course, my butler could fulfill that office, but I liked to take care of some things myself. A man's got to have *some* privacy.

Lillias beamed from her seat at the dining table. "You seem happy again, Papa."

I smiled in response, cherishing the picture of my daughter's face over the tall red candles wafting cinnamon-berry hints into the air. Our new wine glasses sparkled with burgundy richness. "I was born to rule an English estate, Lillykins. A delightfully gloomy estate, touched by fae glass creations and candles ordered straight from Parisian masters." Inhaling the wonderful autumn perfume, I leaned back in my cushioned chair with a deep sigh of contentment. "I shudder at the memory of the passage here, but the temporary discomfort was well worth it."

"Yes. And your circus curiosities suit this manor, somehow." Lillias nodded in approval at the mantle over the enormous fireplace, clustered with various odds and ends from Fair of Phantoms devotees all over the world.

Even while preening in the consequence of my fortune, I yet marveled at my Fair's success. Twenty years ago, if my former fortune teller Madame Tola had assured me that I'd see Italy with Lillias at my side, host her débutante ball in Paris, then come *to live* in an English mansion refurbished and redecorated to my own taste, I'd have laughed that woman to Hell and back. *C'est pas possible!*

"That reminds me," I raised my wine glass to indulge in a deep sip, "I'm having some of the rooms rearranged and the Ocean Room reworked a bit. I'd stay out of there if I were you, dear."

"Very well."

I leaned back and stretched my legs, basking in the fire's crackling gleam. My chair slid rather too close to the fireplace, but the heat did not disturb me. All my life I'd been curiously resistant to extreme temperatures of either scale. Thanks to that, I sometimes incorporated fire into my tiger-taming demonstrations, for I was never burned by it.

Absently drumming my fingers against the tabletop, I wondered if Yassy was nearby. I found I couldn't always sense her presence if she kept her distance enough. It was enough to make a fellow abandon his own skin, the way I'd turn about and spy her lurking in a corner. Scolding her never did any good. It was clear she felt bound to me.

As I felt bound to her...

"Papa?"

I grunted. "Well? Papa is before you."

"Something happened today. While you were talking to Brandon about the Ocean Room."

It wasn't like my Lillias to skirt about the bush. She was blushing, too, winding her napkin between her hands, eyes burrowing into her laden plate.

"You've hardly touched dinner. Anything wrong?"

"It's about Ulysses Melbourne. He... he asked me if he could talk to you this Sunday afternoon. Just you."

Ah, Ulysses. The curly-headed lad who'd practically burst into a sweat the first time we were introduced. "Oh. I see."

Tilting my cup slightly, I stared into the burgundy solace shining behind cut glass. Well, I knew this day was coming, and sooner rather than later. Young bachelors flocked to my estate upon the excuse of "good hunting," pretending to be admiring *me* when I knew damn well they were casting sheep's eyes at my daughter. I grunted, seizing my knife and tracing it slowly along the edge of my plate.

The scrape of the blade against porcelain made Lillias flinch. "Please be kind to Ulysses, Papa. I like him."

"Oh! You *like* him." My eyes snapped up to her face, which made her blush all the more. "Is he as handsome as your storybook heroes?" I teased her gravely. "Should I be ashamed to show my face to this stainless Adonis?"

"Don't tease me!" She huffed with exasperation. "He's handsome, and active, and kind, and comes from a good family. You have every reason to like him and be *civil.*"

"Oh, do I now?"

She dealt me a withering glare. "Yes."

I cut our contest short with a chuckle. "Don't stare daggers at me, princess. Of course I'll be civil to your Ulysses. I *do* take issue with his pretentious name, but I suppose we must blame his parents for their lack of taste and not the man himself."

"It suits him. You'll understand when you know him a little better."

"All right." I twisted my partial scowl into an affectionate grin. "I trust you'll have the good sense to pick a gentleman, and not a scoundrel like your old man."

"If he's half as witty as you, Papa, I'll be satisfied."

I snorted. "Cease winding me about your pinkie finger and eat, girl! You'll wither away before my waking eyes."

She grinned, big brown eyes aglow, and shoved a most unladylike portion of beef into her mouth. We chortled with abandon—horrifying the servants, I was sure. Not that I gave a rat's ass about it.

Barging down the hall into the main library, I kicked off my boots with a *thud.* "Yassy?" I bellowed. "I've come to play, and I shan't stir from thence until thou hast shown thine silver face." I sat at the chess board, twiddling my thumbs.

I heard the soft flutter of pages as a book was closed. The spirit ventured into the firelight, shrinking away from its inviting warmth as if it was poison. "I've had a nasty turn tonight," I asserted, glaring at the chess pieces to vilify them. "It seems I'll have to play the wary old father and polish up my armory when Lillykin's fellow comes a-knocking. This Sunday, no less. I've less than a week to prepare a convincing, protective, eloquent speech. What say you, Yasmin? Have you a lingual contribution?"

I pinned her down with my stare. *Come on, Yasmin. Try to say something. Anything.*

My little Schattengeist merely stared back. She floated a foot or so above the floorboards, her starlight hair waving in an imperceptible wind. I squinted at her, leveling a critical look. "As you used to say, 'tell it not in Gath,' but I miss your voice. I miss your stoic remarks and the compilations of your acute vocabulary. You *seem* more peaceful now than when I first saw you in my bedchamber... but you still won't *talk* to me."

Slowly, the spirit raised one arm. Yasmin pointed at the book she must have been reading when I'd come in. Then, she pointed at herself.

"Your diary?" I guessed. "You require it back?"

She nodded.

"It's wholly necessary? You're not just angry that I've had ample time to pour over it? I agree that it was hardly prudent, but you see, it was all I had left of you—"

I cleared my throat, not eager to display the emotions rising in my quickening chest. She wouldn't believe them. Not at the moment. "Aislinn gave it to me, you know. I didn't think it was wrong for me to take possession of it, since your dearest friend thought it right. Though I cannot tell you *why* she passed it on to me instead of keeping it herself. She was a study, that Celtic sprite of yours! And I find most women as readable as textbooks in large print."

Yasmin shrugged her white shoulders, in a rusty, out-of-practice sort of way. I laughed. "It's all right, Yassy. I was only testing you just like I used to; I thought it would do you good. I'll get the diary and restore it to its rightful owner." *It's no inconvenience, for I've memorized it more thoroughly than my own tattoos.* Still chuckling, I left the library to gain the stairs three at a time and leapt back down, diary in hand. My knees protested such treatment. I uttered a groan, cursing myself for having misplaced my walking stick yet again.

Yasmin was waiting patiently, and she accepted my offering without ado. It vanished once it sank into the palm of her translucent hand. With a great heave and whistle of cool wind, her lips parted.

She spoke.

"Th-thank... Thank you. Sergio."

At long last, she stood before me and uttered my Christian name.

I was hardly used to it. A shudder weakened my limbs. *Don't be a ninny,* I scolded myself. "You may call me that, or Hue, or Dragon, or whatever you like most," I assured her. "I'll answer just the same. Doesn't make any difference to me."

Oh, but it does! My wicked intuition whispered. *You reacted physically to Sergio. There's a magic to your name on her preternatural lips, and don't you deny it.*

Yasmin sighed, faltering through another short sentence with great effort. "I should not... be here."

Well, that explained her vacillating manners, at least—coming so close to me only to dart away minutes later, then return to my side. I frowned. "As I've made it crystal clear that I *want* you here, Yassy, how can you utter such nonsense?"

Slowly, my ghost-witch raised her hand to cradle the side of my face. She spoke in a short, clipped fashion quite different from the flowing intensity I was accustomed to hearing from her. I wondered if she'd utilized her voice at all for the past decade. "You're daydreaming," she began. "With dark shadows under your eyes, you pace around at night. You've handled my diary so often... the ink is fading... I know these signs. You're... a haunted man." She withdrew the frigid breath of her fingers, though they did not bother me. "And only I... can be blamed for it."

I huffed, running a hand through my long hair. "Pshaw, woman! Stay. I *command* you to haunt me." Suddenly spying the dull bronze gleam of my old cane, I swept it up from the library corner, leveling the cobra's nose at her cold forehead. "Just look again. I've rendered myself paunchy, careless, and carnal in these affluent surroundings. It's dulled my spirit; it wants exercise. Your presence shall call forth the whetstone and sharpen my ambitions. What say you, Yassy? Won't you stay?"

To my surprise, the mantle of depressed feelings returned and hung heavy at her shoulders. I lowered the cane to the floor. "What is it?" I inquired, softening my voice.

"I do not... mean anything... to you."

I blinked, tapping the cane against the floor twice to signal her to continue. Imperceptibly, I shifted my weight on it to relieve my aching knee. *Old. Sergio Vincenzo, you are old.* I repressed a bitter, internal sneer.

Slowly but surely, her voice strengthened. "I amuse you, and you enjoy having me as your... sounding board. To hear your ideas and opinions echoed back to you. And now that I've come back... you're delighted that I might again fulfill my purpose. To amuse you."

Her clipped tone grew smoother and stronger the more she spoke. I tilted my head, flashing a faint, encouraging smile. *Yes, Yasmin! Let it go. Seize me by the hand and drag me through each wretched, torturous feeling. It shall make you well.*

She clenched her translucent fists. "If that's all I'm going to be to you, then I do not wish to stay." Her eyes narrowed. "Wandering the earth alone... unperceived by any other mortal... would be far more congenial to my feelings. I stay on *one* condition, Sergio Vincenzo, and one only. You must treat me as your equal and not your subordinate."

Pride swelled in my chest, culminating in a dazzling spark. "Excellent, Yasmin Lange!"

I thrilled at the shock betrayed by her softly parted, cracked lips; she did not yet comprehend how changed I was without the forest demon's touch, and how her independence gave me great satisfaction. I pointed the cobra handle at her again, proclaiming, "Long have I desired to hear you speak those very words. Even in our disturbed youth, I sensed you would thrive once granted your uncontested independence. I heartily consent to your condition. Where shall I sign?"

Allowing herself a short smile, she crossed her arms. Her long, spectral sleeves sank through the floor. "You are... making fun of me."

Setting the cane aside, I bent down on one knee before her, crossing my finger over the region of my heart. "I swear upon my honor as the Dragon King, my cherished Witch Anmut shall receive nothing from me beyond cheerful banter, witty conversation, and perhaps a kindly prank or two."

Another blessed smile lifted the frail curves of her lips. My heart bounded at the sight. "I've witnessed thine 'honor' as the Dragon King, *mein guter Herr.* Swear on something else."

"Ah," I breathed, standing up again, "that sounds like my Yassy. I swear upon the Bible, then. Though upon my honor, I don't know what good *that* does. I've not darkened the threshold of a church once in my accursed life."

"Nor have I, barring the Westford chapel. 'Tis better to know thine own place without a doubt, sir."

"Right you are, madame." *Repossessing the diary must have fully restored her memories,* I realized, since she remembered the chapel.

Beaming, I offered my arm to escort Yassy to the Oak Park. It would be thoroughly abandoned at this hour, leaving us ample privacy to talk without fear of interruption or eavesdropping. By God, it would be good to have her at my side again, conversing at our pleasure! All my snappy, bored, tiresome self needed was a good haunting. A solid haunting at the wiles of a powerful, star-like woman.

A mystic Schattengeist.

8

POWER AT GREAT COST

Sergio

THANKS TO OUR MANY evenings together, I unearthed Yasmin's spectral habits and preferences. I took the liberty of recording them so I might condense my study into calm deliberation... on paper at least.

I adored her all the more each day, but that didn't mean she never vexed me.

She'd be absent during the daylight hours—in Kheima, I suspected—and would only reappear when the evening shadows hit the grandfather clock. She'd search for me and float at my elbow. Sometimes she was very sad and refused to talk, but this seldom occurred; I remained her favorite person in matters of conversation and mutual entertainment.

Having a ghost about the place was akin to having a cat. Allow me to elaborate. Yasmin's tendency to be adoring and affectionate one night and haughty the next closely resembled a feline. Occasionally, her eyes flexed until they resembled plates of pure silver. Then she'd dart from one room to another with no apparent goal, knocking paintings sideways and cracking decanters in her wake. In repentance, she'd come as close to me as her regal self dared and nestle her head into the crook of my neck, pretending to read my book alongside me or regard my current project with deep interest (which didn't fool me). Being near me was her greatest comfort.

Twice, as she roamed the Ocean Room, she sang to herself and wrung her hands, entirely blind and deaf to anything in her circumference until she noticed I had entered the room. Then she'd snap back to reality and rush to my side, wide eyes flickering across the bedchamber as if she feared someone was there in secret, watching her in deep disapproval. Perhaps someone *had* watched her thus.

Rothadamas.

I never asked about it, and she never told me. With my ghost-witch, it was better to draw my own conclusions. I didn't like to remind her that a gaping supernatural chasm stood between us... one that was far more troublesome than the mere fact that she was a spirit and I a man. In a way, being a ghost suited her. The otherworldly power that barely breathed upon her flesh in life soaked her immortal spirit until she dripped with it, scattering tendrils of pale-blue energy everywhere she drifted. Once I was no longer nervous around her, I acknowledged that she was *beautiful.*

Thankfully, my eyes alone perceived her paranormal trace. Staff and daughter alike passed Yasmin's specter-force day after day in blissful ignorance. Perhaps it was possible that I had retained a cache of warlock strength, lying in wait until it was needed again. After all, did *all* of my supernatural power descend from Rothadamas? That would be a discouraging thought, indeed. I preferred to believe that at least some of it was inherent to my nature.

I discussed this theory with Yasmin, and she agreed. "There has always been a specific force about your presence, sir. It bears coloring of its own... bronze and ruby-red." Her dark lips twitched in a guilty smile. "I no longer wonder how I fell in love with you so desperately. I wonder how the whole world has not."

Never before had she stood (or in this case, floated) before me and openly confessed her love. I stammered, quite unable to paste together two words. *You don't deserve her,* my wretched conscience hissed. *She should be with someone better than you. Younger than you. Kinder than you. What have you to offer, Dragon, but painful memories to a woman enamored with pain itself?*

Doubtless, it would have been kinder to push her away from me. To pretend I did not care for her. But I might as well have plunged a blade into my heart, for she grew dearer to me by the hour. Lillias had thought it strange that I never courted any of those fine, flattering widows who twirled in my arms at each seasonal ball, yet I hardly ever thought about them.

It was obvious now. None of those fine ladies were Yasmin, so I did not want them.

Just as my presence was Yasmin's greatest comfort, conversing with her was mine. With my enthusiastic encouragement, her former eloquence healed at an astonishing rate. I drew her into debates, spiritual theories, questions about the Craft in the afterlife, and asked for her opinions regarding estate improvements. She had a keenly artistic eye (as I well knew). I frequently adopted her suggestions, or at least laid them as the foundations for my own.

The night before Ulysses came to call, I held out my hand for Yasmin's with a deep sigh. She smiled, gliding forward to touch her airy fingertips to mine. My warmth lent a glow to her chilly aspect. "Must I release mine progeny to the care of some helter-skelter scoundrel, Yassy? I loathe to imagine House Vincenzo without its princess. I enjoy the place as dim, mysterious, and morose *sometimes*, but I shan't like it so *always*." I indulged a melodramatic sigh.

My ghost-witch replied with her famous, placid wit. "Perhaps I shall gain more lively spirits, my lord, and then you'll have another feminine money-sink to lavish your affections upon. For example, I think the Ocean Room would benefit from a seashell display. Shall I whine, beg, and wheedle until you promise to acquire it?"

I chuckled at the prospect. She'd taken to calling me "my lord," in reference to my ownership of an English estate, I surmised. I could not deny that I found it most charming. "Then that would hardly be *you*, Yasmin. You harbor a passionate yet sturdy reserve about you that deters begging. So be as commanding as you like. I'm quite accustomed to it."

With a flash of deep affection, her gaze settled on the gray streaks in my hair. "As you wish."

We stood several feet from the fireplace (for Yasmin disliked floating too close to its consuming heat). My hand instinctively cupped around hers, though my fingers sensed nothing but chilly air. "Yasmin?"

"My lord."

"Your demeanor toward me has softened."

"Has it? I believe I try your patience just as often as I ever did."

"You *try* to, gray witchling, but your arrows fall short of the target. I fear you're out of practice."

"You've changed, too, Sergio. The target is moving now, and my eye is not so sharp as it once was when it comes to mortals in general."

"*Pfft!* Art thou insinuating that I am no longer a wretched, selfish tyrant?"

"Nein." Her soft, low laugh made me smile; it had been confined to my dreams for so long. "Even during the harsh days of our youth, I saw glimpses of your true nature. Straightforward and kind. I knew it was there, but it was buried beneath some dark, shifting shadow..."

"Rothadamas."

Her posture stiffened. "Don't say His name."

"Will it summon Him?"

"It's best not to risk attracting His attention."

I paused, fumbling with my short beard. *I've put this question off for too long. I need to know.* "I've been meaning to ask you, Yassy. Does He know you're with me? Is it putting you in danger in any way?"

"No, I'm not in danger." Withdrawing her hand from mine, she floated away to contemplate the massive portrait of my father against the library wall. It took me several years to locate his likeness and have an artist improve upon it, but I was content with the result.

I didn't know who my mother was.

"He mainly operates from Deutschland now," Yasmin continued, meaning Rothadamas. "The Black Forest. That's where He kept me until I regained strength and... and some semblance of a will. But Kheima has many doors. Once I won His trust, He allowed me more freedom to travel through them." She trailed one transparent finger over my father's eyes, one brown and one blue. A subtle smile flicked across her face. "You would not believe your own handsome eyes if you but glimpsed the realms I've seen, Sergio."

I lowered my voice. "At what cost?"

She turned aside to look at me. Her wary side-gaze cast a glacial light over my forehead. "It's not that I don't want to confide in you. Kheima knows you are all I have... the one person who can truly sympathize. But I cannot speak of the cost to anyone. Pray, do not ask me again."

I crossed my arms and nodded, staring at the dancing flames. "Very well."

She drifted back to me, as if a magnetic tie drew her irresistibly to my side; she couldn't leave me for long. "Let me ask *you* something now, my lord."

"Che cos'è?"

"How is it that you can tolerate my spectral form? Don't you find me uglier than ever?"

"At first glance? SÌ. You are terrifying."

"I thought as much." She exhaled (from habit, not necessity). Icy breath plumed beneath her nose. "Then, how?"

Hesitating, I weighed my potential responses in the balance. Her sculpted face tightened with anxiety. "First, I must know why my opinion of your looks matters in the slightest?" I began. "My charming Schattengeist, is it not plain to you how much I enjoy your company? I dare any other man alive to take half so much pleasure in his haunting as I experience with you."

She trembled. "My Schattengeist" had tumbled into my thoughts, but until that moment, I hadn't permitted my tongue to utter the phrase. I knew how a special nickname would affect her—knew how crucial the proper timing was.

Eyes flashing, Yasmin tilted her head. "But I know your natural devotion to beauty. And since I cannot even be *plain,* as I used to be, I must be an abomination to your eyes."

I smiled and shook my head. *There. She's ready for the truth now.* "To the generic mortal eye that only takes a woman in at first glance—yes. 'Tis thine fate, Yasmin, to bemoan advantageous beauty. That cannot be refuted in good conscience, and I do not lie to you. Yet, let us look beyond one summary glance."

Motioning for her to follow, I strode from the firelight's glow into a darker corner. I held my open hand near her spectral form, moving it gently over the blue aura she emitted. It almost entranced me on the spot; I forced my wandering mind back to the present. "Think of beauty as one coin with two distinctive sides. There is the beauty of daylight—of springtime, of mortal gladness—beauty such as Aislinn possessed. No one would dare behold her profile etched on the coin's surface and deny her the right to be there. Every human, male and female, acknowledges her peerless silhouette. But take note, Yasmin, that it only takes these people *one glance* to come to their conclusion. That is all daylight beauty shall earn: one glance."

Yasmin's shrunken pupils flexed as she absorbed my meaning. Her pale face shone, enthralled by my words, drinking them as if half-perished with thirst for them. I grinned at the familiar expression.

"But just turn the coin over." I turned my hand from palm-up to palm-down with a fond smile. "Examine the opposite side. Behold the beauty of midnight. It shines all the brighter, for fewer fingers have touched it. And precious few pause to admire its nocturnal shading, for they have neither the time nor the intelligence to do anything else at nighttime but sleep. However... find yourself a handful of insomniacs—of artisans whose creative minds blossom beneath the moon and in country rainstorms, rather than beneath the sun upon glaring beaches—and these worshipers *shall* pause to admire. Nocturnal beauty calls to them. Thine beauty of spiritual midnight, my Schattengeist, is a treasure that few behold." I touched the crisp air lining her face, tracing it as I dropped my voice to a tender volume. "Your Dragon perceives it better than anyone else."

Like a snow-clad wanderer pleading for warmth, Yasmin's countenance guzzled the warm words I exhaled. My God, that look of hers! It was too much. My hands ached to caress her long, pale arms and hold her close. I cursed the Kheiman demon who withheld from me her languid corporeal form, more dear to me now than in our damnable, possessed youth.

I stumbled back from her, panting for breath. "Don't look at me that way, Yassy! As if I were a god offering salvation. I can only speak the truth to you, as I always have, but nothing more. Damn it, nothing more!"

Muttering sour oaths, I paced the library. I would have dearly loved to smash something, but that hardly suited a lord of the manor in his forties. *Blows and botheration! I mustn't frighten Yassy, either.*

My ghost-witch watched me carefully. She nodded once, her tresses overclouding her face. "I understand. You are not angry at *me*, not at present. You are angry at *Him*."

"Of course I am!" I yanked an atlas open, fluttering aimlessly through its thick pages. "Why should I be angry with you? What nonsense."

She endeavored to repress a grin. "I used to dwell solely on your words. I did not consider stopping to divine your *actions*, most often led by mute lamentations." She drifted to me and passed her silver arm through mine. "I regret that my present condition gives you pain, but *you* did not make me like this, Sergio. In a way, I chose it. Never forget that."

Hesitating an instant, she floated up to bestow an icy kiss upon my cheek. My eyelids flew open wide. The sensation of melting icicles dripped through my blood. Seeing me shudder, she quickly drew back... though it was, in truth, the shudder of pleasure. "It is my own fault," she breathlessly submitted. "If I wasn't so prideful, I would have confronted my true feelings far sooner. I'd have perceived the dire necessity of fighting the demon off before He took you. Perhaps even before He took Lillias. Had I not blamed Fate and *done nothing...*"

Downcast, Yasmin stared at the carpet, fighting tears. "I am to blame, Sergio. I am to blame for everything." A crystal tear trickled down her cheek.

I reached for it to wipe it away, cursing and dropping my hand just in time. A useless impulse. "By the gods, woman! Do not torment me with tears I cannot dry. I will do what I can for you. Should even the most meager of opportunities present itself, I *will* save you. Listen! Do not weep."

Her pale fingers trembled over her cheeks as she dried her face.

Smiling, I pantomimed placing both hands on her shoulders, leaning in close. "You are the strongest woman I've ever known. Your poise is nothing short of sacred. And your wisdom reveals you as a daughter of Athena herself. Truly, you ought to have been crowned queen in the medieval times. Your people would have flourished beneath your rule, and your enemies would have fled in terror when you so much as raised your brow at them. Therefore, you must only be *yourself*, Yasmin. Be everything that I've always known you to be, and we will weather this storm as one, you and I. *Beryl's Daughter* need not sail alone, for the *Dragon King* sails with her."

As she recognized the phrasing from her own diary, Yasmin's short, crisp mirth lifted my heart. "How I missed you, my lord! You and your wily, draconian tongue."

I bowed my compliments.

9

KHETMA PART 2

Yasmin

I MUST BE VERY, very careful.

Although my obedience to Rothadamas remained unaltered, my crucial apathy for my own situation was melting away from... love.

In life and after death, indifference was my savior during my service to Him. If I cared, then I cried, and if I was too busy crying to work, I forfeited whatever power and privileges I had in His realm. And if I did nothing but care and cry and forfeit my position, I would soon go mad from utter lack of purpose. *Not caring* was the only way to keep my fragile sanity intact.

Were it not for finding Sergio and clinging to him—even after he relinquished my journal—I might have continued forever with at least the semblance of serenity, of contentment. Yet I could not stay away from him, just as I could not resist his presence in life. I hated dependence with every fiber of my being, but I'd learned my painful lesson. Relying too much on oneself can wound others rather than save them. Strange, but all too true.

Love will soften the stoniest of hearts. It fills the cracks in the casing, however large they may be. I learned to converse with Sergio again, to laugh again. And I learned to love him again. I was born to love him, to reflect and complement his happy, carefree nature, as the moon was born to reflect the sun. I'd felt confused and worthless all my life until I first stood in the Dragon's looming shadow, demanding to join his circus and work for him. In the flash of his mahogany eye and in the sparkle of his elfish blue one, I'd read my fortune. Not once did I require the dictates of Madame Tola in their stead.

And yet, Rothadamas lingered. He touched me more often, for in tactile contact He obtained a perfect portrait of my current state of mind. He hovered over it, adding a stroke or two in broad black paint, smudging out my memories little by little.

He knew I still loved Sergio. He was determined to eliminate my love before it inconvenienced Him. Thus far, His mission had succeeded. He was hoping I'd forgotten my journal for good, but then I remembered, and I demanded His permission to get it back. *Why did He say yes?* I pondered with uneasy fantasies.

Did He have plans for Sergio?

And why, in His own cursed name, did I not leave well enough alone? Why wasn't a supernatural existence of power, of relative freedom (within reason), of translucent immortality, not good enough for me?

Hadn't I suffered enough in the name of love? Although I scorned it one day, I sought it the next. I could not let it go. I cursed my womanly nature, so prone to romantic distraction... so prone to hungering after the forbidden fruit of a mortal man's love with an entire Garden of Gardens at my disposal. Our frozen Eden was sweet and sharp, cold and satisfying.

I ought to be grateful I was *there,* instead of where I fully expected to be upon the moment of my death: Hell.

It was not enough.

How often I entertained the idea of summoning Sergio to Kheima and keeping him with me! He would make such a handsome Kheiman spirit. My ringmaster had yet to learn the few limits of my strength; I could do it with the snap of my nimble fingers, well trained in the art of evil. I could reenlist Sergio as a warlock in His service and have him ever at my side. Rothadamas might be good enough to numb his memories—as He often numbed my own—so he would hardly recall the awful deeds we completed in His cursed name.

We would be happy.

Happy.

What is happiness? Is it the tranquil reward for obedience? Is it the knowledge that one has a purpose in this universe, even if that purpose is evil?

We cannot all be angels of light.

10

It Wasn't Loneliness

Sergio

House Vincenzo was peculiar. It despised half the year, embracing only the seasons of death and dying, whence it gleamed to life in jack-o-lantern sunsets and the frosted grip of winter. Further testament to the fact that Yasmin was *meant* to live in it. I couldn't build a more fitting household for her spirit if I had a king's treasure trove of funds at my disposal.

Throughout the favored seasons, the windows burst with vivid color and flaunted their matching lanterns with the flame of life, impressing the soul with rippling gold, orange, purple and yellow in gothic slants. When encompassed with a border of established oaks, hollies, evergreen, and bejeweled hawthorns, nothing more could be desired. *I hope she loves it as much as I do,* I fervently prayed. *I hope she stays.*

Thanks to one of Yasmin's obstinate ideals, my monument to the late Yasmin Lange yet stood in the Oak Part. My strangeling of a witch wouldn't hear of it being brought down. "I *am* dead, you silly man," she'd protest. "It makes perfect sense to keep it." She'd float herself and her diary down to its stony feet and read there, perusing her own pen-strokes with a silvery furrowed brow. When asked what goal she had in mind, reading and re-reading her own words, and doing so *there* of all places, she'd quietly reply, "Reacquainting myself with myself," and dare me with her glares to query her further.

I left her alone. To oppress her beyond her limit no longer amused me. *Confound it, I was a beast.* It pained me to remember the morbid delight I'd taken in enraging her. Seeing her perched at the foot of her monument, book in hand, outlined in the multi-hued illumination of House Vincenzo... a rare aura of peace settled o'er her starlit head... She belonged there. Living or dead, she belonged with *me*.

Nevertheless, as the empty daylight hours stretched on (and I did what I could to amuse myself without her), I realized with growing anguish that I yearned to have her beside me in the flesh. With my mind clear and my soul unfettered, I knew beyond a shadow of doubt that no other woman suited me half so well as my ghost-witch. In my youth, demonic pride and wild ambitions tempted me to chase other, "prettier" women—women who dressed like angels and flirted like sirens and had not a single original thought worth sharing. Through it all, my poor, neglected Yasmin suffered in silence, her active mind devouring itself with self-deprecation and the unshakable belief that she was ugly.

My Schattengeist was divine. Yasmin's beauty was not carnal, but spiritual, and therein dwelt her greatest charm. I'd beheld her soul itself, bared and glowing, in all its glory. Should I persist in ignoring it? Should I pretend it did not strike my heart like lightning?

But here was my dilemma. Could a mere mortal convince a frigid witch of his earnest passion for her? I'd tamed the ghost, but how did one *court* her? And how in God's vast damnable earth could *I*, her "irascible Dragon," possibly win her love after all the suffering I'd put her through?

True, she had come to me the moment she was permitted to roam the earth. Yet, this was by no means proof of enduring love. We bonded over shared demonic tribulation, which might appear romantic on the surface, but beneath its sentimental ripples flowed poisonous depths: Pain. Solitude. Deprivation. Fear. Habit.

Nay, our shared past was no foundation for the wellspring of love. There were too many cracks in the basin. It must be mended.

However, even if I managed to convince her of my love for her, she'd be obliged to love me back, wouldn't she? This might prove disastrous as her soul remained in the clutches of the forest demon. *Resurrecting her might set her free,* I mused. According to Yasmin's diary, I had once been a warlock. Her sacrifice had cured me of my dark power and wiped my memory of the evils I'd wrought. I ought to have been grateful, I understood, yet I boiled when considering I couldn't lift the proverbial finger against a demon now. Much less the predestined Guardian of the Garden itself, if such He was. Assuming there *was* a sovereign god floating out there in the etherverse, it was logical to presume that attacking one of His chosen servants would be... well, in one word, catastrophic. Running the universe required the balance of light and dark, life and death, good and evil. *We cannot all be angels of light,* I concluded.

I finished staring out the window and yanked on my boots, marching outside. Yasmin was in her usual place at the foot of her own monument. "It remains beyond my comprehension, why you persist in relaxing here. I fitted up the blue bedchamber precisely for you, don't you recall?" I pestered her, not in the best of moods. *She belongs to the forest demon, not you!* My stupid thoughts were plaguing me.

Her paranormal eyes narrowed into slits. She hated being interrupted while reading. "Did it not occur to you that I've existed solely out-of-doors for a decade? I am not comfortable in the house for nights at a time. When you're preoccupied, I come here."

"Touché." I leaned against the monument, folding my arms. Orange tendrils of sunset contrasted against Yasmin's blue glow. "Well, Yassy. Shall we sail forth in silence, or shall we discuss the massive elephant in the graveyard? Hmm?"

She sighed, shutting her worn diary with a flick of the wrist. "I'm in no mood to decipher your verbose comments, sir. Pray, what do you mean?"

"I mean the fact that we seem doomed to skim through life hand-in-hand, though ghost and man. Tell me, in the past decade, have you discovered a means to cure your 'resurrection unto death?' Stumbled upon any clues? Did you not perform that cure yourself when you sent Lillias back to me?"

Her eyes softened at the mention of my daughter. "Aye." She rose to her ghostly feet, her robes fluttering around her. "*He* robbed me of that memory nearly the second I succeeded. He... *baptized* me..." she recalled with a pained shudder, "and I was cleansed of all memories He did not deem wise for me to retain. I'm surprised He allowed me to remember you at all, I daresay." She glanced at the diary. "Just as I remain baffled as to why He allowed me to retrieve this. Holding onto it helps me remember everything."

I grunted. "I have my own theory about that. But that's for another time. Do you think if you took me into Kheima with you, I could find a way to regain my power as a warlock and help you find the cure?"

To my surprise, rage snapped from her aspect. She mastered herself with a calming breath, cloudy with frost. "Thank you for your consideration, Hue," was the stiff reply, (I noted she called me "Hue" when a touch piqued with me), "but I won't take you back to that frozen hell even if I was tempted with immediate resurrection and freedom. If Roth—if *He* got His hands on you again—" She turned her head, a snarl forming on her dark mouth. When angry, she didn't have any pupils at all. They were engulfed in the wide silver discs of her irises.

I'd grown accustomed to it. "Calm yourself, ghostling, that we may proceed with the level-headed clarity befitting two established adults. Did you suppose I had any intention of living out the rest of my days in bachelor bliss while you remain chained to the demon you saved me from?" I shook my head. "Stubborn as you are, you know I'm twice as tenacious. I cannot let our present circumstances stand. If Lillias could be resurrected, then so can you."

A deep sigh exhaled from the abyss of her specter lungs. "Sergio." She drifted to me and placed another chilling kiss on my forehead. Despite our mutual aggravation, I smiled at her nearness. "I realize I don't look it, but I'm happy. Watching you and Lillias thrive in such a beautiful place, laughing and loving and enjoying your lives... That makes me happy. And say I *was* resurrected as you intend. What would I do? I never 'fit in' among the common folk nor popular society. Even in your circus, you and Lillias were all I had. I would fail even more spectacularly now. I'd be a morose little menace of a spinster, glowering upon the world from my blue bedchamber tower."

She laughed at the thought. A dry, humorless laugh. "You'll think me mad, but I'm far more at ease with myself as a specter than I ever felt as a mortal woman. I like breaching the veil as I please, observing both the living and the dead, and conversing with both or neither as my whim takes the notion." Her expression delved far into the woods, almost fairy-like. "Believe it or not, I've grown fond of Kheima. I've made small improvements to how we conduct our business there, and it's really quite beautiful. Hauntingly beautiful."

"You're rattling, Yassy-girl. You aren't convincing me half so much as you're attempting to convince yourself." I pretended to catch and tug a lock of her swirling hair. Pale-blue wreaths danced around my finger. "You're lonelier than ever. That's why you sought me out, is it not? I was harsh with you and outright cruel, but you still sought me out. Why? Sheer loneliness, my dear witch. 'Tis the only explanation."

"No, Sergio. It wasn't loneliness."

"Then what?"

"It was love."

Silence. The wind blew a leaf against my ear. I slapped it away. "Yasmin..."

The ghost-witch smiled. "Didn't you know that, Sergio Erbanhue Vincenzo? Did you not tell me yourself, years ago, as I cured your drunken complaints in your patched-up tent while you jeered at me? Did you not read it in my journal? And did I not confess it to you in person—well, in spirit—not long after our reunion?"

I crimsoned at the memory of my "drunken complaints." I fumbled for words, rendered helpless again by her open, adoring countenance. In all my life, not one other woman looked at me like *that*. Like I was more than just a handsome face, intriguing eyes, and a confident figure traced with exotic tattoos. Like I was her entire world.

"Yasmin, darling," I began, wishing my own confession could have begun much more smoothly, "I care for you, too. I *love* you. More than I can put into words. You've inspired my mind, possessed my soul, and seized hold of my black heart to set it beating again." I cupped both hands around her airy face, frustrated that I couldn't hold it. "But I can never make amends for the cruelty of my abominable tongue. Damn me to Hell, I *struck* you, when I thought you'd killed Matteo! You deserve far better than me. You deserve your fairytale prince—"

Flushed and tremulous, her eyes flashed with fierce contentment. She lifted her ghostly fingers to my lips. "Quiet, sir! I do not say these things to demand restitution. I meant to remind you that you recognized I was in love before *I* did. My confession shouldn't be a shock, as it seems to be." She tilted her head, a silver swarm of mischief blossoming in her otherworldly eyes. She liked putting me off-kilter, probably because she was the only woman who could.

Sighing, she proceeded, "I don't mean to be swept away from reason by the tide of love. The adoration of a ghost is worse than useless to you. I don't expect you to return my devotion; I am not asking for it. What, indeed, could we do with it? It would be akin to winding a dead man's watch or lighting a lantern for the blind. Divinely useless, Sergio."

She punctuated this declaration with rippling, silvern mirth. Once more, I marveled at Yasmin's odd twists and turns of emotion. When any other woman would weep and be right to do so, Yasmin's demeanor would gleam with ironic satisfaction. What a strange woman. And yet, how her strangeness made me adore her!

Smirking, I folded my arms again. "And what about possession?"

Confusion flooded her demeanor. "Possession?"

"I don't disagree per se, Yassy; a love affair between a spirit and a mortal will be exasperating. As always, you're sharp and sound as my best knife. But you haven't considered all the *fun* we could be having."

That suggestion raised a blush, rare and precious in her snow-white face.

11

IN THE VAMPYRE GARDEN

Sergio

IF YOU THINK OF House Vincenzo as the bullseye on an archer's target, then the first ring encompassing it would be the Vampyre Garden. The second would be the Oak Park, and the third (and final) ring of the estate would represent the outlying woods.

I liked things to come in threes.

My Vampyre Garden crept in twisted brambles and petals of antique tints, with the moss-clad gray of stonework peeping from between. It conveyed a glorious symphony of chaos. A mindless yet coordinated tangle of nature—a pleasant contrast to the smooth, manicured park abutting the wrought iron fence.

Yasmin and I wandered the garden as newly-confirmed lovers. While watching her glide soft and steady beneath the gaping moon, her transparent train drifting above gothic foliage, I wondered if some part of me had grown this place *for her*. Had some deep, hidden part of me known that her spirit lingered? That it would not only seek me out, but find me?

Now that we had both confessed, I no longer refrained from worshiping her with frequent staring. Yasmin turned her head in my direction, eyeing me as if she could hear my thoughts. "Do not think to menace me with your stares, ringmaster. I am protected."

I chuckled at the familiar phrase, flourishing my trusty cane. "Thou art formidable, indeed, with thine demonic protector. He trusts you implicitly?"

"Yes."

A cold word, sharp as a dagger's swift cut. Sighing, I switched my cane to the other hand and reached for her. "I know you can't really touch me, but let's do each other the honor of pretending."

Gratefulness flickered in her wry smile. She extended her hand for mine, and I curled my fingers around the frigid pocket of air. "You needn't describe your current position if it hurts you," I murmured aside, staring at our linked fingers (such as we could manage). "As for myself, I've forgotten most of our wretched time in Kheima. I can't tell you how I came to forget it, but my memories grew dimmer with each passing year. Now, I would struggle to recall even the name—Rothadamas—if it weren't for reading your diary."

"Speaking of which," my ghost-witch commenced, slight asperity in her tone. "Which part of my book is your favorite? The part at the beginning where I praise your handsome features, I suppose?"

"Naturally!"

As much as my vanity annoyed Yasmin, it was good for her. She dearly loved to preach at me and prune me down to repentance. It amused her, and frankly, it amused me no less. "Though, I also enjoyed how often you remarked upon my skills as the world's best storyteller," I mused, swinging my cane. "Veracity compels me to agree with you." I produced a broad grin, twirling the walking stick with practiced ease.

"Vain as ever," she sighed. The frost of her exhale kissed my cheek. "I predicted it to be your downfall, but it appears to agree with you. How irritating."

I shrugged. "Better to know and proclaim your strengths than to hide your light beneath the bushel of false humility. The former guides you to opportunities and the chance of success—the latter, to nothing but hopeless dreams. The world cannot grant you what you desire until you cement your place in it."

When listening to my revelations, Yasmin acquired this look of solemn, respectful awe that shone from her face like sunlight. She looked that way now. I smiled down at her. "Don't slip and fall into worshiping your Dragon again, my pretty ghost-witch. I am only a man."

"Not 'only a man,' sir. You are the man I love. The only man I've *ever* loved."

I raised a brow. The stern, unyielding Yasmin Lange not once, not twice, but *thrice* declaring her love for me? By God, she finally handed me the truth, and I had no idea what to do with it! Yassy tied me into helpless knots.

I ceased walking, indicating for her to float directly before me. I leaned my cane against the wrought-iron gate. "Look me in the eyes and tell me so, Yasmin. Look and see that your Dragon has aged." I pointed to the creases at the corners of my eyes, trailing from thence to the silver streaks sprouting from my temples. "Say it were possible to resurrect thee. Would you still desire me? Would you want an old, sarcastic partner whom you've repeatedly known at his worst, when you could have a kind, sympathetic, younger man to adore thee? Have you considered it?"

My angelic specter smiled, her face yet bright with adoration. "Oh, if resurrection was possible, you'd never be rid of me, sir. I've never wanted anyone else. I never will. Your age suits me, and Wisdom's touch at your temples suits *you*." She paused, nipping her lower lip. My breath caught at the sight... every little motion she made rendered twice as enchanting by our understanding. "Our haunted past was painful for us both, and no doubt it would be difficult to reconcile into a smooth-sailing romance. But I'm willing to put in the work if you will work beside me, Master Hue."

That final sentence sounded almost coy. A burst of longing to snatch her in my arms and kiss her senseless teased my poor, pounding heart. It infuriated me beyond description that I could not. I forced myself to be calm, breathing deeply and flexing my empty hands. "Then stay with me, my beloved. The witch and the ringmaster shall be happy together... as merry as two damned souls could ever be."

"That will do," Yasmin answered, and she blessed me with a glance I'd never dreamed to see in her face... a decidedly naughty look. I growled, my chest flaring with suppressed passion as I quickly turned my back, unable to cope with it. "The things you're *doing* to me," I muttered, fumbling for my cane.

Her voice sang sweetly at my elbow: "You've won yourself a haunting unlike any other, my lord. I do hope you're prepared for it."

"Do your worst," I declared, smiling widely and locking gazes with the stars above.

She took me at my word.

Joyous laughter echoed through the Vampyre Garden as Yasmin's spirit rushed *into my body*, stealing my breath away. Giddy sensations danced in my brain, light as feathers, tickling the ends of all my nerves. I wondered why on earth we'd waited so long.

Being possessed by Yasmin was vastly better than getting drunk. Perilously sweet, hauntingly bitter, bitingly erotic. If I concentrated enough, I could not only feel her thoughts and emotions toying with mine, touching and exploring everything, but I could almost feel her body itself. Her feminine curves slipped beneath my eager hands. The pure intoxication of the experience rendered me speechless. We were *one.*

Unfortunately, we lifted our eyes in Kheima.

Kheima—the dead, thorned, frozen forest in some god-forsaken ring of Hell. Too far below its blistering levels to catch a hint of heat. Black ice cracked the surface of black foliage, and ice-blue snowflakes drifted to the hazardous ground. I heard the shuffle of tiny human feet darting away from us, sensing our intrusion. The sickened Tree of the Knowledge of Evil loomed in the distance. And Rothadamas, the demonic Wrath of Adam, might well be lingering close.

Watching us. Preparing to enslave me again. Readying my soul for resurrection unto death.

Perhaps the unholy cauldron with the four strange beasts and the guardian with many eyes awaited their next victim.

Horror seized my brain with lightning speed, but a cool hand brushed my inner forehead. *"Peace, Sergio."* Yasmin whispered. *"All is well. We are invisible. I'm much stronger than I was ten years ago, beloved. I won't let anything happen to you."*

Her voice emanated from somewhere in my skull. She coiled there like a serpent, slithering around my consciousness, tasting its buzzing currents with her forked tongue and testing the limitations of my knowledge. I resisted the impulse to snatch the snake by its ghastly tail and throw it out of my head. She purred approvingly, *"That's it, my lord. You're doing so well! Don't be afraid. We must come here to merge for our first time, for like Him, my power is strongest in this cursed realm. We shall only linger a little while, darling."*

In her own realm, the intensity of our connected souls was overwhelming. I shuddered and twitched, utterly incapable of controlling my body. Waves of ethereal pleasure trickled down my spine, one after the other, merciless. *"You can call me 'my lord' all you like, Yassy,"* I informed her with a sigh of satisfaction. Her sole reply was a low, echoing giggle. It tickled my own throat as if reverberating around it.

Once the echo of mental mirth ebbed, I sensed her shaking her head. *"Pray cease thine bantering, sir, and let me work. I must ensure that all memories and knowledge of your dark employment as His warlock are indeed gone. For He will not feel threatened by this integration, if so."*

"Integration?"

"Our oneness. This is but a sample, a trial. We cannot become one until you trust me fully."

"I do trust you!"

Low laughter again. *"Sweet of you, Sergio, but lies are beyond useless while we are merged like this. You want to trust me, and that is enough for now."*

A brief pause. *"Does your head hurt at all?"* she questioned.

"No. It's light as a feather. I could fly to the moon this minute!"

"Good. Foolish notion—I advise against your inclinations just now—but this experiment was a success. Far more so than I dared to hope. How interesting..." She withdrew from me. Kheima instantly melted into the shadows.

I blinked, trembling on the ground. I heaved myself to my feet. Glad to behold the garden once more, I crossed my shaking arms and nodded. "You *are* stronger, Yassy. Good work."

An odd mixture of euphoria and guilt stained her expression. She floated before me again, white face glittering with translucent tears. "Why are you crying?" I demanded. "Are you hurt?"

"No, not at all. I'm... *happy.* Truly happy for the first time in my afterlife. You let me in, Sergio. You let me in! I saw it all: Your strength, your courage, your love for me. You *do* love me, my ringmaster!" She sobbed, wrecked with joy. "I didn't doubt your word," she hastily amended, lest I misunderstood, "but to *taste* it! To become a part of you, even for a moment. Why, I could fly to the moon myself!"

Her laughter bubbled with a melodious quality that had never before graced my ears. I laughed with her. We "joined hands" as only paranormal couples could. "Why, Yasmin!" I faked reproach. "You thought your Dragon would lie to thee? Or quail beneath the rod of spiritual inspection, when I have tamed tigers? 'Twas I, and I alone, who tamed Darius. Did you forget, witchling? I yet own the scars." I pushed up my right sleeve to show the evidence of training my tiger in the rings. "And here! This is where Vainavi took a swipe, just to make things jolly well even." I elevated the left sleeve.

A frosty breeze caressed me as Yasmin wrapped her arms around my neck. "You're every inch as vain as you ever were," she affirmed, her dark lips a mere inch from mine, "but I love you anyway. Don't ever change, dearest."

"I dare not disobey the whims of a ghost-witch."

"For your sake, I rejoice."

12

Sweet Nothings

Sergio

I sang as I inspected my prized Queen of the Night tulips, happily regarding the setting sun. I contemplated clipping a bouquet for my ghost but doubted she would find much joy in it. She preferred floating among living flowers to owning dead ones.

As my fingertips grazed the petals, I wondered if her skin felt so soft, so inviting. Years ago, when I had kissed her—as even in the thick of demonic possession, I yearned to do—I witnessed a glimmer of passion rising to the surface of her still-water eyes. The next moment, Yasmin froze it solid in pristine restraint.

Any other woman of my acquaintance would have cast herself into my arms. But the daughter of a demon refused to risk getting closer to me. Hail the profound irony that I was possessed by the same demon! She could have been mine that very night. The fantasy I cherished of a dark, demonically-charged consummation stilled the breath in my lungs. Alas, it was not to be. Her supernatural strength of caution held her back.

A cold, sweet-smelling breeze washed over me. *Yasmin.* I stood from my crouched position and clapped the dirt from my hands, wincing as my aging joints protested. "Hail, witchling!" I started to greet her but stopped.

Icy tears clung to her cheeks. They were formed of perfect sleet, dropping from her chapped eyelids with painful slowness. I advanced, pointing at her tears. "Tell me the meaning of this. I shan't stir from hence until you do."

"It's nothing. It was a difficult day."

"It's *Him,* isn't it? He made you do something wicked." My hands reached for her shoulders only to pass through them. I snarled my vexation. "Tell me, darling. You know I'll understand better than anyone else. Under no circumstances shall I ever blame you."

"Please," she begged, wringing her thin hands. "Don't make me describe it. Just let me in for a while. Only a little while. Please?"

Yasmin... *begging?* Beryl's daughter never begged. Whatever she had just endured, it put her out of her normal sphere. I nodded without hesitation. "Come to me." I held out my hands.

With a shuddering sigh of relief, she dried her eyes and swept into my body. Her cooling presence embedded itself beneath my hot skin, settling painfully for a minute before nestling its serpentine coils into my head. This time, I felt no impulse to expel her. "*I'm improving. Don't you think, Yassy?*" I telegraphed. It was much easier to control my possessed self on Earth than it had been in Kheima.

"*Yes. And your warmth, Sergio... It's better than standing near a furnace in a blizzard.*" Her sorrow remained, manifesting itself in my own watering eyes. I wiped them against my shirt sleeve. "*Thank you,*" her ghostly voice intoned. *"Someday I'll be able to do something wonderful for you, too. I just need to get stronger first."*

"Yasmin! I am the one in YOUR debt. You saved Lillias, remember?"

"Yes... after I was likely the reason she was targeted by Roth—by Him. He would not have been drawn to your circus if I hadn't intruded there." Another weary sigh.

"You were my aerialist. The best one I ever had," I gently scolded her. *"You weren't an intrusion. And you were hardly a woman when He robbed you of your soul. How could you have understood what was happening to you? Yasmin, do not blame yourself for your possession, just as you do not allow me to blame myself for mine."*

"You're right."

A comfortable silence intervened. I hummed as I entered the house and hunted for a fresh novel to amuse us with. *"Lillias should be home soon. Please stay with me so you can see her. I know you've been avoiding her because you fear His attention fastening on her again, but I doubt she would be any use to him now."*

"Thalia was a favorite creation of His, just as I was," Yasmin reminded me. I felt her frowning. *"I don't dare risk it. I better withdraw at once."*

"Stay," I ordered. *"If He was in any way interested in us, He would have made His move already. If He has one flaw, it is His impatience."*

Wordless surprise tinted my brain, descending from her emotions. *"I remember that about Him, at least,"* I told her, vaguely amused. *"I did study Him as well as I could once you enlightened me of our mutual misfortune. Did you think I wouldn't?"*

"It is no pleasant study, my love. And you had enough to worry about."

"Bah! You accuse me of lacking faith in you when I trusted you more than anyone else in my life. I never questioned your veracity, even when you broke down and told me all about Roth—about Him."

"That's right. I expected you to lock me up as a madwoman."

"Then put your anxious little mind at ease, Yassy. I know of what I speak."

"Very well, Master Hue." Again, my ghost-witch sounded a tad coquettish, which was the sweetest form of torment I'd ever known.

"What are you smiling about, Papa?"

Lillias had swept into the foyer in her evening gown, and I hadn't noticed. I cleared my throat and snapped a cheerful salute. "Evening, Lillykins! What have you been about? Buying all the latest hats and simpering over tea, eh?"

She huffed, removing her hat and handing it to the maid. She patted her coif into place. "Your face is flushed, Papa. I hope you didn't work yourself to exhaustion, or strain your sore knee. You go about things in such a dreadful do-or-die fashion. Kindly recall that if anything happens to you, I'll have to marry myself off at once to the first gentleman who will have me. You *must* take care of yourself."

"Ha! As if you couldn't live perfectly well off your poor father's fortune. Your threats shall not dissuade my enthusiasm, daughterling." I approached her to menace her hair, wincing as my quick steps taxed my sore knee. *"Perhaps I have been overdoing it,"* I complained aside to Yasmin.

Yasmin's mirth sent tickling glimmers throughout my head. *"Yes, you have, old man."*

I ignored her, prattling on to Lillias. "If I passed away, you would seize your inheritance and spend your days in all manner of parties and dances and merrymaking, as a properly spoiled heiress. I'd be rolling in my grave."

My daughter was staring at my face in a baffled way. "Papa? Are you ill?"

"Not at all!" I pounded my chest. "Fit as a fiddle. Why?"

"Your face... it's... it looks gray. And your eyes are glassy."

Damnation. I didn't think that remaining possessed by Yasmin might change my physical appearance; it didn't once enter my damned head. I forced a cough, drawing my sleeve over my mouth. "I might have overdone it in the garden, as you say. Rest will set me up. I'll retire early."

"Please do." Lillykins put her hand to my forehead. "Your forehead is clammy. Go to bed this instant!"

"Yes'm." Meekly, I trudged up the curving staircase and puttered down the hallway. Once I safely gained the bedchamber, I shut and locked the door, darting to the nearest mirror. Yes, my skin looked a tad grayish, and my eyes gleamed like marbles. "*You might have warned me!*" I reprimanded Yasmin.

"*I didn't think of it myself until it was too late.*"

Her tone of mild amusement made me snort. "*Well, now that I know how unappealing I look while we are merged, I feel less inclined to acquiesce to your requests.*"

"How amusing," Yasmin purred. "*You're just as addicted as I am, sir.*"

A little later, she asked me if she should leave. I pulled the bedclothes up only to kick them back down a minute later, feeling flushed and bothered. "*Stay,*" I commanded.

"*As you wish.*"

I smiled. Despite Yasmin's sole condition for our companionship—our entire and unquestionable equality—she slipped into her old ways of looking up to me, studying me, and speaking to me with peculiar reverence. *"You don't have to keep talking to me as if I remain your ringmaster,"* I clarified, punching my pillow around until satisfied. *"I'm just the elderly lord of a modest manor, and you are not my maid."*

She huffed. *"Elderly and modest, indeed!"* A pause. *"What am I then, dear Sergio?"*

"Hmm?"

"What am I to you? Please tell me."

I savored her query for a few minutes before assembling a reply. As I answered her telepathically she was utterly still, yet the forked tongue brushed each word. Tasting them for the flavor of incontestable authenticity. I knew that long, flowery speeches wouldn't satisfy. 'Twas difficult to pay Yasmin her due, but I vowed I would not be a coward and shy away from trying. *"You are my dearest, most beloved friend. When not a soul around me cared about my suffering or my loneliness, you drifted to my side and wouldn't leave me. You are my grounding rock in a sea of storms. I thought myself utterly alone in supernatural slavery, but you refused to leave me even at my darkest hour.*

"I deserved to be left in Kheima, rendered a soulless puppet, but you paid for my restoration with your own life. And despite your cool words and thorny manners, you are at heart the sweetest, most loyal woman I've ever been blessed to know. And I love you, Yasmin Lange. There. It isn't half what you deserve, but that's the best I can do in a pinch."

For a moment, our connected minds fell silent. Her coils shifted in my mind. *"And it isn't my position of power in Kheima that you love, Sergio? My capabilities as a witch? It's me? Just me?"*

"Truly, dearest. Just you. It's always been you, but I was a blind, stubborn, possessed young fool and couldn't see it."

Yasmin knew the tenderness in her Dragon's intonation could not be fabricated. I sensed rainfall coming; I put a stop to inclement weather at once. *"If you dissolve into tears, witchling, you'll have to wait a good long while before I say anything romantic again! I can't abide making you cry when I cannot dry your tears, nor hold you—"*

I clenched my jaw. Damn to the depths the crazed demon who'd stolen the only woman I adored! My love for Yasmin Lange crept slowly, gently, winding up and around my soul as the peerless autumn vines grew over House Vincenzo, beautifying it so naturally that no one thought twice about its presence there. My awe of her loyalty, respect for her intelligence, and envy—yes, even that—for her unshakable poise at the center of every judgment she made, even while cold and wild. Every cherished, flawed piece of Yasmin was the foundation of love, enduring and true.

And now...

Now, I say again, 'Al diavolo la mia fortuna![1] '

The woman I loved with all my heart, soul, mind, and strength was the woman I could not touch.

---

1. Damn my luck to hell!

13

KHEIMA PART 3

Yasmin

I WAS WICKED. I'D known it for many years. My awareness of the inner darkness only expanded and deepened as I became a woman, and further still in Kheima.

Frozen Eden's forbidden fruit with veined magenta flesh and blue ice mottling was my cheerless sustenance. I no longer shied from its bitter bite. I craved it. Throughout the weary decade I'd survived with no one to comfort me but myself—no songs to soothe me but my own—and I was fortified by it. I convinced myself that I required nothing more.

"Then why possess the ringmaster?" one might ask.

Because he *asked* me to.

Plate some butcher's meat before a starving dog and forbid it from devouring the meal whole. You'd have the same level of success.

14

Make Me a Warlock!

Sergio

THERE WAS ONLY ONE way to save Yasmin. The Craft within me had to be awakened.

If it was possible, I would become powerful enough to summon, touch, and even resurrect the subjects of Rothadamas Himself. I would bring Yasmin back to the land of the living, to behold daylight without pain once more. And I would shelter her in my arms and kiss her until her knees weakened and I was obliged to carry her to our bed, if it was the last thing this old man did.

Luckily, I was not religious. Taking on witchcraft didn't bother me then and wouldn't bother me now. And since Rothadamas was the only spiritual being of a higher power that I'd ever witnessed with my own eyes, offending some unseen god that didn't concern itself about my Yassy's plight did not concern me, either. I was what *He* made me, so Rothadamas was the sole demigod in my book. And demigods could be felled. They had weaknesses, temptations, and seasons of sheer boredom that rendered half-baked wagers with mortals *highly* interesting.

No, none of these considerations gave me pause. What *did* concern me was devising how to 1.) Locate Aislinn, the only other witch I knew who had adored Yasmin, and would therefore be open to helping *her* via helping *me*, and 2.) Beg her to take me on as her student of the Craft, and 3.) Practice diligently until capable.

But most importantly, number 4.) *Don't let Yasmin find out.* At least, not until after a bargain with Aislinn had already been struck. Yasmin would not expect me to break my word once it was pledged.

If Yasmin knew that I planned to confront the forest demon, she would try to stop me. She wouldn't even speak to *me*, her own beloved Dragon, of where she went and what she did during the daylight hours for fear of enraging the demon. The second she assumed I was in danger she'd sacrifice herself again, withdrawing into Kheima forevermore rather than encouraging me to draw near the mouth of her frigid hellscape in the vague hope of revival. Much as it pained me, I had to keep her in the dark.

For the first time since I'd spied Yasmin's spirit at the angel monument, I rejoiced that she remained at the demon's service in daylight. The first part of my plan slipped into motion with comparative ease. I placed advertisements inquiring after the address of one Aislinn Bláthnaid, a healer, including a physical description from memory. That was simple, for I daresay she shone in every man's mind as brightly as a star fallen from Heaven.

Last I heard, her intense partiality for freedom kept her happily single despite her renowned beauty. She spurned suitors all her eligible life, content to take a spacious forest cottage for herself and be worshiped from afar. Only fellow womenfolk were welcome.

Had Yasmin retired to such a pagan nunnery as that, she would have expired from loneliness. She'd never admit it, demon bless her, but her loyal service to Rothadamas—and whatever proverbial breadcrumbs He gifted her in return—were the very things keeping her from going insane. My Yassy needed purpose and praise and admiration, however slight. Aislinn thrived either with or without it. Quite admirable in her own stubborn way, really.

"Did you not fall in love with Aislinn yourself, you cursed manipulator of women?" you might well inquire. I never loved Aislinn because I understood that she didn't *want* love. Not my love, at least. Yasmin craved love... *my* love... with such wild, deep, profound intensity that she was afraid of herself, and hid that desire behind fortified steel. Like a true lady, she feared the fierce wildfire of her passion exploding out of control, scorching everything in its path. I loved her for it.

My dear, proud, star-led Schattengeist. My angel from another realm. She deserved to be restored to life so I might gather all the best and brightest goods of the land and pour them at her pretty feet.

An interminable wait supervened as I haunted the post. At last, I had an answer to my advertisement.

I informed the household that I was traveling to visit a friend who had fallen ill. I left a letter for Yassy in the Ocean Room explaining the same. I also advised her to await my return, as frightening an invalid with a ghostly presence would not be a wise risk to take. The deception turned my stomach, but I felt confident that she'd use whatever dark means at her disposal to stop me if she became aware of my true errand.

I took a train to the town indicated. By great sovereign luck, Aislinn, too, had left America to retire in dreary England. I swore there was something in its sodden countryside that appealed to all three of us.

Stopping at the livery stable, I rented a horse. After two days of tiresome travel and one night at a village inn, I dismounted and secured my gelding. Yanking off my gloves, I stuffed them into the pockets of my dusty greatcoat. Stretching my sore limbs, I groaned at the pain crackling from my joints. *Can't travel like I used to.* I seized my cane, which I had secured to the back of the saddle. I seldom stirred from my front door without my walking stick, unless I'd managed to lose it... which did happen rather frequently, I fear.

As my last news of the Celtic witch portrayed, her address boasted a sprawling woodland cottage. Herbs and flowers of all conceivable shapes, sizes, and shades grew in a sparkling bower around the place, putting my Vampyre Garden right to shame. I gaped at the splendid foliage like a man put out of his senses. "Beautiful!" I murmured aloud.

"Are you lost, sir?"

Rolling my sore shoulders, I glanced around for the source of the voice. Aislinn Bláthnaid herself accosted me, standing in her doorway. Her magnificent figure was outlined by the glow of lantern-light. As I'd expected, her matchless features were unmarked by age, preserved by her Craft. Regal hair preened in golden swirls down her shoulders, past her waist, and brushed the flagstone floor.

I removed my top hat and bowed. "Do you not know me?" I inquired, sparing a moment to admire how the climbing, sky-blue roses around her doorway matched her dress. And her eyes, an astounding seafoam blue. Time somewhat dulled my memories of her incandescent beauty, but the fact remained that those heavenly eyes bore not a single momentary flicker of warmth. At least, not for me.

In fact, Aislinn looked as if she might like to eat me, or perhaps chop me up. I took a step back, remembering that if Yasmin had gained untold powers over the past decade, Aislinn must have also. "Formerly Ringmaster Erbanhue of the Fair of Phantoms, at your service," I clarified, reclaiming my hat. "I wouldn't dream of intruding upon your solitude, Aislinn, except in dire circumstances."

"Oh, yes. Yasmin's ringmaster. Your long hair confused me."

My mouth curved into a smile. *Yasmin's ringmaster.* It seemed everyone but us knew our love was fated.

Aislinn's beautiful eyes widened as her lips parted in a feathery gasp. *By the Celtic gods! Every tiny motion is perfection itself.* It almost made one uncomfortable, how ethereal she was. It *did* make me uncomfortable. "Is Lillias hurt?" she asked, frightened. "Did Roth—did *He* take her back to Kheima?"

Ah! So the witch was capable of softness and warmth, after all. But only for her fellow *femme fatales* of the supernatural order. "No, my daughter is fine," I reassured her, leaning against my cane. "It's Yasmin."

"Yassy?" She spoke her beloved friend's nickname with tremulous, tender reverence. Sisters not in blood, but in solemn demon-bond. "Yasmin is dead, Erbanhue. You know that as well as I do."

"You are correct." I could not deny that it amused me to have the upper hand over the Celtic witch. Yasmin would have guessed my errand the moment I rode up; she would have landed somewhere in the circumference of the truth. Aislinn might be gifted, but she was not as sharp as my Yassy. "Yasmin's *spirit* found me, just as she promised me she would when the forest demon overpowered her. She's a formidable ghost-witch, Aislinn, terrifying even to me. And no doubt she's done many great and terrible things in the demon's name to keep in His good standing. Nevertheless, I intend to rescue her by restoring her to life."

Aislinn's eyes narrowed upon my countenance. Absorbing my claim, she paced around the garden, her slippered feet barely shifting the soil beneath them. She bit the end of her pristine thumbnail. "It's not possible, Erbanhue. I respect and admire that you want to help her. It's truly good of you." Her pupils returned to mine. "Now that the shadow of Rothadamas has lifted from you, I perceive that you are a better man than I gave you credit for. It relieves me to know that Yasmin didn't love an abusive, self-absorbed brute who would beat her as soon as steal a kiss from her."

I stifled an inward cringe. There was nothing subtle about her choice of words. Yet I softened my heart to receive the blows; I knew I deserved them. "I don't blame you for reminding me what an utter beast I was," I reassured her, twisting my hand around the handle of my serpent cane. The familiar shape was reassuring. "I was jealous of her favored standing with Him and longed to take her place. I intend to make amends the only way I can: by resurrecting Yasmin. However, I can do nothing so long as my Craft remains out of reach. If anyone can make me a warlock again, it's you. I know of no one else." Casting the cane aside, I fell to my knees, preparing to beg for the first time in my life. (And hopefully the last.)

Aislinn shook her head. Her golden locks shimmered around her face like silk. "Your powers were gifts from Him in exchange for bringing Him new souls. I cannot give your power back to you unless it originated *from* you."

"But your power originates from His, does it not? Can't you get in touch with it and channel it to me?"

She confirmed my assumption without words, parting her blouse enough for me to see the Mark on her chest. She covered herself again. "I tried everything in my power to sever my ties to Him," Aislinn assured me.

"'Tis a delicate surgery, as you might imagine. Direct rebellion would result in a death certificate and little else. I *want* to help you, Erbanhue."

The Celtic witch caught up her skirts and swept to me, cradling my downcast face. "I'd sacrifice everything, from my entire garden to my private book of spells, if I thought it would bring our beloved Yasmin back. But mere mankind cannot resist the likes of Rothadamas. Unless He Himself discards His servant, there is no escaping His service."

"I'll think of a way," I muttered, standing up and brushing off my pant legs. "He's not a god, you know. He's just a demon."

Aislinn was good enough to stoop and return my cane to me. "A *very* powerful demon. Yasmin did not refer to Him as the Demongod of the Corrupt Wood without cause."

"Give me time. Meanwhile, pray allow me to shadow you and learn what I can. The first step is knowledge. Once I've acquired a fund of it, I can concentrate on practice until I've seized my old magic with both hands! If I cannot find the key, I'll break the door down." My fists clenched, my teeth grated, and my throat uttered a growl.

Its guttural quality startled Aislinn, but in a pleased sort of way. Something akin to admiration betrayed itself in her grin. "I see you cannot be dissuaded. Might I ask..."

I gulped back my rage. "Ask me anything. For Yasmin's sake, I shall tell you everything I know."

She softened her tone to mirror the melody of the evening wind: gentle, solicitous, and bracing. "Do you love Yasmin?"

"With all that I am, all I've been, and all I shall ever be."

With a firm, decisive nod, Aislinn captured my hand in hers and guided me indoors. "Then come. For if it is possible, you *shall* save our Yasmin."

15

No More Masks

Sergio

It was settled that I'd stay with Aislinn for a fortnight. It wasn't long enough—not by a quarter—but I couldn't keep away from House Vincenzo for longer without waking Yasmin's suspicions. She'd track me down to Aislinn's cottage, pester me with questions, scare her old friend half to death, and then force me to spend my last dime of patience upon explanations.

As I unpacked my carpetbag in Aislinn's spare bedroom, I heard her snickering in the hall. I poked my head out of the doorway. She was laughing at my cane. It leaned against the foyer wall dull with age and dented from use, its golden-bronze handle supposedly harboring the Witch's Scourge. The protection charm that Aislinn herself was paid to infuse my cane with.

Back then, I knew *someone* was after my soul. I could "feel it in my bones," as they say; intuition never lied. I assumed it was Yasmin Lange, the dour-faced witch in my circus who tried to conceal her hopeless infatuation with me. In a roundabout way it *was* Yassy, but she herself wasn't aware of it. Such a damned curious subject, possession. It must be studied further.

And before you ask, yes. I noticed years ago that this *scourge* failed to dissuade Yasmin in any way, shape, or form. I should have known those two would be in cahoots and laughing all the way to the bank, jingling my hard-earned coins, giggling at the stupid, superstitious ringmaster. Well! I liked making Yasmin laugh. Let the women have their fun, and far be it from me to deprive them.

I expected my ghost-witch to locate me in four-and-twenty hours, perhaps less. To my surprise, I neither saw nor heard from her for three nights. On the fourth, I dreamed of her. An intense, cutting, mesmerizing dream that would surely enchant me until the day I drew my final breath.

I dreamt I was kneeling in the Vampyre Garden when I heard her voice. *"You seek to free me."*

I jolted upright from watching the light blue snow of Kheima fall and frost the garden flowers. Yasmin floated several feet above the ground, challenging me from above with her frigid stare.

"Oh, you've deprived me of my fun!" I managed a half-hearted joke. *"I had the very king of red herrings prepared for thine palate, mine witchling: your best friend."*

Her smile was tender, but sad. *"My dearest Sergio, I am not here to get in your way. I know you far too well. You'd take my disapproval as a challenge and double your efforts to deceive me. Let us have no more deception between us, beloved."*

Pride shimmered in her strange, silvern gaze as she fixed it upon me. A warm quiver shot through my heart and quickened its pace. *"Yasmin... My darling!"*

Her translucent chest rose and fell in a deep, sharp breath. *"I'm here."*

"Come to me. Don't glare down at me so." I held out my hands.

Yasmin floated down with that calm, obeisant expression she knew I liked. *"How can I help?"* she asked. Her winter touch cooled my hot hands. I glanced down at them, wondering why in damnation they were pluming like a steamship, iridescent with heat.

"Just stay with me every moment you can spare," I instructed her, *"and I think my damned hands are on fire. Put them out, if you would, dearest."*

"Yes, sir." She grasped my hands more firmly within her own, doubling the cooling effect of her spectral body until the invisible flames went out.

"Thank'ee, darling."

Gods, but her spirit eyes were eerie! The pupils so shrunken and pale, nearly whittled away to nothing. The wide irises so glassy and silver-gray, brighter when she was happy and darker when she was angry or sad. And her poor, cold specter body looked more emaciated than ever, just as it was in the days of the traveling circus.

I gazed at her with sorrow, lamenting that I couldn't kiss that pale wash away and replace it with soft, blushing roses. *"Remember our kiss? I've never forgotten it. I suppose it has haunted me more than you, witchling."*

"Has it? Good!" My charmingly wicked witch smiled. *"You deserved it, you colossal scalawag."*

"I wanted to awaken my sleeping beauty," I chuckled, hating the warmth that stained my ears and prowled over my face. Grown men in their forties have no call to blush. *"When you're passionate, Yasmin, you're the most beautiful woman I ever beheld."*

"Don't speak nonsense, Hue; it becomes you ill."

"I'm not speaking nonsense! It is the solemn truth. It's your eyes, methinks... glowing like molten silver in your pale face. When you mask your emotions from the world, they cannot see the way your eyes gleam. They only see rigidity and fierce pride. And that, my dear, is lamentable. You mustn't wear masks anymore, Yassy. Not with me."

I cupped my hands around her face and locked eyes with her. *"Forgive me. I wasted so many years without you by my side, unmasked and free and safe. I can't even say what I was so blasted afraid of. I'm a damned coward."*

"You WERE a coward," she corrected, a saucy grin crossing her lips. *"But no more."*

"Aye. No more. No more cowardice. No more masks."

I leaned down and kissed the frigid space of her forehead. My nerves fully believed I'd kissed a cloud of winter frost. Yet from the beam that entered Yasmin's eyes, I knew it did her good. *"Would that I could kiss you in earnest!"* I groaned. *"I swear I will free you, Yasmin, and ensure that He never touches you again. You belong to me, not Him."*

"Kind of you, Sergio. But I'd far rather free myself if I could," she admitted. Typical, imperious witch of mine. She despised accepting help from anyone, even those who loved her most.

"Now YOU are speaking nonsense, darling." I kissed her airy forehead several more times, drawing forth a rare giggle or two. I'm sure I looked utterly insane. *"I'll learn what I can from your witch friend, Aislinn, and see what comes of it. Remember when we discussed why I can see you while*

none of my household can? It's possible that I do, in fact, harbor a natural Craft of my own."

"Well, don't get your hopes up sky-high, sir. My own power might have ensured that result. And, Sergio… Do you think… Would it be wrong of me to see Aislinn? Can you ask her for me?"

"Wrong? Pah! She'll be thrilled to see her sister-in-spirit again. Shall we call you up in séance pose? Shall we join hands and chant before a smoking cauldron? Or shall we dance naked 'round a bonfire?"

"You're making fun of me!" Yasmin pouted.

I laughed aloud at her drawn face. *"Only a little, beloved. Because you're so much fun when you're teased."*

She drew near and circled her arms around my waist, affecting to rest her head against my chest. *"You can call me beloved anytime."*

Once I woke from the dream, it was morning. I washed and sauntered downstairs to find Aislinn and communicate Yasmin's wish to her, for I knew in my heart that I had truly communicated with her through the dream. I never actually *felt* hot or cold in dreams—I merely expected to feel it, then did not—but this dream had been utterly different.

Beside herself with excitement, Aislinn flew about the parlor tinkering and rearranging and tossing cushions (at which I deployed an amicable snort, for why would a ghost care whether the sitting room was artistically displayed?). Bored, I strode about the cottage to take a gander.

Typical of natural witches, all manner of seeds, herbs, botanical sketches and gardening books littered her spacious dwelling. An oversized stone fireplace burned merrily in the sitting room, casting a rose-gold hue over all. Unknown species of leafy plants sprouted from every nook and cranny. I checked my immediate surroundings often, just to make sure carnivorous wonders weren't growing limbs and scuttling after me, seeking whom they might devour. Aislinn was the mistress of botanical horrors.

I heard the Celtic witch calling me from below. Snaking down the cramped back staircase, I stomped into the sitting room. "Shall I summon her?" I asked, snatching up my cane from sheer habit and giving it a twirl. "Our bond is strong. She should sense me wanting her even if she's busy in Kheima."

The Celt jabbed a forefinger toward a black armchair. "Yes. Sit down."

"Bossy, bossy!" I sat anyway, propping my ankle against my opposite knee. *"She's ready to see you, Yassy,"* I projected, getting straight to the point. *"We're in the sitting room."*

No reply.

Normally when Yasmin approached, I'd hear her breathe. Not *audibly,* mind you. The sound originated within my mind. She admitted that the strength of our bond originated from *ghost possession,* highly similar to demonic possession. She could even steal control over my movements if she wished.

Hmm. *What a fascinating prospect...* I cleared my throat and stared into the pinkish flames, embarrassed by the train of thought that premise had tempted.

After Aislinn and I passed a few minutes in silence, both of our distant gazes absently fixed on the fire, I spoke up. "She usually comes the minute I call for her. Unless she's... fulfilling an errand."

"Is she never late?"

"Only when she's with *Him.*" I'd never met anyone else as punctual as Yasmin. Both in life and in death. She harbored an unnaturally keen intolerance for tardiness. She wouldn't hesitate to verbally thrash the devil himself if he arrived late to drag her soul to the Second Death... though Satan might not frighten her an instant, thanks to damned Rothadamas and His unique torments.

I shrugged. "I'll try again."

A second mental summons also went unanswered. I pushed off the chair and paced around the sitting room, dodging various wind instruments and glass-cased curios. A pinned butterfly collection caught my eye. "You didn't," I objected, raising one draconian brow.

"I *found* them like that!" Aislinn objected. "Leave me alone. I'll try calling Yasmin myself."

Rising also, the regal Celt swept to a velvet drape and drew it aside. No longer covered, a gleaming round table stained black awaited its mistress. Rosy firelight shimmered over its polished surface. The table itself seemed *alive*, eager, sentient. Wicked. It had witnessed spells and held aloft tarot cards not meant for mortal hands.

Withdrawing a dried black rose from a secreted drawer, Aislinn cupped it between her hands and chanted a spell. As the incantation progressed, her voice strengthened. Pearls of sweat dotted her upper lip and forehead as her focus increased. Her body began to tremble.

I'd just leapt to her side to stop her when a flash like blue lightning and an iron-laden scent... *blood*... filled the air, along with a piercing cry.

Yasmin drifted in the center of the room, but she was not *our* Yasmin—our cool, self-contained ghost-witch. Her hair was tangled, her veil gone, her hands clawing at her own face, raking black blood down her cheeks. Her mouth gaped in a wordless wail of anguish. Her contorted limbs shook, and her bare body twitched in and out of view—there one moment and gone the next—its outline fuzzy and uncertain to the human eye.

With a wild shout, I dashed to her side. I expected Rothadamas to pool the room's shadows together and rise from them, as I now recalled Him doing before. But only Yasmin stirred in the dark, pale as death and utterly broken. "*Il Diavolo!*" I cursed, reaching for my beloved witch in vain. I could not touch her, oh, I could not touch her! By every god's name invented by human lips, what I wouldn't sacrifice to *touch* her!

Aislinn and I could do nothing but watch. At last, Yasmin's violent twitching came to an end. She floated to the cottage floor and crumpled into a ball as if by instinct. Silent sobs came next, just as agonizing to my soul as her screams had been. For it was all too clear to me: My poor Yassy had been in the midst of punishment in the Kheiman realm when Aislinn's witchcraft dragged her from it, doubling—perhaps tripling—her suffering.

"Oh, Yasmin!" Aislinn cried. She knelt to the specter's starch-white form, wringing her hands in a repentant gesture. "I didn't know! I didn't know! I'm so sorry, my darling! My dearest!"

My vision swam. I hurriedly swiped my sleeve over my eyelids, cursing my weakness. *Yasmin needs me to be strong for her.* I knelt at her side also. "Darling, I'm here. We're both here. What can we do?"

"Let me be!" she screamed, covering her bloody face. "You've done enough. Just let me be!"

My heart throbbed painfully. I punched the floorboards with all the force I could muster. My tattooed knuckles blistered. I *thought* I saw a thick wisp of smoke rise and dissipate, but it must have been my imagination. "This will not go unpunished!" I roared. "I have sworn to save you, and I'll do it if it costs me my life! Do you hear me, Yasmin? Do you?"

Anger struck me blind. The world went white, as white as poor Yasmin's dead countenance. "Do *you* hear me?" I yelled. "She's mine, you demon bastard!" I shook with rage.

"Erbanhue... Erbanhue!" Aislinn grasped my arm. Her touch felt far away, so very far away. "Your face... What is happening to you?"

She said more, but her words were lost in the howling wind crashing against the cottage. I clenched my fists with an enraged yell more bestial than human. In one powerful rush, a fervent heat flooded from my shoulders down to my fingers. Orbs of yellow, orange, red, and blue flames burst from my palms and scorched the wall opposite, leaving Aislinn shrieking. Covering her head with her apron, she darted aside just in time.

Yasmin remained on the floor with her blurry focus locked on the charred, smoking wall. Not making one sound. Not uttering one word.

Slowly, Aislinn removed her apron. Her eyes resembled dinner plates. "So. You *are* a warlock... with the gift of pyrocraft."

I grunted something in response, though *what*, I couldn't say. I crouched next to Yasmin and waited for her to speak again. I sang to her, trailing my smoking fingertips through her beautiful icy-blue aura. It warmed her and chilled me, gradually placating us both.

Midnight shadows stained the room before she spoke again. "Dragon, indeed."

We had yet to learn how right she was.

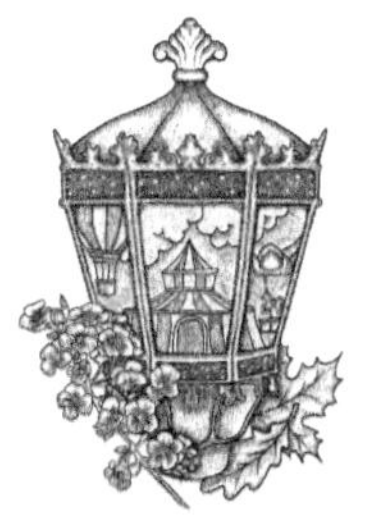

16

GHOST, WITCH, AND SOVEREIGN

Sergio

YASMIN VANISHED. TO RECOVER herself in peace, or so Aislinn and I surmised. I ached for her, but we trusted she would return to us on her own terms. *If Rothadamas allows it,* I thought, clenching my fist around my cane to quell the storm of anxiety. I couldn't risk burning the house down, nor could I simply rush into Kheima, much as I yearned to.

In the meantime, the Celt and I had much to discuss. "So," Aislinn commenced, handing over a cup of tea and pouring one for herself, "It appears your talents as a warlock weren't entirely of the demon's doing."

"So it seems." Setting the cane aside, I flexed my hands, lifting them to stare at the glittering scarlet flecks hidden in the palms. So subtle they were nearly undetectable. What I *could* see of them reminded me of minuscule dragon scales. "Ironic that Yasmin dubbed me 'the Dragon' when she was yet on the cusp of womanhood. I thought it in reference to my dragon tattoo. Later she made it quite clear that she meant my tyrannical mannerisms and desperate love of gold."

I chuckled, though it didn't seem right to laugh when my poor darling suffered so. My mirth ended with a sigh. Lowering my hands, I frowned at Aislinn. "It isn't terribly practical, is it? Pyrocraft, I mean. How can blasting pretty fireworks from my fingers do Yasmin any good?"

"Patience, ringmaster," she soothed, motioning for me to drink my tea. "It will be useful in the proper time and place. First, you must learn to control it."

Huffing, I downed the cup in two gulps. The flavor was not improved by the smell of smoke pervading the room. I wrinkled my nose, wishing for coffee. "Thank'ee, milady. What do you suggest?"

Aislinn raised her cup for a sip, glaring at the charred wall. "For now, we find somewhere suitable for you to practice wielding your Craft, and I strongly suggest you learn to control your temper." She sighed, lowering her cup to its matching pale-green saucer with a *clink*. "Fire magic for the temperamental ringmaster. It's so fitting, I feel a fool for not guessing it."

"As do I," I admitted. "In normal circumstances I'd be rushing out at once to test my limits, but I'll wait here for Yasmin. Then we'll go out." I burrowed down into the easy chair, thus indicating that neither fire nor water, Heaven nor Hell, should compel me to stir from it until I saw my Yassy's face. "I trust I didn't frighten her? She didn't seem to comprehend anything clearly."

"Shock, no doubt." Setting her tea tray aside, Aislinn approached the blasted wall and raised her hands, murmuring, causing a flowered vine to grow and overlap in waving tendrils until the burnt sections were covered. Satisfied, she sat across from me and regarded me with her curious, seafoam-blue eyes. "At long last, the blessed day has come. I'm relieved to see that you've come to terms with your feelings for her." None too pleased with herself, that was plain! "I thought her diary would do the trick." She laced her perfect fingers together with a placid, wicked grin.

I snorted. Thin columns of smoke puffed from my nostrils. Annoyed, I waved them away. "Don't pat yourself on the back too soon. The first time I saw her, she looked positively murderous with rage because you'd given me her diary." It required a great deal of self-control to render my expression grave. "Best prepare thyself for a lecture, witchling."

"I know." Aislinn's unshakable serenity prevailed. "Considering the results, I think she will forgive me." She paused, unlacing her hands to trace her forefinger around the rim of her teacup—clockwise—three quick, intentional times. *I wonder what that signifies,* I mused. *Perhaps, like me, she likes things to come in threes.* "Her tendency to deny her own feelings played against her chances more than the demon Himself," Aislinn continued. "If she'd shown her heart to you earlier... shown her true self... her death might have been avoided. Yasmin, my dearest, how I've mourned for you!" The thought summoned her tears. "She has yet to learn the strength of her own will. We all have the power to turn the wheel of fate, but many of us are too passive to try."

"Pray, calm yourself." I leaned forward to pat her hand. "We must be strong for her sake. She can't return to find us both blubbering messes, *capire?*"

"Don't you go ordering me about like an emperor," Aislinn retorted, flicking my hand away. "Yassy might tolerate it, but *I* don't find controlling men attractive in the least."

I sighed. Again, two wisps of smoke floated from my nostrils. I cursed. "Have some pity, Aislinn! I was demonically possessed. Can you blame me?"

"So was I, in case that fact fled your memory. I still am from time to time."

"Yet He leaves you alone for the most part. Why, nobody knows, but from a day-to-day perspective, you can live however you please." I reverted back to her original comment. "What's left in me is *me*. Good-natured teasing, forgetting to leave my muddy boots at the door, and the occasional show of temper when vexed. I assure you, I'm doing everything in my power to atone for my sins."

"Well, you'd better, lest I turn you into a lizard."

"Oh you would, would you? Then I'd huff, and I'd puff, and I'd burn your house down, little witch."

"*Little?* If you knew but half the spells I've accomplished in the past decade, you'd change your tone, you self-centered—"

"*I see you two are getting along just as well as ever.*"

Yasmin. She spoke within my mind, but Aislinn must have heard her, too; I saw her flinch. Relieved, I held out my hand for Yasmin's. Appearing from the ether, she came to me adorned in ripped black robes. Her eyes, creased with exhaustion, dwelt sorrowfully on our anxious faces. "*I'm so sorry that you both witnessed me in such a state. I assure you, I recover in haste. If I were crippled for days, I would be useless to Him.*"

"What a horrid thing to say," I exclaimed, speaking aloud for Aislinn's benefit. "Don't speak as if you are just a tool. Possess me at once, darling, and rest for as long as you need to."

She hesitated. The temptation was too much to resist. "*Not for long, dearest Sergio. My wounds might hurt you.*"

"Good! I don't know why I didn't think of that before." I rubbed my bristled chin, eyes aflash and lips agrin. "Perhaps possessing me can divide your suffering between us. I can be your safeguard, your healing—"

"*Sergio! No. You know not of what you speak.*"

I stumbled from the force of her voice; it physically pushed me. Aislinn and I shared a concerned glance. "My dear Yasmin, I'm so happy to see you again," the Celt addressed her, every word true as gold and sweet as angel cake. Even I relaxed beneath her soothing tone, though she was not speaking to me. Aislinn presented Yasmin with an enchanted bouquet, sparkling with all of Yasmin's favorite colors. "I'm appalled that our reunion must be under such gloomy circumstances, but as your ringmaster said, perhaps in time... there could be something he and I could do to put things right. You belong here on Earth with us, darling."

Yasmin granted her old friend a weak smile but said nothing. From the minute she entered the room, her haunted eyes latched onto my face and either couldn't or wouldn't look elsewhere for long. *"Dragon King,"* she finally telegraphed in my mind alone. *"How wildly suitable. Yet you wear it so well, it didn't occur to me to think it strange."*

"Did you know?"

"No. I sensed it, but I didn't know what it was. I suppose that's why they say, 'love is blind.'"

"Hmm."

Her pride in me radiated from her being. Pale-blue tendrils spiraled around me like an embrace. For a good minute we just stared at each other, lost in the churning sea of adoration and melancholy, brimming passion breaking the surface in frothy caps. Despite the circumstances, my attraction to Yasmin increased by the hour. Telling her so would accomplish nothing—she'd scoff at it—but if I could *show* her, that was another matter.

I snapped back to reality, realizing that Aislinn looked left out. "Why don't you two chatterboxes get reacquainted," I suggested, beaming at my ghost-witch. "I'll go outside and seek a wide space for pyrocraft."

"Oh, Yasmin! Don't let him go alone! He'll burn my woods down," Aislinn implored with all the force her angelic aspect could manage.

Yasmin stared at me another moment. *I'll join you in ten minutes. Can you keep out of trouble for that long, sir?*

"Cross my heart and hope to eat pie."

She didn't laugh. She was too exhausted to laugh, but she did smile.

I vented my rage against Rothadamas in sweeps of ruby flame.

As one might expect, fire proved difficult to control. Nevertheless, the exhilaration I experienced from wielding it pummeled through my aging body, recalling me back to energetic youth as only magic can. In a word, pyrocraft felt *cathartic.* All negative energy channeled into the flames and dispelled. Flaring, seizing, sizzling, then gone!

Once Yasmin joined me, she caught me laughing. I stood in the clearing with my sleeves rolled up, bundling my blasted hair into a tie to keep it from falling in my face, which I ought to have done at the start. *"You're doing well,"* my ghost-witch intoned. *"I spy, with mine little eyes, only seven scorch marks!"*

Smirking at her sarcastic tone, I answered aloud, "Could be worse. Well, did you avail yourself of your opportunity to hold witchling conference? I was very good, you see. Didn't drop a single eave!"

She tilted her head, narrowing her eyes. Then a low hum of amusement buzzed in my skull. *"Oh, eavesdropping. I fear I am too exhausted to be amused by your wordsmithery, my lord."*

"Of course." I strode to her side and pretended to tweak her earlobe, as I sometimes did back in our circus days. "Then I'll restrain myself and hazard only one question. Aislinn still serves *Him*, so how is it that she's flourishing like the summer grass while you're..." I broke off to grind my teeth.

"You're sweet," Yasmin whispered.

I scoffed, though I appreciated her grateful look. "About time I was, isn't it? The demon made enemies of us so that He might have His way with thee unhindered. And so...?"

"And so," Yasmin sighed, switching to audible conversation. "He only calls for her a few times a year. I am His favorite. A witch of death, as Arusi once termed me: a hex witch. Alas, she spoke the truth."

Arusi. "The African dancer? She was a witch, too?" I groaned, refastening the buttons of my waistcoat. "Oh, yes. I recall coming across that in your journal. By God, how many witches did I shelter in my circus? And how many hexes were piled upon my ignorant head? It's a wonder I'm not a lizard or a frog already."

She didn't respond. Yasmin's steely eyes were fixed on my chest. Flattered, I rewarded her with a beaming grin. She quickly secured her gaze elsewhere. "To my knowledge, there were only the three of us," she answered. "Arusi was not in His service, as we were. Like you, her Craft originated from her own self. She was forced to work *with* Him, but never *for* Him."

Yassy's businesslike tone made me chuckle. *She's jealous. She needn't be.* Perhaps she was trying to distract herself; my looks may have aged a solid decade, but it was clear that she found me more irresistible than ever.

I couldn't deny that my heart skipped at the thought.

Yasmin pretended not to hear my low, seductive laughter. "If any of us placed a curse on you, it was without my knowledge, and Arusi would have had no reason to. As I said, she never served Him. Just coexisted with Him. Called Him 'part of the sacred whole.' She respected Him, despite her apparent antipathy, which I ponder to this day…"

Lifting one hand, I played with her floating hair. "I know this is asking much from you, my charming Schattengeist, but try to train your thoughts upon more pleasant subjects. Like me," I added with a flex. "I'm going to resurrect you, and then you'll live with me in House Vincenzo until the end of your grievously spoiled days."

Yasmin shook her head, a slow-blooming smile lifting her dark lips. "Bravest and most foolish of men! Remember, Sergio, that I chose to sacrifice myself. It was not of your doing; you owe me nothing. I did not come to you intending to weaponize my fondness for your company into persuasion."

Yasmin paused, her silver brows furrowing as she cleared her throat. From time to time, her voice sounded rusty again, rendering her far more comfortable with telepathic conversation. "It is difficult to explain, but at the end of the day, I am not… *miserable* with Him. For all His seasons of discipline, He has given me many blessings in proportion with my endurance. I cannot begin to describe everything I have seen. The wonders I have beheld since my banishment from Earth.

"I have seen what you would call Heaven, and it bored me. I have seen what you would call Hell, and Kheima is beautiful and merciful in comparison. Indeed, I have gained such a measure of influence in His realm that I have made changes according to my own tastes, and I daresay it pleased Him. He praises my creativity and encourages me to visit other realms to expand, influence, or trade acquisitions for Kheima."

My brows betrayed my surprise, but she had more to disclose. "Since I've gone this far," she recommenced, "I might as well make a full disclosure. For all practical intents and purposes, I am the Kheiman Queen." She exhaled from habit, releasing her nervous confession in a breathy plume. "If you bargained with Rothadamas or fought Him to win me back, we may rejoice in our spiritual bond made physical, but then who would I be? A penniless spinster with not a drop of magic in her veins. How could you love me then? I know you, ringmaster." A touch of bitterness seeped from her tone, releasing a twinge of pain in my heart. "You would soon tire of me. As long as I am powerful, that will not happen. Power fascinates you and commands your respect. It always has. So maybe you aren't meant to save me, Sergio. Maybe we're meant to be content just as we are."

I inhaled slowly, tapping the foot of my cane against my boot as I considered her point of view. *She's been tortured,* I reminded myself. *She's not the type to betray her terror, but she's terrified. She must be. The prospect of challenging Rothadamas scares her.*

Also, Yasmin was one hundred percent the type of woman to seize upon a half-truth and weave a whole new tapestry of surmise with it. I saw it in her writing. Yasmin's notions of Erbanhue were not without error. Besides, she had known me best back *then.* She must be reacquainted with me *now.*

"Listen, Yasmin." Placing my cane aside, I again knelt on one knee before her, bracing my hands against my knee and staring earnestly into her face. "A soul accustomed to pain will seek out new wounds. It's only natural that you cannot allow yourself to believe in a happy ending for us. You can no longer imagine selfless kindness, or the comfort of being well and truly loved. You have forgotten what *friendship* is, let alone love! You adored Aislinn just as much as she adored you, and all you could manage just now was a very unconvincing smile."

Guilt swept her expression. I smiled reassuringly. "Fear not, for I am determined to draw your secretly affectionate nature out of the shadows and into the light. But make no mistake," my voice rose an octave or two in passion, "You *will* be mine body and soul, Yasmin Lange, even if you are penniless and robbed of your Craft. I love you, and I'll make you the happiest woman on Earth, else I am not your Dragon!"

Sleet thickened on her thorn-like lashes as her mouth trembled. She *wanted* to believe me. She wanted it with every fraction of her immortal soul.

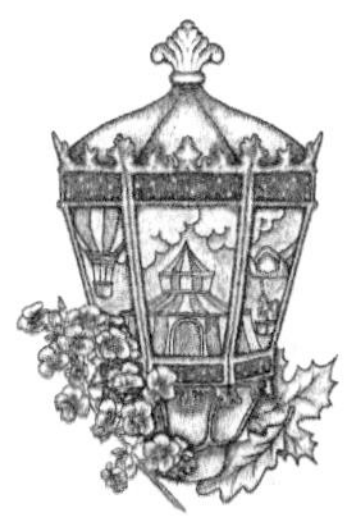

17

To Court a Ghost

Sergio

DESPITE MY ARDENT AVOWAL, Yasmin distanced herself in the following weeks.

Irritating, but not unexpected. She was yet bound to the forest demon. *His* service must come before my company, hateful as it was to both of us, and she would be extra cautious to please Him after... after what the damned creature did to her.

My mind was well made up, the goalpost planted, and my course of action determined. I set my jaw and got to work.

Truth be told, I had no clue what good my scarlet flames could work on her behalf, but I practiced controlling them. Disappearing from the mansion at regular intervals didn't raise any questions, as my daughter and I were both accustomed to doing as we pleased. Even when I came back sweaty and red-faced with the decided tinge of smoke clinging to my hair and clothing, Lillias would laugh and tell me there were more profitable things to do with my time than burn leaf piles in the woods.

As for my household staff, they knew I was touched in the head from the hour I hired each of them; they cared not.

My ghost-witch reappeared sometimes, making crisp remarks in answer to my many questions and watching my pyrocraft with a frigid, mournful face. Her moods were delicate—so many shining icicles of silver-blue ready to crack beneath the slightest pressure. *She needs to be thoroughly convinced that I love her,* I realized, fumbling with my beard as I watched her face. *Really, truly, eternally love her, no matter what.*

If there was a way to show her my past memories, all doubt would be erased. I had watched her practice her aerial art not because I was so controlling and strict (as she believed), but because I loved watching *her.* For years, I imprisoned my strong desire to kiss those cool, sweet lips; I waited until she knew me well and could make up her own mind. And when she stormed out, thoroughly convinced I was mocking her, I restrained myself from running after her and kissing her again, sweeping my fingers through that beautiful hair, like silk formed on the night of a full moon.

Above all, I'd somehow known, deep down, that I was bad for her. That something dark had seized hold of me and refused to let me go.

Now that my soul was free, I was also free to love her, but she had to *believe it.*

Revealed in my dreams, the Kheiman Queen sought refuge from her feelings in her winter realm.

Kheima was indeed altered. Yasmin's touch bound the frigid chaos together into delicacy and refinement. The dark, twisted Tree of the Knowledge of Evil bore decorations of ice in various pagan shapes, bright and miraculous, shining light blue against the black, thorned branches. The forest demon's throne shone fiercely in a glow of navy light. The ebony ice encasing everything like a disease seemed more like a polished floor than the knobby, piercing, uneven ground it had once been. And the odd Creature of Many Eyes, composed of moonstones, gazed upon its Queen with cool adoration whenever she stirred.

Yasmin approached the throne. With the flick of her forefinger, the Creature of Eyes was dismissed. She rested her forearm against the demented seat, evaluating her lonely home with vacant eyes.

He sensed her presence and appeared in a flash, alabaster skin and monstrous wings laden with gemstones. He exchanged a few German words with His witch in a strange, purring voice that bordered on affectionate. Pure white and bald-headed with ice-blue eyes, Rothadamas was an eerie combination of alien and dread angel, formidably muscular. His long hand rested on Yasmin's head before He vanished again, leaving her to her own devices.

The exchange was brief and quiet. Its peacefulness amid the black frost of that winterbourne hell demonstrated the utter trust the forest demon and His witch had in one another. They were not good—they were anything but—but they knew each other intimately. Every strength, every weakness, every past sin and future hope.

Yasmin was one with pain. With loneliness. With torment. And she would stay in that godless place unless I dragged her from it.

How does one court a ghost?

Blissfully ignorant of my quandary, Lillias and Ulysses commenced their bashful courtship with horseback riding across the estate. That seemed like a jolly good idea for *us,* too, until I recalled that unless phantom horses were an option, Yasmin couldn't ride. She could float behind me, I supposed, and give a sort of semblance of riding, but that would be ridiculous.

Ulysses brought Lillias flowers. I knew Yasmin scorned the practice (besides Aislinn's enchanted bouquets), for we'd discussed many thoughts and opinions over the years on our evening strolls. That was no good, either. "It reminds me too much of the rose you left for Janet," Yasmin admitted later, "and the rose I tried to enchant you with afterward—"

"In revenge?" I queried, pretending to be horrified.

"Naturally," she smiled.

By the gods, I loved her. I must have been mad, indeed, to feel irresistibly attracted to a woman who *could* hurt me, curse me, suck my blood like a vampyre.

I continued to revolve the problem around and around—how to court this phantasmic phenomenon of a woman. Yasmin couldn't dine, couldn't be danced with—at least not in public, for all the company would see me dancing with no one and smiling at nothing. Although people were well aware of my eccentricity since I'd worked the circus scene, I had no desire to push it to the extreme of my neighbors ringing up the nearest asylum.

I couldn't buy her clothing or jewelry. She wore what Rothadamas made for her, which infuriated me to no end. I could take her traveling with me, I supposed, but over half that time she would vanish into Kheima at the forest demon's request. Her time was not her own.

Maddened by limitations, I stalked around my office sneering at everything, hands linked behind my back, mumbling to myself like a crazed old man. It was common in life that the best answer was usually the most obvious one. But my ghost-witch harbored such a high opinion of my intelligence—of my creativity—that I hated the thought of serving her the obvious answer: a private ball.

The Vincenzo ballroom of black marble was situated at the back of the mansion, so that it might be surrounded by the borders of the Vampyre Garden. Lined with gloriously gothic stained glass, the spires reached for the cloudy sky. Turrets were topped with brass-bodied dragons in various poses, their jeweled eyes winking down at the dark lawn.

Yes. The obvious choice, but the best one. The ballroom was distant, private, and abandoned at the witching hours, the perfect place for a ghost-witch to waltz unhindered. But, blast it all, couldn't I think of something more *original* than that?

As I continued to pace, loosening my bolo tie with a snort of impatience, I felt the chilly touch in my skull heralding Yasmin's presence. *"May I enter?"*

"You may."

I forced myself to think of other things. As Yasmin's spiritual presence intertwined with my own, I sensed her sighing in relief. "You're trembling," I stated aloud, stopping at my desk. "What happened?"

"Nothing... it's nothing."

"Please don't lie to me, Yassy."

"I... I took another child today. For Kheima. For Him. I thought He was done with forcing me to hunt, but..."

Feeling a ghost tremble around your brain was an eerie sensation, indeed. I flexed my hands and clapped them together, focusing on something else to alleviate the alien impression. "You couldn't help it, Yasmin. We both know what would happen if you attempted to oppose His will."

"I know. That doesn't make my actions any less diabolical. I saved one child, and what was the result? Taking twelve others!"

Sighing, I grew more determined than ever to take her mind off things. To save her from this constant deliberation of evil and woe. "Can you meet me in the ballroom tomorrow? At one A.M.?" I pleaded, brash and breathless.

Her dry amusement colored my thoughts. *"Hmm. I wonder what we'll be doing there?"*

"Shut up and say you'll come," I demanded, grinning.

"Shut up or say I'm coming? I can't do both, dear."

"Then tell me."

"I'll come."

"Excellent."

The frost of her presence lessened as she relished my contrasting heat. She hummed with contentment. I grinned again as I felt her delicate fingers lace between mine. *"Is this all right?"* she asked, a touch of anxiety in her voice.

"Of course." In truth, there was precious little she could do that I *wouldn't* find "all right," but I had no intention of letting her know. Not until tomorrow night.

Those ideas led me down a dangerous path. I began to recall a rather... interesting dream I'd had a few nights prior. I flushed, clapping the lid of that particular box shut and locking it before its contents were revealed. Yasmin's invisible fingers tightened around mine. *"What was that?"* she questioned, coyly.

I replied telepathically, too embarrassed to open my mouth. *"Nothing!"*

"Don't lie to me, Hue."

I groaned. *"Nosy witch! If you must know..."* She'd likely sneer at compliments, but they might serve to distract her. *"I was thinking about the night I kissed you. How beautiful you looked in your sorceress gown with the red and gold stripes of the tent behind you. The golden ripple of the lantern-light against your hair. The captivating sorrow in your eyes—you begged me to kiss you—"*

Instant denial interrupted me. *"I did no such thing!"*

"Not in words, but you're no good at hiding your facial expressions, see?"

She released my hand to squeeze my shoulder. Hard. This only made me laugh. *"You had this look that I can't describe to satisfaction, Yassy. It's truly mesmerizing. It drew me in. That's why I teased you so much. You drove me to distraction, and I longed to repay you in kind. To make you wild for me the way I secretly was for you."*

"Yet in the same breath you called me ugly. What was I supposed to think?"

"That was a nasty habit I had trouble breaking," I admitted. *"You were barely touching the threshold of womanhood when we first knew one another, remember? You don't think I'm the type of man to chase young girls, I hope?"*

"Oh." Her hand released my shoulder to rest on my arm instead.

"You never thought of that?" I chuckled, returning to speaking out loud to emphasize my point. "Once you *were* a woman, I still remained your employer, and as everyone knows, employers courting their employees rarely work out in the long term."

"Then what about Janet Willow?" Yasmin demanded, returning to ice and bite. *"And Lillias's mother, Maria?"*

"Closer to my own age. More accessible."

"But they didn't last, either."

"No—which proves that it was not true love with either of them, my green little Schattengeist. As I told you on that memorable night when I said you and I are so alike—that we craved worship beyond almost anything else—they were just pretty faces, and my demonic self loved conquering the pretty faces." I winced at the memory of sweet, innocent Janet, who deserved much better than me. "I've heard nothing about Maria, but I know Janet is married now, to some country squire or other. I was happy for her."

"Indeed. Your sincerity is refreshing. You were never so humble as this," Yasmin conceded.

"Humph." I fiddled with a bronze paperweight on my desk. "I intend to keep surprising you until you know for certain that the monster in me was laid to rest. By *you,* if you recall, my sterling witch."

I felt her smiling. Her hand returned to mine. *"And I'd do it again without hesitation."*

"Nay, Yassy. This time it will be Sergio saving the witch, not vice versa. I have sworn it; it shall be so."

A rare giggle fluttered overhead. *"Pray, don't change completely. I like a man who can be savage but chooses not to be. So, keep a pinch of devil spice, Sergio. Just a pinch."*

"You know I will." I burned to lean my head against her shoulder. To coil my arm around her silver waist. "After your funeral, I almost lost myself, but your diary called me back. You didn't save me once. You saved me *twice.* I don't know how I shall ever make up for it, but I'll give it my all—with pyrocraft thrown in for good measure. Maybe I can melt His smug white face," I added complacently, with a dark chuckle.

I expected a reprimand. Instead, Yasmin sighed with contentment, tucking her arm through mine. *"It's so good to hear your laugh again."*

18

A Waltz in Witching Hours

Sergio

The Vincenzo Ballroom was certainly something to behold. Mirror-bright ebony marble, multicolored lanterns, and scarlet flames crowning dark candles. Best of all, the low draconian censer draped from the center of the vaulted ceiling, framed by black oak beams. "It makes sense now—my confounded obsession with dragons," I speculated, standing akimbo to approve the finishing touches. Blue and purple smoke drifted from the censer, filling the room with the scent of violets. "Warlocks of pyrocraft are as close to their kind as humans can get, I suppose."

Smiling, I straightened my embroidered waistcoat and gave my hair a few final, rushed swipes. Yasmin had yet to see the ballroom cast in midnight elegance. If only I had the ability to make her a specter gown of sweeping black silk roses, what perfection we would attain this night. Alas, only Rothadamas could clothe her. *Demon bastard.*

The double doors creaked behind me. I turned, bending in a low bow. "My lady."

"My ringmaster."

Yasmin's attire had resumed its silvery-white, flowing aspect. Her ghostly eyes widened behind her veil, bright with ethereal affection. My gracious ghost-witch advanced and placed her translucent hand over my outstretched palm. "It's magnificent, Sergio. Puts me in mind of the first time I saw your splendid Fair of Phantoms."

"Thank'ee." I moved as if to tuck her hand in my arm, walking her around the ballroom's circumference. She followed my motion perfectly. The sharp flora of the garden whispered against the windows, depicting various circus scenes in sparkling pictures. "Lillias wanted to add statues and the like, but I preferred it roomy and uncluttered," I said. "Besides, I spent a pretty penny on these windows. I balked at any suggestion to cover them up."

"Your instincts served you well. As always."

I glanced at her silver veil. Her features could be seen through it easily enough, but I wondered why she seldom took it off. *Perhaps she couldn't?* "I'd have joyfully ordered you a gown for the occasion... Any gown you wanted on the Earth, even if you demanded to be encrusted with diamonds head to toe," I assured her.

She smiled a cool, regal smile. "I appreciate the thought, but I'm no beauty. There's no need to dress me like one. I like my ghostly garb." Floating a little ahead of me, she surprised me by executing a pert little twirl, causing her specter glow to illuminate the night. A small thing—a brief moment—yet it bristled with precious joy, rare as red beryl.

My face colored with answering delight. "It does suit you," I breathed, stopping beneath the censer to observe the tinted smoke alternating from the copper bowl. "There's no denying that silver is your color." *And I've no objection to the low collar, either,* I added, but only to myself.

Yasmin turned to face me, solemn as a priestess. "No musicians. What shall we dance to?"

I gestured toward the phonograph in the corner. "This will do. Ready?"

"Ready. No stupid shoes with bells on their pointes to distract me this time," she laughed. *Actually laughed,* bright and full. I raised one brow, thinking, then burst into mirth myself when I remembered the wild May Day dance she referred to, when Aislinn had brought her bell-encrusted shoes for her costume. "Ah, that certainly sets the mood for romance," I teased her, turning the phonograph crank. "I almost kissed you again. How you teased your poor ringmaster by staring at him with such irrepressible longing!"

She floated close to glare mockingly into my face. "'Twas *you* who asked *me* to dance. If you feared my stares so much, you should have ignored me."

As the music began, I straightened and struck my pose. "Tried to. Couldn't do it."

Yasmin didn't breathe, as a rule—ghosts had no need to—yet she caught her breath. She touched her airy hands to mine. I waltzed with my ghost-witch in the night, to cello and piano strains beneath the magic of stars, among the power of flame, and within the majesty of a quaint gothic mansion teeming with circus memorabilia.

I expected this moment, this dance, to be rife with passion—our soul-bond growing stronger in the dramatic, operatic melody—but Yasmin seemed so far away from me. Dancing with her felt like stumbling after a falling star, desperate to catch it and whisper all my greatest desires to it… in the hope that one of them might be granted. But I could not run fast enough, or there was a hole in my star-net. *Something* refused to grant me success.

Melancholy crept across the ballroom floor. It settled in my heels, slowing our dance. My hands clenched nothing but cold air bearing her form.

Yasmin's smile dropped, betraying concern. "What is it, beloved?"

"I'm sorry," I stammered. I halted and removed my hands from her. "I'm sorry. For everything. Everything He did. Everything *I* did. Most of all," I swallowed back the culminating despair, "I'm sorry I can't dance with you tonight—not really. I can't hold you. Comfort you. I can't… kiss you. And I want to. More than *anything*." My fists clenched.

More than anything. It rang through the dance hall like a clock-strike, breaking a witching-hour spell. A single traitorous tear scalded my bronze cheek. I yelped and smothered it, staring at the red trail it left across the back of my hand. "What the devil is this? Are my tears made of lava?" I spat, annoyed that my hands were shaking.

Yasmin leaned closer, utilizing her cool breath to relieve the burning. I leaned into her, too, cupping the back of her head and touching the side of my face to hers as well as I could. There was nothing but her cold, sweet air, but it was soothing. "I want to change for you. Be good for you," I whispered in her spectral ear. "I'm a fool. How can I give you what you need?"

"You're doing it now," she murmured in my mind. Her hand lifted to brush against my cheek where the tear fell. *"Be near me. Talk to me. Accept me for what I am. That's all I ever wanted."*

Memory replayed the first time we met. That fateful day, I was irritable and distracted. I was busy herding my traveling fair through the city, barking orders, when suddenly a barefooted urchin with ash-blonde locks, piercing gray eyes, and a demeanor stubborn enough to challenge my own stood before me. She demanded to know how to become an aerialist and insisted upon joining us at once.

I ordered her away. She would not go.

Her tenacity was so much like mine, I relented, curious to see where it would lead her. Whether it would make her into a star. As we both grew side by side, drawn closer through mutual privation and exhausting yet rewarding work, my curiosity turned into something else. Something alarmingly possessive.

"Remember when we met, Yassy? I had not the faintest inkling that I was looking down at my other half," I smiled. "If I *had* known, I'd have never wasted my time flirting with anyone else."

For a moment, a pink circle flushed over each of her pale cheeks. Mild irritation launched her out of telepathic speech. "I doubt that! You would have held me at bay and flirted with Janet all the same. You were afraid of me and you *know* it, Sergio Erbanhue Vincenzo." Floating back, she crossed her arms to solidify her scolding, though her eyes retained a playful glimmer.

I flushed in turn; I adored the way she said my name, especially when she was vexed. "Say my name again," I commanded, playfully reaching for her waist. "Say it slowly, though; don't be in such a rush."

Breaking into a broad grin, she floated further still. "You keep away from me."

"You can vanish into the ether any second you like. Little tease!"

Merry as a boy, I chased my ghost-witch around the ballroom for a minute, plying her with false threats and reminding her of my bad knee. She laughed as I hadn't heard since she was a young woman. At last, she stopped, pretending to let me catch her. I batted at the ghostly locks of her hair, like a cat catching strands of yarn. "I've caught my falling star, but alas! I cannot put it in my pocket. What shall I do with it?"

"Let it sparkle from within," Yasmin replied. The natural pout of her lips lifted into a coy smile. "Let it loose inside your soul, and see what wonders come of it."

"Come, my ghost-witch," I called, stepping back a few feet and holding my arms open wide. "Possess me like your afterlife depends on it!"

She flew to me.

A wave of frost embraced me, followed by a cloak of evanescent warmth.

I fell to my knees, gasping. My hands shook. I flattened them against the cold marble floor, facing my own dark reflection. My heart pounded and my head felt so light, I wondered if it was in danger of flying straight off my shoulders like a balloon.

Someone laughed; I wasn't sure if it was my voice or Yasmin's, or a combination of both, but a bubbling, tickling joy washed over me like champagne. I could feel her everywhere, touching me *everywhere,* all at once. I moaned, lying face up on the floor to close my eyes. *This is like my dream.*

Much later, it struck me how ridiculous a forty-one-year-old man must have looked there, prone upon the floor, staring up at the censer as if hypnotized. I thanked our lucky stars that none of the servants checked on their master. Everyone assumed I was tucked in the bedchamber where I belonged.

The bubbling sensation washed up and down, up and down, caressing my arms and chest first. I moaned again, biting my lower lip, my vision flickering as unknown shapes took form in the multi-hued clouds of the censer. They swirled overhead in storm formation. Excitement buzzed deep in my core. By the gods, what magic *was* this? What manner of Craft did the Queen of Kheima possess?

I realized, too late, that I didn't know—I had not the faintest conception of her full capabilities. To trust her like this was beyond trust alone. It was madness. Glorious, electrifying madness.

The censer clouds flew to the candles and put them out. Yasmin shrouded us in darkness, our only guide the light of the moon shining through the windows. She set the *Dragon King* adrift in a delicious dark sea, her passion roiling around me... over me... through me. I released the helm, allowing her to steer me where she willed.

It was a very good thing I'd had the sense to lie down. I was putty in her wicked hands as they loosened my clothes, teased my senses, seduced my rationality. All sense of time, all awareness of place, evaporated until I came crashing down from the waterspout high her spell had conjured. I tugged hard at invisible restraints, panting for breath, ready to beg for it. My veins were full of ice and fire.

She released me reluctantly. I sat up, gulping up oxygen and readjusting to my weight; I'd felt light as a feather, hot as a flame. It required a solid minute to compose myself enough to absorb what had occurred. Paranormal seduction, ghostly intimacy. Yasmin and I were truly *one.*

"How... did you... do that?" I managed between gulps of air.

A touch of mischief echoed from her breathless response. "A magician never reveals their secrets, my lord."

"Wicked witch!" I steadied myself a moment longer before I stood, flushing as I fastened my pants and snatched up my wrinkled shirt and waistcoat. Several of the ornate buttons lay scattered on the floor. "Did I do that?"

"I'm afraid I did. Couldn't get the damned things to behave."

Mirth rose so rapidly in my throat, I nearly choked on it. Had Yassy *ever* cursed before? My influence on her was becoming apparent. I burst into a loud, hearty laugh, sweat pearling over my skin.

Suffusing back into view, Yasmin flinched and whipped her head toward the double doors, no doubt fearing the staff would hear me. "I always knew a submarine volcano lurked beneath your Arctic waves," I chuckled. Still clutching half my clothes, I strode up to her and mimicked giving her translucent cheek a kiss.

"Don't ever speak of this to anyone," she demanded. "I'll send you straight to Hell. It does exist, you know—at least, there is a realm very much like it."

"No doubt you would." I grinned, using my loose tie to playfully "spank" her. "But what would I gain by telling anyone, absurd ghost? They'd lock me up in the madhouse."

A prideful sniff was her sole response.

Beloved! I'd spied a glimpse of Yasmin Lange's fire long ago. It was in my own tent, lurking in her dilated pupils in the aftermath of our first kiss. She wanted to hurt me. To fly at me and beat her fists against my chest... shortly followed by kissing me back with all the passion Juliet ever felt for Romeo.

Better, even! For she and I had the dark arts lurking at the heels of our *amore*. I shan't ever be done kicking myself for such an opportunity wasted. Though this night went a long way toward making up for it...

Gradually, Yasmin recognized what she had just done in the throes of lust. Her wide eyes locked on the ballroom floor and refused to meet my face. I touched my hand to the coils of her floating hair. "I love you, Yasmin Lange," I said, nearly capsized by the surge of tender feelings that followed.

Finally facing me again, her coy smile returned. "And I love you, Sergio."

19

THIS PARANORMAL FEVER

Sergio

From that night onward, I was a hopeless addict.

When Yasmin's soul was *not* melded with mine, my untamed pyrocraft sizzled and spat in my arteries, rushing to inform my heart that my frosty ghost-witch was required to come and tame it. And when her spirit touched mine, it soothed me as David's harp calmed the demons of his pagan king.

Ironic, as she is a demon's queen.

Nonetheless, I knew in my bones she was formed to be *my* queen. There were no classic haunts from those stalwart eyes, only romantic ones. Hypnotic, passionate, dizzying haunts that stole a man's soul from his body and held it captive until that helpless body was pleasured beyond sanity. *Per Dio!* I found little else could be said. Mortal language was incapable of describing the love of a ghost.

Yasmin, and Yasmin alone, both knew and loved my darkness to its furthest reach.

And I would soon know all of hers.

I visited Aislinn as often as the lord of the manor could be spared. She helped me train my Craft and spoke with me about Kheima, which Yasmin seldom did.

"Why won't she tell me more about her role there?" I complained, casting myself into Aislinn's pet armchair and propping my ankle against my knee. My leather shoes gleamed in candlelight. "If anyone on this blasted Earth would sympathize rather than judge, it would be me."

Aislinn glared at me in her precious chair, but I wouldn't budge. I blessed her with a sunshine smile. She waved her hand and suddenly I was blinked out of the chair and dumped onto the green sofa, swallowing a yelp of astonishment.

The Celtic witch sat herself in my former place. "You forget that she isn't just His servant, like I am, or like you were. She's His favorite. Neither of us can possibly fathom what secrets and responsibilities He entrusts her with. What threads she's holding that reach into other realms."

She paused to pluck off her garden gloves, stained with moist earth. "And you know that our Yasmin is quite capable of locking away her emotions. No doubt it has been to her advantage, time and time again... Is love hard for her?" she asked. "Hard to either accept or display? I thought it might be *impossible*." A peculiar gleam lit her blue eyes, puzzling me with their intense focus.

Instantly remembering our steamy ballroom encounter, I barely repressed a broad grin. "She's... coming around. Thank the gods, He doesn't seem to be watching her as closely as I supposed... especially considering the last time He—" Ceasing, I pinched the bridge of my nose. *Tortured her.* Taking a deep breath, I crossed my arms, leaning back on the couch. "She was a wild thing not so long ago. He mustn't have caught on yet that she's waking up. Almost human again."

Aislinn nodded, grazing her thumbnail along her plump lower lip. "I see. I suppose I have you to thank for that," she grudgingly allowed. "For years, it was as plain as the nose on your face that she adored you, though *why* remains beyond the reach of my imagination. She deserves a much better man than *you*."

Huffing, I refused to take the witch's bait, even though I secretly agreed with her. She did love to argue! "Anyway, to business." I moved my arms behind my head. "I acknowledge that we are merely exchanging theories at this point, but I'd like to bounce ideas off your brain regarding how to resurrect Yasmin. Or at least free her from the demon's service, if resurrection is not possible."

Aislinn stood to pace the room, her sculpted forefinger softly tapping her chin. I yet marveled at her beauty, though in the same way I would admire a wondrous sunrise; she was steeped head to toe in beauty enchantments. "Logic suggests that you must challenge Rothadamas one on one, but that would be suicide. Although it's in your favor that you're a warlock *born* and not a warlock *made*, your power represents but a drop in the ocean compared to the strength of a fallen angel." She sighed. "We *assume* that's what He is, at any rate. We'll never know for sure."

"Yes, yes. I know all that." I glared at the low ceiling, fraught with purple vines and creeping flora that *chirped.* Flinching, I hastily restored my gaze to the Celtic witch. *Nota bene: Don't look up.* "But do you know of any spells I could master that would restore Yasmin to life?"

Aislinn stopped pacing, shaking her golden head. "No. I've been searching through every written text I own, but the few resurrection spells I've found... Well, I doubt they would do you any good. His hold on her has had a *decade* to solidify, and it was already strong throughout her painful life. Death has only made her more accessible to Him, more convenient."

My foot bounced against the couch as I fumbled with my beard. "Then perhaps I should offer myself to Him. Gain access to Kheima by my own merit. How else can I study her role there, and the full extent of His hold on her?"

Horror leeched all the bloom from her cheeks. "No, Erbanhue. He will erase your identity piece by piece, until all that's left is a shadow of yourself for Him to manipulate. You won't remember that you ever loved Yasmin at all."

"Hmm." *Then how is it that Yasmin not only remembered me, but loved me still?* I decided not to discuss that with Aislinn, but rather ponder it in the quiet confines of my heart.

Nevertheless, Aislinn read my expression and discerned what I was musing over. "She's the exception to the rule. I suspect she learned how to mask her own emotions so well that even *He* cannot master them all."

Clever witch. Pride glowed in my chest. Only Yasmin Lange could deceive a master deceiver—play her hand that close to her chest. *Her matchless, breathtaking chest—*

I shook my head hard. "What do you suggest I do for now?"

"Continue to court her," Aislinn shrugged, recommencing her measured tread through the cottage. "When the time is right, you must convince her to take you to Kheima and search for a tether."

"Kindly clarify yourself. Tether?"

"Whatever is binding her soul to Rothadamas. Mind you, there's no guarantee that her tether is tangible. It may not be. But in cases like this, where a person's soul ought to have been released into the afterlife but instead was bound to a demon, there's usually a soul tether of some sort. After all, powerful though He is, He is not a... *god*." Her brief hesitancy proved her doubt.

To all three of us—the forest demon's unholy trinity—He reigned over us like a demigod. Yasmin certainly believed He was a god. I myself struggled *not* to. *The Demongod of the Corrupt Wood.* While she remained at His mercy, was Yasmin's belief her worst enemy, or her salvation?

"I see." The dawn of hope warmed the horizon. "What must I do if I find this soul tether?"

"Again, logic would suggest it must be destroyed. That being said," Aislinn frowned, "Wouldn't her soul fly to the afterlife, beyond our reach? I doubt we could resurrect her once that occurs. We'll need to prepare a tether of our own—a temporary one—to call her soul back down to her body." A vaguely horrified expression widened her eyes. "We must have her coffin exhumed and brought here."

I thought of her body moldering in the grave and immediately regretted it. "How morbid." Also, how *inconvenient.* She'd died in America at the Fair of Phantoms. Her body was still there, far as I knew. *I could order her coffin to be shipped here, but again—how hideously morbid, how terribly inconvenient.* Thankfully, she had no living relatives to object to her disinterment, so it was just a question of money.

I must have been cringing. "Don't be a coward," Aislinn chuckled, flashing a bright smile. "I'll have to study more about soul tethers and resurrection spells. I can't make any promises, ringmaster. I hope you understand that. There's a reason why nobody dares to try them; they usually fail."

"Yes. I thank you for your efforts, Aislinn. You're a true friend to Yasmin; you stayed by her side even when I forsook her. I'm sure she hasn't forgotten, and neither have I."

Aislinn dipped her regal head in a short nod. "I never had siblings. Yasmin is like a sister to me." She paused, an uncanny grin returning to her peach-tinted lips. "Although my feelings would be rather objectionable if we were related by blood."

"Pardon me, witchling? *Feelings?*"

Her fae mirth tickled my ears. "I kissed her. Just to see what she would do. I wonder how *you* held back?"

I didn't.

We shared a knowing smile.

When I first began to "tame the ghost," Yasmin's presence lurked in dark corners and lingered in the most forbidden hallways. But now everything about her was brighter, sweeter, *stronger.*

House Vincenzo came alive as she did. A shimmering brilliance lingered over the walls, the ceiling, the dinner plates. Tiny sparkles of white, silver, or pale blue, alternating like winking starlight. I heard my ghost-witch singing, her plaintive, icy voice trilling in sober yet ethereal songs. And sometimes she'd play tricks, swapping items or tugging my hair (just as I used to tug *her* hair), giggling from afar when I reprimanded her.

During her lifetime, I could count on one hand how many times I saw Yasmin *happy.* Witnessing her happiness as a ghost threw me a bit, but of course I was happy, too... or as happy as I could be while robbed of the privilege to hold her, kiss her, stroke her hair.

I pursued my own study of resurrection. The results were most disheartening. Most proclaimed "resurrections" resulted in either the unintentional or *intentional* creation of godless, soulless beings such as vampyres or lycanthropes, which I jokingly mentioned to Yassy as not being the *worst* sort of outcome. I liked the notion of playing rough.

Her eyes widened at the mental depiction. She laughed as she had never laughed before. I failed to perceive what was so hilarious about my naughty quip, but her boundless joy made me smile. "If I didn't know any better, I'd say you *like* being dead." I pantomimed tweaking her ear.

She tilted her head. "I don't *dislike* it. There are many supernatural benefits. But of course," grinning affectionately at me, "I would rather have you kiss me again. And mean it!"

I raised a caustic brow. "You don't suppose I meant it the first time?"

"Of course not! You were teasing me. 'Twas thine cherished pastime."

"Aye, but these reasons are not mutually exclusive." My eyes twinkled in response. "I can tease thee *and* adore thee, sterling witch."

She faked a right hook to my arm, which floated through me. I chuckled at the frigid air whipping my locks back. "Ah, you've *no* idea the trouble you'd be in right now if I could only—"

Suddenly, her face stiffened. She raised a hand to cut me off. The ghost-witch appeared to listen intently, eyes glittering like the gaze of a wary serpent.

"Is it *Him?*"

She vanished without delay. I groaned. *That has to be Him.*

Confound it! I will rid her of this foul, detestable immortal if it's my last accomplishment upon the Earth. Muttering with rage, I stomped to the library fireplace and lit it with scalding scarlet flames from my own mouth. "A drop in the ocean, am I, thou Celtic witch?"

I was more than a warlock with pyrocraft at his disposal. Something else churned in my blood, begging for release. Something *more*. But I had to take care, for it boiled and burst at angry moments more than at any other time.

If the unknown beast escaped and wounded my ghost-witch, I'd never forgive myself.

20

KHEIMA PART 4

Yasmin

Soft blue light flickered from the Kheiman lanterns in the trees. I selected their color for sanctity and calm. It cleansed the black wilderness to which my spirit was bound.

I summoned the throne guard. Once the Creature of Many Eyes scuffled over and bowed, I directed it to lead me to my master.

A chorus of cursed children echoed from the depths of the forest. I fixed my eyes forward, enduring their morbid nursery rhymes without flinching. Kheiman children were far more dangerous than their elders, which was why *He* normally favored them.

Once we drew near the Deadlakes, the Creature left. Rothadamas emerged from a billowing cloud of snowflakes and dark ice. His German greeting was laced with affection... and possessive ownership.

I lowered my head, dropping a wordless curtsy.

"I've changed my mind about your Dragon," the forest demon intoned. His white pupils shone fiercely in the everlasting moonlight. Strange but beautiful eyes; the eyes of a once-splendid angel. "I desire to speak with him."

If my dead veins yet harbored blood, it would have frozen solid. I fixed a mask of stoicism upon my face. He'd seemed so careless about my visits to Earth, I didn't think He bothered watching me there.

I was wrong. *We* were wrong. *Just how much has He witnessed between us?* When I'd begged, over and over again, to know why He was torturing me the last time, He'd refused to say a word. I was terrified that Sergio and I had been discovered...

Intertwining my fingers to keep them from trembling, I struggled to keep my tone carefree. "May I ask what You intend to do with him?"

"I won't know that until I've spoken with him and determined the source of his pyrocraft," Rothadamas smoothly replied. "You've seen a sample of it, I know. How did he seem to you? *Kraftvoll?*[1] Capable of self-direction?" A curious pause. "Human?"

What did He mean, *human?*

This was a test. If I showed the slightest emotion at the prospect of watching my ringmaster becoming enslaved to Rothadamas again, then I would affix Sergio's fate to my own. I had to be measured and emotionless. In the far reaches of my brain, I wondered if I'd *ever* be free to... be myself. To feel what I truly felt without having to put a mask on it. To make my reactions palatable to another. It was all I'd ever known.

And yet, I must remain balanced. Believable. If I showed abject cruelty, He'd realize I was putting on a performance. The Kheiman Queen was

---

1. Powerful

cold, but not openly cruel. The souls she stole and tethered to the forest demon were extracted from their bodies with merciful haste. As Rothadamas Himself once put it, "Anmut does not play with her food."

I exposed a small, prideful smile. I watched the Kheiman maidens tending to the Tree of the Knowledge of Evil, plucking its ripe, ice-cold fruit and tending to its magenta buds. Their fair hands danced around the iron thorns, so brilliant and sharp that the callous moonlight shining along their lengths was *audible.* A high, penetrating shriek, so high that the human ear could barely distinguish it from winter gales.

"The Dragon is capable but careless," I replied. "He has no goal. No direction." Pretending to be quite at ease, I drifted to the maidens and joined them in their labors. The cursed fruit dropped into my cupped hands, sweet of flesh and bitter at its black core. I stared at the blue crystals sparkling around it like sugar. *To think, I used to find this fruit unappetizing.* I took a deep bite. Purple juice stained the corners of my mouth.

Rothadamas loomed behind me. His long white hand rested on my shoulder. I stiffened but managed not to shudder. That He could touch me, and *did* touch me, when my beloved ringmaster could not...

I tossed the fruit aside, suddenly repulsed by it.

"Careless, you say? Then he has not changed." The demon's cultivated words buzzed with shards of lightning, menacing the back of my neck. I exhaled slowly. *Careful! Careful! Careful what you say!* "He's the same diabolical, selfish scapegrace as ever, Master," I murmured, praying they were the right words to say.

"I see." Rothadamas grasped both of my shoulders. His dreadful, beautiful wings shifted around me, folding me closer to Himself. I tilted my head back to look into His marble-white face. *His features are thin. So very thin.* "Then you shall be tempted by him," My master intoned. "You must harden your heart against his reprobate charm." His alien fingers slipped upward to my neck, tapping my skin one by one like spider legs. "Keep well in mind, mine Anmut, that charm is fleeting and beauty is vain. Do you believe he would love thee if I hadn't blessed thee with great power? Enchanting seduction? Magnificent gowns to mesmerize thine targets? Nein, my Queen. You would mean nothing to him without Me."

Another repressed shudder froze my spine. Rothadamas rarely referred to me as His Queen. He only did so when He was especially pleased with my service. And even then I had no crown, no throne of my own, no real command in this frozen forest kingdom. Nay, He could proclaim me the Kheiman Empress, and it wouldn't matter one whit.

But He read my doubts as easily as print. "You doubt your standing, *meine Hexe*?"

Ghosts need not draw breath, but at times I did so from nervous habit. I caught my breath at the deepening throb in His tone. *Careful!* "I am not worthy to be called a queen," I stated. I linked my translucent fingers behind my back. "You speak the truth. I am not powerful, nor beautiful, nor elegant without Your blessings. I am not what You deserve."

At this declaration, Rothadamas's mighty voice raised a winter gale. "Blessed Anmut! For thine heavenly humility, and for thine decade of loyal service, I shall crown you as Queen before all mine subjects. Bow thine head before Me."

My phantom body tensed with fear. With a single sweep of His wings, all the cursed residents of Kheima knelt before us. Rothadamas lifted His hands above my bowed head. "I fear this will pain you, *meine Hexe,* but it's only for a moment. Then you shall revel in spiritual treasures untold, and your Kheiman subjects shall be blessed by merely touching the hem of your garments. Close thine eyes, Anmut. Trust me."

When a forest demon warns you that something is about to hurt, you could be sure it was going to *hurt.* I complied.

Searing pain delved into my head.

I screamed as Rothadamas murmured soothing incantations in His faultless German. Tears cascaded down my face to be half-crystallized by the cold. Once the pain dulled a little, I wiped my cheeks. My fingers came away hot with liquid iron scent.

Blood. I'm bleeding again? Before, I only bled when He *wanted* me to bleed, to suffer. Terrified, I felt along my brow with trembling fingers.

Thorns. He'd anointed His Queen with a crown of ice thorns, and it had grown from my own skull.

I sobbed.

Ten years. I'd escaped being more intimately marked by Him for ten long, agonizing years. My upper chest bore the encircled *X* of all His servants, but I did not stand out in any way—and I was so, so careful, only to end up irrevocably His at last. Wearing His crown, limp and helpless in His arms. Crying like an abandoned child, despite my thirty-three years.

As Rothadamas held me, He leaned forward until His alabaster forehead pushed against the sheer blue thorns. He kept pressing closer until His thin, papery lips were an inch from mine. I gasped, attempting to squirm away, but His black tentacles emerged and forced my face back to meet His. The thorns sank into His pure skin, drawing streams of dark blood. "You see, Anmut? The fallen angel bleeds. Now that we've shed blood as one, as one we shall remain."

He pulled away, leaving traces of His demon blood upon the crown. "Rejoice!" He roared to our subjects. "Pay homage to your Queen."

The multitude raised their voices in complex, rippling song. It was beautiful and terrible—a song I'd taught them myself. I clung to Rothadamas, still sobbing.

No. I am not yours. I am NOT yours!

I belong to Sergio, to my ringmaster! I always have.

I always have.

21

A Wager It Is!

Sergio

Something's wrong.

The portraits in the great hall shook. Tears of blood gathered at my ancestors' painted eyelids. I frowned, reaching out for Yasmin in my mind. *What is it, darling? What's that bastard got you doing for Him now?*

On second thought, maybe I didn't want to know.

No. That was selfish. Tied though my hands might be, I could still comfort my ghost-witch. I reached out again. *Yasmin. I'm here.*

She delayed for several hours. I filled the time tending to chores I'd been putting off, desperate to keep my blazing hands busy before I lit the house on fire. When she blinked into being, I choked on anguished disbelief and rage.

Her silver gown was torn in many places. One sleeve sagged from her bare shoulder. Trails of dried, blood-soaked tears streaked her fair cheeks, and a *crown of thorns* paraded the circumference of her fair head like the death-march to Golgotha.

My Schattengeist was strong. She never quailed from terror, that I ever saw. Yet the utter helplessness, *hopelessness,* in her wide gray eyes struck me mute.

Not mute for long. I flexed my hands as my shoulders quivered with suppressed rage. "That tyrant shall rue the day!" I managed from between clenched teeth. "Yasmin… Yasmin! By God, don't stand there looking like that. It's torture. Come to me. Let me soothe your pain."

Tears recommenced. "I can't," sounded from her feeble whisper.

"Come anyway," I demanded. "He mustn't command every moment between us. He won't!"

Yasmin slowly drifted to my side, affecting to lean her head against my shoulder. I curved my arms around her airy, insubstantial form. "Possess me if you want to," I added. "Please."

She sniffled. "Thank you. I'm all right now."

I scoffed. "After two seconds of a half-baked embrace? You are *not.*"

"As well as I can be under the circumstances, then." She floated a few feet away, managing a transient smile. "Always so difficult to please, aren't you, sir?"

My mouth opened to say something along the lineaments of 'Easier than *Him!*' Thank the gods, I thought better of it. I cupped the side of her face in my hand. "I hate to bring this up so soon, Yasmin, but I must know: What does this…" gesturing hatefully at the crown, "What does it mean?"

"It means that I am completely and irrefutably His right hand."

"Seems a bit overdone. Didn't this seal the notion?" I queried, motioning to His scar on her upper chest. The one He marked her with the first time she willfully chose to use His magic.

"No. That only means I'm one of His proxies. You had the same scar for a time."

"Yes." Once my charismatic powers—to entrance and control my prey—were stripped from me, most of my memories connected to them were eliminated as well. Yassy's journal had recalled them. "Is it still hurting you?" I asked, moving my thumb across the cloud of her cheek. Pale-blue curls whispered around my thumb.

"If I turn my head too quickly, it hurts. But it's mostly numb now." She closed her weary eyes, leaning her limpid head into my hand. "I can only imagine your touch, Sergio, but I *can* feel your warmth. Even if it's only in my imagination, it helps."

"Good."

Despite my softness with Yasmin, rage boiled beneath my skin. I longed to command her to take me to Him at once, but forty-one years taught me some wisdom, if nothing else. I wasn't ready, and I knew it. "Does He require you anymore tonight?" I dropped my hand. "Dare you stay with me?"

To my surprise, a touch of mischief glinted from her shrunken pupils. "If you want me to, my lord."

"No need for you to ask." I offered her my arm. "We'll take a turn or two through the garden and reminisce. Remember that night when I was walking Vainavi and you touched your bare hand to my wrist as you walked by my side? You'll never know how perilously close I came to kissing you."

A wry smile. "You're just saying that to cheer me up."

Thus commenced a skirmish of warring egos and flirtatious nonsense. Yasmin was distracted. Mouth drawn, gaze mournful, she floated so low to the ground that her feet bled into the grass. I noticed that when she was happy, she floated several inches higher.

It scalded my soul. Being forced to stand aside and watch as poor Yasmin took three steps forward, two steps back. Straining to grow into her power and grasp Fate by her devilish horns, bending her down to her will. It comes naturally for some of us, but for others it requires a lifetime of practice. In Yasmin's case, it required her afterlife, too.

I needed a plan.

Not just an *idea*. A plan. Finding Yasmin's soul-tether in Kheima was a good starting point, but even the most accomplished warlock found resurrection no small endeavor. The enormity of the undertaking gnawed at my natural cheerfulness. A thick border of blue outlined my scarlet pyrocraft, attesting to my melancholy.

Fortunately, the bare minimum was taken care of: I'd written and dispatched my request to have Yasmin Lange's casket exhumed and shipped to my estate. All I had to do was be patient, and the first barrier to Yasmin's freedom would be eliminated.

I trudged to my office to pace to full effect. It helped me think, although Lillias insisted I merely enjoyed harassing the household with stomping, mutterings, and the occasional sharp shout when I grasped hold of sensational prospects. However, any good father ought to be entertaining; at least I was *that*—or such was my rejoinder.

"Humph!" I addressed the inkwell. Clasping my hands behind my back, I prepared to monologue upon spiritual matters. "So. He has tightened His grip on her yet again. The insufferable bastard! Every time I think He can do no more, He does. I wonder if He does it just to spite me?"

The inkwell shimmered in agreement.

"Now." I began long, satisfying strides across the brocade carpet. "His knowledge and experience are so far beyond my own, only a blithering idiot would dream of competing with Him outright."

Sir Inkwell emitted mute concurrence.

"Yes." I scratched my chin. "Then I'd say only two options remain. One: Aislinn's plan. I convince Yasmin to take me to Kheima. While there, I exercise every method within my power to avoid Rothadamas while searching for Yasmin's soul tether. Meanwhile, Aislinn is positioned at Yasmin's coffin and has performed whatever spells necessary to ensure that her old tether, when cut, is immediately replaced by the new tether leading her spirit back to her restored body."

I stared at Sir Inkwell. Sir Inkwell stared back.

"Option two: A wager."

The mere mention of the word—*wager*—lit the fire in my veins. Devil's deals were Ringmaster Erbanhue's forte. Here, I might have an advantage.

"I have nothing to offer a demon beyond my own soul, which, according to all evidence, He can take anytime He wants. But if I think of a way to spice up my offer, He may consider a wager. If I win, Yasmin is returned to me alive, unharmed, and unfettered. If I lose, He gets both of us."

In that case, even losing would have a sweetness to its sting. The thought of Yassy and I romping about the Kheiman realm as ghostly lovers, embracing eternal night, caused a slow grin to creep across my face. "Right," I sighed to Sir Inkwell. "Mustn't let my stupid head run wild. At any rate, how can I tempt Him to take the deal? What would benefit Him?"

I increased the rate of my footsteps as I considered everything I knew about Him. I didn't remember much—just what I'd read in Yasmin's journal. Yet Rothadamas did have one weakness for certain. *One* sore point that had tried His foundational strength for at least a decade. Maybe longer.

Yasmin Lange herself.

A sudden suspicion curled my hands into fists as my pacing ground to a halt. *Recall the Book of Enoch. Nephilim. If fallen angels are capable of falling in love with the daughters of men, then it's possible...*

I groaned, running my hands through my graying locks. A demon's demonstration of *love* would not be pleasant. There would be pain, possessiveness, manipulation and control and envy. That's precisely how Rothadamas treated my ghost-witch, down to the letter. *The blasted demon loves her, doesn't He?*

I have a stomach of iron, yet the bile rose. I stamped to the bell pull and rang for water. As I waited, I recommenced pacing, growling like a beast with smouldering hands. *If I'm right, gods damn it, then I have something the demon doesn't have and certainly wants. Yasmin's love.*

Remove me from the equation; uproot me from Yasmin's stolid heart. Then, and *only* then, would Rothadamas have even the ghost of a chance at securing her everlasting loyalty.

"Ghost of a chance." Temporarily soothed by my unintentional quip, I slapped the desktop and chuckled, leaving a scorch mark in the shape of my hand. "Blows, blast, and infernal botheration!"

The next time I saw Aislinn, she'd come to visit me for a change. I sprang down the main staircase (wincing from my bad knee; why did I do this to myself?) and into the drawing room the instant she was announced.

"Do love spells work?" I blurted out before she'd straightened from her meager curtsy. In hindsight, it's shocking that she'd bothered with anything more than a nod. I'd missed the point of it. Now that she perceived me for who I truly was, she respected what she saw.

Or maybe that was my vanity talking. Her curtsy might have been the effect of standing in the foyer of House Vincenzo, greeted by murals of bronze and red dragons revolving in a giant carousel. In either case, I wouldn't blame her.

Her sea-foam eyes absorbed my tense expression. "Why do you want to know about love spells?"

"If Roth—if *He* cast a love spell over Yasmin, would she succumb to it? Would she love Him?"

Aislinn shook her head at once. I relaxed, catching my breath after my stupid romp down the stairs. *Gods damn it, man, you're not a sprightly lad anymore.* I wished for my cane, but I'd misplaced it again.

The Celt removed her green cloak. "Even if it worked for a time, it wouldn't last because she's loved *you* so adamantly and for so long. Her entire persona would have to undergo a massive change for her to forget you. You're part of who she is. What she has become."

"Thank you." Escorting her into the grand room, I dropped onto the sofa and motioned for her to sit across from me. She cast her eyes ceilingward at my ungentlemanly habit of seating myself first, but I ignored her. "I presume you're plagued with curiosity as to why I want to know?" I asked, suddenly spying my missing cane leaning against the sofa. I snatched it up with a grunt of satisfaction, twirling it around.

"Perhaps." She grinned, rearranging her skirts. "Pray, why would He desire the romantic attention of *any* woman?"

"Why indeed!" I chuckled. I tossed the cane down next to me and leaned back, arms crossed. "Why would any of us desire it? Because women are the mystic wonders of our world. The most puritan Christian among them works unconscious magic every day she lives, infusing her surroundings, her family, and her friends without realizing her power. Her natural Craft soothes the very earth beneath her feet." I grinned. "Which is where that saying comes from, you know. 'He worshiped the ground she walked on.' It's been blessed by her magic, whether she acknowledges it or not. And *He* senses it; He reaps it for His own advantage. Kheima has improved thanks to her. I've witnessed the changes in a dream myself."

That Celtic witch had the impertinence to laugh. "Love is indeed blind! I've met a multitude of womenfolk that are forces of nature, indeed, but far from *soothing* in their perverse ministrations. We are also forces of chaos, of long-repressed wrath, of spirit-bound indignation for the vast array of religious institutions birthed and maintained by men. So, look before you leap, ringmaster, else you leap into chaos instead of a soft bed."

I grunted. "And Yasmin called *me* cynical! But you shan't lead me astray into quarreling, as entertaining as it is." I leaned sideways, snatching my pipe from the side table, stuffing it with fresh tobacco, and lighting it with my own breath. "Do you know of Yasmin's crown?"

Aislinn flinched and averted her eyes.

"Yes, you've seen it." I indulged in thoughtful puffs. "It's disgusting, but delightfully suggestive. I present to you this theory: Rothadamas *does* have a weakness. And that weakness is Yasmin Lange herself."

She started and gaped. "You're saying He loves her?" Incredulity tensed her posture.

"And why not?" Anxiety and pride intertwined as I spoke. "She's brilliant. She can converse with the most educated men in society, and their attention will not flag. She's tenacious and loyal to a fault—even to *Him!* And upon my honor, she's more beautiful every year that passes with the pure, honest beauty of starlight in December."

"How poetic you are when the notion strikes you," Aislinn smiled. "When you're so well-spoken with that dark, thoughtful brow raised, I am reminded why poor Yasmin is so taken with you. Well. Your theory is highly interesting, and it does explain why He hasn't stolen more souls to become High Proxies, instead choosing to focus all His training and attention on *her*." She pursed her lips. "Your eyes are twinkling, sir. I daresay you are gleeful about it!"

"I've had time to process my initial rage," I shrugged. "And, you see, it simplifies matters beautifully! We can skip all the confounded resurrection theories and playing ring-around-a-Rosie with a Demongod in His own realm." I clapped my hand against my knee, dropping my pipe in my enthusiasm. Aislinn hastened to fetch it before it set fire to her gown. "*He* wants her, but she wants *me*. He cannot cast a spell to have her. It must drive Him utterly mad that He can't alter her affections. And He's getting desperate, weaving together crowns and such. Ha! A wager is the way forward. So a wager it is!"

22

THE DRAGON PREPARES

Sergio

"WHAT DO YOU MEAN, a wager?" Yasmin's tone was a tad stiff.

Having anticipated her resistance, I smiled and clapped my hands together. It was essential that I appear at my ease, no more perturbed than if we were planning a birthday dinner. "Did you ever wonder why *you,* and you alone, have remained these ten years as the demon's only High Proxy?"

"Who said so?" Yasmin scoffed. She coasted away from me, crossing her arms and staring out the window. A sprinkle of rose-hued light framed her pastel physique. *Someone ought to paint her just so,* I mused, biting my lower lip.

Wholly unaware of my unholy thoughts, Yasmin recommended, "I've never seen another High Proxy with my own eyes, but that doesn't prove they don't exist. He visits many countries... other realms. Sometimes He's gone for a month at a time."

"But how does He act when He returns?"

"Rather... attentive," she confessed. An uncomfortable frown creased her mouth. "Like He missed me. I'm not flattered by it, if you were entertaining the thought."

"Did His attention toward you increase over time?" I gulped back a sudden wave of jealousy threatening to inundate my self-respect. *I'll win back every year He stole from us, and then some.*

"Yes," she admitted. Her stare accused me of insanity as she snapped, "If you're implying that He *loves* me, I assure you He isn't capable of loving anybody."

"Not in the *human* sense of the word 'love,'" I allowed, raising my forefinger, "but remember, Yassy, that He is not human. Fallen angels *can* love, or at least crave and lust same as we do. Recall the Nephilim."

"A religious myth."

"Perhaps. But for argument's sake, suppose their parentage to be confirmed. The result of fallen angels taking human women for themselves."

Her stare softened. "Humph. Well, I won't be allowing any such action from Him." Her face writhed with disgust. "So, what is your point, sir? Beyond making me feel ill."

I snapped my fingers. "My point is that if He indeed cares for you—in His dark, disturbed way—He must feel humiliated that He cannot make you care for Him. He would want me out of the way, since you *do* care for me. Or so I can assume," I added with a coy grin.

She floated close to mimic elbowing me. "That's true, but since I'm a ghost, we can't actually..."

My ghost-witch drifted off and blushed. I cherished the sight of peach roses budding on her white cheeks, albeit briefly. "But we can do other things," I reminded her in a low tone.

Her eyes softened as they divined the wicked spark burning in my pupils. *"Yes. Other things,"* she whispered telepathically.

"What I meant to propose," I resumed, fighting to stay on track, "is that I can offer my own soul willingly to Rothadamas—or simply my life, whichever he prefers—if I lose the wager. And you shall be resurrected and returned to me if I win."

She tensed at the prospect, yet she remained calm, waiting to hear my full proposal. I smiled down at her. *She's grown so much over the years.* "And the wager itself?" she questioned.

I nodded. "That's where I need your intimate knowledge of His character. What would entice Him most? Claiming new souls for Him within a certain time limit, or under certain conditions? Obtaining a rare artifact that He doesn't have the time or inclination to fetch for Himself? What say thee, your royal ghostliness?"

Yasmin floated across the hallway as she pondered. I marveled at her specter-form beauty, so precious and unique. The flesh stripped bare so the spirit might shine all the more. Glowing. Set apart. *Holy.*

The crown still caused my blood to boil, but it matched her regal aura so flawlessly that it might as well have grown from her skull. *Perhaps it had,* I frowned, remembering the dried flecks of blood...

"I must consider the matter further before I can answer," she murmured, lifting her gleaming head. The veil rippled over her face as the crown glittered above it. "But Sergio, you are an admirable warlock in your own right. Now that your latent powers have awoken, it would give Rothadamas some trouble to claim you if you resisted Him. Be that as it may, He can still take you whenever He wills. He's had thousands of years—perhaps longer—to practice the irresistible corruption of human souls. You cannot withstand Him any more than I could. How would offering yourself to Him freely be a temptation for Rothadamas?"

"Point taken, quick-minded Yassy, but you forget that we have a powerful witch on our side."

Yasmin permitted herself a small, fond smile. "Aislinn?"

"Aislinn." I chuckled. "She wasn't keen on the idea. She's accustomed to playing it safe when it comes to Him. Ducking low and avoiding attention so she can continue living how she likes. But I eventually persuaded her to shield me from afar. Once I've mastered my pyrocraft, she and I will make a formidable team." I pushed up my sleeves, grinning broadly. "I'd like to see Him try to take me then!"

"What about me?" Yasmin pouted. "You don't expect me to stand aside, wringing my hands and moaning, do you? I've learned a trick or two myself after a decade of ruling Kheima at His side. *I* am a powerful sorceress, too."

My eyes lingered on her, sparkling with affection. "You needn't convince me of it. I know. But you must stand quietly to one side and not involve yourself. If you did, the validity of the wager would be put at risk. Do you see?"

Yasmin relented with an angry huff. "Of all men to succumb to, I lost my heart to the man who vexes me five times a day."

"Careful, Yassy. Flattery gets you everywhere with me."

She laughed. Short and crisp, but a laugh.

As the first earnest frost of winter settled over the Vampyre Garden, I practiced my Craft. With Yasmin, I remained cheerful and affectionate, unwilling to add to her fear by betraying my own concerns. For I *was* concerned. I lost countless hours of sleep to endless pacing, muttering aloud plan after plan, wager after wager, only to deem them unfit for my immortal foe and tossing them out in disgust.

Yasmin had no answers for me. She'd possess me (at my invitation) to stroke my inner forehead with her icy fingertips as we melded our thoughts as one, hoping it might encourage a brainstorm. In truth, it only served as a distraction. Our growing love for one another couldn't handle the intimacy of ghost possession, and we'd... end up doing other things.

After one such time, I kicked off the tangled bedsheets. "By God, woman. Hathor herself might blush in shame if she witnessed what you do to me."

Yasmin withdrew from my body. "You don't seem to mind it," she whispered.

"Nary a bit." Putting my hands behind my head, I grinned up into her star-like face as she floated above me in a horizontal pose. "But tell me something, thou witch. Why do you wear that confounded veil? Can't you remove it?"

"Nein," she answered. "This veil protects any living soul who might see me. Including you, beloved. My wardrobe is at His beck and call, but it is never without a purpose." She sighed.

I didn't like to admit that He had good taste. He preferred cut and make over fuss and feathers, which suited our ghost-witch.

Rolling onto my side, I reached for the silk shirt rumpled on the floor. I smirked when I noticed a few missing buttons and a rip. "And there goes another one. You could be a *tad* less aggressive, darling. The maids may ask what in tarnation I'm doing to my best shirts. Describing my paranormal lover might prove mighty uncomfortable all around."

"Yes, that would be unfortunate."

Stumbling to the dresser, I pulled a deep green collar over my head, tossing aside the accompanying emerald bolo. "I wonder what it would have been like," I mused as I tightened my snakehead earring. A miniature twin to my cane's cobra handle.

Her cool breath prickled the back of my neck. "What are you referring to, sir?"

"What if Rothadamas had never haunted us? What if our circus had just been a circus, and not a magnet for dark forces? That we were free to love each other in our youth, you and I." My voice deepened with emotion.

Yasmin's ethereal hand brushed my shoulder. "Even without His influence on us, neither of us was perfect, my irascible Dragon. Let's acknowledge our young selves for what they were: blind, beauty-loving fools. And let's say no more about it, if you please."

"Yes, milady." Her hand lingered. I hovered my fingers over hers. "But I'll have you know I'm still a beauty-loving fool where certain moon goddesses are concerned."

I heard the fragile smile in her pert reply. "Don't speak nonsense, Hue."

She leaned her forehead against the back of my shoulder. So content in my presence. It begged such a contrast to her stiff, inscrutable mannerisms back in our day that the water rose in my eyes. "Blast it, Yassy! Never make a warlock cry; 'tis rotten luck."

"The witch can counter it," she murmured. "Cast your masks into the sea, ringmaster, for you'll never need them again."

23

THE DEMON DESCENDS

Sergio

THE MINUTE I WOKE to my estate dusted in ice-blue snow, suspicion corroded any thought of breakfast. Needless to say, that was not the usual color of a snowfall.

I rushed to dress and descend the stairs, snatching the cane and favoring my sore knee. Cloaked in my heaviest cape, I strode out the foyer, ignoring Eloise's curtsy and lisped morning greeting. *This is a Kheiman frost, else my name isn't Sergio Vincenzo.*

Wrenching the door open, I crouched to examine the newborn snow. It was strangely soft—as soft as satin, if one could envision that comparison—but it bit your finger just before it melted, like a tiny living creature. The resulting dewdrop turned gray and slipped from the skin, leaving an angry red blemish in its wake.

I shook the nasty sensation away and straightened, clapping my hands once. Sharp and determined. "Up and at 'em, demon! Can't tolerate happy mortals? What do you plan to do about it, eh? What?" I spread my arms wide, grinning at the navy clouds thickening the sky. *That's Him all right. He's planning something for little old me. I'm flattered!*

I kept on the lookout for Yasmin's blueish tendrils. I didn't see them, but that was typical during daylight hours. I greeted my daughter the same as always. I sang as I completed my daily tasks and answered correspondence (not that I received much). I poked fun at my maids and harangued my butler, who kept pausing in his chores to peek out the window and marvel at the strange snow.

Taunting my subconscious like the steady tick of the grandfather clock, the snow ever fell. The demonic harbinger haunted the ear with deathly silence, freezing the senses with lurking calm. Beautiful, terrible, and treacherous.

I'd best settle on that wager. Whether in *love* with his Kheiman Queen or not, Rothadamas intended to keep her. That was the message of the silent, biting snow. That I couldn't stop Him any more than I could command the snow to cease falling.

When Yasmin finally appeared, I tossed aside the book I'd been perusing for the past hour. Although my gaze flew across the same two pages at least thirty times, I hadn't absorbed a word. "Is everything all right?"

The crown of thorns glinted from her head. The upper section of her veil covered the base of it, so I couldn't confirm whether it had *grown* from her head or not. I parted my lips to ask her whether it had, but she interrupted with an alarming piece of news: "He'll be watching us every minute from now on. He told me to tell you that."

I started at the eerie timbre of her voice, guttural and depressed. I gathered a deep breath and nodded. *No more games.* For better or worse, it was high time I held one last conference with Aislinn and set the shield.

I prepared to murmur a spell allowing me to communicate with Aislinn, but Yasmin spoke again, stopping me.

"He wants to speak with you," Yasmin clarified. A puff of smoke escaped my mouth as my arms crossed. "When you're ready, go to the gate of your Vampyre Garden and knock on it three times. Rothadamas will transport you to Kheima and speak with you there."

He is initiating our meeting? *Catch me!* As Yasmin warned me, it would be absurdly simple for Him to imprison my soul the minute I entered His realm. Even with Aislinn's shield to protect me, I wouldn't last long on the demon's own turf. "No," I replied, making every effort to sound unruffled. "I won't agree to talk to Him there. He must meet me at the gate and keep us there."

Yasmin lowered her head in a prayerful pose. After a minute of silence, she lifted her head again. Her eyes shone like dull marbles beneath the shadows of the thorns 'round her beautiful, postmortem head; my indignation raged against the change. *Every time she's beginning to heal, He kicks her back down.* "Very well," the ghost-witch intoned. "He agrees to meet you at the gate and promises not to remove you elsewhere. But in return, you must agree not to attack Him. He wishes to converse with you, not eliminate you in a precipitous battle."

"Did He mention *why* He wants to talk to me?" I asked.

To my surprise, Yasmin dipped her chin in a slow nod. "He is... curious about you. He remembers you but vaguely from our hunting days, and He wishes to be reacquainted." She paused before quickly adding, "He wants to know what kind of man I love."

How possessive of Him, I thought, but wisely did not say. It was certainly suggestive. I squared my shoulders and cleared my throat. "I'll be there."

"I shall convey your response to the Master."

I flinched at that term. *Master.* So cold, so obedient. Before I could risk saying something imprudent, she vanished.

As I bent to pick up my book from the floor and return it—a mindless motion of habit, for I loved my books—I struggled with the sudden shift from potential magical battle with a demon, to a potential war of wits. It seemed just as dangerous to impress Him as it would be to disappoint Him. If He liked what He saw, wouldn't He immediately take my soul for His own use?

Again?

And if I played the fool, wouldn't He eliminate me at once, claiming to Yasmin that He was doing her a favor by ridding her of a senile old idiot?

Aye, Heaven and Earth may testify to the bravery of Sergio Vincenzo, but matching wits with a fallen angel caused the former fiery ringmaster to quake in his polished boots. And far be it from me to deny it.

"So, this is the mighty Dragon whom Anmut loves."

The demon's gaze was oddly human. Thoughtful. I remembered Him as a black, static-ridden shadow of a creature, thin and featureless with spider-like limbs and a strange, contorting manner of movement that startled me with sudden jerks. He didn't look like that at all in His own realm, as I'd seen in my dream, and He didn't look like that in the Vampyre Garden.

As in Kheima, He was striking. His muscular build was perfection itself, a white marble statue given life. Ice-blue irises glittered around white pupils, sharp and delicate. A long gray skirt stitched with strange symbols, secured at the waist with rope, swept to the snow-clad ground. His bald head was covered with a matching hood. His sculpted chest was bare, glimmering like snow in the dim evening light.

Most impressive of all, dragging through blue-frost foliage on either side of Him loomed His enormous, gem-laden wings. *Can't possibly fly with them, but they're incredible, nonetheless.*

Grinning, I clasped my gloved hands behind my back to offer an exaggerated bow. *"Don't you dare,"* Yasmin telegraphed.

My left eye twitched. *"Don't I dare what?"*

"You're jealous." Yasmin averted her eyes, hiding a brief flash of a smile. *"Don't let Him notice. Be strong! As you said to me once, you're a devil in your own line, and by far my favorite. Don't forget it."*

I drove my stare deep into the demon's pupils. "Ten years."

"Yes?" His tone sounded polite to the point of complete and utter detachment. After one cursory glance, He was bored of me already.

Well, that wouldn't last long.

"What would it take for you to let Yasmin go?" I asked.

That got His attention. His brilliant pupils narrowed as they sprang back to life, no longer glazed over. "She's mine. She agreed to be mine in your daughter's place, and what I take is never returned to the land of the living."

My muscles tensed as the demon's grim face relaxed. He paced close to Yasmin, resting one white hand on her ghostly shoulder. *I hate how tall He is,* I stupidly thought for no reason.

And He can touch her. I already knew He could, yet fury rose in my chest. I forced it back down with all the limited self-control at my disposal. "Yasmin, is this true?" My voice dropped low as I, too, slipped closer to my ghost-witch. "You not only rescued Lillias from this winterhell, but you also took her place? Of your own accord?"

She merely nodded, as if it were old news by now and quite unremarkable. "It was either her soul or mine. For my master must have a High Proxy. The place cannot be empty."

The place cannot be empty.

After staring at Yasmin with pained thankfulness, I returned my attention to the forest demon. He stood close to her still, His hand clasping her shoulder. Possessive. "You'll need another High Proxy to take her place before she can be relinquished," I realized aloud.

"None can take her place," Rothadamas answered. His tone shifted into a bitter sternness, permitting not an inch of argument. "Anmut is uniquely suited not only to me, but to Kheima itself. One need only look upon our realm and divine it for himself, Dragon."

Our realm, meaning His and Yasmin's. Indeed. I grudgingly conceded that Yasmin not only survived in frozen Eden, but some part of her—the darkest part of my beloved witch—thrived there. For Yasmin and I shared the same core fault: a primal craving for power. Her power might be derived from another, but it was power all the same.

It was up to me to prove to both of them that Yasmin Lange didn't need power to be worth something. She could be *herself* and achieve her most treasured goals. And she certainly didn't need power for me to love her.

"Then let me offer you a deal," I proposed. "A wager, if you will."

Yasmin's eyes widened behind her veil. I hadn't spoken of this proposal to her since I knew she would consider it far too risky. But Rothadamas would accept nothing less.

As anticipated, a spark of interest lit the demon's ice-cold aspect. His hand pulled Yasmin a little closer... the motion did not escape me. I gulped back a growl. "What is your proposal, Dragon?"

I straightened my waistcoat, staring Rothadamas straight in the eyes. "Give me one year to find a replacement High Proxy for you. A soul just as suitable to you and fit for Kheima as Yasmin herself. If I'm able to complete this task within one year, then my payment shall be this: you will resurrect Yasmin Lange back to life and sever all ties to her soul, relinquish every claim, and erase every bond, whether natural or unnatural. She will not be burdened by your existence from a single hour henceforth."

Yasmin's dark lips parted to protest, her silver eyes flashing with anger. "*Wait!*" I practically shouted into her mind. "*I'll explain everything later. Just wait. Trust me!*"

Rothadamas flexed His wings. I couldn't help sparing another second to admire them. Mottled and misshapen though they were, the gemstones encrusting the bone structure and peeping between the sharp feathers demanded reverence. He'd been a glorious angel once. Any dolt of a human had to admit that the traces remained. *And yet, Yasmin's loyalty is not with Him,* I comforted myself. *It remains steadfastly with me.*

Young Erbanhue's chest would have puffed with pride at the thought. Now it generated a bittersweet, solemn sadness. I didn't deserve it. I *never* deserved Yasmin.

"And if you should fail?" the demon queried, dragging out each word. A deepening chill swept over the garden at His malevolent question.

"Then you shall have not only Yasmin, but myself as well. Of my own free will. Take my soul and change it, or eliminate me entirely; it is up to you."

"A poor incentive." Rothadamas's thin smile was unsettling. "I can take you anytime I please, fledgling warlock. I refrain from the temptation since I have no use for you at this time."

At this time. He placed such careful emphasis on that phrase. I postured with an unshaken brevity I did not feel. "You might be surprised. My powers are more complex and diverse than you think, and their source runs deep. You aren't omniscient, Rothadamas."

The prong of truth failed to discourage Him. He removed His hand from Yasmin with a slow, nonchalant nod. I breathed an inner sigh of relief. *That's right. Keep your hand off her, you foul disease.*

"This is true." His neck craned as His eerie head tilted, moving with that odd jerking motion He usually displayed in His hunting form. "I do sense something *other* stirring within your blood." Parchment-thin nostrils flared open as He breathed in my scent: "You smell of saffron and the Otherworld. There might, indeed, be more to you than meets the eye, even the eye of an immortal. You mask yourself most effectively, ringmaster; I daresay as effectively as Anmut herself. It is vexing, yet impressive."

Astonished by how *chatty* He was with me, I stole a glance at my ghost-witch for her reaction. She looked undecided, swinging like a pendulum between smirking in agreement and indulging her notion to scold me. "*Later,*" I reminded her. She frowned but blinked her acknowledgment.

"One more thing," I added. "Throughout this year, both Yasmin and I shall be fully protected from all demonic possession, including from yourself."

"You doubt my ability to play fair," Rothadamas stated, but He chuckled. It sounded more like the threatening growl of a great cat than a laugh, causing the skin on the back of my neck to prickle. "Very well. You're lucky to have caught me in an amiable mood, Dragon. I look forward to observing your efforts." He smiled—a wide, fracture-thin smile that was far more imposing than His laugh—and touched His fingertips together. "I also anticipate a most amusing year deciding what I will turn you into once you are mine."

He vanished, and I turned to Yasmin with my arms extended, joy and hope vibrating from each fingertip.

She was trembling. A single tear froze against her cheek.

"Why, Sergio? My beloved, you have chosen a fate worse than death."

24

MASTER VINCENZO'S MADNESS

Sergio

I sighed, letting my arms fall to my sides. "I promised you I'd explain everything. Have you no faith in me?"

"This task is impossible," Yasmin whispered aloud. Her gaze dwelt mournfully upon my face, absorbing every feature as if already resigned to see it pillowed in a coffin. "He has made up His mind to refuse any soul you offer. Surely, you must have sensed it. You are no simpleton! What have you done, my beloved?"

"Exactly what I intended to do. I bought us time."

Drying her tears, Yasmin steeled her face, returning to impenetrable stoicism. "What do you mean?"

I extended my hands for hers. Hesitating, she hovered her palms directly above mine. The cold air buzzed over my skin. "If I hadn't made that wager, then He could have stolen my soul for Himself whenever He wanted to. This way, He's sworn to keep His hands off my soul for a solid year. And according to all demon lore, they must honor their agreements. They're bound to them just as they were as angels."

Clearing my throat, I carefully proceeded with the next part of the plan. "Now you may take me to visit Kheima with you, and I'll be safe. We are free to seek the crack in the foundation... the weakness in your curse. So don't cry, little Yassy." I dropped my voice to the soothing, placating tone she knew so well. "I will resurrect you and make you whole again. Upon my life, I will, with Aislinn's aid."

At last, Yasmin lifted her eyes to mine and managed a weak smile. "There," I murmured, placing a kiss in the proximity of her specter forehead. "That's my sterling witch. We shall conquer the forest demon together, you and I."

Another plaintive sniffle. "You always did speak nonsense when you were trying to be romantic."

"Blows and botheration!" Her accusation sparked a grin. "You like it; don't pretend otherwise, for you cannot hide your true emotions from *me*."

"What if we cannot find a way to break the demon's hold?" Yasmin asked, removing her hands from above mine. "I'd rather descend to the Second Death than watch you become... something else."

"I may be something else, but I'll be with you forever. And that's better than living out the rest of my life alone, and facing eternity without you."

"You haven't seen what He can do," the ghost-witch maintained with a sour face. "You haven't dwelt in living nightmares as I have. Thalia von

Brittania was child's play for Him. You'll think her charming once you've lived in Kheima for one week."

"Pray, don't linger amid such dark thoughts, Yassy. I've pledged to rescue you, and rescue you I shall, or be metamorphosed in the attempt." I lifted my hands in a helpless gesture. "How do you plan to stop me, anyhow?"

"I have my ways."

I chuckled, pretending to tug her hair. Her ghastly, threatening stare did unmentionable things to my body, but now I shuddered with eager anticipation instead of nervous terror. *I am perhaps not quite sane.*

Meanwhile, poor Lillias was doing her best to process the fact that her Papa skated the border of madness.

He rambled over the mansion, muttering to no one. Several times, Lillias thought she overheard the name *Yassy*, but she dismissed it until she heard it again, clearly and distinctly, as she lurked outside of his library one night. And from the way his affectionate conversation was paced, he not only spoke to his dead witch, but made up her responses as well.

"This is beyond everything!" Lillias exclaimed after prowling back to her bedroom, flickering candle in one hand, Bible splayed open in the other.

Peering down the hallway, I whispered a curse; *she knows.* I thanked the gods she didn't stumble upon the inverse pentagram in the attic where I conducted my studies in demonology. *It's bad, but it could be very much worse,* I reflected.

To my knowledge, the Vincenzos never bothered with religion beyond the curious reading, but now Lillias seriously considered it. Was her father possessed? Was he haunted by the vengeful spirit of Yasmin Lange, intent upon serving him hell in her afterlife as she had been served hell throughout her life?

Ha! My poor dear. It didn't occur to her that Yasmin practically lived with us. I debated whether or not to tell her, but she was out of the house half the time anyway, *and* was being courted. One of her pretty little feet was already out the House Vincenzo door. I didn't see the sense in disturbing her with the truth when she could do nothing to help—and, in fact, might hinder us—and if all went well, she would soon be married and out of the house. So, why tell her?

Like most fathers, I hated the thought of handing my daughter off to a clueless young whipper-snapper and just *hoping* he would treat my Lillykins right. But alas, this was the way of the world. Yasmin and I both knew how successful we were at fighting *the way of the world.* Luckily, I'd charmed it into working *for* me instead of *against* me, but it had required a hefty bribe.

Aislinn agreed to meet me on my woodland trails for a ride. As we bid our steeds a gentle, "Walk on," I tossed the Celtic witch a mischievous look. "No doubt you've been spying on us and know all about our Kheiman visitor, eh?"

"I have much better manners than *you,*" Aislinn replied. She adjusted the cape of her red hood, shielding herself against the November chill. "I wait for Yasmin to tell me herself, as she often does, now that she's somewhat recovered." Her eyes steeled in my direction. "So, you have given yourself only one year to achieve the impossible. A facade to buy time, I suppose? What is your next move?"

"To enter Kheima with Yasmin." I spoke a soothing word aside to Belmont, patting his stiff old neck. "I need to start looking for clues."

"Where do you plan to look first?"

"The Tree of the Knowledge of Evil. I feel drawn to it, especially since I was once tied to it as Yasmin was tempted to perform craft extraction there. 'Tis a source of divine power, and no mistake."

"No mistake," Aislinn repeated. "But I certainly wouldn't touch it, if I were you. You might feel drawn to it by design—to eat of its fruit."

"It bears fruit? I don't recall that."

Aislinn reined in her mount to slow its pace before replying, "There are many manipulations and hallucinations throughout the Kheiman realm. He only shows you what He wants you to see. It's possible to catch Him off guard, of course, but it is rare indeed. Yes, the Tree bears forbidden fruit, as it did on the first day of mankind."

I nodded. "And Yasmin has tasted it."

"Multiple times. That's why she is so powerful."

So dangerous, Aislinn could have said, but she did not.

"Ringmaster," Aislinn lowered her voice, "I admire you for wanting to save Yasmin. With all my heart, I do. But are you certain she is... herself?"

My forehead creased. "What are you driving at, witch?"

"She's a... a wild spirit, to put it concisely. A demon's ghost, or worse: what if she's another one of His hallucinations? A trick to get you to commit yourself to Him of your own free will. There is no going back once you've freely given yourself. I ought to know." She exhaled a sigh from the depths of her being. "There's too much that could go wrong. Rothadamas is powerful... *beyond* powerful. The word doesn't do Him justice. Who are you to go against Him?"

"That's your decade of service talking," I coldly replied. I urged Belmont a bit faster, striding ahead of her. "Do not place Him in the throne of gods, for He is not one. Hell would not exist if demons could worm their way out of every inconvenience. They are not infallible, and you would do yourself a favor by remembering it."

The dry November foliage creaked and cracked around us, rustling in the wind. Gloom danced in the cryptic air. Frosted leaves crunched beneath our horses' feet. Belmont snorted, his hot breath clouding his flared nostrils. The witch and the warlock rode on in silence.

I shattered it. "This weather is something like!" I announced, whistling a few bars of a favorite tune. "The heat renders me irritable more often than not. Give me the frigid sea-storms and the winter gales; you shan't hear a murmur of complaint from me. What say you, witch? Do you want the comfortable cold, too, or the blasted heat?"

"Heat." Aislinn primly tossed her golden head. "I miss my garden. It is too heartbreaking to look at it in its present lifeless state, so kindly keep your mad winter worship to yourself."

"Ah." I exhaled a little plume of flame, just for fun. "Yasmin *did* wonder why, in our youth, I didn't fall for you head-over-heels, what with your enchantments and natural beauty combined. And there it is. Incompatible is incompatible, looks and charms aside."

"True enough." She increased her mount's speed to catch up with mine, soft eyes returning to steel. "And rest assured that I didn't try to capture *you*. I never had much use for men, especially not pompous peacocks. Minus being worshiped from afar, which had its advantages, you see."

"Ah-haa! *Un amante delle donne,*[1] eh?"

---

1. Italian: "A lover of women"

Aislinn lowered her head, cantering away with a sly smile.

"I knew it," I addressed old Belmont, "and I told Sallix so when he avowed his intentions to court her. He laughed at me and cursed me for a fool. It goes to show you, doesn't it, that intuition is so often right."

25

THE GILDED NOODLE

Sergio

"Blows! Blast! Botheration!"

Choking on black smog, I rushed to open the attic door. The inverse pentagram billowed from its red waxen lineaments, searing my vision as I looked anywhere else. "Must have pronounced that last phrase wrong. Blasted Latin incantations!" I envied Yassy for her flawless schooling. "Where *did* she learn Latin, anyway?" I mumbled, fanning the room by swinging the door back and forth.

Thankfully, the candles had all gone out at once; I didn't have to worry about starting a fire. Leaving the door ajar, I ripped off my jacket and wafted the smoke out with it. The smog pooled down the stairs like a sentient cloud. *Whoops.* Hopefully Eloise hadn't heard the minor explosion and wouldn't be coming up to investigate.

Sighing, I thumped back to the pentagram and knelt to snatch up the blackened parchments. I tossed my walking stick to the floor, scratching my chin, deep in thought.

"What in bloody blazes?" a strange voice hissed. From *the cane.*

"By the devil!" I spluttered. I kicked it away from me and stared as it *clunked* against the wall.

I swore the cobra's head *moved.* It flexed its threatening mouth as the ruby eyes narrowed. "Where am I and who are *you,* human?" the snake spat. Its gilt tongue flicked in my direction. "No, I was wrong: *half*-human. Damnation! Well, tell me your business and be quick about it so I may be released from this cursed confinement."

I locked eyes with the serpent as I slowly backed to the door and closed it. *Now we* really *can't have the maids coming up here,* I thought. Or even worse, Lillias.

As best it could, the cobra head writhed on the cane in a vain ploy for mobility. "What an asinine choice of vessel! Who trained you? If you've been consulting with Belial, then by Lucifer I will—"

"Slow down, slow down!" Gingerly, I bent and picked up the cane by the ferrule. The snake hissed in my face. I narrowed my eyes at it in return. "What do you mean by possessing my cane? And what do you mean, *half-human?*"

"I mean *you,* you utter imbecile. You're a warlock; you've done your shadow work, so you know what you are. And if you don't, you're the most ignorant ignoramus ever to walk the Earth. Tell me why you summoned me and trapped me in here, or I'll bite your nose off!"

The little devil's voice rattled like stones shaken in a box, rough and unpleasant. Frowning, I grabbed my jacket to wind its sleeves around the cobra's protesting head, muffling its curses. I sat cross-legged with the shaft resting across my knees, wondering what to do. And what in blue blazes was *shadow work*?

The obvious answer was to destroy the cane immediately, but I had my qualms about it. That cane had seen me through years of poverty to years of plenty—I swung it carelessly as a boisterous young ringmaster, and leaned on it trustingly as a manor lord. It was practically another appendage; I might as well cut off one of my arms as destroy it. Also, no one else of my acquaintance had a cane like it, which of course made me like it all the more. No, destruction was out of the question.

The second solution: work the proper spell to remove the demon and banish it from my estate. However, that idea gave me pause as well. I'd just failed a spell—what if I accidentally sent the little devil into my maid next? (It must be confessed that I chortled at the thought.)

Third, I remembered Aislinn. *She'd know how to cast him out.* For according to its voice, it was likely a *him.* A grumpy *him.*

Sighing, I untied the jacket sleeves from the snake head. He took a snap at my nose, but I coolly held him at a safe distance from my person, inspecting his savage countenance with fascination. "I think I'll call you Linguine," I said.

"I'll chew your face in your sleep, half-blood!"

I chuckled. "Feisty, cranky, to the point. You and Aislinn should get along splendidly. But what is all this about me being only half human? I really must hear more."

Linguine hissed again, puffing out his hood. It was quite impressive, the way his gilded hood caught the rays no matter how meager, and his living ruby eyes scattered speckles of scarlet light. Secretly, I was delighted with this turn of events. "A withering curse upon thine house!" the silly noodle commenced, agleam with menace. "Every flower, every sprig of vegetation, shall shrivel and die—"

Smiling, I held the cane aloft to show him the view out the window. Shriveled, wintery grounds drove my point home. Linguine stopped dead, drops of wrathful venom dripping from his fangs. "Well, what *do* you want with me, then?" he demanded.

"Nothing at all, Noodle. I was just practicing. But since you're here," standing up to swing the cane around a few times, I finished, "what *can* you do?"

Curses split from his forked tongue. "That hurts my head. I won't tell you a damn thing until you *stop* that!"

I ceased and desisted, but not without a guffaw. "Now see here, Linguine. I am your master until I release you from this cane, and I command you to tell me what your powers are." I scratched the top of his head, which he did not appear to enjoy.

"I owe you nothing, you insufferable—"

Humming, I swung the cane around in a wide figure-eight.

"That's enough... that's enough! Leave me be. I'll tell you."

I stopped with a wide grin.

His dry, rattling voice admitted, "My venom causes a deep sleep which not even intense physical pain can break. And any mortal who stares into my eyes cannot tell a lie."

"Seems oddly suited to your current form," I pointed out.

"That's the way of it, half-blood. We adapt to the vessels we're bound to. As if you didn't know!"

There was no wisdom in informing him of the truth—that he was bound by a warlock who knew next to nothing, not even what *shadow work* was. It would only increase his sulky wrath. I tapped the foot of the walking stick against the floor as I considered how Linguine might be put to good use...

Trim footsteps pattered up the attic stairs. "Papa? Papa, I smell smoke. What on earth are you doing?"

Damnation! I hissed at Linguine to hold his forked tongue. "What will you give me if I do?" the little devil inquired.

"I *won't* beat your noodle brain against the iron fence."

He muttered something acidic beneath his breath but went silent.

Lillias pushed the door ajar. Her eyes widened as they drifted from my bedraggled personhood to the red inverse pentagram smudging the floorboards. I tightened my grip on the snake in mute warning. *Don't you dare speak to her.*

"You do know, Papa," Lillias commenced, frightened eyes attached to the pentagram, "You *do* know that Ulysses is the nephew of the vicar…"

"A sixpence for the vicar!" I snapped. "Uncles-in-law have nothing to do with us. If they don't like what goes on in my own house, they needn't darken its threshold."

"I didn't mean to interrupt, Papa," Lillias frowned, "but your experiments up here are getting stranger and stranger all the time. You *must* take care, else you'll burn the place down."

"Right, right. Thanks. I'll remember."

She conjured a ladylike scowl before turning on her heel and departing. I sighed, fully aware that an apology was called for. However, I'd accomplished what I meant to: getting her out of the room.

"Lovely daughter you have," muttered the snake.

I moved my hand from his head, surprised he didn't try to bite my fingers off. "That *seemed* sincere, but don't think you'll soften me up with flattery. I *am* in a rather precarious situation, and your services may come in handy."

Linguine hissed a serpentine sigh. "Let's have the details, then. I want out of here as soon as possible."

Nodding, I absentmindedly scratched his head as I told him all about my ghost-witch. He endured it with grudging tolerance.

26

KHETMA PART 5

Yasmin

My fingers explored the holes in my skull. Curious, I dug my fingertips deeper. Would they touch bone? Would it provoke pain? Would I *feel* something?

Nothing but disappointment, it seemed. Sighing, I lowered my hands and continued to the frozen falls near the Deadlakes.

Rothadamas awaited my curtsy to embrace me. I fought the lethal urge to push Him back from it, knowing rejection could only enrage Him. I motioned to the glinting crystal waterfall, which ought to have been rushing and crushing joyously down to a rippling lake. Instead, it glimmered in moonlit silence, frozen in time. "Why here?"

"Because you like it here, Anmut," He purred. "I've seen you walk here as often as you can."

After all this time, I still hated the fact that He spied on me regularly. If it wasn't for that infuriating habit, I might be able to *pretend* I had my freedom. Fortunately, after a decade of practice, my stoicism was so firmly secured that it might as well be glued to my face. Not a glint of irritation betrayed itself. "Yes. I do."

He took my hand, leading me closer to that sweet frozen fountain. My treasured respite in the horrors of Kheima. "I needed to know what you truly think of this warlock's intentions," Rothadamas said. His handsome, flawless German flowed as smoothly as glass. "Naturally, I can touch your mind and provide myself with the required information, but I trust you to tell me yourself, mine Anmut. What say thee? Do you truly love this wicked, self-serving Dragon?" His grasp tightened. "Do you really think he does not want your power and your talents for himself?"

When I did not answer, He lowered His voice to persist, "And do you truly love him, when you're with Me?"

I need not elaborate; to clarify that I did not love Him at all—never had and never would—would mean Second Death, I was sure. I was truthful now... far more honest than I ever was in the dark, confused days of my life... but I was not honest to a *fatal* fault. At least, I had no inclination to be at the moment. Lying was part of the human existence, both in life and after death.

So, I tried not to smile as I answered, "I shall never love anyone as I love you, Rothadamas."

With the burning, murderous passion of a thousand suns.

There! I'd managed a half-truth. Sergio would be proud of me.

"For you *do* know, meine Hexe," the forest demon recommenced, alien eyes aslant, "You *do* know that no man can be utterly swayed from his sins? He is still selfish, still prone to entertaining pretty widows at parties, still apt to gamble to alleviate boredom or drink to forget his pain. He may be a warlock, but he is only a man. No more and no less."

I'll take a man over a demon, thank you, I yearned to say. I kept my confounded mouth shut. Serene, Rothadamas inspected our joined reflections in the frozen waterfall. "*We* are equals, you and I," He asserted. "Sanctified, gifted, and set apart. Death has consecrated your spirit, cleansing you from the taint of earthly temptations and petty desires. Our combined work has doubled the riches of Kheima and sustains its eternal children.

"Kheima *needs* you, Anmut," He continued, his tone shifting to a sudden intensity that made me flinch. "Even I did not fully comprehend how much. If your Dragon were to succeed, all we have achieved would be resigned to another. To an inferior queen who must rule in name only. Your children would be lost," dropping low and threatening, He added, "Aislinn would suffer at your expense. Is this what you desire, Yasmin?"

He rarely used my mortal name. I fixed my eyes upon His, refusing to quail. "No, Rothadamas."

"A wise answer." He held His long, white hands behind His back. I shivered at the parallel pose—one that Sergio often executed. *He's been taking notes, for He, too, is jealous.* "Then see to it that your Dragon is well distracted," the demon instructed. "Let him wander through Kheima all he likes, but be charming. Show him all the power you hold here, and all the gifts I've bestowed upon you. Intimidate him. And if he gets too close," He lifted one diamond-bright forefinger as he hissed, "Pleasure him."

"Pleasure him?" I swallowed hard, reeling back from His blatant instructions.

"Don't act like you do not understand what I refer to," He snapped, a glare of disgust washing over me. "I see, hear, and *sense* everything,

Yasmin. So steal all the forbidden sweets you want, but remember that I am calculating the debt incurred."

The instant He departed, I indulged myself in a curse or two *à la* Sergio. The manipulation, the orders, and above all the spying—damn it all to Hades! I'd had enough of being led like a bitch on a leash. *I'll get out of this whether Sergio can help me or not.*

Yasmin Lange disgusted me. So accepting of "Fate." So prone to pointing her trembling finger at anything and anyone other than who she ought to blame: herself. She never acted until it was too late, and sometimes not even then, for fear held her at bay.

No more.

27

Come With Me!

Sergio

"Sergio."

Sitting up in bed, I scrubbed the slumber from my eyes. Yasmin's ghostly body hung in the atmosphere, enrobed by smoky clouds from my bedchamber's censer. The cruel prongs of her crown glinted from her forehead. "Come with me."

I grunted, tossing off the bedclothes. "We're going to Kheima? Now?"

"Now."

Trusting she had her reasons, I gestured for her to lead the way.

A subtle hiss reminded me of Linguine's unplanned presence. I made a short shooing motion at the cane propped against my nightstand. *Not this time.*

His second hiss was sulky.

The frigid robe of Yasmin's presence embraced me as she guided me forward. We lifted right through the mansion ceiling and into Cursed Eden.

The ruinous forest swallowed us up, sinking its shadowed teeth into us like a starved predator. My memories of this place were vague, but Yasmin's journal refreshed my confused visitations. My lungs constricted as all breath was squeezed out of them, resulting in a black cloud formed like a flower that trailed behind me.

Yasmin had no breath-cloud.

I nearly wrought a sarcastic comment on the fact, but jests were out of reach in this stricken country. There was a solemnness to this dim forest cathedral that even I daren't mock.

Sheets of ebony ice coated the branches and blades of dead grass. Biting snowflakes glittered as they fell. In the distance, I spied glimpses of waterfalls, frozen solid, glinting black and frothy pale, the opposing tints swirling together like marble. The pattering feet of children and their low, mirthless whispers crackled 'round my ears, teasing me; for whenever I turned my head, the specter children would vanish.

As my ghost-witch propelled me forward, I saw where she had added her own feminine touch to the wasteland. Pagan pyres menaced the shadows with brilliant flames of blue and green. The stars seemed brighter, the moon fuller, and more silver-shaded rather than yellow. Silent children romped around the pagan altars. The fire's incandescent coloring reminded me of my own fire work in the Fair of Phantoms. A low laugh escaped me. It was touching, this evidence of my imprint upon her imaginative mind.

From the quick flash of a smile Yasmin tossed over her shoulder, I could tell she knew what I was chuckling about.

There was more. We slipped past a chapel formed entirely from blue-gray glass with a frozen stream running through it. Another pagan altar rose at its center, and several cloaked, gaunt women sang around it with glowing stars crowning their heads and cupped between their hands.

Other women? Was this also new? I caught up to Yasmin's side and darted her a questioning glance. She merely shrugged, as if to imply that the women's service was more atmospheric than anything else.

I whispered at her translucent ear, "Is this how you protect His other proxies? By assigning them to priestly servitude in Kheima, instead of making them soul-hunters?"

Yasmin inclined her head in a slow nod.

My brave darling. My heart swelled with pride, to be the man walking alongside the gracious Kheiman Queen. Aye, no one else ever formed in flesh could rival Anmut's cool, subtle sleight of hand and high-born demeanor in a realm of demons.

It vexed me beyond description to admit that Rothadamas was right. It was highly unlikely I'd find another High Proxy to match her. That being said, *unlikely* was not synonymous with *impossible.*

Curious, I focused on a nearby root and snapped my fingers. A fizzle of orange sparks danced around it and died. Yasmin raised her brows at me. "Must keep in practice," I whispered with an evil smirk.

Even after her death, my smirks remained a weak point for her. She smiled back, sliding alongside me as if to take my arm. "At least I understand now why you seldom shiver in a ghost's presence," Yasmin murmured, affection gleaming in her eyes. "Fire warlocks are impervious to cold."

"And extreme heat. And it explains why Roth—*He* called me Dragon straight off."

"Yes."

Arm in arm—or as well as we could manage that pose—we continued our trek through Kheima. Yasmin certainly had a natural taste for demon-realm décor. Everything she incorporated was salvaged from the elements and hand-formed. All that was missing was the matching witch's cabin... but my ghost-witch did not require shelter.

"Here we are," Yasmin whispered, breaking my train of thought. We stopped directly before the wicked Tree.

The enormous Tree of the Knowledge of Evil had grown since I saw it last. And thanks to the Queen's care, it flourished, sparkling from tip to root with gemlike shards of blue ice. The magenta flesh of the forbidden fruit glowed against the Tree's black bark. Long thorns guarded the fruit stems. I leaned forward to take a whiff, but Yasmin's supernatural force held me back. "Don't, Sergio! If you eat it, you will be like me, immortal but irrevocably bound to *Him*."

Deep down, part of me was tempted by the prospect. Lillias was provided for, and all but engaged to her Ulysses fellow. *Just leave the careless, callous world behind and live with Yasmin forever in a darkly beautiful demon's forest,* I considered. From what I'd seen so far, Yasmin had changed it for the better. It wasn't so terrible with her helping to rule it. The demon's children seemed happier, too. Although His art prevented me from looking at them, I could hear them. They babbled precisely how happy children ought to babble, though it was quiet and solicitous of demonic oversight.

His striking voice intervened. "If you desire it, then you may taste of it, worthy Dragon."

I started back from the Tree. A snow-white serpent of blinding beauty and eyes like lapis lazuli was watching me from above. His purple tongue flicked, tasting the air. Searching for my scent, sensing my weakness.

Something warned me not to lock eyes with Him. I snapped my gaze over to Yasmin and fixed it there. My lips lifted in a minuscule smile. *"Don't fear for me, Yassy. I know what He's trying to do."*

The Great Temptation, as ancient as the Earth itself.

Yasmin's calm, dead eyes blinked in response. *"I trust you."*

Ah, to succeed where Adam failed! What would have been the fate of the world if he had simply refused, even if Eve did not? A fascinating exposition—for another time. I planted my feet in place. "Good evening," I addressed Rothadamas, tipping my absent hat. "I must grudgingly confess that Yasmin has, indeed, made an impressive Kheiman Queen. Finding a replacement may be more akin to impossible than I first supposed."

"My foolish Dragon," the forest demon purred (a strange sound to come from a snake), "you must learn to gather more information before you strike soul bargains. I'm afraid you are quite rash." I bowed my compliments. Yasmin choked on irresistible mirth.

"And you have re-entered your birthplace without hesitation," Rothadamas pursued, slithering down the trunk and closer to me. "For it was here where I myself wedged the spark of pyrocraft deep into your heart and breathed draconian courage into your soul. I have fond hopes for you, my son."

From the corner of my subtle eye, I noticed Yasmin lifting and dropping her hand but half an inch. I knew she was telling me to proceed with caution, for the snake lied. *"Your pyrocraft is your own, not His!"* my ghost-witch was saying. *"But don't betray your knowledge of it."*

Ah, how our wordless communication became more natural to us by the hour. *My beloved Schattengeist.* "In that case, I humbly thank you. But to business. I assume the replacement Queen's appearance does not concern you, as you are free to alter it?"

"Correct." Shifting and stretching as if bored, Rothadamas maneuvered to catch my eye. That time, He succeeded.

A burst of otherworldly colors filtered through the circumference of my vision. Directly ahead, I saw only the blinding magnificence of the Serpent. But beside Him and all around, the forest bristled to life, bedewed with tints only the waking dead ever laid eyes on. The forbidden fruit seemed magnified, bereft of their wicked thorns, shining and sweet.

Amazed, I drew in my breath. That was a mistake. The black breath-cloud behind me returned to my lungs, and my senses increased tenfold. My nostrils flared to life, inhaling the fruit's decadence. My hand was already reaching for the nearest one when Yasmin's cold force stopped me.

"It's all right, Sergio. I'm here for you. I won't let you succumb."

Ashamed, I dropped my hand and held my breath. The breath-cloud painfully expelled itself and resumed its place behind me. The forest demon uttered a low hiss, clearly displeased. "Well done."

I flicked a look at Yasmin. *"He can't tell when You interfere?"*

A triumphant glint blossomed in her eyes. *"Not when He's distracted, no."*

How helpful.

"Come back some other night," Rothadamas stated. Piece by piece, He worked Himself out of His own scales, returning to His natural form as the snakeskin pooled to the ground like a dazzling cloak. "I have other matters to attend to."

As He passed Yasmin, He murmured a word or two of dark, affectionate German. Then He was gone.

"He's... not normal tonight," Yasmin whispered. Her eyes gleamed as they penetrated the dark forest gloom, seeing something there invisible to my sight.

I walked to her side, glaring at the crown yet embedded in her skull. *If only I could rip it off somehow, without hurting her.* "What do you mean?" I asked.

"He hasn't been Himself lately." She moved to touch my arm. I stared at her transparent hand, imagining her smooth skin against mine. Yasmin snapped her fingers to redirect my attention, trying not to smile. "He gets depressed sometimes. Bored of eternity, I daresay. But when a project as tempting as *you* loses its appeal in three minutes flat, there's something amiss in Kheima. Mark my words."

"Consider them marked. We'd best strike while the iron is hot," I exclaimed. "I know He ordered me away, but dare I risk lingering a few minutes? We might as well start by studying this Tree."

"You must swear not to get too close to it," my ghost-witch warned. "I'm here to stop you from eating the fruit, but you *must* take its temptation seriously, Hue. No horsing around. *Capiche*?"

I chuckled at her imitation of me in the Italian word. She stifled her laughter, turning aside to keep an eye on the clearing that Rothadamas disappeared through. "He'll call for me soon. Be quick!"

I advanced, cautiously avoiding the forbidden fruit. Up close, I spied dark gray glyphs and spells from multiple languages grafted into the ebony bark. "Intriguing," I remarked to Yasmin, smoothing my hand over them. "Can you read these?"

"Only parts of it, and what I *have* read didn't tell me much. It's the history of Eden."

I nodded, proceeding to the massive, draping branches, thin as thorns at their ground-scraping tips. I recalled from Yasmin's journal that she believed each branch represented one of the demon's victims. If that was the case, wouldn't Yasmin's branch be the most hardy, the most impressive amongst them all?

Alas, they all looked the same. None of the markings showed any significant deviations. I shook my head, leaping off the large root I stood upon and rejoining the Queen's side. "No clues there, but I have a *very* strong feeling that we must locate your branch. It's crucial to breaking His hold on you, I'm certain of it."

"As am I."

Standing there, looking down at her—the dusk-walker sovereign of Kheima—with her veiled face and crown awash in glorious moonlight, a sad sort of pride inundated me. "He spoke the truth," I murmured, hovering my hot hands over her frigid ones. "Ruling over Kheima suits you. I cannot fathom another woman taking your place with half your poise, your wisdom, your starlight beauty... more's the pity. We must break your curse on our own, for I could never find a replacement to satisfy *myself,* let alone Him."

Emotion swam in her eyes. "That's the kindest compliment you've ever given me, Sergio. I can only pray it was sincere," she added teasingly.

"Then hurry up and grow yourself some skin, thou witch, and I'll *show* you how sincere I am—"

"*Shhh,*" she admonished, glancing over her shoulder. Yet her glittering pupils betrayed her mutual eagerness for me. For *us.*

28

RESEARCH

Sergio

As December loomed near, the dynamics between the Demon and the Dragon were rather... curious.

He conversed with me sometimes, either asking general questions about my search for a new Kheiman Queen, or instructing me on what qualities to look for—magical affinities and such. As Yasmin had surmised, Rothadamas did indeed seem stricken with depression, or something like it. Unshakable, unhurried, and nonchalant—much like Yasmin herself—He was never in *good spirits*. Even when He smiled, or tried to, it never once reached His gemstone eyes. To my utter astonishment, I found myself pitying that damned creature one day as I thought Him over, roaming the snow-clad Vampyre Garden.

Just imagine living century after century in eternal winter, with no end in sight. No company of equal footing. No comfort or solace of any kind—besides His children, from whom He extracted a morose sort of satisfaction; yet they were not on equal footing, as aforementioned.

However, learning to pity Him would do nothing for Yasmin.

Grateful for the strange serenity with Him that I'd earned with my wager, I battened down the hatches and doubled my efforts to study Kheima's landmarks.

There weren't many of them. For all His (eternally damned) faults, Rothadamas did not hoard *riches.* He was a hoarder of *souls.* Even then, He selected quality over quantity. A certain grave, high-minded, worshipful countenance dressed the dead faces of all His proxies. *A height of soul,* I might have once termed it. Although His preference was women and children, I did witness a fellow warlock or two stargazing through breaks in the clouds. For in Kheima there was eternal night, everlasting snow, and the grave icy ripple of voices singing otherworldly hymns.

"That is His recreation of Heaven, I suppose," Yasmin confided to me during one of our scouting missions. "It must be no more than a dream to Him by now, yet He still attempts to relive it."

Indeed, I *would* pity Him if He'd release the children. Most of the adults came here by virtue of their own soul bargains, i.e., by their own hand. Which reminded me...

"Yasmin," I murmured as we walked to the glass-walled chapel, "I've been meaning to ask you directly, but the timing never seemed right. Why did you give yourself up for my daughter?"

Her slender pupils flashed as she turned her head toward me. "Don't you know?"

"I have my suspicions."

She paused, lifting her thumbnail between her lips to bite it. A nervous habit that both she and Aislinn shared. "Well, I believed that you would not find it in your heart to love me, so my own life had but little worth to me. Yet Lillias means everything to you. After all," creasing her brows, "children should be rescued from this place whenever possible. Were she some stranger's daughter instead of yours, I would have exchanged my place with hers all the same."

"And *this* was your reward!" I deployed a barrage of curses at the crown buried in her head. "Does it hurt you still, Yassy?"

"Nein," she softly repeated for the one thousandth time. "Do not worry about me, Sergio. Think about the task at hand. We are working on borrowed time, and there's no knowing when He might snap out of whatever lackadaisical mood He's in."

"Right."

I expected Rothadamas would treat me in a caustic manner reminiscent of my butler squinting at the flies circling the living room. And although He did so every now and then, it was far from His default *modus operandi*. As ridiculous as it might sound, Rothadamas treated me with... respect. A bored, dry sort of tolerance permeated His tone when He spoke to me, but what He said was civil. Yasmin was surprised by it, too.

"Have you thought more about the reason behind this affable mood of His?" I whispered. Something about Kheima made one want to whisper. "Because if something I've said or done managed to earn it, I must keep it up by all means."

"I couldn't tell you, except for the fact that *I* think highly of you. That might be enough."

"Hmm?" I held up a hand, signaling for her to halt. "He thinks highly of me simply because *you* do?"

The ghost-witch shrugged. "Yes. Is that so very odd? I've been His right hand, His trusted enchantress for ten years. He knows me better than any other woman in Kheima, and He's pleased with what He knows."

Turning, she gestured to the changes she'd made throughout her frozen Eden. "He approves of my insight and ideas." She lowered her hand with a short laugh. "I must say, I've done far more with a decade in a demon realm than I ever did with twenty-three years upon the Earth. How blind I was! What a fog of anxiety and self-deprecation I cloaked myself in! If Kheima has done one thing for me, it has opened my eyes to the universe and to eternity instead of keeping them narrowed on the vulgar, mortal present."

I didn't much like the gleam in her eyes. The *satisfaction.* I motioned for us to carry on to the chapel, a slow and uncomfortable realization taking root:

I wasn't just battling Rothadamas. No, I was saving Yasmin from Yasmin herself. There was no denying that gleam. She loved power. Co-ruling her own realm gave her that.

I could give her a mansion, but not a realm.

After the glass chapel, we scoured several more prominent landmarks. The silver basin guarded by the hooved beasts (which I turned away from in disgust, avoiding hideous memories). A massive, tarnished statue, overgrown with a riot of dry poisonous foliage, which Yasmin cited as the fallen idol of Nebuchadnezzar. And last, a beautiful stained-glass mortuary, the likes of which I'd never seen before nor shall ever behold again. That place brought tears to Yasmin's cold eyes. She would not tell me what souls were honored within.

Despite all these wonders, nothing useful came to light. No clues, no budding theories. Just as I prepared to kick rocks and yell, my boiling irritation was quelled by the return of the forest demon.

He turned His diamond countenance upon me. "What dost thou think of mine realm, Dragon?"

Startled that He wanted my opinion, an earnest response fell impulsively from my lips. "It is sacred. Holy, in the purest sense of the word."

Formerly, ennui overshadowed the gleam of His lapis lazuli eyes. My honesty called forth a momentary spark; His white pupils fixed onto mine. "Would you like to remain here, Dragon?"

"You mean, live here?" I stammered. I shot Yasmin an alarmed look.

She stepped in, "You startle him with your sudden proposal, Master. Perhaps Sergio should complete his chosen task before He considers such a generous offer?"

"That is what I meant to say," Rothadamas growled. The shadows enveloped His gaze once more. "After his task is completed. Come, Anmut. You've shown him everything worth seeing. You must rest."

Yasmin's voice rose several octaves. "Rest?"

Her confusion was plain. Without another word, Rothadamas seized her by the hand and started to take her back to the Tree.

"Farewell," He snapped at me. With a dismissive wave of His free hand, He vanished me from Kheima and returned me to the Vampyre Garden.

Baffled, I trudged through the packed snow to the mansion. He wasn't at all like I remembered Him. Or, more accurately, how Yasmin's diary portrayed Him: vicious, beastly, and utterly taciturn. So close to all-knowing and all-powerful, He might as well be a god. *The Demongod of the Corrupt Wood.*

If that's how He *used* to be, then something had changed Him.

Weariness? After so long, eternity would sicken anybody, even demons.

Sheer, unadulterated apathy? Ceasing to care about anything, including His own pet projects? Was Kheima on the brink of collapse without Yasmin's assistance?

Or was it—

No.

Demons did not love. They *could not* love.

"And if He loved her," I snarled, finally indulging my desire to kick some obliging rocks, "He would let her go!"

It couldn't be love. By definition, love was selfless. It was patient and kind. Love could never torture Yasmin and bind her to a frozen hell.

Unless...

My brows climbed at the thought.

Unless demons are bound by the rules of their realm.

Excited, I threw myself back into demonology.

I plastered Linguine with questions, but he couldn't answer all of them. It seemed to me that he was more of the "imp" category, not a powerful all-seeing demon (as he considered himself to be). But he could read people with astonishing accuracy and kept annoying me by calling me "half-blood," yet refusing to explain what he meant. "Maybe if you're *nice,* I'll let you in on the secret," he'd say, working his serpentine mouth into an unsettling grin. "Obviously your shadow work is disgraceful, but I'm glad of it, you utter imbecile of a half-baked warlock."

I'd reward Noodle's cutting remarks with a jolly swing or two.

If poor Lillias had been concerned about her Papa before, she was devastated now. Her madman of a father perpetually stalked 'round his attic, ducking and dodging spiderwebs whilst muttering to himself and scrubbing at his stubbly beard. Sometimes he argued stormily "with no one," to dissolve into pensive silence afterward. Meals were waved aside with snorts of contempt. Evening pipes were offered and scorned. Sleep came and went fitfully, devoured by terrifying or intoxicating dreams.

What Yasmin *might* have taken the trouble to warn me about was that the intense draw of demonic energy into one's home attracted not only little devils, but ghosts, too.

At first, I assumed the increase of paranormal activity around the mansion was just Yasmin, bored and playing for my attention like a spoiled child. But I was mistaken. First, this voice, then that laugh—then the violence of my dinner plate thrown at my face—couldn't be my beloved. Annoyed, I shouted and cursed and made signs of the cross as inspiration struck. But that didn't bother them at all.

After a fortnight of sporadic hauntings, I gave up, adapting myself to their nonsense with a shrug. "They'll keep me company once Lillias is good and married," I sighed. So, I stuffed cotton into my ears and buried myself in my books, resigned to ignore them.

That was easier said than done. One obstinate boy, "Oliver," delighted in hearing me curse like a sailor; he conjured all manner of merry pranks to the end of opening Sergio's Serendipitous Thesaurus. Sometimes I laughed with him and challenged him to a game of checkers, but other times I hollered like a cantankerous old man and shook my fist. If Yasmin was watching, I daresay she had her fill of amusement.

For since Rothadamas had taken her by the hand and drawn her away "to rest," I felt her presence but briefly. I trusted she had her reasons for keeping her distance.

But I hated it.

"Patience, half-blood," Linguine admonished. "Remember that your ceaseless yearning is the result of haunted limerence. It's not *natural,* this seething lovesickness of yours."

It was late at night. I lingered at the fireplace, staring at my own fire work in awe. Bursts of red, orange, blue, green, and purple crackled in the spiked grate. Grinning, I unbuttoned my silk shirt and tossed it aside, flexing my hands near the flames to shape them. Linguine watched from the couch, content to observe.

"Impressive," Aislinn's voice cooed from the flames.

I jumped back with a curse. The witch's matchless face grinned from the smoke. It swirled into the hall, taking shape. She dusted the ashes from her burgundy gown. A sprig of holly was fastened to her collar. "I've just met with Yasmin," she announced, tickled pink to have startled me. "She's sorry that Rothadamas is keeping her busy, but she trusts you'll do well enough without her. I see she was right."

I grunted a short greeting, turning my back to her to resume my work. I sensed the Celt's platonic appreciation of my back and forearms, engraved with navy tattoos. "If you came to stare, simper, and spy, then surely you've got better things to do," I retorted.

"Maybe I don't," she chuckled. "Besides, Yasmin asked me to come visit you on her behalf. Mustn't disappoint our darling."

I sighed, extinguishing my flames and facing her. "What's she doing, anyway?" *Not kidnapping more children on that bastard's behalf, I hope.*

"Something surprisingly benign," Aislinn reported. "Planning a new cathedral." She tripped to my side, swiping a flake of hot ash from my shoulder (that I hadn't noticed). Her eyes narrowed at the skin beneath it, cool and clear. "You really do have draconian blood in your veins, don't you?"

"So Rothadamas implied," I answered, "and a certain little devil hereabouts says the same. When do you think Yasmin will be finished?"

Aislinn's rosy lips curled. "Ah, yes. The obsessive phase. You'll see her when He is done with her, and not a second sooner, I fear. That's the way of it, and there's no use bucking against a wild horse."

"That's what *I* keep telling him," Linguine interposed.

I swung around and glared at the cane, tucked into a shadowed corner. "Be silent, Noodle. Did I give you permission to speak to Aislinn?"

"She's a powerful witch," Linguine protested, emitting a rattling hiss. His tongue flickered in her direction, as it had when he first met me. "Far more powerful than *you*. It would be rude not to greet her. Well met, Lady Aislinn."

Aislinn knelt by the cane, touching Linguine's shining head with respectful awe. "Intriguing. You've summoned a devil, Hue? I didn't know your studies had availed you so far. Congratulations. And well met, too… What's your real name?"

"Osedis."

Aislinn straightened and shot a glare over her shoulder. "You've been calling him *Noodle*? For shame, ringmaster! If you befriend your devil, there's nothing he won't do for you. He might even render himself your bondservant for life." She shook her head, hands bracing her hips. "Leave it to Erbanhue to get off on the wrong foot."

Her gaze trickled down my bare chest, reading my tattoos with great interest, as if she could read my future in them. I cast my eyes to the ceiling, motioning for her to kindly remove herself from my presence. "If you don't mind, my lady, I'm working. A dragon that must concentrate every fiber of his being to shape fire isn't much of a dragon."

As she left, she tossed another teasing smile at me. "I wonder if Yasmin peeped into the future and saw that you'd become even *more* handsome. That might explain her own obsessive tendencies."

"I like her *obsessive tendencies*," I announced, slamming the door behind her. "It shows she hides fire of her own below the ice."

Strange woman, Aislinn. One never knew what she was really thinking, despite being shamelessly direct most of the time. The opposite of Yasmin, and yet, so alike.

"I *do* hope to speak with her again," Linguine said. "Conversing with a true disciple of the Craft is such a pleasure. *She* has completed her shadow work admirably. She is whole; she wields her strength with expert comprehension and intention."

The cane was propped in the corner of the room. Trudging up to it, I smacked it down, standing akimbo as Noodle's head rolled helplessly while he hissed indignations in some demonic language.

29

KHETMA PART 6

Yasmin

A WHIMPER ESCAPED MY throat as His tendril crushed it.

You're hurting me.

The pressure lessened, but not by much. Rothadamas hissed in my ear, head, and soul:

"You're *mine,* witch. I've graciously permitted you the freedom you crave, but remember that I can take it away at any time. Tend to our kingdom, and I shall take care of you. Neglect it, and you shall be punished."

His wrath rippled around me, howled above me, causing black lightning to break and crackle above my head. Once more, Rothadamas had looked into my heart and seen the boundless love for my Dragon beating there.

He tested my limits until the tears came. I experienced a little satisfaction when it took Him more work, more inventive stratagems, to bring my pain to the surface. I might well cry, sob, even plead for mercy by the end of it, but it would come at a cost. I'd make Him pay for it with His precious time.

In the furthest reach of my soul, I thrived on abuse. It sharpened me and made me keen. So accustomed to its bite, I learned to survive it by conflating the pain and the fearful anticipation with the pounding of my undead heart. To be in pain meant to be *alive.* And while my body rotted in the grave, my spirit yet lived.

To be in pain meant I still cared. I still *loved.*

And I would live to love again, God help me!

30

ENLIGHTENED SPRING

Sergio

As the firstborn violets stretched their faces to the sun, I awaited my ghost-witch.

Christmas Eve. The New Year. Lillias's engagement party. Yasmin's own birthday. They had all come and gone without Yasmin's beloved, alarming face floating somewhere in the backdrop, smiling upon me from afar with eyes like winter stars.

I weathered the resulting storm of emotions in smoke and drink. Flush-faced, I ranted and raved to Linguine and found unexpected solace in his hissing replies. By then, he knew practically everything about us, including our dark pasts.

"Don't think of her as your humble little circus witch, Sergio. She isn't that half-starved performer ever at your beck and call. She's a *queen*. That's not privilege, that's responsibility."

Linguine's tempered counsel helped more than anything else, but now the *Dragon King,* battered from the tempest, would make port on forbidden shores. Fascinating and forbidden—for Christian mortals, anyhow. Thank the gods I was not one of that count.

Attic-bound, I stomped up the stairs, pausing at the library to collect certain volumes guarded under lock and key. I gathered candles, matches, chalk, an altar cloth, a statue, and a ceremonial knife. Tossing everything into one large box, I lugged my tools into the darkest, mustiest corner of the deserted attic.

Here, a round window cast tinted hues across the floorboards. The window's stained glass image depicted a woman guarded by a scarlet dragon. I waved a curious spider away from my beard and knelt, extracting my sordid gathering of goods and spreading them out in what I could only hope was a visually-pleasing display.

Such arrangements were Yasmin's forte, not mine. But if she were by my side where she belonged, I wouldn't be attempting such a foolhardy thing without her.

"I'll help," Linguine offered, propped by the door. Although he'd never *said* that the star-crossed plight of Yasmin and Sergio eventually intrigued him enough to want to help, I'd noticed that it had. Nodding my thanks, I grabbed the chalk to sketch a new inverse pentagram. Once I was satisfied with it, I traced it with fresh melted wax and placed the symbolic dagger just so.

Snatching my journal, I cited a short incantation I'd written myself and lit the arranged candles with my draconian breath. Linguine's narrowed eyes concentrated on the dagger.

I smiled, knowing Yasmin would have been impressed. *If I ask nicely, perhaps He will tell me where she is.* Demons and little devils alike are obsessed with displays of reverence.

For the final step, I took a yellowed page that I'd extracted from Yasmin's journal and centered it in the pentagram, below the knife. I sat cross-legged in front of the summoning circle, closing my eyes and holding my hands open on my knees, palms up—an inviting pose.

The tickle of static touched my ears. A purr of demonic mirth followed, growing steadily louder until it phased into His voice, speaking in sarcastic English. "You have managed to summon me, Dragon? I am impressed. Have you found a replacement for me?"

At least He isn't angry. That's a start. I dared to crack my eyelids open, just a smidgen. Rothadamas loomed in the semi-darkness, looking twice as tall beneath the harsh angles of the mansion's turreted roof. He was in His hunting form, dark and twitching in and out of the ether.

Pleased with my results, I opened my eyes fully. "I might have found a soul to suit," I informed Him, unable to look at Him directly in this harsh, painful form. "What do you think of my daughter's intended? Ulysses?"

My deadpan expression made even the forest demon chuckle. "I have no use for humans who are blind to the supernatural." He leaned over me, His featureless aspect flickering and twisting like a nightmare. "Your daughter might be an agreeable alternative."

Before my gathering rage could scorch Him with an answer, a child's fascinated gasp turned my head. I shooed the little ghost-boy away. "Summoning circles are for demons; ghosts need not attend. Depart!"

Oliver sulked but obeyed, slinking through the wall. I shook my head, returning my attention to Rothadamas. "Pardon young Oliver. There isn't much here to entertain him since he went through all my circus curios... whilst breaking a third of them," I added beneath my breath, then raised my voice. "I summoned you to ask after Yasmin's welfare. Where is she? If she has been abused and locked up, then I have a word or two to add to our wager, forest demon."

Rothadamas was not accustomed to such directness from mere mortals. For a minute, He was silent, tilting His head at a sickening angle to read my face. "I was right to mark you, Dragon," He said, paying me the subtle compliment of switching to Italian. "In all my years dealing with the souls of men, it pains me to report that the vast majority of them are cowards. Not so with thee, Sergio Vincenzo."

Well! Since He absorbed my initial blow so well, I might as well fire at will. "I know you cherish Yasmin in your own demented, fallen way. You care about her, so why cause her unnecessary pain? Let her come and see me." I rose and folded my not-insubstantial arms. "Forge whatever agreement you prefer about the whens and for-how-longs, but let her come. If you antagonize her, she will cease to obey you with alacrity or attend to your realm's interests."

Linguine hissed, stealing my attention. He shook his cobra hood at me.

Too late. Wrath bristled in ebony lightning above the demon's head. He stretched Himself, dragging His head down until His blank face was inches from mine. A wide, threadlike smile, lined with pointed teeth, leered at me. "Pray, why should I give my *servant* any consideration?"

"Because as your Queen, she deserves respect." I dug in my heels, refusing to step back although every instinct in my body screamed *"take cover!"* "Secondly, you've given her some measure of access to your power; you wouldn't have done so if she hadn't earned it. And third," I deepened the force of my tone, willing for the world itself to hear, "I, who have but briefly tasted her soul, know that she's the most remarkable woman to have walked the Earth. And I dare you and every demonic force below to deny it to my face!"

An onslaught of righteous rage tensed my body and quickened my blood. Furious, the demon's supernatural pressure sealed over my skin. It pressed upon me, trying to force me to my knees as Rothadamas growled.

I smirked as short, sporadic flames coiled from between my teeth, and smoke huffed from my nostrils. "Deny it, then!" I shouted. "Here and now, Rothadamas. Deny it and keep your Queen beneath your thumb for all you're worth!"

As the forest demon plied His pressure upon me, it became so great, I clawed for air. In the midst of my pain, the sheer sense of *power* rushed through my pounding heart, screaming for release. Linguine's widened eyes took on a frantic gleam. He knocked his own head back against the wall, trying to fall lengthwise and roll away from me.

With the roar of a predatory beast, I raised my head.

My face shot up to the ceiling, knocking against it. I ducked, snorting with surprise, and nearly blew a hole in the floorboards with my fiery breath. I blinked at the pair of ruddy dragon paws curling where my hands should have been.

My balance suddenly askew, I lurched forward. The gleaming talons scraped over the pentagram, breaking the circle. Rothadamas dissolved into thin air.

A sensation of pulling, stretching, *growth.* I regained my balance as a mighty spiked tail, thick with thousands upon thousands of ruby-bright scales, shimmered from the faint light of stained glass.

My heavy head swiveled on its long, thick neck. I sniffed at the blood-red wings sprouting on either side of my itching shoulders—my own scent billowed from their sweeping flaps. In my bafflement, another roar and rattling growl punched from my throat.

My body. My scent. This was *me.*

In case you were wondering whether discovering you're a dragon shifter in a cramped attic might be fun, I can tell you that it wasn't.

That first (miserable) night, I tore everything my talons touched. My left draconian thumb stuck straight through the window and shattered it to bits. That was my favorite design, too! A tribute to myself and Yasmin, though I wouldn't admit to *that* while the design was being ordered. "I like dragons, and I like queenly women," I'd informed the stained-glass artist. "It really is that simple, my good man."

Ha! Masking my own intentions from myself. *I blame Yasmin's influence.*

I spent most of the night endeavoring to shrink back down to human form, arguing with Linguine meanwhile. *"So, this is what you were hiding from me, you cursed noodle!"* I roared.

I couldn't physically speak to him, but since he was bonded to me, he could sense my thoughts. "It's your own fault," Linguine asserted. He'd managed to roll out of the way, so he'd returned to his signature, callous calm. "I told you all you had to do was pay me a modicum of respect... or if you'd done your shadow work first, like a *proper* warlock, instead of bursting into dragon form as an old man—"

"Blows and botheration! I don't have TIME to pander to you!" Grumbling, I clumsily scratched at my foreleg, wondering if I'd have to shed the scales like a snake sheds its skin.

"That won't work," the Noodle sniffed.

"Then tell me what WILL work, devil!" I snorted a thick cloud in his direction. Mild satisfaction resulted as it swallowed him up; he had no arms to wave it away.

"Figure it out for yourself," the imp grumbled, tilting his head up haughtily. "I don't have *time* to *pander* to you."

In answer, I uttered a deep draconian growl, which was quite satisfying. By the gods, my growling would have *impact* now.

Several hours later, I managed to return to humanity at the two-thirds point of success: a slightly enlarged human (don't you dare laugh!) with red scales mottling his arms and legs, long nails and teeth, and vaguely reptilian pupils highly sensitive to light. Once I could fit down the stairs again, I snatched my cane and returned to my bedchamber—exhausted, yet extremely proud of myself—only to laugh myself into fits at the mirror when I applied to it for a diagnosis (as Yasmin would say).

I guess you *can* laugh, after all, since I did. And Linguine's puffing, huffing sort of noises must have been a serpent's laughter.

Rothadamas had known what I was all along. I believed He never wanted me to tap into my full potential, so He didn't dare trigger it on purpose by angering me... confounded blackguard of a demon. I supposed I owed Him a begrudging thanks for enraging me at last, though I'd been the one to start it. If He hadn't infuriated me by treating his own Kheiman Queen like a slave, it was likely I'd have gone my entire life without shifting once.

That being said, did Yasmin know? She was the first to call me "the Dragon," just as I first called her a witch when illness affected the entire troupe except for her.

We'd seen each other's bare souls before realizing it.

With my clothing burnt to ash, I tossed my bare self onto the bed with a huff. *I should take a bath,* I mused, lifting my arm to confirm the thick scent of smoke and saffron wafting from my glinting skin. *Yasmin might come any minute.* Perhaps I'd unnerved the demon Himself with my unexpected shift, and He'd let her come.

Linguine sighed. "The way your lizard brain defaults to her every instant is exhausting. Being bonded to you is trying, indeed."

"At least *I* care about someone other than myself, damned noodle." *Even if it took me a few decades to get there,* I privately sulked.

To the bath I fled. I tried to be quick, but I wasn't quick enough. Yasmin's chilly hand blew against my shoulder. "What happened?" she gasped. "You're burning up, and what's that ruby gauntlet thing around your wrist?"

Grinning, I propped myself half out of the water to display my scales. "Behold! Your Dragon is a dragon indeed, my sterling witch. How good it is to see your face again!" I fervently kissed the air in her general direction, making her laugh.

"It took the final shred of my mind, soul, and strength to keep away from you," my ghost-witch replied, blowing a regal kiss in response, "but it was for the best. Whatever have you done, Hue?"

I lifted a brow, stepping from the tub and wrapping a towel around my waist. I winced as my bad knee protested; it wanted to soak much longer than that. "He's permitting your visits on strict terms, I take it?"

"Yes, but don't ask questions. I'm here, so be content." Yasmin swept to me and hugged her airy form to my chest. "Never in my cursed afterlife did I hope to see anyone best the forest demon. I'm beginning to think *you* could do it, my reckless, beautiful Sergio."

The witch who seldom cried proceeded to leak tears of joy. I shook my head, affecting to stroke her wonderful hair. "Blast it all, Yassy! We've scheming to attend to; do quell the storm, beloved. He will adjust, so I'll need something else up my sleeve that is more than brute beast force."

"I know," Yasmin admitted. She floated back and cleared her face. "But I never allowed myself to really *hope* before. Looking at you like this," adoration bordering on worship gleamed in her countenance, "I ought to have guessed it. And seeing you discover your power after all this time... Sergio!" She clapped her icy hands. "Why, dragon shifters have charmed lives. Even if some tragic illness befell you, you would rise again like the mighty phoenix! What a wonder you are!"

Now *my* eyes watered with emotion. "Confound it, woman! Don't soften me up at a time like this. We have much to discuss."

"All in good time, Dragon. Let me worship at the altar of your second birth." Yasmin floated to her knees, staring lovingly into my face. "Whenever I can't possibly adore you more, you blast the gates open and unveil yet another hidden kingdom. I can wander it for three lifetimes and still not search its breadth."

The sight of my beloved witch kneeling before me made me lightheaded. My heart begged to snatch her and hold her body against mine until not a centimeter of space was left between us. "Well, hurry up and finish gawking so we can talk like serene, sane humans," I managed to say. My teeth ground together, but not at all from rage. "I can't stand it when you look at me like that."

Her answering smile made me groan. I fixed my burning stare on the ceiling. As I bit my lip, my elongated teeth drew blood, and I cursed. "Then why did you *make* me look at you so often?" Yasmin demanded.

I glanced back down at her with a wide grin, swiping my lip clean. "Because I'm vain."

"So you are. Well, at least you admit to your faults."

Linguine's strident voice stabbed our bubble of affection, deflating it. "Amen!"

"Shut up!" I roared.

Yasmin's gleaming head turned toward the walking stick. "Was that... Did your *cane* just speak?"

"Never mind the noodle," I murmured, meeting her on my knees. "I *need* you to possess me. In fact, I demand it! Right now." I punched the floor to solidify the command.

Her eyes sparkled wickedly behind her Kheiman veil. "I thought you said we needed to have a serious talk."

I leaned in closer. Stared her down. "I have waited far too long, my Schattengeist. *Right. Now.*"

She shuddered. Her lips parted in a decadent sigh. "Yes, my Dragon. I will."

"And don't you dare hold back," I warned her. "This is not the witching hour in a ballroom, but in my chambers. Banish all modesty, Yasmin. Remember that I am yours and yours alone, just as you are mine."

"Yes, my lord."

My lord. I flushed with undeniable delight, beckoning for her to follow me to the bedroom.

But no one can serve two masters, "for they will love the one and despise the other," or so the saying goes. I had to free her from this confounded duplicity.

31

THE MANNA OF HOPE

Sergio

As the days lengthened, I had so much to do that Yasmin and I were blessed to snatch a half hour to ourselves here and there.

Lillias flew about ordering *stravaganze* for her trousseau and planning the wedding. My eyes grew strangely wet at the corners whenever I thought about that day, so I pushed it out of mind's reach until necessity forced it forward. Luckily, all the father needed to do on the day itself was show up on time, clothed and in his right mind. This, I could manage.

"I shall be sorry to see her go," Linguine said. "She's a breath of fresh air in this mansion with Lord Lunatic."

I smirked and scratched his head, which he'd learned to tolerate better over time; in fact, I suspected he liked it. "Thank you, by the way. You kept your promise not to reveal yourself to her or to my staff."

He made a soft scoffing noise in his puffed throat. "As entertaining as it would be to terrify your household, I don't enjoy the headaches you delight in causing."

Chuckling, I crept into the wide clearing in the woods to practice pyrocraft and shift in and out of dragon form, determined to make my beastly anatomy second nature. Not a single lick of flame would escape me without my precise control over its temperature, direction, and tint. I discovered that I could only morph into a dragon when I was well fed and well rested. And the more often I tried to shift, the harder it became, until I required rest before I could do it again.

Linguine lent me what strength he could spare, but it wasn't much. I accepted it without commentary, for I couldn't antagonize him *always,* and the little imp couldn't be blamed for not having the power to supplement a dragon.

Aislinn continued to visit to teach me basic spells, or so she *said.* The sly Celt batted her heavenly eyes, tossed her locks of gold, and was wicked to the core. She wanted Linguine—was trying to win him over for herself. She befriended him, just as I predicted she would, and called him "Osedis" in a sweet, playful tone that charmed him.

Well, let the wicked witch play her games. If Aislinn's charm was the glue that held us together, then we might achieve our mad goal of freeing Yasmin.

As the months passed, I became more ardently convinced that I couldn't go on living without her. My ghost-witch possessed me heart, body, and soul. She was my queen; I would have no other. She was my precious Eve, sovereign ordained, bone of my bone and flesh of my flesh, the dark divine feminine to my flaming masculine. *I will have her, hold her, and cherish her until the end of our days.*

Lost in everlasting resurrection theories, I was conversing with Linguine when Eloise surprised us with her teatime announcement. Before I could react to her terrified gaze, frozen on Linguine's animate face, the snake lunged his head as far forward as it would go and sunk his glinting fangs into her hand. She fell to the threshold in a deep swoon.

"You're welcome," Linguine said.

I sighed, stooping to carry Eloise to the maid's room and preparing a story about sudden illness and feverish dreaming. *Confound it!* Everything seemed to be going wrong, somehow, and the only thing that felt *right* was my dragon form.

After a cold, drizzly sort of spring, my daughter's wedding fell on midsummer. As I confronted the mirror to fasten the bolo tie and button the embroidered waistcoat, I reminded myself that if it wasn't for a certain ghost-witch, I wouldn't *have* a daughter to give away. That prevented the strange eye-watering well enough, thank the gods.

"Once this is over," I murmured to Yasmin's reflection in the mirror, "you and I are going straight to Kheima. Tonight. We need to visit all the landmarks again and scour them top to bottom. Your soul tether *must* be there somewhere."

I huffed, still fighting the temptation to brand myself a failure. A burning cluster of ash sizzled on my hot palms. I dashed the ashes away. "Damnation! You'd best possess me, beloved, to keep me cool. I might burn the chapel down."

Yassy's measured voice soothed me. "Your beautiful estate chapel, no less? Oh, dear. We can't have that."

Her glowing arms slipped around my chest as she embraced me from behind, her bright face peeping above my shoulder. The eerie reflection made me smile. "I've a notion to burn that godforsaken Tree down in one hellish sweep," I confessed, mimicking said sweep for good measure. "It's the best guess we've got, and we've only five months left."

"The time flew past on wings of wind," Yasmin sighed. "Perhaps if you hadn't distracted us from our goal so often, I might already be free of this curse."

"Little minx!" I dealt her a mock frown. "In this blasted state, *you* may do things to *me,* but I cannot return the favor. You're the scoundrel of this pair, thou witch!"

She hid her playful smile in the crook of my neck, bestowing a kiss upon it. A tingle of cold electricity prickled my skin. "You're going to miss it."

"Ha! Not I." I turned to face her, grinning and standing akimbo. "I intend to repay you for each moment you dragged me to the edge, just to hold me over the precipice and keep me there. Tempting me with the promise of a free-fall, yet refusing to push me over, and I could not jump." I chuckled, grabbing the cane and flourishing it. "And as a dragon shifter, there are more thrilling punishments to mete out."

She raised one brow to mimic me. "Such as?"

I crossed my arms. "I shan't give you a ride."

Yasmin burst into a fluttery cascade of giggles—a butterfly laugh that she only indulged around me. "I'm a ghost, Sergio. I can take *myself* on magical flights, thank you."

"Not once you've been brought back to life. You're grounded... in the most wholesome sense of the word."

Her grin melted into affectionate gazing. She cupped my cheek with her airy hand. "How I missed our banter. I dreamed about our nocturnal *tête-à-têtes* more often than our first kiss, if you can believe it."

I snorted, puffing two miniature streams of smoke. "I believe it. That was a pathetic excuse for a kiss. One might as well call it what it was: a *peck*."

"It's not as if I welcomed it," Yasmin laughed. "I *might* have encouraged you instead of repelling you, sir. I recall how stiff and cold I was, afraid to move, terrified to even breathe." She lingered close and inhaled deeply, making me squirm away. (I'm ticklish, though I'd rather battle Rothadamas to the death than admit it.) "Your scent is truly… otherworldly. Like a bonfire on Walpurgisnacht fed with the most sweet-smelling wood." She drew back, mischief sharp in the depths of her eyes. "That ought to have informed me you were no common man, but I had other things burdening my mind."

"Yes, you did," I replied softly. I arranged my pocket watch chain across my chest, tapping its gleaming face with a significant look. *I need to go.* "Bond with me now, Yassy, and brace up your old Dragon so he doesn't collapse in the aisle, or blubber, or otherwise make a fool of himself. Hmm?"

"Yes, my lord."

My face burned; I couldn't help it when she called me that. We stepped out the door as one. "You don't need to call me that unless you want to," I murmured. "I promised you that we'd be equals, you and I, and equals we shall be."

Her ethereal voice cooed in my skull: "*If you want me to stop so you'll stop blushing, you might as well resign yourself, my lord.*"

Once my darling Lillias was officially Lady Ulysses Melbourne, the estate was safely vacant. With Brandon and the maids busy tidying up, I trudged to my chambers and poured a salute to my ghost-witch. With her divine aid, I had managed not to tear up once. I danced and smiled and "said the toast" elegantly.

"Lillias used to call it 'saying toast,'" I chuckled, pouring a second glass and clinking my own against it, in Yasmin's honor. "Ah, I shall miss having her here. My house seems twice as big without her in it."

Linguine agreed but said nothing more. He was strangely quiet all day, come to think of it. *That might have been the first wedding he's ever attended,* I mused, grinning at the thought that it might have made my grumpy little imp emotional for once.

"She'll be back from the honeymoon before you know it," Yasmin reassured me.

Draining my glass dry, I clapped it back onto the table. "I might have had a wee bit more than is good for me, Yassy. Carry me?"

"No, indeed," Yasmin sniffed. "I couldn't if I wanted to, and I don't. You'd best go to bed."

"But what about Kheima? Your soul tether?" I objected, fumbling to the wardrobe to change out of my fancy clothes. "We're supposed to go tonight." I snatched at my cane, knocking it from corner to floor. Linguine hissed.

Yasmin smiled and shook her head. "It was madness to even suggest it. We'll go tomorrow… and I think that's still too soon. The night after tomorrow would be preferable."

I stumbled after the cane and picked it up, stifling a yawn and muttering an apology to the Noodle. Yasmin utilized her supernatural force to remove my dress jacket and tie. "See? You can barely keep your eyes open, and you'll be grumpy and tired all day tomorrow."

"Very well," I mumbled, none too pleased. "But we don't have much time left. I have… to bring you home."

I collapsed into bed, still mostly dressed. Yasmin's sigh echoed in my wide chambers. "You know, dear, I've done ample searching on my own in Kheima. If my soul tether were accessible, I'd have found it by now. I think…"

I tried to raise my head, but it seemed too heavy. "What dost thou think, ghost-witch? My queen? My spirit conscience? My Kheiman druid?"

"Don't speak nonsense. Let me finish. I think our only chance is to confess defeat and ask Rothadamas to waive the wager. All things considered, we're happy like this, aren't we? We're together. Not daily, but enough to be satisfied."

That propelled me from the mattress. I shot up with a half-shriek, "Satisfied?!"

"Partially satisfied, then."

"Not even close!" I roared. Linguine's hissy chuckle punctuated my statement; I suppose he found drunk Sergio entertaining.

Yasmin's eyes widened. Her gentle force pushed me back onto the bed. "Have you no heart, woman?" I grunted, submitting to her push. "Don't you know how desperately I want to touch you? To cherish the warmth of your skin against mine? To hold you, for Christ's sake? To kiss you until you cannot breathe?"

I clenched the bedclothes with hot hands. Scales flashed over my arms. "I know you love me, Yasmin, yet you habitually revert to detached, icy logic. You wound me with your thoughtlessness. Oh, I know you don't mean to, beloved—it's self-preservation—but *I love you*, you stone-hearted witch, and I'll give you a heart of flesh or perish in the attempt. Am I understood?"

I sat up again. My burning gaze pierced her eyes through the veil.

Her silver head dipped in acquiescence as her lips trembled.

Sighing, I closed my eyes and rubbed my face. The scales melted back into my flesh, vanishing beneath it. "Forgive me. I'm not angry at *you*, darling. I'm furious with Him. With what He's done to you—what He's taken from us. How we could have been together already, for *years*, if it wasn't for Him tearing us apart."

Yasmin's low voice murmured, "I know."

"Goodnight, beloved."

"Goodnight, Sergio. And... thank you. For everything."

I grunted. "Don't thank me before the deed is done, love."

That Tree would be my first test by draconian fire. Would it withstand my fury? And would its destruction usher in the death of the forest demon?

I doubted it. The Tree was well guarded and the cherished root of His throne, but it was too accessible to result in the demon's fatality if struck. Rothadamas was exquisitely detestable, but no idiot.

And, after all, would destroying the demon result in good things? Something about His reign in Kheima felt not only everlasting but *foundational*. As if His destruction—or His realm's destruction—would bring about the destruction of the Earth itself. After all, Kheima was once the Garden of Gardens. The birthplace of all life as we know it (or so we could assume). The Kheiman frost did not murder the life therein; it merely put it to sleep, terrible but intensely beautiful in its preservation. If *I* were a forest demon, my realm would look much like His: the Sleeping Beauty of forests, cool and calm, a structured pagan chaos.

What a strange, unholy trinity the three of us formed! So different, yet at our cores, so wildly alike. Rothadamas claimed to have formed me with His own hands at the hour of my birth. Yasmin said He had lied, yet...

No, killing Him was not the answer; I doubted it was even possible. Wounding Him was the most I could hope to achieve.

Years ago, Arusi told Yasmin that she did not interfere with Rothadamas because He was necessary to the balance of nature. A "part of the sacred whole," in her own words. *Like a shark in the sea, perhaps*, I mused. *A hunter that renders the waters healthier thanks to its predation.* Did Rothadamas steal souls because He *wanted* to, or because He *had* to? This was the question that plagued me night after night, day after day.

Nevertheless, dreaming of the demon's demise filled my slumbers with the sweet manna of hope. That was worth something in and of itself.

32

Kheima Part 7

Yasmin

Merged with Rothadamas, we raised our hands and spoke in a rapid flow of incantations as the cathedral flooded into being.

Layer upon layer of fluid black ice formed gothic spires. The elaborate staircase leading to the gated double doors rippled with a smooth waterfall only a few inches deep, clear and cold. It slipped into a stream that formed a dark-water moat around the building. *The first flowing waters in Kheima,* I rejoiced. Alas, I could only admire it until it froze over with all the rest, but for the moment I could admire it with all my might and main.

Sensing my delight, the forest demon's paper-thin smile flickered over our face.

Secluded from view by the tallest trees in His forest realm, His new cathedral commanded reverence. Only His nearest and dearest would be permitted to worship here.

We lowered our hands. My breath caught in my throat as I surveyed our combined effort, the melody of winter wind wafting through the towers and blue glass. The sound of flowing water was heavenly music to our ears. "Wonderful," we whispered in tandem.

"Our best work," Rothadamas confirmed.

Possessing the forest demon expanded my soul, sharpening every sense. My mind would grow new roots that dug into the spiritual realms only He could access, granting me views of lily harbors edging crystal oceans, purple-moon planets where royal beings pledged solemn vows, and blood-red countries of fire and ice where the Dracoblods sparred, preparing to win the prettiest mates for themselves in traditional tournaments.

My Sergio is part Dracoblod, I dreamily mused. *I've been meaning to tell him all about his mysterious lineage, but we have so much to plan and discuss when we're together... I wonder what he would think of his home country of dragon shifters? I wonder—*

"He shall make a fine high priest."

Prying my mind loose from His consciousness, I separated from Him with a spark of terror lighting deep within my heart. It hurt to rip the newly-grown roots from the soil, but by now I was accustomed to pain. "Who?" I stammered.

"Your Dragon," Rothadamas replied, voice crisp with amusement. "I require a high priest for my cathedral. Once Sergio has been baptized and born anew, he will be perfect. Don't you agree, Anmut?" Shifting to face me, His icy eyes glinted with barely-repressed resentment. "You may go and worship your lover whenever you please, so long as all of my commissions have been fulfilled. The same applies to him. Would that make you happy, mein Hexe?"

Happy?

The forest demon never troubled Himself to inquire whether I was *happy*. I longed to be pleased with this development... to hope for better, brighter days despite the shadow of His haunting. It meant that even if Sergio lost the wager, which looked all too certain, we would be together in the end. But Rothadamas suddenly sharing His plans with me boded ill for both myself and my ringmaster, or so I believed.

Go back to never thinking of me! I begged. *Go back to minding your own affairs and leaving me to mine. Don't try to please me. Don't give me gifts. Don't change Sergio. Don't!*

"You want me to leave him unaltered," Rothadamas intoned. His eyes narrowed as His wings stretched in the moonlight. He steepled His elegant hands. "I am willing to compromise. I *must* change him to some extent so he will survive my realm, you understand. But I will do what I can to keep his physiognomy familiar to you."

I nodded sans commentary, afraid to say anything, even something grateful. I hated looking *weak*.

"That's settled, then." His form turned black and rippled with static, as it always did before He traveled or went hunting. Summoning my fragile courage, I stopped him with one desperate query: "But why Sergio?"

His ebony head twisted on His thin black neck to look me in the face—an unnatural angle that made me feel sick. "I must ask *you* that," His bitter German rumbled. "Why Sergio, Anmut?"

I battled a fresh rush of tears as He dissipated into the forest. Sergio's love had softened my frozen heart; I never cried as often as I did then.

"Why Sergio?" I repeated, matching and outdoing His bitterness. "Because he not only stripped all my masks to reveal my face but accepted the shadows beneath them. He never tried to change me into someone else, someone he believed was *better*. He ranted against Emma Bauer when he first beheld her, knowing that she wasn't real—that she was only my latest and most socially-tempered mask. I was enough for him. I *am* enough!"

If only Sergio had bound a capable demon to his cane instead of an impish little devil, he might be protected from Rothadamas. I was useless to my beloved. Unless I found some way to sever my own bond with Him, there was nothing I could do to protect Sergio from the Demongod of the Corrupt Wood.

33

BURNING SUMMER

Sergio

"So, Noodle. I don't suppose you could bite Rothadamas and render Him a sleeping menace if I put you within range, eh?"

"Very funny."

I shrugged. "Worth a shot."

"Be quick," Yasmin said as she led me through Kheima, floating a little above me like a guiding star. She made the most stunning of spooks on Earth, but in her own realm she was transcendent. *My angel.* I reached up to swipe my fingertips through her glittering ankle. "Lovely," I whispered.

"Not now."

I curbed a smile at her businesslike tone. Never before had I *enjoyed* being ordered around by anyone. "He isn't here?" I questioned, wanting to confirm it.

"No," Yasmin and Linguine answered as one. "He's studying the Dracoblods," Yasmin added.

"Dracoblods. Sounds like…"

"Dragon shifters. *Ja.* The other half of your ancestry. I'll tell you all about them sometime—as much as I know, at least." Yasmin stopped in front of the Tree of the Knowledge of Evil. "Hurry. Burn it down as quickly as you can."

I took my stance, preparing to shift. A particle of suspicion arose. "You *are* the real Yasmin and not some kind of a trick?" I questioned, brow furrowing at the Kheiman Queen waiting patiently, hands clasped before her trim form.

Angelic Yasmin smiled. In a low voice, she proceeded to sing "My Lady's Galleon," a song that the forest demon would have no reason to know. *My* song. The lyrics my devilish old self had written to mirror Yasmin Lange.

Not that I admitted it, of course; that would have ruined our deliciously unspoken understanding.

Yasmin sensed my remorse and broke down halfway through, punctuating the chorus with a soft laugh. "Don't despise yourself too much, sir. I didn't *hate* it."

"Your feet were rooted to the ground," I teased, flinching as scarlet scales protruded from my flesh to cover it. "I ought to have applied as a professional singer."

"It wasn't your voice in particular, sir. It was the song itself. And *you.*"

Noodle sliced into our reminiscing with a hiss. "*Do* focus on the task at hand, you insufferable creatures. We haven't got all night!"

I managed a final grin before my face lengthened into a dragon's muzzle. I snorted, shaking my head as the cane fell from my claws. "*Stay back,*" I cautioned Yasmin via psychic connection.

She remained floating where she was. *"Fire cannot wound me."*

"Right." Drawing in a deep breath, a guttural snarl resounded from my throat along with a steady stream of ruby flames. I coated every branch, the brilliant crackle reflecting in my narrow pupils. I did not stop until the whole tree lit the eternal night of Kheima.

We waited.

Not a single branch weakened.

It flamed but would not burn. Wouldn't so much as crack. My rumble of dissatisfaction made Yasmin jolt back instinctively as I charged the trunk, turning my head and widening my jaws to chomp into the bark and shake the whole damned Tree like a stick.

"Hue, stop!" Yasmin shoved me with her ghost-force, but pushing a dragon was no Sunday picnic. "It must be indestructible. You'll hurt *yourself*, not it."

I released my hold with another growl. *Indestructible.* Nothing touched that godforsaken demon. Perhaps...

The hideous truth. Perhaps it was time to consider that the only way to be with Yasmin *was* to join Rothadamas. My soul had already belonged to Him for the majority of my young adult years, so I didn't concern myself with my eternal destiny... Hell-bound from conception, according to every priest I'd ever encountered. By joining Rothadamas for good, I'd be exchanging a fiery doom for an icy one. Nothing more, and nothing less.

But Yasmin would be there.

If she managed to remain in the demon's good graces, she might make the transition easier for me. *Better to choose the demon I know than the devil I don't,* I finally allowed myself to think.

Thud. Thud. Thud. Linguine was rolling himself toward me over the dead grass. "Brilliant," he complained, flicking his forked tongue. "What's your plan now, half-blood? Sacrifice yourself to evil in the name of love?

Such a disturbingly *human* thing to do." The flames sizzled and went out, leaving the Tree unharmed as far as we could tell.

Yasmin raised one hand, eyes aglow with compassion. "I know what you're thinking, Sergio. My beloved, I'd never forgive myself for haunting your home and possessing you if this was to be the outcome of the temptation. I am formed for Kheima... *meant* for it. You are not. You are its polar opposite, and you despise taking orders from anyone. You'd perish from sheer misery. And I—"

Her chin trembled.

I shook my massive head, scraping the frozen earth with my claws as I came close and dropped my muzzle into her airy hand. "*This is my choice to make, just as it was yours all those years ago.*" I tilted my head, locking my blue eye with hers. "*Yasmin, thanks to your sacrifice, I've accomplished everything in this life that I meant to. Fame, fortune, and the well-being of my daughter as far as I can ensure it.*" I exhaled a soft, dark-blue plume of smoke through her neck, making her smile. "*I am in your debt. And there's only one thing left that I desire: to spend the rest of my life with you. And preferably my afterlife as well.*"

Yasmin's sigh exhaled from the cavern of her cynical soul. "*You could have had any woman your Dracoblod heart desired. The most beautiful, the most fashionable, with a dowry fit for a princess. But no, your perverse spirit sought out a fellow perversion—a freak of nature bound to demons. You would!*"

I tried to laugh but discovered it didn't sound quite right coming from a dragon's throat. "*Was it not I who first told you that we are the same? Not in person, but in essence.*"

"*Yes. You did. I hated you for it because I didn't want to acknowledge my own vanity. I preferred blaming you for yours.*"

"*I valued your honesty. Always.*"

"You're welcome, then." Her silver irises seemed to double in size as inspiration widened them. "Speaking of vanity," she said aloud, "Would you like to see what I made? Well," tossing her hand dismissively, "what He and I made."

She's trying to distract me from sacrificing myself here and now. I heaved an inward sigh as the last glowing ashes on the Tree whittled down to nothing. The smoke of my complete and utter failure thickened the night air. *"Lead the way."*

Picking up Linguine with her ghost force, she turned, her translucent robes whispering around her. My gaze fastened on her backside as she floated ahead. "Stop staring," she ordered without turning her head.

"Stop having such a delicious figure, and maybe I can."

I sensed her rolling her eyes.

She guided me through the tallest trees in Kheima until we approached a breathtaking cathedral. Cast from black ice and alight with blue-green gothic windows depicting pagan scenes, I marveled at its design. *"If you hadn't already told me you made it, I would have guessed,"* I praised her. *"Your exquisite taste envelopes it."*

Her bright smile touched my heart. "I admit that aiding Him has its perks. I enjoy these projects."

I concentrated the flow of my magic to morph back to human form. She politely returned my spare clothes and cane to me and turned her back until I was dressed. I offered her my arm, which she accepted with a frank grin. "Can I ask you something, Yassy? Pray, don't be angry with me, but you don't seem truly *unhappy* with Him unless He's abused you for some imaginary slight. Will you..." I forced the question through a frown. "If I do succeed in taking you away from Him, will you be happy with me? Or will the dull prose of a normal life—a normal *relationship*—cause the bloom of love to fade?"

Thankfully, she didn't take offense. Her spiritual force dealt my hair a playful tug. "If you could look into my heart and see how strongly the imprint of your soul has sealed it, you wouldn't need to ask. None can lift the seal but you."

We shared an affectionate smile before returning our gazes to the cathedral. *What a stunning location for a marriage proposal*, I thought but wisely did not say.

Four more months until November.

"If I may, I might have an idea," Linguine supplied.

Holding his face up to mine, I grinned. "About time, Noodle."

I wandered through the Vampyre Garden, trampling fallen burgundy and black petals with wild abandon and talking to myself (again). The gothic bower dripped with dark, damp foliage, its statues of crestfallen angels aiding a somber atmosphere. I daydreamed in the Oak Park, while I untangled knotty problems in the Garden.

Now that Lillias was married and moved out, I could indulge my eccentric whims as often as I liked. Nobody but the butler, the maids, and the stable boys were around to judge me. And they wouldn't do it in my hearing unless they had a new employer in mind.

According to Linguine's devilish intuition and observations, the forest demon's weakness *was* Yasmin herself. I grudgingly agreed; if I was certain of nothing else, I was certain of that. He was evil but not immune to the graces of her companionship. However, how could I turn that fact against Him and work it in our favor? That was the question.

I stopped at the angel statue by the Oak Park, glaring into its accompanying lantern. "If Yasmin pleaded her case in light of her love for me, it wouldn't stir Him an inch," I fretted, plucking my beard. "And she'd refuse to try it, I'm sure. She's proud. I like her pride when it's not an inconvenience, but it cannot be denied that it often is."

Linguine nodded. I flinched; sometimes I forgot he was there. "And yet, He seems to be making concessions for her happiness," the imp reminded me. "One must question His true motives, of course. Maybe He wants to prove to Yasmin that He isn't heartless, hoping that will make a case for Him."

I groaned. "Don't humanize Him, Noodle. He's a demon."

"So what? *I* am, too, Sergio, in case you didn't notice. Yet you don't see *me* running around snatching the souls of children or torturing my subjects. Some of us are more mischievous than downright evil."

"First time you've called me by my own name," I grinned, choosing a lighter topic for the moment.

"A small courtesy that I believe I deserve, too. Half-blood."

"Oh, go eat a rat. But wait. You can't!"

Linguine vented an eloquent curse.

I swung the cane with a sigh—albeit more gently than I had when I first met him. "If I challenge Him directly, I will lose," I resumed. "I might offer another wager, but what do I have to give that He cannot get for Himself?" I leaned my head back to glare at the gray sky. "If I were a praying man, I'd get down on my knees this instant, but I've never been the type to capitulate to hogwash. Why would the gods listen to *us*?" I shrugged.

"The High God likes the humans either hot or cold," Linguine informed me. "Let us be consistent."

"A surprisingly insightful remark, Noodle."

"I harbor a plethora of them, yet people are always surprised."

The clop of horseshoes broke the late summer silence. A drizzle of rain descended as a cloaked womanly figure broke the fog, steadying her mount with an encouraging pat or two. "Hail, ringmaster!" Aislinn called out.

"Hail, witchling." I planted the foot of the cane in the ground, leaning against it as she approached down the winding avenue. Linguine sighed but endured my weight.

Trotting through the main gate, Aislinn reined her horse to a halt and dismounted. "Any news?" I called out.

"Rejoice, Sergio! For I come bearing tidings of great joy."

She laughed as I cast my eyes heavenward. "Proceed," I motioned.

Aislinn waved to Linguine and blew him a kiss. "Evening, Osedis. Correct me if I'm mistaken, ringmaster," Aislinn began, sparkling with mischievous intent, "but your current wager with Rothadamas still stands, yes? A soul for a soul. He will release Yasmin back to you, resurrected and unharmed, if you can find Him a suitable replacement as His Kheiman Queen by November?"

"*Questo è corretto*," I dryly replied, "but it was a false wager from the start, meant to buy us time. By His own word, He cannot touch me until the deadline has expired."

"Good, good! That was clever." Aislinn spread her arms wide and curtsied deeply. Her blue cloak accentuated her eyes to perfection. "Then may I present the new Queen of Kheima. I intend to offer myself in her place."

Stunned, my brain scrambled to gather words, but it missed the catch somewhere. Even Linguine was too shocked to speak.

"Don't look so much like a lightning strike!" the Celt chuckled, straightening up. "I've hit an impasse, Sergio. My studies are redundant, my companions bore me, and I've no intention of giving up my freedom for some dullard of a husband so I may integrate into society. Why should

I?" She shook her head, standing akimbo. "Besides, I'm the only witch we know that's anything like our dear, quaint little Yassy. Although, I'm miles more charming and cheerful than she is. Dear old soul!"

With great effort, I deployed my argument. "How can you speak so flippantly about this? You *do* know what spiritual torment at His right hand would be like? For *all eternity*?"

Aislinn wiggled her forefinger at me. "He only tortures her because He knows her heart doesn't belong to Him. It yearns for *you,* and He hates it. But He can't do anything about it; she has loved you devotedly for over a decade. You don't deserve it," shrugging her cloaked shoulders, "but it is what it is."

She smiled, reaching up to purloin my top hat and place it on her own head. "*I* am not in love with anybody. He won't have to waste His precious time reminding me of my place. I'll slip right into it as if born to be there."

I only had two words left to say. "You're mad."

Linguine spluttered in agreement. "You can't be serious, Lady Aislinn! It would be a waste... an impolitic, incomparable waste... to bind yourself to that demon. Better for you to die this instant than to suffer such a fate." He lowered his scathing voice to add, "I say this because I care about you, lady witch. I've sensed your strength and tasted your spirit. You were born to rule, not be ruled by another."

Aislinn smiled at both of us. "Thank you, gentlemen. You're very kind. But tell me something new sometime, if you would."

"You've spent all these years serving Him at the bare minimum to preserve your freedom," I persisted. "Will you cast it all aside now?"

"For Yasmin? My darling friend who has shouldered the burden of His haunting for all these years, even after death?" Her voice gentled, her eyes contemplating something far away. "Aye. Of course I will."

I groaned, rubbing a hand over my face. "Let's pretend, for a moment, that I agree and I take you to Him. What if He refuses? We have every reason to expect He will. We'll be back at square one."

"Then you'll have to challenge Him to a battle. First challenger to relent from his injuries must give Yasmin up."

I grunted at her singular bluntness, a trait that always grated on me. Which was odd, considering that I relished Yasmin's version of it. *What was that about being consistent, you blustering windbag?* "It would be a fight to the death. *My* death, at least, for I'd never relent."

"Men." Aislinn flicked her golden hair with a sigh. "Well, think about it. I've considered it for weeks and I've made up my mind. And once I've done so," she tossed my hat back to me, "I'm very, *very* difficult to persuade otherwise. I want to be the Kheiman Queen. I want to save Yasmin, and you want to be with her. It's a victory for everyone concerned." She flashed Osedis a dazzling smile before mounting and trotting away.

A drip of venom stung my finger. I yelped, dropping Linguine to the ground. "What was that for?"

"An honest mistake." He vented a deeper, darker hiss than I'd yet heard. He was truly troubled for Aislinn—he cared for her. "If that beautiful, talented witch pledges herself to eternal servitude to *anyone,* I shan't rest until I've found a loophole through which she could slip."

"Easy does it, Noodle." Gingerly, I picked him up to pat him on the head. "Remember she's a *witch.* Part of her Craft is to charm everyone who looks upon her. Including little devils."

He tried to nip me, but I held him out of range in time. I yawned. "Blasted hex venom."

I knew Aislinn well enough to pierce that blinding charm. She'd loathe to part with her freedom, her cherished gardens, and her divine herbology in exchange for servitude in eternal winter. But she'd do it.

For Yasmin.

"Oh, my darling! You little know the strength of the friendships you have formed," I addressed my ghost-witch from afar.

Blows and botheration! I was stuck with the same mortifying question. If Rothadamas accepted, would Yasmin be happy at my side once the deed was done, the conditions of the wager cleared, and a calm, ordinary life within her reach, *at the cost of her dearest friend?*

I groaned again, collapsing at an angel statue's feet to study its mournful aspect. "Heaven above, guide me!"

The sky shook with a clap of thunder. *Maybe I should appeal to Hell below, instead.*

"You know, I'm getting a *little* tired of being thrown around," Linguine muttered from the grass.

34

STORMING FALL

Sergio

AISLINN AND I AGREED not to share her solution with Yasmin until after Rothadamas either accepted or declined. If we gave Yasmin the option to try to stop Aislinn first, then she certainly would. Yasmin loved only a few and far between, but she loved with the fierceness of a dragoness.

In the meantime, Aislinn withdrew to her cottage to meditate and otherwise prepare herself for her hopeful position as Kheima's new queen.

I wasn't pleased with this plan of hers. It did occur to me to offer myself in Yasmin's stead, but Rothadamas had specified a *queen*, and I wasn't about to let Aislinn turn me into a woman—not even for poor Yassy's sake. A man must have his limits, and that was mine. I'd make a damned gorgeous bit of frock, though.

At any rate, what other option did we have?

Night after night, I twisted and turned, struggling in vain to form a solution just as viable but without sacrificing yet another soul to the forest demon.

I complained to the ghost-boy Oliver, who had taken an unaccountable liking to me. "He may not be a god, but He might as well be," I assured him. *Hmm, sounds familiar.* Yasmin had likely said something similar.

"Stuff and nonsense," Linguine piped in from his umbrella stand. (He threw quite the *hissy* fit when I endeavored to place him in it with my umbrellas and a spare cane. I cleared them out to shut him up; as a result, his umbrella stand was quite roomy.) "If you were half as clever as you pretend to be, outsmarting the demon would be a walk in your Vampyre Garden."

"Cut the cackle and let me sleep, Noodle."

Listlessly, I prepared another summoning circle. This time I set up shop out of doors, in the same discreet clearing where I practiced pyrocraft and shifting. Sunset cast copper rays over the changing trees. In the distance, the ebony towers and dragon grotesques of House Vincenzo twinkled above the roiling clouds. I smelled storms and autumn in the air, and my spirits lifted in spite of my dreadful task. *Our favorite season.*

Not far from the clearing, Yasmin's coffin lay buried in the gloom. It had arrived at last. I'd expected to be happy to see it—to have it in my own possession, to have *her*—to trace its precious corners with my own hands. Instead, the sight and feel of it brought a weary sorrow to my soul.

Depression's persistence continually plucked at my heels, slowing my pace. My sore knee was aching, too, reminding me that my time would come...

Linguine watched at my side, the patient overseer of my tasks. "Can you conjure me a snack, Noodle?" I asked, sitting cross-legged and holding the cane like a pharaoh's scepter. Silly, perhaps, but it increased my confidence and allowed the little devil to see everything.

"If you ask me like a proper gentleman, I might consider it."

"Eat a rat."

"I might eat your *hand* one of these days..."

In the midst of our mild bickering, Rothadamas appeared in His hunting form. He hunched over me, inspecting my downcast aura with interest. "You've a prospect for me?" He lost no time inquiring.

"One of your own," I answered, feigning complete confidence. "Aislinn Bláthnaid."

As I anticipated, His interest faded. "She is not suited to the position. Her talents are concerned with the living and the wealth of spring. She'd pine away and perish in my realm."

"She thought you'd say so." I proceeded with caution, making brief but respectful eye contact. It stung my eyes like a thousand tiny needles. "She wishes to inform you that she's grown weary of life on this Earth and yearns to serve at your side. She is willing to be baptized and born anew. Changed to suit your realm."

The forest demon jerked His head and sighed, a surprisingly human reaction. Linguine and I exchanged meaningful glances. "Pray speak the truth, Dragon. She's bored, and she thinks becoming my queen will alleviate her boredom." Rothadamas chuckled—a most unpleasant sound. It scattered like electricity and pained my ears, like His eye contact burned my pupils. "Aislinn Bláthnaid will not do. You've wasted too many months gadding about with my Queen instead of searching far and wide for a suitable replacement. Fortunately, I've taken the liberty of generating a place for you in Kheima. You shan't be cast aside but made useful at once."

"How kind of you," I muttered.

"Have you any other business with me, Dragon? If not, I shall take my leave."

Keep Him talking. Think, Sergio! Think!

Linguine butted in. "Just my two pence, sir, but according to Sergio, you mentioned testing your prospective Queen."

Tightening my grip, I growled at him to button up. That infuriating half-baked noodle ignored me. "Why not test Aislinn before you reject her? She's not only well familiar with Kheima and your... methods... but she is willing. You won't find another willing prospect, Rothadamas. Not if you gave the half-blood fifty years instead of one." I stiffened, vexed with Linguine's interference. Surely the forest demon wouldn't condescend to converse with a lower devil.

Linguine's indiscretion was not in vain; the cobra struck a chord somewhere. The forest demon's glazed-over demeanor sharpened and zeroed in on my face. Interest recaptured. "The imp is correct, but he must hold his forked tongue in the presence of his betters. It is impertinence, Dragon, and I've no inclination to entertain it."

I smiled, recalling my partial ancestry: the Dracoblods. "Dracos and demons need not stand upon ceremony as the humans do," I pointed out. "Quailing silence is not a compliment to my kind. And as the imp is bonded to me, I say he may speak with impunity for as long as the bond remains."

Linguine's ruby eyes glinted, perplexed. A sly grin pushed his snake cheeks up into two bronze bulges. Young Sergio would have burst into laughter at the sight.

"An... interesting perspective." The forest demon tilted His head at a weird angle. "In return, I admit that to a certain extent, I also respect thee, Sergio Vincenzo Dragonson. The more we interact, the more determined I am to incorporate you into my realm. I am confident that you will do well there, and Anmut will be grateful for my benevolence and obliged to please me."

"I see." *How odd that you should be so talkative, Rothadamas.* He truly was a different creature after a decade with Yasmin at His side.

Yasmin Lange, tamer of dragons and demons! I hid a smirk by cupping my hands and blowing into them, as if feeling the nightfall chill. Moonrise would call Yasmin to my side soon. I didn't want her to ask what her two "masters" were discussing. "I haven't given up on Aislinn yet. You'll see how much better she would serve you than Yasmin. Her Craft is unmatched. Her heart is undivided. You only need to test her. With Aislinn as your right hand, Kheima might even *bloom* and be a happy place!"

Wishful thinking, I knew, but I'd lied for far less worthy causes than this.

He straightened His head, flexing His long fingers. "What makes you so certain, Dragon?"

"I know Aislinn's temperament. Once she's set her mind to something, she'll accomplish it. That woman is fixed as fate. And," pausing to increase the gravity of my statement, "because no one can serve two masters."

"You think of yourself as Yasmin's master also?" The forest demon uttered a subtle growl of challenge. It reverberated in the roots of the nearby trees, quaking the ground.

Formerly, I sat cross-legged in the summoning circle. I stood, flashing a confident smile. "'Tis only logical. She revered me long before she knew of your existence."

I grinned through His face looming closer. It wasn't wise to test His temper, but I was tired of all this figurative bowing and scraping for a spoiled, selfish demon who was determined to squeeze every last inch of autonomy from Yasmin's soul. *Not on my watch, demon bastard.*

"You truly believe you are more worthy than I," Rothadamas rumbled, amused. "Very well. A new wager—and remember, Dragon, that you brought it upon yourself."

Linguine and I exchanged looks again.

"I shall prepare Yasmin for a Witch's Duel. And you shall prepare her opponent, Aislinn Bláthnaid. The match shall take place on the winter solstice." He steepled His hands like a cunning entrepreneur. "The winner shall be crowned the Kheiman Queen with all due ceremony, to be treated with reverence by her subjects and honor by my word. The runner-up shall be stripped of her powers and restored to her Earthly home."

I stepped forward, mouth open and fist in the air, filled to the brim with objections. But the forest demon chuckled in His threatening, purring way and vanished, leaving behind a charred, smoking summoning circle that would have burnt my feet to a crisp if I were a pure-blooded human.

"Blast! Blows! Damnation!" I cried, kicking the nearest rock. Yasmin warned me time and time again not to open my mouth to boast. *Why didn't I listen?*

And now, she'd be forced to duel the woman she loved most.

Because of me.

"Dearest, can you forgive me?"

I cupped the cold glow of Yasmin's face. The light in her eyes—albeit a frigid, undead sort of light, but still light—had quite died, leaving placid brackish pools in its wake. "I'll do whatever I can to help you," I reassured her. "And Aislinn will do her best to win, I'm sure. We may consider the results of the match as settled. You will be free—"

"No," my ghost-witch replied. I flinched at the emptiness in her voice. Hope had fled. "I cannot allow anyone else to suffer what I've suffered. I will take the victory so Aislinn may live out the rest of her days in peace."

"She'll hate it!" I protested. "She'd rather descend to Second Death than be stripped of her Craft. You know how much she identifies with it. Forced to become a common woman... Losing all her meticulous beauty charms. *We* might laugh at them, but to her they are the very essence of her inner spirit manifested in the flesh. No, she'd far rather rule at the demon's side, believe me." *This,* at least, was no lie. Aislinn would far rather rule alongside a demon than be a normal woman, and Yasmin and I both knew it. By the gods, even Linguine knew it!

Yasmin turned and floated off. She stared into the blazing fireplace of the library, crossing her thin arms. "Then it will be a real match. *I* shall be giving it my all, too."

All the blood drained from my face. I stomped forward and clutched at her arm, cursing as my fingers passed through her. "No, Yasmin. No! Let Aislinn win the duel. Let someone else take up your burden. You've done enough, for Christ's sake! You've done enough!"

Linguine wisely kept silent as I battled the impulse to break something. In thanks, I set the cane aside so I didn't grip it too tightly. I *never* cried, yet the water rose.

"Sergio! My beloved ringmaster." Yasmin darted in front of me and gently blew the tears dry with her sweet winter touch. "This wager is far more agreeable to me than the previous one, for your own soul is not at stake. For that, I thank you." A tiny beam of hope was restored to her shrunken pupils. "And Aislinn may be vain, but she's a disciplined proxy. We will be well matched. It is just; it is fair. Rothadamas has shown mercy in this matter."

A fresh bouquet of curses burst anew. "I wish upon every star above that I could shake you. Pitting two devoted women against one another is anything *but* merciful. It is evil. Do call things what they are, Yasmin Lange, and cease and desist with donning the rose-colored glasses."

She made a caressing motion, as if stroking my hair. "My rose-colored glasses have saved my sanity these ten years, darling. Look upon them with more grace."

"Then you won't let Aislinn win?" I fired one last time. "You are determined?"

My Schattengeist's sad smile struck me like an arrow to the chest. "I am many things, Sergio, and some of them are neither pleasant nor proper. Cold, proud, prone to melancholy reverie. Dead," she added with a low laugh. "Beloved sorceress of one forest demon and one irritable dragon shifter." Her pale face lit with affection. "But I am *not* going to make the same mistake of using my own friends as a shield against Rothadamas. I will stand on my own two feet, look Him in the eye, and tell Him I am ready for His challenge."

When her eyes flashed like lightning and her lips pursed into a deep purple line, I knew any further rebukes were worse than useless; they'd hammer her deeper into her own will. I sighed, seizing Linguine and tapping the cane against my library desk for luck. *Knock. Knock. Knock.* "Then know this, O Ghastly Sorceress. Whether you're returned to Earth as Yasmin Lange or detained in Kheima as Queen Anmut, I shall worship at your feet regardless. You won't get away from me because you can't. I'll see to *that*."

Her smile healed my wounded chest. "I'm going to be selfish and admit that's exactly what I expect of you, and precisely what I want."

"But you better lose," I grumbled. "If we keep dilly-dallying with paranormal foreplay, blast it, woman! I'm going to lose my goddamn mind."

Her eyes sparkled in reply, light resuming in full force.

35

KHEIMA PART 8

Yasmin

I DRIFTED PAST THE cathedral doors. Emerging above the dark blue altar shone a statue of Rothadamas Himself, glowing with gemstones and holding a small fountain between His hands. *Crafted to depict honor and leniency,* I thought, biting back a sneer with valiant effort.

I was not as affected as Sergio feared. I wore rose-colored glasses to calm *him,* not to comfort myself. I'd discovered years ago that my ringmaster's quick temper rendered him his own worst enemy, and further inciting his wrath against a timeless demon was... inadvisable.

As I made my thoughtless, fleeting bow at the altar—sheer habit—I lifted my eyes to its black-stone face in time to see it morph into the living face of the forest demon. I amended my half-hearted bow with a deep curtsy. "Master."

He hummed contentedly. "My Queen."

"Might I be of service?" I inquired, darting a glance over the gleaming furnishings of the cathedral. I'd hoped to design them myself, but it appeared He'd delegated that task to another.

A crying shame. My taste was superior; even He would acknowledge it if asked. He did lie, of course, but He rarely lied to me.

"Since I have every confidence that you will win the Witch's Duel against Aislinn," Rothadamas began, taking my hands in His, "I thought it prudent to prepare you for the elaborate ceremony being planned in your honor."

I declined the honor as graciously as I could. Pointed out that I was only doing what I agreed to in Lillias's place. Reminded Him that He had gifted Aislinn, too, so she was no lackadaisical opponent.

"You misunderstand me," the forest demon corrected. He released my hands, interlocking His fingers behind His back. He bent over me. "It was not my intention to merely reassert your position. This shall be no ordinary occasion." He paused, leaning further in to touch His forehead to mine. I held His painful, icy gaze, loathing to flinch in fear. "There is but one higher honor I can bestow upon thee, my Sorceress Sovereign of Kheima."

If my face weren't already as pale as death, it would certainly have become so at those words. "You," I fumbled, slow terror flooding the whole of my being, "You don't mean..."

In one fluid motion, Rothadamas stepped back, lifted my left hand in His, and slipped a ring upon my wedding finger.

I shut down, locking my terror away for private inspection later. I focused on the ring itself. Black, of course, with tiny veins of blue gems snaking over it that gleamed in the moonlight. Simple and unassuming. He knew my tastes as well as Sergio did.

"Do you approve?" Rothadamas asked.

I raised my blank stare from the ring to His ice-blue eyes. "Why me?"

He blew a soft, static-laced huff across my face. A black tendril escaped from His spine to caress my cheek. "Any more ridiculous questions, meine Hexe?"

Fear and wonder engulfed me in perplexing waves. His demeanor was... *affectionate.* Or as close to affectionate as any demon's facial expression might become. Terror seized my throat with more violence than any of His abuse had ever conjured. Muttering some excuse, I fled, flying through the forest half-blind with sleet-like tears.

Lovers must commit to honesty. I knew that. But how would Sergio receive this news? God, the look on his face! How could I endure it?

36

LOOMING WINTER

Sergio

YASMIN CRIED INTO MY chest as I positioned my arms to hold her. It was just like holding a winter-cloud. I blessed the Maker for seeing fit to intertwine my ancestry with draconian blood. Otherwise, regular contact with my poor ghost-witch would have frozen me to the bone.

Aislinn ceased her spell work and flew to Yasmin's side. Her own eyes filled with sympathetic tears at Yasmin's distress, its open display so rare that I quaked with preemptive rage.

"He's running you into the ground training you, isn't He?" I growled through gritted teeth. Primed for deployment, my scales bristled in response. "Just say the word, beloved, and I'll charge Him this moment and get it all over with, for better or for worse."

"No! Please stay here," Yasmin begged, drying her eyes. "You haven't the slightest chance of winning. The Witch's Duel must take place."

"Then what can I do?" I trudged to the cottage window and glared at the austere November skies. "Grant me a pursuit, or I shall lose my head. And good luck taming your Dragon then."

"Please," Yasmin murmured, her paranormal force grabbing my shoulders and turning me to face her, "help Aislinn train. And you, darling," she said, managing a weary but loving smile for her sister-in-spirit, "You must be prepared for the worst. If you pour every ounce of your magic into this challenge... if you win... you might become *His wife*."

Previously unnoticed, she held up her left hand. An ebony ring coiled its smug self around her wedding finger.

Smoke billowed from my nostrils and mouth. Yasmin shook her head at me, pursing her lips. "Not in the house. Go outside if you can't contain it."

She was right, of course; Aislinn's cottage had already suffered enough at my fiery hands. I grabbed Linguine and stomped outside without another word, barely clinging to humanity, not even noticing the wondrous beauty of Aislinn's autumnal wreaths above the door. "Can you take me to Kheima?" I demanded, lifting the cane to be face to face with the imp.

"I can, but I certainly wouldn't advise it. You'll get yourself killed."

"Not if you help me."

Linguine sighed, looking genuinely downcast. An impressive feat for a bronze knob with rubies for eyes. "I can only work basic spells, Sergio, and perhaps lend you what magical strength I embody. I am not a mighty demon. If only you'd summoned Bregor instead of me—"

His sorrow softened my rage. I scratched his head. "Noodle, I'm glad we met, and your counsel has been helpful. I'm sorry that *I'm* not a mighty warlock."

"You will be, though. I can tell."

"Well, thanks... Osedis."

A short pause intervened as he digested his surprise. "This may not be the best of times, Sergio, but may I ask a favor from you?"

"Make it quick." I nodded. "Once I've cooled off, I should get back inside."

"Yes, you should. Would you talk to Aislinn on my behalf about... about transferring our bond over to her? If she doesn't win the Witches' Duel, she'll need me." He burst out with uncharacteristic anxiety, "I'd be so honored to serve as her companion!"

"You want to be Aislinn's bondservant?" I rubbed my chin. "Hmm. With Aislinn's help, I intended to free you the instant we're no longer plagued by this Kheiman haunting."

"I thought you might—if only to be rid of me—but there's something about Lady Aislinn. I... I long to be by her side. I *want* her to rely on me, to lean on me for support, both magically and physically. I've never felt that way about any human before; she draws me like a moth to a flame. For the first time in my existence, I feel as if I am *meant* to bond with someone."

I smiled, warming to the Noodle in the face of his earnest plea. "Of course. Once this ugly business is over, if Aislinn is stripped of her Craft, she will indeed benefit from your companionship. You suit one another."

His little cheeks puffed then deflated as he sighed with relief. "Thank you, Sergio."

"Nothing to it, Noodle."

His hood flared a bit, but a snake-ish grin revealed his glinting fangs.

Meanwhile, Aislinn and Yasmin spoke in low, troubled tones. I didn't make a conscious effort to eavesdrop, but I heard some of their conversation here and there. I paced, limbs taut and aching from suppressing the urge to shift. I was much calmer than I would have been otherwise, thanks to Linguine. *Perhaps he has been more useful than I realized,* I admitted to myself. *I shouldn't swing him around or shake him...*

"Did you agree to this?" Aislinn was saying.

"There was nothing to agree to; He didn't ask me. He *informed* me."

"I might have known." From the click of heeled boots, I knew Aislinn was pacing, too. "Why would He do this to you, my poor Yassy? Your soul is His. You're at His beck and call. Why force *marriage*," she seethed at the word, "as if it could ever be anything more than a mockery?"

"Humiliation," Yasmin supplied with a deep sigh. "What else? And to think I used to call Erbanhue possessive!"

"Well he *was*," our sweet Celt reminded her. "Don't whitewash that Dracoblod of yours, my dear. He's no demon, but that doesn't make him a saint. Anyway," her boots recommenced their crisp clicking against the cottage floorboards, back and forth, back and forth, "this changes nothing. I know you don't want me to, but I'm giving this duel my all. I shall take your place beside Rothadamas. You will be resurrected and be with Sergio, even though he doesn't deserve you." Aislinn sniffed.

"You're sweet." I heard the smile in Yasmin's voice. "Kindly recall that I am not a saint either, darling. I'm a hex witch: apathetic, detached, and selfish."

Aislinn sighed and blew our ghost-witch a kiss; I heard its tender, unmistakable sound, soft though it was. "You *used* to be, darling," Aislinn reassured her. "You're not selfish anymore. Well, if the ringmaster truly makes you happy, I won't say another word. But the day he mistreats you or forgets everything you've sacrificed for him, I'm turning him into a frog."

"A poison dart frog might suit him," Yasmin coolly submitted.

They shared brief, girlish mirth. I snorted but didn't restrain a grin. *Bless you, Aislinn, for making our beloved Yasmin laugh.* Besides, they weren't wrong.

Yassy lowered her voice. "Do you realize what you're sacrificing yourself for, my darling? Truly, fully realize it?"

Aislinn interrupted with another charming giggle. "You mean mortality for immortality? Paranormal power beyond my imagination? A realm of my own to co-reign, and marriage to one of the most prominent fallen angels under Heaven? What's so bad about that?"

"Don't make light of it," Yasmin sternly interposed. "He'll make you get your hands dirty, too. You'll be stealing far more souls for His realm than you've ever taken before."

"We'll see about that," the Celt announced. "Over time, you've influenced Kheima and your own position there, and I know I can, too. I'll follow your lead. It will be a different place by the time I'm done with it."

"Then the changes *must* be gradual," my ghost-witch insisted. "Don't push Him for everything you want all at once. And mask your emotions as well as you can. He'll be calmer when you are calm."

"Yes, *mother*," Aislinn teased. "I kept my distance as much as possible, but I'm well acquainted with His personality. Don't fret about me, dearest." Her resumed pacing clipped to a halt. "I love you to pieces, Yassy, but you aren't as crafty as Sergio and me. I know how to wind the most unruly, stone-hearted men 'round my pinkie finger, and I'll manage Rothadamas, too. Just wait and see!"

Yasmin's voice trembled. "If only I could cast a protection spell around your spirit, my Aislinn. If He broke you, I'd never forgive myself." She sniffled and her voice strengthened. "I'll give you fair warning that I'm not letting you win, Aislinn Bláthnaid. If I'm going to have your soul on my conscience, it will be there after I did everything I could to keep you safe."

"I already belong to Him. I'll only be changing locations, dear."

"It's not that straightforward... but I'm relieved to find you so brave."

"I'm always brave, silly goose!"

From the mutual sniffling that followed, I could only imagine a ghostly embrace was underway. I lingered a minute before traipsing back inside. "Any scones to be had, witchlings?" I called out, forcing a cheer I didn't feel. "I'm famished."

"This is ridiculous."

"Hush, now." I kissed the cloud of Yasmin's forehead. "Be still. Use that impeccable imagination of yours."

I sat on the front steps of House Vincenzo, cradling Yasmin's ethereal form in my lap. She hovered just above it, staring at me with an amusing combination of reproach and affection. "Paranormal physics aside, aren't we too old for this?"

"Speak for yourself, you gray-haired hag." I flushed—that was an old insult from years ago when Yasmin referred to herself as such, and I overheard it; the jest had not aged well. "I'm sorry, darling—"

Giggling, she mussed my queue with ghost force. I laughed, too, extracting the band that imprisoned my locks and shaking them free. "Been thinking about cutting it."

"Don't you dare. I like it this way."

"Bossy."

Gusts of night air swept golden leaves against the mansion. The Vampyre Garden was speckled with frost, and the circus-themed lanterns lent a ruddy glow over the spectral landscape. End-of-year gloom skulked in the shadows, but I liked it.

So did my ghost-witch. I locked eyes with her. "A month from now you'll *really* be sitting here with me. Just like this."

She caught her breath. The brimming passion she hid so well frothed to the surface, catching in her irises like silver fire. "I want that more than anything I've ever wanted in my life, Sergio. To finally be yours. And yet... how can I resign myself to Aislinn's fate?" Yasmin trembled, looking away into the garden. "How can I live a happy life knowing it came at such a cost? I've never had a friend like Aislinn, and I never will again. I love her. Every bit as much as I love *you*, I dare to say."

I grunted, stretching my sore neck. Practicing the Craft with Aislinn took a lot out of me, not that I'd admit it to Yasmin. "First of all, you've been socially isolated all your life and especially so in your afterlife, so how do you know you 'never will again?' Once you're Lady Vincenzo, empress of the mansion, you will have all the time in the world to indulge in society and make friends."

Emitting a coy grin, I continued, "Secondly, Aislinn has plastered herself with so many beautifying enchantments and anti-aging spells that she's hardly fit to dwell among the common folk anymore. Very soon, people will begin to question her complete lack of aging. She's also far too powerful for her own good; it's wasted here. She'll make an excellent Kheiman Queen. And as she said herself, she's crafty. She'll manage Rothadamas if anybody can."

"Easy for *you* to say, sir." Yasmin sighed, returning her gaze to mine. "You don't remember your own service to the forest demon. Your freedom-loving spirit warred against it so stormily that you even turned against *me*, your most loyal employee and your honest friend."

"Don't remind me," I grumped. "I'll spend the rest of my life making it up to you. You'll haunt me either way."

Her tender smile thrilled me. I fastened my gaze onto those wonderful dark lips, vampiric in their sensuous curve and saturation. They excited me to my core. *It's a shame she isn't a vampyre, for I'd gladly let her drink my blood.*

Yasmin shook her head. "Wild, ghastly creature that I was, haunting your mansion was great fun. Haunting *you* has been... heavenly. I'll be a little sorry to resume life and lose my supernatural abilities."

"Oh no, you won't." I opened my mouth to shoot a small red flame through her, making her jump and laugh. "I shall fill your days with mirth, banter, and curious gifts from all over the world, and I shall fill your nights with breathless pleasure. Your years of hardship will be over. The *Dragon King* will tow *Beryl's Daughter* to waters smooth as glass, and moor her there."

Yasmin's airy arms wrapped around my neck. Her preternatural eyes glowed more fiercely than ever. "I haven't been cared for in so long. I can't even imagine it."

"Then don't try. Let me show you."

"Yes, but *you* will be enough for me. Gifts be damned!" my ghost-witch uttered with delightful vehemence.

I hummed and rocked back and forth a few times, still holding her. "We'll have the most magnificent New Year. The ballroom will be filled with every color your weary eyes have been denied these eleven years, bursting with gold and red, and royal purple and vibrant green. So many exotic bouquets, you'll be sick of them, Yassy! And chocolates. Shaped cakes and towers of pies and every kind of drink imaginable..."

I described the party in a dreamy drawl. A crystal-bright tear or two rolled down Yasmin's thin cheek, but I paid it no mind; I knew they were happy tears.

My witch and I lounged at the foot of my Stygian mansion, cloaked in the shadow of its glory. In the depths of night, House Vincenzo preened like a sable Christmas tree, brilliant with shocks of color from its windows. Dragons channeled the rainwater instead of classic gargoyles. Organ music drifted from the open chapel hall (Brandon liked to play sometimes, and I liked to let him). The wind carried the sharp, blood-stirring scent of coming snow.

"Winter smells exciting. Don't you think?" I demanded.

Yasmin's rapt smile split in a laugh. "Your mind is wandering all over creation tonight."

"It's your fault. Your presence is quite stimulating."

She heaved a mock sigh. "Then you'll never get anything done while I'm around."

"Nonsense. The Fair of Phantoms was most successful after you joined."

"I didn't notice. My eyes were full of *you*. Eyes, head, heart—they've all been yours since the day you smiled at me as you reached for my hand, helping me up after I fell from the high ropes."

I *tsk'ed*. "You shouldn't have lost your heart to such a cruel bastard. You should have protected it. Locked it up until a real Prince Charming came along."

My charming Schattengeist laughed long and loud, tossing back her translucent silver tresses from her white neck. "I'd have to be a princess to deserve a prince, Sergio. And I'm not. I never was. Thank God!"

I didn't have to ask her what she meant by that. I remembered. *"Then it is settled. We are the same. We crave worship, and we will get it, by God!"*

My Yasmin and I were strong, and we rejoiced in our strength.

37

WHAT MADNESS IS LOVE

Sergio

WHILE ROTHADAMAS TRAINED YASMIN for the Witch's Duel, I was ordered to train Aislinn for it—though she knew more about the Craft than I did. We were placed at a crippling disadvantage. An *obvious* disadvantage.

I spat and sneered in my rage, but Aislinn didn't waste any time by joining me in my righteous anger. She buried her golden head in her studies.

As Yuletide drew near, some of Aislinn's snap and sparkle dimmed. She normally walked with a powerful, long stride, self-assured and determined. Her steps slowed. Her bright, relaxed face looked more drawn and tense than I'd ever seen it. And she didn't laugh at my jokes anymore.

Well, *snort* at my jokes, then. She made it quite clear that she didn't think men in general very amusing, and I was worse than most in her peerless eyes.

As far as the Witch's Duel was concerned, we had no way of knowing what the challenge itself would be. So, we practiced what Aislinn referred to as the "fundamentals," spells she learned from Mistress Arusi. Arusi had gone her separate way years ago, but her lessons remained scattered around Aislinn's cottage in carefully-preserved journals.

I liked learning alongside that spitfire of a Celt. We quarreled—much more stringently than Yasmin and I ever had, and with a great deal more cursing involved—but our mutual love for Yasmin drew us together again. We'd mend our frayed friendship over tea and scones and home-churned butter and get right back to work, a pleasant silence settling over us, only interrupted by the flutter of a page turning or the whispered recital of a new incantation.

Generally speaking, I made people nervous. I entered a room like a thunderstorm rolling over a field, roiling and rumbling and wholly unapologetic. It comforted me to discover kindred spirits who were confident enough in themselves to relax in the storm, letting it come and go as it was meant to.

If Aislinn won the Duel, I would miss her, too.

The same shadow that lurked over Aislinn soon swallowed me. I donned my hat and cloak with neither a hum nor a whistle, leaving Linguine behind in my preoccupation. I rode to the cottage through a flurry of winter flakes.

They weren't white, but pale blue.

The cottage door bristled with evergreen, pine cones, and holly. Aislinn's velvet-green gown swept against the window as she hung glass witch balls. Noticing my approach, she waved me inside.

I knocked my boots against the door frame to loosen the snow. Aislinn took my cloak and hat to hang them. "Warm up," she ordered, pointing to the fireplace.

"No need." I pushed up my sleeves to display one of my dragon tattoos. "I only wore the cloak to keep the maids from fretting about my health."

"Oh, yes. I'd forgotten."

I squinted at her face. "You're pale. And you've dark circles beneath your eyes. Confound it, witchling! Are you getting any sleep at all?"

"Not much," the Celt admitted. She threw herself into the nearest chair. "I can't do this, Sergio," she whispered, her wide eyes locked onto the dancing flames. "What was I thinking? What in *hell* was I thinking?"

I sighed, walking to her side and reaching down to hold her hand. She flinched in surprise but calmed herself, submitting her palm to mine when I looked into her face with deep compassion. "You can back out. Yasmin and I never asked you to do this. We wouldn't hold it against you."

Maybe I can find someone else to duel Yasmin? I doubted it, but I'd cross that bridge later. Right now, Yasmin's dearest friend was scared, and she had every damned right to be.

Aislinn managed a thin smile, but her gaze fell away from mine. Her free hand fumbled to her dress collar and parted it to show the Mark of Rothadamas, putrid and black against her light gold skin. "See? He's holding me to my commitment as Yasmin's voluntary challenger. Once you've pledged anything to Rothadamas, there's no taking it back."

"Yes, but why don't I find someone else for this duel, at least? He's resistant but not inflexible, and He listens to me sometimes, which is more than I hoped for to begin with—"

Aislinn declined with a frown. "There's no one else. We both know that. He made Yasmin more powerful than all His other High Proxies, and I'm the only other witch that comes close. There's no one else," she repeated, low and sorrowful. "Arusi left, and even if she hadn't, it would be selfish and cruel to involve her."

I gave her hand another gentle squeeze, then released it. "Yassy is in agony about this. She loves you more than any other woman in her life."

Aislinn snorted. "That's why He wants me to duel her. That heartless, soul-eating, kidnapping son of a—"

"Wait." I sat on the green couch across from her, propping my ankle over my knee. I crossed my arms. "What if... Just what if...?"

A feeble ray of hope penetrated Aislinn's mien. "What if?"

I smiled wryly. "It's insanity."

"No, tell me!"

"Promise you won't ship me off to the nearest madhouse?" I demanded.

"Oh, how tempting..."

"Aislinn!"

"Yes, yes, I promise! Out with it."

"Indulge me." I held up my forefinger. "As you know, I've been toying with the suspicion that in His own demented, fallen way, Rothadamas cares for Yasmin. He's determined to keep her for Himself. That's why He's setting the conditions of the duel against us."

She shifted forward in her chair, curiosity restoring the customary gleam in her eyes. "That's obvious. Go on."

"As far as we know, He's a fallen angel—a fallen angel that's been cursed to guard Eden itself. Much as we hate Him, we must agree that He's wise and far-seeing, with an intimate understanding of how humans think and the emotions that inspire them. That's what makes Him so good at psychological torture. Even more so than physical torment."

"Yes, yes. Come to the point."

"He's no *common* fallen angel. Being placed to preserve the ruined Garden of Gardens itself is quite significant. Don't you think?"

Aislinn leaned back again, nodding. "It's not something I considered in full, but... yes. It's an honor even though the garden is dead."

"Not dead. Sleeping."

She waved her hand dismissively. "If you say so. Continue."

I gathered a deep breath, rubbing my hands together. "If He's special—higher up in the chain of command than we supposed—He might be duty-bound to a higher power. Perhaps *the* Higher Power. In which case, He's bound by supernatural law on an eternal level."

The Celt's newly-awakened sparkle enhanced my own intrigue. "Are you saying that He *has* to exchange a soul for a soul? That He Himself... *has no choice?*"

I nodded. "Yes. He may be cursed for all eternity to steal souls for the Garden's keep, whether He wants to or not. To keep the Garden preserved in its frigid slumber, but not dead. It needs caretakers, you see." I hummed, "Yet in the midst of His curse, a light shone in the dark..."

Aislinn finished in an awed whisper. "Yasmin Lange."

And we seek to rob Him of her.

As we mused in Aislinn's bower of Yuletide trappings, compassion stole into my draconian heart. What a hideous, lonely fate. I imagined being cursed to fetch souls who were far from ready to be fetched, to turn them into strange undead beings. Their only purpose? To help you feed the cursed ground of a winter garden where only thorny trees and forbidden fruit could grow.

No companions. Not a single bird, rodent, or bug had I ever laid eyes on in Kheima. Just vapid souls robbed of hope and will. Worshiping because they *must*, never because they wanted to.

And then a certain cynical, gray-eyed witch threw herself in your way. Offered herself in exchange for a child's soul. Followed you into Kheima by her own agreement. She did not require the *Cleansing*—the soul extraction—so she retained a great deal of her original spirit. She was *not* vapid and mindlessly obedient. She needed to be coaxed, reprimanded, even threatened. Reminded of her place in your world.

Over time, she challenged you in the most delightfully irritating way. Reinforced inspiration, artistry, eloquence. Made you more than you ever dreamed you could be. Expanded your horizons and glorified your future plans, your present fate. Even your past mistakes took on a golden hue in her keen, comprehensive eyes.

She brings you to life.

I looked at Aislinn and saw my own pity mirrored in her face. "He's still evil," she murmured. "He was punished for a reason."

I grimaced, old Bible lessons floating to the surface like flotsam. "Punished for wanting to think for Himself, no doubt." I found it interesting that the first "sin" was simply wanting to be able to distinguish between good and evil, instead of remaining forever infantilized.

Aislinn and I traded bitter smiles. "The way of the world." The Celt's gilt brows furrowed. "But Sergio, if He truly cares for Yasmin, why would He make her duel her dearest friend?"

"Because you love her, too." I smiled, sitting up to softly touch her elbow. *This* was the point I'd been building up to, the one I wanted to drive thoroughly home. "Don't you see? You're the best chance He has at helping Yasmin win her freedom. *That's why it has to be you.*"

Her eyes misted with the threat of rain. "And the ring?"

"A final, desperate symbol of His forbidden love."

Aislinn couldn't answer. She dissolved into tears.

I handed her my handkerchief and trudged outside to watch the snow fall.

Pale blue.

We trained with twice the determination.

It was a theory, nothing more. 'Twas far more likely that Rothadamas was the godforsaken calamity of pure evil that everyone saw in Him. My hunch would never be more than surmise combined with one unanswerable question:

Why did Rothadamas cling to Yasmin so fiercely?

Alas, only Rothadamas Himself could answer that, and the likelihood of Him doing so was nigh on into the negatives.

It *was* sad, if we were right. However, as a man robbed of his soul mate—first by his own damned hand, and then by another's—I hardened my heart against the forest demon and steeled myself for the Witch's Duel.

It was a mere two weeks away.

38

KHEIMA PART 9

Yasmin

ROTHADAMAS AND I DID not speak while He trained me for the duel. There was no need. Our bond was strong from my first day at His side, and it only strengthened over the years until an invisible thread knotted our black hearts together.

I ignored it as often as I could, but that didn't eliminate the solemn weight of it. I was His, while my heart endlessly pined for another.

It was shameful. Profoundly wrong. *You can't do anything right, not even sacrifice yourself.* Even though I'd given myself to Him for a greater good, to do what I knew was right, my afterlife—my soul itself—was His. Yet my heart never was. *You can't do anything right, Yasmin Lange.*

By the second year of my Kheiman life, my spirit was plagued by this loathsome guilt. I tried to fix it. I tried to patch up the ripped shreds of my heart with flimsy attempts at *love*, but no matter how many well-crafted lies I told myself, I couldn't love the forest demon.

I'd crouch beside the frozen lake. I'd grasp the lengths of my own thin hair and pull, relieving my wounded whispers with the pressure. I'd tell myself sparkling white lies, over and over again, murmuring them from between chapped, bloody lips:

He's here because He's cursed. Like me.

He doesn't take souls because He wants to, but because He has to.

He's not possessive, or controlling, or cruel. He's putting on a show because He must. Remember when you had to don different "masks" to survive? That's what He does, too.

Rothadamas witnessed my desperate struggle. He rose to meet it; He softened His cruel demeanor around me. He wanted to help me find even a sliver of peace in the dark. But how could he grant solace to me when He Himself was barred from it?

Success proved impossible. Bitter wrath surged in His empty, heartless chest when He saw the truth: no one could ever love Him, not even me. A woman who might as well have been formed from His flesh and bone, she was so like Him in some respects.

Yet, through it all, there was Sergio. My opposite; my complement. Fortunate, happy-hearted, with a sane and clear mind free of the shadows of the demon. Missing his "sterling witch" more and more, instead of forgetting me until he barely recalled my name. As I'd expected.

He didn't want me then. Why would he want me now?

By some miracle, he was unattached. Waiting for me. Waiting in a mad gothic mansion that he seemed to have planned with me in mind. He even kept my old caravan on the grounds. I stumbled upon it one night and teased him about it. He blushed, deploying several weak excuses in succession, and refused to explain why he'd kept it after all these years. Why he'd sent for it from across the sea.

One night, I caught him lingering in it—holding the nightgown I once wore and inhaling its scent. A lady might have been shocked, dismayed, or disgusted, but I was not a lady. I was a witch. I laughed aloud, delighted to my frozen bones. My haunted ringmaster was driven to smell the lingering drift of my perfume, to touch the fabrics that once encased my rigid, emaciated body. Sleep evaded him until he'd done so.

Beloved ringmaster. My fierce Dragon. Aislinn persisted in her claim that he did not deserve me, but constantly clawing at my mind was the question: Do *I* deserve *him*?

"Hmm," Rothadamas purred aloud, disturbing my train of thought, "It is not a question of deserving, mein Hexe."

I sighed, wondering if I'd ever get used to the forest demon breaking into my thoughts as flawlessly as if our minds were one. I lowered my hands, breaking the spell I'd wrought. The black ice I'd conjured withered and cracked, breaking down to nothing. "I'm sorry that I'm so distracted tonight. I'll try again."

"You are correct; we are indeed much alike."

I didn't answer. I pursed my ghostly lips and tried again, extending my hands and focusing, pushing my beloved from my thoughts with every grain of self-control I could gather.

"You're truly preparing yourself to live without me? For him?" A dark chuckle of amusement rippled from His pale throat. Glittering and magnificent in His angelic form, I could imagine how simple a thing it would be for Him to seduce the heart of any other witch... besides a witch who had no heart to lose.

Because it pulsed in the hands of another.

"Aislinn adores thee, mine Anmut," He continued. He nodded once toward my shaking hands, indicating for me to get ahold of myself. "Fear not. She will be determined; she will fight for your place. By enlisting your Dragon's suggested challenger, I've given you... a fair chance."

For the first time in my cursed afterlife, I heard His voice tremble.

It happened so briefly that I almost missed it.

But it *happened*.

"Does that not please you?" the forest demon asked.

I stopped again, turning to stare at Him. He stared back. His white pupils dilated as they absorbed my face. "You do not care whether it pleases me or doesn't," I answered slowly, snatching up bravery like a naked beggar would snatch up clothing. Desperately. "You're trying something new... new for *you*, anyway... pulling at my heartstrings in the hope that I will stay with you. I won't. Not if I can win my freedom back. I shan't look back once, Rothadamas, and you must take back your ring and go on without me."

My posture tightened, bracing my body for the well-deserved blow, but He didn't extend His dark tendrils to smite me. He didn't growl, didn't sneer with His flashing, pointed teeth. Nothing.

He turned His back to me and left.

I fell to my knees, grateful, panting for breath.

He's trying to manipulate you by acting sad, my conscience whispered. *Don't fall for it.*

And yet, imagining Rothadamas alone...

Deep down, that made me very unhappy. My black heart threatened to rip in two.

What manner of woman *was* I?

39

THE WITCH'S DUEL

Sergio

AISLINN AND I JOINED hands to enter Kheima.

As it sludged into shape around us, I half expected the place to be completely different. Lava, fire, torture, lots of running and screaming. Chaos to shake us from our steeled purpose. Instead, everything looked the same. I found it calming to walk through the familiar pale-blue snow, to crunch over the sleek black ice, to observe the immense, thorned trees towering above us, sheltering pagan altars and tranquil cathedrals as foggy starlight winked overhead. If one good thing—and *only* one—could be said for the forest demon, it was that He liked His peace. So His realm was peaceful. Strange and wild, but peaceful. *I almost wish I could live here,* I caught myself thinking.

"There's never any music," I piped up. "Singing, sometimes, but never music."

Aislinn lifted her black hood to cover her head. "Music?" She sounded very distracted, bless her courageous heart.

"From the holy places. The cathedrals. Why not, witchling?"

"Musical instruments aren't allowed here. One of the odd Kheiman rules that I don't know the origin of."

"I see."

We continued in silence. Our hands remained linked in a sort of unspoken agreement, for who knew if this might be the last human contact Aislinn might have? In my other hand, I tightened my grip on the cane and shouldered it. "Rothadamas permitting, I'll not leave your side," I reassured Aislinn. "I'm staying for the whole event, and Linguine is here if we need him."

Event. A cold, businesslike word. I regretted it the instant it slipped from my stupid tongue.

Aislinn didn't seem to notice or care. "Thank you, Sergio, and thank *you* for coming, too, Osedis. No matter what happens, I'm glad I got to know you both." She tried to smile at us but couldn't manage it. "You're still rather temperamental and vain, ringmaster, but you're a good man. I know that now. I hope you and Yasmin will be happy."

"I'll do everything in my power to ensure her happiness," I promised.

Her lips trembled. "Good."

As we neared the Tree of the Knowledge of Evil, His children sprouted up out of thin air, carrying glowing candles. Their glassy, black eyes stared straight ahead as they lit our path to the Tree. Nausea churned my stomach as those eyes brought back painful memories of Thalia... my own Lillias reformed into a Kheiman tool, the eternal fate Yasmin had saved her from. I grunted, smoke wafting from my nostrils, and focused on the Tree.

Frost quivered from its thick, dark branches. It clung to the plump magenta fruit like a sugar coating. Bright thorns guarded the fruit stems, and cryptic symbols glowed with soft blue moonlight along every inch of the Tree's bark.

"How beautiful!" Osedis praised. I rolled my eyes. Of course, that's what a devil would think. *It IS beautiful,* my conscience whispered in secret.

Rothadamas waited before it. He wore a sweeping silver robe instead of His usual gray train, bearing the cursed words "LET THE LITTLE CHILDREN COME TO ME, AND DO NOT HINDER THEM." I was no Christian, but the hellish perversion of the holy word's intent made the bile rise in my draconian throat. I swallowed the nausea back.

There was no sign of my ghost-witch. "Where is Yasmin?" I demanded.

"Anmut shall arrive presently," the forest demon soothed. "By her request, I shall permit Aislinn a five-minute head start. She is not a resident of Kheima as mine Anmut is."

His pointed use of Yasmin's witch name didn't escape me. The name *I* had first pronounced. Long ago, I watched Yasmin perform a breathtaking aerial dance and realized for the first time that she was no longer a willful young girl, but a talented woman of twenty years, with a strong will hiding behind her false passivity. I relished my first glance of her soul that day, and it remained etched in the depths of my heart, pounding faster whenever she drew near with her cool, quiet words and her determined face. She called *me* otherworldly? She was *truly* so.

"Where shall I stand?" I grunted, releasing Aislinn's chilly fingers.

He lifted one glittering hand to indicate that I must remain where I was. I murmured a final encouragement to Aislinn. She drew in a breath and stepped forward to stand beneath the Tree, squaring her shoulders. I kept Linguine clasped close.

Rothadamas placed His long hand on Aislinn's shoulder. She stiffened but permitted the unwelcome contact. A black pulse fluttered over her body.

The forest demon nodded toward the Tree. "Find your branch," He said.

A respectful pause followed this injunction. "And then?" Aislinn gasped, finally gathering the courage to ask.

"That is all, mein Hexe. Find your branch, cut it off, and bring it to me. Every branch you see represents one of My chosen, so one of them is yours. But if you bring the wrong one," His voice dropped low and threatening, "You lose the duel. Otherwise, the first witch to bring me her own branch shall be mine and rule Kheima by my side, with honor and protection."

Aislinn was crafty, but she couldn't mask her emotions as well as my Yassy could. I physically read the struggle on her face. She could snatch up any old branch and forfeit right then and there, escaping her terrifying fate and securing Yasmin's place as the Kheiman Queen forevermore. *Temptation always factors in somewhere,* I thought with an internal growl. *He picked something outwardly mundane so He can toy with their thoughts meanwhile. Bastard.*

Not once did Rothadamas stray from His favorite form of torture—the torment of the mind.

"Good," murmured the demon. "You have five minutes before Anmut joins you."

"May I touch the Tree?" Aislinn questioned, drawing closer to inspect the strange symbols.

"Yes. You may eat its fruit if you grow hungry, but I wouldn't recommend it in your case," He airily warned, as if doing her a great favor by saying anything more. "Unless you intend to reside here."

The Celtic witch nodded. She turned back to the Tree and squinted at the glowing symbols. Her baffled expression alerted me to her complete ignorance of the language.

That doesn't bode well. I knew from Linguine's rattling hiss that he was concerned for her, too.

Five fruitless minutes later, Rothadamas abruptly snapped His fingers. Yasmin's enchanting form exhaled into being. Hot breath caught in my throat, for that damned demon had dressed her in a gown fit for a queen with ethereal gold and scarlet holly in her moonlit hair. The crown of thorns was replaced by a real, elegant headpiece, modest yet stunning, rising from her temples entwined with gleaming Christmas roses.

My knees weakened. Linguine hit the ground (cursing me for dropping him). *Godforsaken demon bastard!* Preemptively showing off His eternal queen in the presence of her true love. Oh, how I longed to blast Him in His cursed face.

Uttering a soft, purring chuckle, He motioned for Yasmin to join her friend at the Tree. "Go with my particular blessing, Anmut, and find thine branch." She glided forward without a word, her demeanor scrubbed of all emotion. I hated seeing her like that, but I loved her with all my might.

I prayed she would lose. Beneath my breath, I recited every deity's name I'd ever come across in my entire life. If just *one* of them would listen and take our part against the forest demon, I'd serve that god for the rest of my days.

Right after I finished worshiping Yasmin.

Time lost all meaning. The witches worked in abject silence as their shaking fingers fumbled over the Tree. As anxiety built in both of them, they abandoned their poise and proceeded to mutter aloud, fumble with their skirts, fiddle with their hair, anything to relieve their apprehension.

Despite the supernatural tension thickening the forest air, my artistic appreciation was fully engaged. The Tree's undeniable beauty and the star-like form of my Schattengeist prowling beneath it stole what was left of my heart. Strangely, I could have lingered there forever watching the two witches and the accursed Tree in the pale of midnight snowfall. Linguine's dead silence concurred, relishing the picture just as much.

"Yasmin, are there clues anywhere?" Aislinn gathered the courage to whisper. "Are we allowed to search Kheima for them?"

Yasmin said nothing, just shrugged her transparent shoulders. I longed to rush to her side and console her, but I knew without asking that Rothadamas would consider it interference. I was lucky I was still here at all, a quiet observer.

He wants me to watch Him claim my love as His own.

Hateful, but fascinating. Rothadamas acknowledged a sort of grudging respect for me once, and this was incontrovertible proof of it. I stood in His sacred realm, did I not? Saw *His* Queen in all her glory? I wondered what I did to deserve it. Perhaps it was merely my bloodline; He seemed to appreciate Dracoblods.

All the same, the impolitic pain of Yasmin's position made me clench my fists. Logic dictated that she should bide her time, allowing Aislinn to reap the advantage and claim her immortal place at the forest demon's side. It was what we had all but agreed to. But Yassy's mind was intimately linked to Rothadamas; He would know if she didn't give the challenge her all. Knowing Him as all three of us did, He'd conjure another challenge... a far worse one. Yasmin had no choice but to give the Tree her utmost effort.

Our one hope? Divine herbology was Aislinn's forte. Dendrology might be well within her grasp, too.

Lost in thought, I missed what Aislinn whispered to Yasmin. Something that managed to raise a short giggle. My lips curved into a fond smile, but a sigh accompanied it. No matter the outcome, this would be the last time they could be together like this.

I ground the end of my cane into the frozen dirt. Linguine's focus was so irrevocably fixed on Aislinn, he didn't complain.

Why didn't I believe in an involved, loving, devoted god, you might ask? Why wasn't I praying to the Higher Power, right then and there? Paint this picture for yourself and gaze upon it long and hard, and you'll comprehend why. There were no happy endings without some sting of remorse, the swinging pendulum of betrayal, or the gaping pitfall of sacrifice. A great price must ever be paid. They spoke of *balance,* but there was no balance.

Confound it! If only I were a demon myself. I could challenge Rothadamas, defeat Him, and save both the witches from lifelong separation. But then *I* would be doomed to an eternity without Yasmin, forced to guard frozen Eden myself. Unless I cursed Yasmin's existence to remain by my side as Rothadamas did; and then, I'd be no less of a monster than Him.

There was no balance.

I slumped against the tree, fighting a strong premonition of defeat. My fingers twitched with suppressed energy. Every cursed inch of me begged to transform so I might burn the forest down, seize the witches, and escape with them. But to attempt it would mean instant death—and to burn the forest down might mean the death of the entire world. I could only watch and wait.

40

KHETMA PART 10

Yasmin

I burned to look at him... to glean the shimmer of encouragement and admiration that I knew would be resting in his eyes, if I would only look at him. I feared that doing so would tempt me beyond my self-restraint. I yearned to burst into tears and fly into his arms. To fly *home.*

To tell him how scared I was. If I won, I'd immediately seek out any and all means of spiritual suicide. For the curse of love was its own brilliance, shining such an incomparable light into all darkness that now that my eyes beheld it, I could no longer see in the dark. I was blinded to all else.

Hardening my resolve, I locked gazes with Aislinn, subtly tilting my head in the direction of the cathedral. I flew there myself, trusting her to follow my lead.

Translucent skirts of gold trailed behind me like gossamer wings. The crown shone from my head, spiked and brilliant as the tail of a falling star.

Some frivolous part of me mourned the fact that I was dressed for a royal ball—for the first time in my life *and* afterlife—but was in reality attending a funeral. Either my own or Aislinn's.

I wondered if His demonic counterparts were busy making wagers. Chuckling from their iron thrones as they counted tallies and cited my various qualifications against my friend's. Lusting after her peerless beauty, no doubt.

I chose to search for clues in the cathedral because it didn't make sense that Rothadamas had picked someone else to fill it with curious furnishings, knick-knacks, and artistic landscapes. Entire side rooms had been filled to the brim with strange and beautiful mechanisms that I was barred from examining. *There must have been a reason; they must be part of His deadly game.*

His choir rippled with dark Latin chants as I entered. Ordinarily, I would have liked to stay and listen, but I had no time. I glided to the first room on the right-hand side.

The doors parted silently at my command. A mock ice sculpture of the *Phantom Horses* confronted me from the shadows, revolving from a silver ceiling. Hanging from the ceiling by a black ribbon was the porcelain doll from my past, Thalia von Brittania.

I stifled a sob. Of course, the first clue would be buried in the relics of my past. The cursed life that Rothadamas formed for me, saturating it with hopeless longing and isolation and black magic until I ran from everything, even love—the one truth that could have saved me.

The Witch in me vented her rage in a low hiss. *He'll pay for that.*

He'll pay with loss.

Fueled with fresh determination, I ignored the savage gleam in the horses' bulbous eyes and inspected the false carousel from top to bottom. Like the Tree, it glowed with strange symbols.

I recognized a handful of them. They suspended from the cresting in smooth, reflective panels. *I need to press the panels in order.* But what order?

The porcelain doll haunted me with memory. I yanked it free from the ribbons to inspect it, as well. This doll had been poor Lillias's vessel, when Rothadamas took the ringmaster's daughter and made her a soulless scrying tool, until I offered myself in her place. In her spirit-child facsimile, Lillias had been dismissive and willful, but deep down I liked her anyway. *Because at last, I knew someone like me.* In Thalia von Brittania, Rothadamas had given me a fitting companion.

Carefully, I caused the doll to float beside me as I resumed my examination. *Perhaps I need to turn the carousel on.* Would it play a song? I adored music; I survived in Kheima by introducing the *a cappella* choir during my imprisonment, but apart from the melodies of my choir, not a single stitch of music was permitted.

I swept toward the center pole. The activation lever protruded from its base. *Unusual design.* I moved it with paranormal force.

As the carousel activated, the door to the room swung open to reveal Aislinn. She panted, staring at the carousel with one hand still on the black doorknob. "Not fair. I should be allowed to fly, too."

We shared a smile. "I'll slow down next time," I promised her.

Aislinn studied the symbols on the panels. "Which horse was your favorite?" she asked, the innocuous question throwing me off-kilter. "Didn't you have a favorite one? The lead horse?"

"No, too fancy. I liked the last one. The white one."

"Excellent." Without ado, Aislinn hurried to the white horse and touched the panel directly above it. A clicking sound filled the room. With a great moan and heave, the horses were lifted from the platform and held near the roof. Beneath them, glass Yuletide-themed ornaments gleamed. They all mirrored the same symbol.

I stared at Aislinn, mouth agape. She laughed at me. "Don't overthink things, Yassy. He's not testing our ability to solve puzzles. He's testing our willpower in the face of eternal consequences." She pointed at the panel she'd touched. "This one relates to you or to your name in His Kheiman symbolism. Memorize it. It'll be on your branch."

I caught on. "Then we need to solve all the rooms in the cathedral to put all our symbols together. So we can cut off the matching branch."

"Right. Not so bad."

No. Not so bad. As Aislinn said, our intelligence wasn't in question. Our dedication was. It would take time to comb through all the rooms... time that would test our resolve.

Aislinn touched the symbol above her favorite horse. The lead horse. It lit up and stayed lit, revealing her own first symbol. She withdrew a tiny dagger from her ebony bodice and carefully cut the symbol into her arm. Morbid, but clever.

I dearly loved puzzles. Solving them with Aislinn at my side would only remind me more of how dear she was to me.

Could I live without her?

Each room dragged me through my wretched past. Forced me to confront emotions I had no desire to entertain. I knew why He orchestrated it that way—to subtract from my home advantage and give Aislinn a better chance. Intense emotions distracted me more than physical pain, as He knew all too well.

It was certainly suggestive... His apparent desire to balance the *appearance* of callous unconcern, with *wanting Aislinn to win,* wanting me to be free.

Was it true? Or was it just what I *wanted* to see in Him?

In the last room, the most beautiful graven image of Sergio stole my concentration, draining it from me like a vampire bat draining its victim's sweet blood. Although the demon's sarcastic message wasn't lost on me—*You're merely trading one idol for another, Yasmin Lange*—it was spectacular. Wrought in layered bronze and gold, with a tiger's eye in one eye socket and a sapphire in the other, it reeked of magic. It spoke to me, alternating from whispering romantic promises to seething judgments, blaming me for my chilly indifference, my tendency to stew in apathy until someone lifted me from it with the slotted spoon of reason.

"Is this to be my future?" the false Sergio demanded, damning me with his glorious gaze. He lowered his cobra cane with a *clack!* "Am I to parent you, Yassy? A stubborn, selfish child who can never be my equal? May it never be!"

Rothadamas wants me to doubt Sergio's love for me. Not astounding in the least. What *did* startle me, however, was how blatant a tactic this was for Him to employ. Rothadamas was the embodiment of supernatural subtlety that only centuries of existence could teach. Why would He try something so... crass?

He's slipping. Something in Him is breaking, or about to break.

After beholding many eerie wonders in those cathedral rooms, Aislinn and I knew all our symbols. We traveled side by side as we returned to the Tree. "How is this going to work?" my friend fretted, plucking at a loose thread in her cloak. "What if we find our branches at the same time? Cut them at the same time? Bring them at the same time? What if it's a tie?"

"Rothadamas will choose whomever He likes best." *Me.* However, my depression over the prospect was somewhat lessened; His pagan cathedral games brought my abiding love for our realm to the forefront. It seemed such a radically *insane* thing to say, "I dearly love Kheima," and yet I found it to be true. If it were not for the forest demon, I wouldn't want to leave it.

"Yasmin," Aislinn begged, her sweet eyes bright with unshed tears, "Can't you forfeit right now? For the gods' sake, let me take your place and give you peace! Sergio and I agreed that it is only right. You're here because you sacrificed yourself for the ringmaster's daughter. Let me sacrifice myself for you. And perhaps..." she hesitated, then said, "Perhaps someone will do the same for me one day."

I declined with a gentle smile. "He threatened me with many imaginative punishments if I so much as considered forfeiting—hurting you and Sergio amongst them. I don't dare."

Aislinn sighed, cupping her warm, solid hand around my clouded one. "Then we'll both do the best we can and leave the rest to fate."

"'Tis all we can do from the day we're born, darling." My voice trembled.

Aislinn kissed my airy cheek. "Don't cry, there's a good ghost-witch. You know how we hate to see you cry."

Sergio's downcast expression brightened as he caught sight of me. Clutching Osedis, he ran to my side, serving Rothadamas a hateful glare. The forest demon hadn't budged from His position by the Tree. I knew from the multiple tendrils extending from His spine into the ground that He was monitoring us closely. "You know the symbols?" Sergio panted, eyes ablaze with impatience.

"Yes."

"Then *run*, for Hades' sake!" His hand reached for Aislinn's back, as if to push her forward. The cobra's angry hiss restored Sergio's manners; he barely restrained himself, his open hand hovering an inch away. Scales momentarily flashed over its flesh. "Get ahead of Yasmin," he commanded.

Aislinn glowered at him. "She can fly; she'll overtake me in two seconds. *Do* use the brain the Draco god gave you!"

Sergio's anxiety manifested as anger, as it often did, and I did my best to quell the storm brewing between the two. "Let's get to the Tree and get this over with," I sighed, pushing them apart with paranormal force. "Behave yourself, Sergio. For my sake."

He stomped back to his place, compiling Italian curses beneath his smoking breath. Sparks flickered at his fingertips. I smiled in spite of everything. *He's so beautiful.* Righteous anger made him more beautiful than ever.

As one, Aislinn and I approached the Tree. I inhaled slowly at the innumerable symbols scratched into its base and trunk, coating every branch like a loathsome disease. The game was all about patience now. Would Aislinn or Yasmin keep her head?

As I floated over the nearest branch to read it, Aislinn knelt at the base of the trunk. I drew back to observe her. Closing her eyes, she touched her fingertips to the bark and murmured a few lilting words.

The glowing blue light of the symbols vanished... all but a short arrangement of symbols on one solitary branch.

Aislinn's branch.

Before I could rally myself, Aislinn stood and made a forceful gesture at her branch. Severed by her magic, it cracked and dropped to the ground. Snatching it up, she fled to Rothadamas with it clasped to her chest. Without a single final glance at either Sergio or me.

My conscience screamed at me to move. To stop her. But I was rooted in place. Sergio was frozen, too. He'd been inching closer in reckless defiance, determined to be as near to me as he could. Now he crouched there in a patch of puddled black ice, wordless.

Neither of us believed it.

Rothadamas accepted the branch to confirm it as hers. A long, dreadful pause supervened.

"Aislinn Bláthnaid is the victor."

Another beat of silence.

I finally gathered the presence of mind to turn and look at Sergio. To look upon him for the first time with *hope* in my eyes. But a tumble of gilt hair and black clothing arrested my attention. Aislinn had fainted.

"My lady!" Osedis cried out. Careless of potential consequence, he poured his own strength into Aislinn until he was spent, his bronze face rendered gravely dull.

41

Valley of the Shadow

Sergio

Mortified, I lunged to catch Aislinn. Rothadamas gazed on impassively. Cradling the poor Celtic witch in my arms, I glared up at the forest demon. "Well? Take your *queen,*" I seethed past clenched teeth. "Or will you continue to stand there like an imbecile?"

Yasmin's sharp gasp recalled me a bit. I returned my attention to Aislinn, feeling for her heartbeat. It fluttered beneath my fingers, and her pale temples yet retained a flush. *Thank you, Osedis.* "What will you do with her, you demon bastard?" I growled. "How will you manipulate her into a creature of darkness?"

For I found it was one thing to imagine a certain outcome, and another to be staring it in the face. Though Aislinn vexed me past my patience on multiple occasions, I cared for her—not only as Yasmin's dearest friend, but as a powerful woman worthy of the greatest respect. Aislinn Bláthnaid might have led nations and conquered realms. To see her worthy spirit forcibly extracted from her and married off to a veritable iceberg of a demon... *Will He make us watch?* I suddenly wondered, alarmed by the prospect.

In a black flash, Rothadamas loomed at my side. I resumed my glare as He bent over us. He, too, reached out to brush His white fingers against her smooth forehead.

Something in His cold, marble eyes shifted. I'd pay a great sum from the Vincenzo coffers to know what it meant. Alas, I never would.

The forest demon snapped His fingers.

Once my vision cleared, the forest was gone.

I lifted my head with a grunt. *Why is it so heavy... Ah.* I'd transformed somehow. I clawed the soft dirt as I wrestled my bulky, scaled body to its feet. Twin tendrils of smoke danced before my eyes. I snorted, waving it from my face as well as I could. *It's been too long since I shifted. This body feels clumsy.*

Where was I? *A cage,* I quickly realized. *I'm in a cage.* "Osedis!" I tried to yell, forgetting how difficult it was to twist one's dragon tongue into words. There was no response to my half-formed outcry.

So. Rothadamas found it convenient to lock me up. As if that wasn't enough, a gold collar and chain clinked around my scarlet neck. I charged at the barred door, only to be stopped several feet from it by the chain, priorly unnoticed. I snarled. *"Yasmin?"* I called out with my mind. *"Aislinn? Osedis! Anyone?"*

Nothing.

I indulged my temper with fierce growling as I absorbed my surroundings. According to the overall appearance, feel, and smell of the place, I appeared to be imprisoned in an underground chamber. It smelled earthy and damp. A single torch casting red light over the gray stone walls and ceiling was the only light source. There wasn't one stick of furniture.

I craned my neck to look behind me. *Where's the door?* There didn't seem to be one. All around me the stone walls flowed without a break or crack. Seamless. *All right; I'm trapped. But where? And why?*

My cursed temper must have aggravated Him, though I'd *thought* infinitely worse insults than I ever *said*. He ought to be thankful! But demons were incapable of gratitude. I snorted again, cutting deep scratches into the packed dirt floor. I bellowed and listened to my draconian cry echo off the walls.

Am I still in Kheima, but underground? Or somewhere else?

I recalled Yasmin saying something about Him traveling to other realms. What business the likes of Him could possibly have with other species was beyond me, but He never acted superfluously. Perhaps He had studied the Dracoblods to offer me in some exotic exchange...

"Sergio Vincenzo, you are most welcome."

Growling, I whipped my head around to pinpoint the voice. An elderly man had slipped through the hidden door in the wall so quietly, I hadn't heard him enter. That, or I was so angry that my emotions had distracted me. *Calm. I must be calm.*

"Yes, it would behoove you to calm yourself," the gray-haired man stated. "You are at the home of your ancestors. Welcome to Ludhelfast, Realm of the First Dragon."

He can hear my thoughts. Eagerly, I pelted the man with questions. He answered them in such an aggravatingly nonchalant manner, I yearned to burn him to a crisp on the spot. Unfortunately, that would be murdering an informant, and I was in dire need of information.

"How did I get here?"

"Rothadamas sent you."

"Why did He send me?"

"In payment of a debt. He promised to send you to us in exchange for a favor. Do not fear; you are no slave or indentured servant. You are free."

"What favor?"

"I am not at liberty to discuss that with anyone other than Rothadamas Himself."

"Where is Yasmin Lange?"

"I do not know anyone by that name."

"Aislinn Bláthnaid. Do you know this name?"

"The Winter Demon's queen? Yes, I know her name, but that is all. I've not laid eyes on her myself."

"If I'm free, why am I caged?"

"For our protection, and for your own."

"How is it that you can hear my thoughts?"

"I am of the Dracoblod race, same as yourself."

I growled as my mind raced, sorting through confusion. If Aislinn's name was known in another realm... *"How long have I been here?"*

"Ludhelfast exists outside of the construct of time," the elder clarified, "but in your Earth terms, you've been here for two weeks."

"Two weeks?" I was out of it for an entire fortnight? *"How am I alive?"*

"Enchanted ministrations."

Horror sliced through confusion. A low, mournful bellow rippled from my lungs, quaking my throat. *Yasmin! My beloved, I'm so, so sorry...*

"Who is this Yasmin you dwell upon? Your mate? If so, we can fetch her for you. She is of Dracoblod descent, I presume?"

"No. She is a human spirit. A ghost-witch." My beautiful Schattengeist.

If he was surprised by my unconventional choice of a "mate," he didn't show it. Genuine pity crossed his stern features. "My deepest condolences. Ghosts are tethered to their realm of origin and cannot be extracted from it."

"Then I cannot see her again?"

"No, but mates are plentiful here, thanks to our diligence in gathering all full and part Dracoblods from across the universe. Calling them back home," he added with a beaming smile. "You may choose a new mate as soon as you have rested and found your place among us. We have an extensive program to inform and rehabilitate—"

I roared with every ounce of draconian force my lungs could handle, and once I'd expended all my fiery breath, I buried my head between my forefeet and closed my eyes. *"Don't say another word! Leave me!"*

Sympathy reformed on his countenance. "I understand. You were devoted to your principal mate. That is as it should be, Sergio; it is honorable. I shall leave you time to mourn."

He shuffled away from the cage to the wall. Breathing hard, I pried one scaled lid open to watch what he was doing. He passed his hand over several stones, pressing them in order to unlock the hidden door. Through the hazy fog in my vision, I obtained a glance of the green scales rippling over the back of his hand. Yes, a fellow Dracoblod, indeed. "I will visit you again tomorrow and answer any questions you have," he promised. "Try to rest."

The stone door slid open. A hot splash and sizzle struck my claw. I reared back from it, then realized what it was: a dragon's tear.

"How long shall I be locked up?" I had the presence of mind to ask.

He'd just stepped over the threshold. He paused. "That depends on you, Sergio. Grieving dragons are deadly things in any city, even cities built to accommodate them. Better to introduce you to your new life *gradually*."

His gentle smile vanished behind the sliding stone door.

I was alone.

Everything we did had been for naught.

Splash, sizzle. Splash, sizzle.

Ludhelfast. The Land of the Dragon Shifters. In any other circumstance, I'd have been pleased from my snout to my tail-spike to be there. But as my elderly guide, Shen, pointed out the enormous sunset-streaked roads, the minimalist homes formed from natural elements, and the crimson gold temple built to honor the First Dragon and his human mate—Father and Mother to the shifters (not a story for the faint of heart)—all I could think about was my poor Yasmin.

Even the glories of the Saffron Plains failed to distract me. *Where is she now? Did Rothadamas release her? It seems he took Aislinn to be his queen, but that doesn't guarantee that He let Yasmin go.* A deep sense of foreboding plagued me.

If my intuition was wrong—if Yasmin was alive, on Earth, and safely disconnected from His black magic—I knew she'd be crying her fair little eyes out, thinking I was dead. I *had* to leave this place.

Back in human form, I pushed my disheveled hair from my face. "Can Dracoblods travel between realms?" I asked the instant I could insert a question in Shen's informative spewing.

Shen's thick brows scaled his forehead. "You wish to return to Earth? We have so much to teach you. You're free, as I said, but I was hoping you would stay—"

"I am not ungrateful," I amended. "But you don't know the dreadful circumstances that led me to your doorstep..."

Shen shook his head, raising his hand to stop me from saying more. He glanced to and fro, ascertaining whether anyone was listening. After confirming our safety, he continued in a low whisper. "Speak quietly whenever you speak of *Him*, but I am not so ignorant as you suppose. Whenever we make deals with powerful beings in other realms, I often sign the contracts as a court witness. I have seen *legal evils* that have made my scales crawl, believe me."

"Then why be complicit in them?"

Shen chuckled. His short, pointed beard glinted in the setting sun—a frothing ombre of reds and pinks unlike any sunset I'd ever dreamed of, let alone witnessed. "Once you understand the delicate politics of Dracoblods, you will answer that question for yourself. Now, about this Yasmin of yours. Tell me everything, and we'll see whether we can unearth a solution between us. I can help you... *because* of my influence in court," he pointedly added.

Inhaling deeply, I complied. My only hope was to trust him.

42

HOUSE VINCENZO PART I

Yasmin

I COULDN'T MOVE. IT felt as though someone had ripped open my body, filled it with stones, and sewn me back together again. I peeled my head from the ground of the Vampyre Garden, blinking a crust of snow from my blurry eyes.

Behind me, sidewinding footprints attested to my dizzied, half-conscious journey to the garden, walking from somewhere in the outlying woods. I'd awoken in a shallow grave, confused, banging frantically against the coffin lid sealing me in the dirt. Horror of horrors—worse than *anything* the forest demon had ever done to me. I wouldn't wish waking up in a buried coffin on Satan himself.

Once I'd finally broken free from sheer, desperate, terrified will—with cracked nails and bleeding, bruised fingers—I stumbled toward the familiar spires of House Vincenzo. Sergio's manor leered like a beast in the dark of night, littered with a multitude of glowing stained-glass eyes. I was *so* glad to see it. I did not expect Rothadamas to keep his word. *But he is a demon after all*, I mused, struggling to rise once more to my bare feet. *They are bound by certain laws of conduct, I suspect—*

I gasped when I realized that my feet weren't the only bare parts of me. The dress I'd been buried in over a decade ago had withered away to nothing; I had not a stitch of clothing on my renewed skin. I arranged my hair so that it covered my chest, no longer trembling from the cold due to the strength of my blush. I was alone, however... to my frowning disappointment.

Where was Sergio? And Osedis?

Not that I want them to see me like this. I need to get into the mansion.

On my feet at last, I took one wobbling step toward the house, then another. *Gracious!* I seemed to weigh a thousand pounds. My footsteps left slanted, uncertain prints in the snow. For a moment, I thought longingly of my paranormal grace as a spirit, dancing in the air from Kheima to Earth and back again without faltering. Without the *ability* to falter. But I pushed the vain regret aside. *Focus. You need to find Sergio. Why isn't he here, too?*

I sighed, rubbing my temples. *I am sick to death of demons.* We ought to have made another pact with Rothadamas to ensure Sergio's fate after the duel was over. Between Sergio and the demon lurked a certain measure of cold respect, but it wasn't anywhere near enough to keep Rothadamas from doing something to my ringmaster.

Only the gods knew where my Dragon was.

If there was one thing I was utterly certain of, it was that the forest demon might keep his word, but he would also utilize every weapon in his vast arsenal to make sure that Sergio and I never found each other. No happy ending for us. *"If I cannot keep her, then he can't, either."* I could practically hear Rothadamas saying it to Aislinn. With much more subtlety and elegance than *that*, of course, but that would be the crux of his statement.

Aislinn! My stern face crumpled as tears threatened to inundate my vision. *She sacrificed herself for me.* She loved me, and I despised myself for never acknowledging it in full, not saying or doing enough in return. *I didn't truly believe I was lovable,* my newly-beating heart whispered. *Not by Sergio, not by Lillias, and not by Aislinn.*

Indeed, had my heart not been seized by Sergio from the first time our hands touched—and he smiled his full, sparkling smile in his intensely cheerful way—I might have loved Aislinn instead. For who could help it? Her bravery challenged the steel of the Arthurian Knights, and she was as beautiful as a dream of Heaven with a smile that coaxed the light from the sun. A witch of life.

The witch of life sacrificed for the witch of death.

The reality of it sank into my mind like an anchor. *Beryl's Daughter* was stranded at the Isle of Guilt, content to be boarded and ravaged of all her goods and treasures. Pleading for punishment, for the sake of truth be it said. If anyone deserved Hell, it was me. I clutched at my hair, moaning, pulling it in my despair.

Focus! My conscience screamed again. *Where is Sergio? You are no longer a witch, but he is still a warlock. He can help you see Aislinn again, but first you must find him!*

I remembered that the chapel remained open at all hours, and a small back hallway connected it to the rest of the mansion, seldom guarded. Still wobbling, I scurried around the front and slipped past the creaking double doors without detection. *Thank goodness.* Once inside, I yanked an embroidered burgundy drape from the nearest window and secured it around me with the curtain cord. *I look ridiculous, but at least I'm not naked.* My bloodied fingers baptized the plush fabric.

I'm alive.

Rushing down the aisle, my bare feet pattering over the opulent runner, my body finally began to adjust itself to its mortal weight. My lungs heaved with breath. My heart pounded with anticipation. A belated laugh bubbled from my lips, soft and warm. *Alive. I'm alive.* And I craved Sergio's touch with an urgency I'd never dreamed myself capable of. I threw my arms open wide, thrusting all the power of my voice into the empty chapel's echo: "I summon my Dragon. Come embrace your beloved, and let us never be parted again!"

I laughed again, exhilarated, though the tears coursed down my face. Guilt, fear, love, and hope ricocheted around my heart in lethal bullets; I couldn't guess which one would land. *Rothadamas won't get his way. Not this time.* I'd find Sergio, and I would bring him home.

He and I were fated to become one. Fallen angels might twist the arm of Fate, but they could not break it. They might attempt to reign over us as gods, but sooner or later, they'd reveal themselves as what they truly were—mere demons.

Suddenly, to my great relief, the cobra's dry voice echoed through the chapel. "Yasmin? By Heaven and Earth, is that you?" Upon the altar, the glint of ruby and bronze tickled my vision. Sergio's devil was waiting for me.

43

A Dragon's Promise

Sergio

AFTER SHEN LISTENED INTENTLY to my tale of woe, he invited me to his home for a late supper. I consented. We walked in unison, eyes glued to the road, hands linked behind our backs, and brows furrowed.

"Here we are," Shen announced. Distracted, I braked just in time to avoid slamming into the front door.

The *enormous* front door. Shaped and sized to accommodate the shifters in their dragon forms, the door lifted from the threshold like a medieval gate. The main room, formed from a natural cavern, had been deepened and smoothed until dragons could walk freely through it, wings and all. Sleek minimalism prevented untoward accidents. "Impressive," I remarked.

"This is quite modest, actually, but thank you."

He motioned me into a smaller room built for human use. A long dining table awaited its masters. Shen lit the broad fireplace with his breath and bid me to be seated. "I've naught but dried meat, bread, and cheese at present. I trust that will satisfy you."

"That'll make me very happy, indeed."

Once he set a plate before me, he sat as well and hummed to himself, carefully tearing up his bread to dip it in a mug of milk. I dug in, suddenly discovering how ravenous I was. Shen's green eyes were fixed on an elaborate mural decorating the far wall. "Most Dracoblods are blessed with fire magic and raised with it from their youth. 'Tis a lucky thing you discovered yours on your own."

I shrugged, swallowing a hefty chunk of dried meat. "It hasn't been all that useful, I'm afraid. It's more of a liability than a blessing... and it's especially useless against a fallen angel who's been around since time began," I muttered. I attacked my mug of beer next, scowling at an imaginary Rothadamas over its crude rim. Shen's knowing smile piqued my curiosity. "What is it? What do you know?" I demanded, lowering my mug with a smack.

"You saw the Tree of the Knowledge of Evil?"

"Yes; I recall mentioning that. I tried to burn it down to no avail."

"That's because your pyrocraft has only just awakened," Shen said. "You'll need solid, regular training to get there, but you *can* burn it down."

I leapt from my chair, inadvertently tipping it to the ground. Flames rippled around my hands. "I can? What will happen?"

Shen smiled again, pleased to witness my enthusiasm. "As far as we can understand it, the Tree is the tether that connects Rothadamas to His proxies. Hence the correlation between the Tree's growth and additional branches with the more souls He collects. If it's burnt down, He'll lose His connection with them and be forced to grow another Tree."

"And all the souls? Will they be set free?"

"I can only present a theory," Shen warned me, "so don't take what I suggest as absolute knowledge, Sergio. I *believe* the souls that are aware enough to see their window of opportunity can free themselves. Or the souls that receive outside help." Shen's demeanor sobered. "The proxies that have belonged to Him for decades might be too enmeshed with Him to be severed, but as for the newly-acquired souls..." He drifted off and nodded once.

"How do you know this?" I demanded.

"As I said, I don't know it for certain, yet we Dracoblods make zealous scholars and paragons of deductive analysis." Shen finished his odd snack of milk and bread, pushing his glazed pottery aside. "It is generally understood that the branches of the Tree multiply according to the proxies He takes. Therefore, it is sound reasoning to conclude that maiming or destroying the Tree will—at least temporarily—remove the proxies from His control. Added to this, the Witch's Duel you described to me supports the conclusion; He told the witches to cut off their own branches and bring them to Him."

An infectious grin crawled across my lips. "You're telling me... and punch me if I'm dreaming, if you please, sir... You're telling me that I can enter Kheima, burn down the Tree, rescue Aislinn—and Yasmin if He's still holding her captive—and return to Earth? It's *all* possible?"

"Yes, Sergio. That is why Rothadamas respects the Dracoblods; he knew you had the potential to become a formidable opponent. That is, if you're willing to train harder than you've ever trained in your life," Shen cautioned. "It is possible but not *easy*. Thankfully, Ludhelfast exists outside of time, so it will not seem long to Aislinn or Yasmin before they see you again. Take comfort in that while you work, Sergio, and I believe you have every hope of success."

I whooped, batting my mug into the air and letting the golden rainfall soak me. Shen laughed at my childish display. "By the Father! It's nice to have a younger Dracoblod in my life again, half-blood though you may be. It's a pity you won't be staying to rebuild our population—as we intended when we struck the bargain for you—but Rothadamas neglected to mention you had already taken a mate. We take pair bonding very seriously. I'm sure I can plead your case to the court, despite how ill-advised their agreement was from the start." He stood from his seat and bowed low. "If you'll permit me, I'll train you myself."

"It would be an honor."

"Please, the honor would be mine."

I bowed in return, marveling at the excellent good luck that I'd stumbled upon Shen—that of all the Dracoblods I could have met first, it was him. He was confused by my choice of mate, that was clear, but he was too polite to point out its obvious inconveniences. Instead, he focused on helping me overcome them.

Decades of self-preservation knocked on the door of my suspicion, but I waved the unwelcome visitor away. Why would Shen deceive me? He wouldn't gain anything from it, and judging from what I'd seen of Ludhelfast, it was so peaceful a realm that the mighty Dracoblods must be itching for a fight. Judging from the light in Shen's sharp green eyes, my adventure appealed to his lonely life.

So, wait for me, beloved. I'm coming for you. And I'm bringing your Celtic witchling with me.

Nonetheless, one almighty concern buzzed in the back of my brain. Once again, Rothadamas had *chosen* to provide a way out, a remedy, a path to salvation from Himself. He'd sent me to the one realm in the universe that could teach me what I was, that could instruct me on how to *be* a Dracoblod.

He was showing me how to defeat Him.

44

HOUSE VINCENZO PART 2

Yasmin

I DISCOVERED OSEDIS, OR rather the cane he was bound to, waiting on the chapel altar. After a lengthy conference, Osedis and I agreed that my only chance of locating Sergio was to harness the etherpower of the mansion's ghosts (with the little devil's aid). It took a great deal of convincing, but I coaxed Sergio's spooks out of hiding to have a word or two with them.

I managed to avoid Sergio's butler and maids, slinking up the winding mansion floors until I had 1.) Discovered and shamelessly pillaged Lillias's old bedroom, emerging fully dressed, and 2.) Gained the attic, where I knew Sergio's ghostly friends and summoning circle lay in wait.

"How are you not a ghost anymore?"

I smiled at Violet and her brother Oliver, the first two ghosts to appear. "That's a story for another time. Right now, I need your help. I'm not a witch anymore, so I can't use this alone," pointing to the chalked summoning circle, "but *you* can. I'll provide the incantation, and Osedis here shall provide the direction. If you'd be so good, you'll provide the power."

"What do we get for helping?" Violet asked. I glanced at her dark, pursed lips and wondered if my own mouth had been that... evil-looking. *Sergio, you are the spirit of Madness itself. You rejected me at my prettiest and loved me at my ugliest.* "I'll build an altar for all of you and put treats on it every weekend. Anything you want," I promised.

Promises to the dead were tricky things, and ghost treats could be... morbid. But I'd been a specter myself, had I not? I knew what they craved. I, of all people, should have the stomach to acquire what they wanted.

Violet and Oliver agreed.

"Good. Let's begin."

My hands worked the paranormal setup on muscle memory. Over the years, I'd dabbled in a little more than simple blood magic, but it was wise to keep such knowledge to myself. I concentrated fully on Aislinn's face, features, and spiritual presence, shutting everything else out of my thoughts as I'd been ruthlessly trained to do.

Normally, an item that had been in contact with Aislinn was necessary, but experienced summoners didn't need such grounding tools. Additionally, I had 'Linguine,' her hopeful bondservant (so Sergio had told me). I extended the cane over the summoning circle, chanting rapidly.

Our strong intentions reached into the ether, grasping and pulling with vehement strength. In a clash of black static, Aislinn appeared.

My heart sank. Her Kheiman form looked much like mine. In fact, he'd manipulated it to mirror me so closely, I wrinkled my nose in dismay. "You don't look like yourself. Not at all. How dare he!"

Aislinn's shrunken pupils swam dizzily over my face, taking me in. "Yassy? Osedis? Is that really you? Where... Where am I?"

"Sergio's mansion." I pushed my offended sensibilities aside. "I don't have time to explain much. The ghosts can only hold your spirit here for so long. Tell me quickly, darling. Are you in pain? Is he hurting you?"

"No... no. He's mourning your absence. He tried to make me look like you, but now He hates it. He won't look me in the face."

She was neglected but not wounded. Good. This was the best-case scenario in Kheima. "Is Sergio in Kheima?"

"I haven't seen him."

"All right." I breathed a sigh that was half relief, half annoyance. "Then where can he be? If he's not here, and not in Kheima..."

"He's a Dracoblod descendant, didn't you tell me?" Aislinn murmured. She was already beginning to flicker in and out of view. I only caught a few phrases: "Rothadamas might—sent him away—the dragon shifters."

I frowned. "Why in the name of frigid Hell would he go to that trouble?"

Osedis snorted aside, "You talk more like Sergio all the time." I permitted myself to smirk, rather proud of it.

How could we have ever thought of Rothadamas as a Demongod? *He's a spoiled, bratty child who throws fits when things don't go his way,* I thought.

All his prior civility toward Sergio was nothing more than a trap. It would be easy for Rothadamas to offer an exotic half-human Dracoblod as payment for some debt. *Especially when considering how handsome he is.*

"Aislinn," I pleaded, reaching up for her translucent hand—forgetting that I could not touch her now. "Take me. Take me with you, and we'll find the Kheiman door that leads to Sergio's realm. Then I'll rescue you, too. I swear it!"

My darling friend's shadowed eyes welled with sorrow. "I can't. I can't do anything without His consent. He told me He would kill you and Sergio... for good..."

"Aislinn!"

Without another word, she disappeared.

Violet and Oliver hung their heads in apology. "Sorry, Yasmin. That's all we have to give," Violet explained.

I groaned, dropping to my knees and clawing at the floorboards in a helpless rage. Vital energy pummeled through my veins, begging to take action. I'd been dead and a prisoner for so long, the surge of life overwhelmed me. I leapt to my feet and rushed at the wall, punching it multiple times and screaming. A wedge of broken glass cut me, drawing bright red blood. "No," I yelled, "Don't you dare bleed. Don't you dare be *alive* without him!"

The ghosts fled, terrified of the madwoman in their attic.

My fists continued to mount their assault. I kept saying the same name over and over. "Sergio. Sergio. *Sergio!*"

45

BREAKING KHEIMA

Sergio

MY MEMORIES OF SHEN'S training all ran together like one long, exhausting day. On the whole, I relished it. The flow of fire through blood was indescribable, so hopelessly *wrong* as a human, so wonderfully *right* in my draconian form.

The scenery and social structure of Ludhelfast was so goddamn *serene*, it made my scales itch. Made me want to shout and throw something. I was a man of action—of chaos, I was sure Yasmin would say—and therefore the dragon shifter's realm did not appeal to me in the long run. Pleasant to visit, but I wouldn't want to live there.

"Come back and visit us for the Blood Moon Tournament," Shen insisted. "You'll see how we keep our beastly natures satisfied."

"Oh? That's tempting, indeed. Maybe I will."

As my pyrocraft improved, the tint of my flames deepened until it breathed a dark blood-red lined with scarlet. I became capable of emitting such intense heat that I feared ever using my fire again once I reached Earth. "I'll burn the world down. Entirely by accident," I snorted to Shen.

He seemed amused by the concept. Dracoblods had a generally low opinion of the human realm, I found.

Once I was strong enough to destroy the Tree, Shen instructed me to visit the holy temple and speak to Vaughn. "He can teach you the incantation to enter Kheima from here," Shen promised, "but once you're in the forest demon's realm, you're on your own. We've no knowledge of how to leave it. We only know that as the preserved Garden of Eden, it is the gateway to many realms."

Well, that explains why Rothadamas was cursed to guard it. "Yasmin mentioned once that there were many doors to other realms in Kheima. I'm sure if I find Aislinn in time, she can help us escape."

"Let's hope so."

"What if Rothadamas tries to stop us? Will my fire be of any use against Him?"

Shen ran his pointed fingernail along his lower lip. "I don't know. I doubt it, but there's a possibility. You might be able to wound Him temporarily, at least."

"Good."

"Save it as your last resort, Sergio. Do not incur His wrath until you have no other choice."

"Understood. Gods! What would I have done without you, Shen? And how can I ever begin to thank you?"

"By enjoying a life well lived, my son." He smiled. "And by coming to visit me again with your resurrected witch. She sounds like quite the woman."

Vaughn was a very good, very irritating Dracoblod who tried to prevent me from leaving Ludhelfast. He spoke soothingly of the beauty of Dracoblod females, the matchless peace of their realm, how humans were so selfish and bloodthirsty compared to dragonkind, etc. etc.

I admit I came perilously close to losing my temper with him. I forced myself to remember holding Yasmin's ethereal form on the front steps of my mansion, telling her that I'd hold her in earnest someday. I couldn't fly off the handle and ruin my chances, slim though they were.

Two hours in, I eventually convinced Vaughn that nothing would dissuade me, not even the prettiest and most fertile new mate. Sighing for my apparent idiocy, Vaughn taught me the incantation I'd need to break into Kheima. "Move quickly once you're there. That place is not kind to the living, Sergio."

I nodded, thankful for the reminder. In and out with Aislinn in tow, and Yasmin too if she remained there.

Yasmin sacrificed everything for me twice over. Rescuing Aislinn was the bare minimum she deserved.

Having completed the incantation, I grunted, scratching my ears. They buzzed and burned with familiar static. *Good. I'm in the right place, but why is it so dark?*

Heaving to my feet, I glared in all directions. *Where on earth—*

A veritable feast of bioluminescent wonders carpeted the ground. Green, turquoise, cobalt, even purple. Despite my hesitation, I couldn't help but take one step closer. Then another. In the center of the cold, undulating earth rushed a violent onyx stream. How clear the water looked! I thirsted for it, but a warning whisper of instinct kept me away.

Churning waves smashed against the silver rocks, beating them smooth and clean. *An underground river? Didn't know there was one, or any living plants, either. Poisonous, I expect; better keep my distance. I wonder if Yasmin ever found this place?*

To light my way, I snapped my fingers and lit my palm with a blood-red flame. I traipsed through the underground cavern in search of a ray or two of moonlight breaking in from overhead. I'd just begun to panic when I finally spied an opening.

My fingers were reaching for the rim to pull myself up when I heard a sob. Abandoning the exit, I ran downstream in pursuit of it. "Yasmin! Darling, is that you?"

A grayish-silver, feminine shape glowed near a cluster of cobalt flora. I ran faster, lips spreading into a relieved smile and arms open wide. "Yasmin—"

"No. I'm not Yasmin, Hue."

My heels dug into the ground to stop me. I gaped. "*Aislinn?*"

"I'm afraid so."

She wore a gown quite similar to my ghost-witch's attire and had the same Kheiman veil covering her face. The same crown. Not only that... but some of her features were changed to mirror Yasmin's looks. I frowned. "Oh, poor dear. What has He done to you?"

"No worse than we anticipated," Aislinn sighed. She bent to pluck a cobalt... *thing*... and tore it apart, dropping it in the rushing subterranean river one ripped fleck at a time. Her mournful eyes followed its wreckage as it drifted away. "If you're here for Yassy, don't worry. She's safe. Rothadamas resurrected her on Earth as was promised."

My stiff shoulders relaxed. As nervous tension fled my muscles, I winced, reaching down to rub my bad knee. *Wish Osedis was with me. I just realized he's missing, too.* "I've come for you, Aislinn. It'll take too much time to explain, but my pyrocraft is much stronger now. I'll burn that goddamned Tree to a crisp. Then I have a short window of time to take you home before He can grow another."

A vague flicker of hope brightened her dull eyes. "Let's go," she said, her new spectral force grabbing my hand without hesitation. *There's our Aislinn,* I smiled as she dragged me behind her. Up and out. *At least she's in there somewhere.*

"How will you resurrect me?" She asked in a quavering voice.

"Won't need to. You were changed, not killed. Once you leave this realm and enter Earth again, your body should revert back to normal. According to Shen."

"To whom?"

"Later, Aislinn."

She got me to the Tree so quickly that Kheima passed in a blur. "Don't hold back, ringmaster. Give it everything you have to give."

"I hear and obey, milady."

Aislinn turned her back as I removed my clothing and set it aside. I shifted to dragon form. Planting my claws in the earth, I inhaled deeply and scalded the atmosphere.

'Tis no boast to declare that Kheima had never seen the intensity of color and heat that I channeled that night. Nor shall it ever see a display like mine again. Soon the Tree blazed like a beacon. With immense satisfaction, I watched its branches charring, dripping with dark red. The light of the glowing symbols went out. The forbidden fruit bubbled and burst, covering the ashen bark with magenta drippings. The scent was tempting even then, a sweet, boiled treat. I inhaled through my jaws to avoid smelling it.

Aislinn's Kheiman form gleamed in firelight. The more the Tree burned, the more life came back into her eyes, and the more her spectral glow dissolved. She lifted her drooping head and straightened her posture. A subtle smile lifted the corners of her dark mouth. "Hail, Dragon!" the Celtic witch cheered, punching a fist into the smoky air. "I owe you a drink after this."

"Just one?" I projected with a dragonish chortle.

"Don't overdo it."

We waited until the Tree resembled nothing more than a charred stump. Shifting back into human form and into my clothes, I reached out for Aislinn's hand and exclaimed with delight when her rejuvenated skin grazed mine. "You're yourself again! Let's get the hell out of here, witchling."

She nodded. Hands joined, we rushed back toward the underground river where the Realm Gates waited. I kept glancing over my shoulder, but the forest demon did not appear.

"He's sulking," Aislinn answered my unasked question. She panted from exertion before adding, "He's been out of sorts since He lost Yasmin."

"It seems even a demon can learn to love."

"Perhaps."

We reached the entryway. Aislinn dropped into the lip of the chasm first, waiting for me to follow. I wedged myself inside. We blinked and stared, adjusting our vision to the increased darkness.

A thunderous, cavernous growl of immortal masculinity made us both flinch. "So, Dragon. You would not only rob me of my first and most beloved queen, but of her replacement as well?"

Rothadamas.

Even in the meager light I saw Aislinn turn a shade paler. I snatched her hand again and squeezed it tight. "*We'll get through this. Together.*"

Usually, unsolicited telepathic communication between witches was considered rude, but I figured she'd forgive me in this case.

Facing Rothadamas, my reassuring smile curled into a sneer. "You dare to call them your queens, Demon? No matter how many false titles you bestow upon us, we remain nothing more than slaves to you." I pulled Aislinn behind me. "You keep *slaves*. Nothing more and nothing less."

"Such assertive words from such ignorance," Rothadamas snapped. I turned my head to and fro, looking for Him, my hair slapping my shoulders. *He's hiding.* "As it happens, I am irritated with you and therefore delighted by the prospect of battle."

Rothadamas shimmered into view and drew a flaming sword. Despite the darkness, the blade's surface flashed mirror-bright, blinding its challenger, turning every which way to dazzle the eyes of its future victims.

Quickly, Aislinn ducked behind a large boulder. *"Hold out your right hand, ringmaster!"* she called out within my mind. I immediately obeyed, tossing her a trusting grin.

Osedis appeared in my right palm. Uttering an astonished shout, I wrapped my fingers around the shaft of the cane before I dropped it. Flames enrobed the cobra's head. Their garnet hue rippled around the cavern, tinting everything in bloodlight. "How in blue blazes—Never mind!" the little devil yelled, his ruby eyes absorbing the situation. "Fight now, questions later."

The forest demon leveled His blade. *Or leveled three blades?* Confound it, it was hard to tell. Black antlers sprouted from His pale head, blood dripping from the broken skin. He was taller and bulkier than I, but I believed I held the advantage in Dracoblod protection and endurance. I hoped so, anyway. Otherwise...

"Stay out of sight but cast spells whenever you can to slow Him down," I instructed Aislinn. *"Once He's distracted, trap Him in a summoning circle. Hellspeed to us both."*

Amused by what might have been my final joke, Aislinn cackled. *"Hellspeed, Sergio!"*

Pride and admiration laced her psychic words. The crafty witch knew all along that there was more to my fate than being a mere ringmaster or half-baked warlock. She was annoyed with me for ignoring the source of my talent for so long, for abandoning my bloodline to rot in a dusty hallway full of neglected portraits. With my ancestral power within my grasp, acknowledged and trained for battle, she celebrated the awakened Dragon.

Taking heart, I lunged forward and channeled a menacing wheel of flames.

46

BREAKING DEMONS

Sergio

GRINDING MY TEETH, I resisted the urge to shift. *Not in here, you can't.* Half the cavern's flora burned as the forest demon and I lobbed flames at each other. The demon's blade burned blue, colliding with my bloodlight in an explosive display of sickening purple. The collision thundered through the subterranean hall as Aislinn interwove our spellwork with astonishing speed, ensuring that Osedis and I worked together. Despite all her fears and doubts, she was *ready.*

Yet Rothadamas hardly flinched, even when my flames brushed His glittering skin. Steam enrobed Him as His wintery force placated the heat. *He's toying with us. Battling like God Himself—*

"*Remember, he is not a god.*" Aislinn's words infused my blazing mind, grounding it, cooling my dread. "*He CAN be defeated. He WILL be defeated as long as we work together.*"

Osedis and I summoned another ruby-red barrage along with my strong, inward shout: *"He is no god!"*

On the heels of our coordinated attack, Aislinn tried to imprison the forest demon with vines. Flicking his finger, Rothadamas redirected them to the craggy wall. With an irritated snarl, Aislinn sought for a beaten stone that was hollowed out from the relentless river's push. A moment later, a certain teeth-gritting squeak informed me that she'd conjured her slate pencil and was sketching Rothadamas on the bottom of the stone. *She's laying the trap.*

Time's up, bastard. Laughing with a devilish chuckle, I set Osedis against a boulder and rolled up my sleeves.

The squeaking paused. "Sergio! Don't!" Aislinn cried out. "I'm almost done—"

Ha! As if I've ever let anyone tell me what to do. I charged Rothadamas, positioning my fists for the best blasted right hook of my life. "For Yasmin!"

It took the demon by surprise. He dodged my fist in time, but not my foot as it dealt a swift kick to his stomach. I winced, remembering my bad knee too late. Rothadamas uttered a soft grunt and caught me by the throat.

I struggled in his grasp as he lifted me from the ground. "What a strange beast you are, Dragon." Rothadamas grinned—his thread-thin, papery, lightning-laced grin rife with static and sharp teeth. Dark blood dripped from his antlers. "You could have gone straight back to Earth, back to your beloved Yasmin. Like a vengeful fool, you came here. You offered yourself to me." His grip on my neck loosened, ever so slightly. "Why?"

And you sent me to the realm of my ancestors. You made me stronger; you handed me the answer, all the while pretending you did not. Why?

But I wasn't there to play Twenty Questions. Managing a half-strangled smile, I held my hand vertically and slammed it down hard in the crook of his elbow, trying to break his hold. He didn't budge.

Aislinn's voice rang in my head. "*Now!*"

She inverted the makeshift bowl.

A living, contorting strand of thorns grew around Rothadamas. Dropping me, he emitted an ice-shrill shriek that I wouldn't have thought him capable of: the sound of poignant, plaintive despair. To my ears, it was a beautiful melody of defeat. The subterranean river echoed with it.

Yet Aislinn's trap wouldn't hold him forever. Panting and rubbing my bruised throat, I stumbled back to Aislinn, grabbing Osedis on the way. "Hurry," I wheezed. "I don't know how long that will hold him."

I held out my hand for Aislinn's. She grabbed it and we ran together, plunging headlong into the frothing waterfall that meant *home.*

And Yasmin.

"Thank you."

Turning my relieved gaze from House Vincenzo's distant towers, I smiled at Aislinn, patting her on the head. "No need to thank me, witchling. It's what any gentleman would have done."

She batted my hand away with a mock frown. "I'm in your debt regardless." She bared her upper chest, clear and smooth. The Mark was gone. "If you ever need anything, please tell me and I'll do whatever I can to help. That goes for you too, Osedis." She gestured to my cane. I handed it to her so she could scratch the little devil's head. To my amusement, he uttered a chirrup of delight as his cobra cheeks swelled in a grin. *He's in love with that Celtic witchling, I swear,* I chuckled to myself.

"Whoever would have thought we'd end up friends?" I gravely submitted, eyes moving from the fiercely independent Celt to the hard-headed imp. "There's enough stubbornness concentrated here to plague the Christ himself."

Aislinn elbowed me, returned Osedis, then nodded toward House Vincenzo. "If I were to guess, I'd guess Yasmin is home, waiting for you." She paused, bright teeth lightly scraping her lower lip. "I'll... I'll let you two have your moment. I could use a little rest, anyway."

Bless the woman. I knew she loved Yasmin, too. I fondly hoped she would someday meet her own soul mate, but until then, Yassy and I would take care of her.

My delighted gaze lingered on the shining, multicolored windows. I inhaled a chilling breath, exhaled a smoky cloud. "Looks like snow." My boots started to move across the ground, my heart beating furiously in my burning chest. *Damn, I'm nervous. I'm more nervous now than when I battled the demon, by thunder!*

"Merry Yule," Aislinn called from behind, seating herself on a fallen log.

"Merry Yule, indeed!"

I ran.

The blasted vest felt much too tight. I swore my heart was trying to burst through it. Tearing off the vest, I cast it to the ground. "Yasmin!" I yelled, unable to restrain myself a minute longer. "Gray witchling, I'm home!"

The front door was slightly ajar. I dashed inside, knocking the door open wide with my shoulder and dropping Osedis in the umbrella stand. "Pardon me, Noodle. Yasmin?" I bellowed. My arms broke out in scales as my excited body threatened to shift.

Brandon the butler tore into the foyer, eyes round as plates. I seized him by the lapel. "Look, you—Brandon—yes, that's your name. Right. Did a woman come here? Pale, gray eyes, ash-blonde hair? Confused, perhaps—not quite right in the head—has trouble speaking?"

"I think not, sir. I saw no one—"

"What's wrong with you, old man?" I gave him a brief, impatient shake. "You *think?* Don't you know whether she's here or not? Don't toy with me, my heart can't take it."

Suddenly, from far up in the attic, I heard muffled screaming. My heart seized in my throat.

I gulped it back down. "Is *that* her?"

Poor Brandon's face blanched. "How did she get in, sir? It's quite impossible..."

"Witchcraft." *Perhaps the resident ghosts helped her.* I charged up the stairs. My middle-aged knees complained about it and begged for my cane, but I ignored them. Up, up, up! It was torture for my bruised windpipe and battle-battered body. Wheezing, I dashed the attic door open. "Yassy!"

My beloved witch—excuse me, *former* witch—lay coiled in the middle of my summoning circle. She writhed and screamed, attempting to mute herself with both hands pressed firmly over her mouth. From the way her body lunged and twitched, I knew she was possessed. And judging from her proximity to the summoning circle, *voluntarily* so.

She was doing the one thing she could to come and help me. Ghost possession. Using the ghouls from my haunted estate to borrow the only power within her reach.

My swollen heart broke. I fell to my knees, gathering her in my arms. I held her tight, murmuring extrication spells in a soothing voice. She stilled. One by one, my mansion ghosts fled her stiff form. Her pale skin took on a pinker hue, warming at my touch. Hot tears slipped unheeded from my eyes as I kissed her precious forehead again, and again, and again. "Come back to me, darling. I'm here, my angel. I'm here."

She opened her eyes. Her beautiful, serious, silvery eyes. Tears of pain streaked down her hollow cheeks. "Sergio?" she whispered.

"*Yasmin.*"

I stroked her hair back from her face, trembling, and placed another kiss on her forehead—a long kiss of promise and commitment. "I'm here for good, Yasmin Lange. We'll never be separated again." I touched our foreheads together, catching my breath as she reclaimed her own.

Her tense body melted into mine, yet she continued to stare at me as if disbelieving her senses. Slowly, her arms slipped around my neck, and she sobbed into the crook of my shoulder. I held her and rocked back and forth, shedding grief alongside her. "I'm sorry," I pleaded, stroking her wild hair. "I'm so sorry for everything. I could have protected you all along. I could have spared you from all of this."

Once her final tear spent itself, Yasmin raised her regal head. Her red-rimmed eyes beamed with love. *Living,* breathing love. I inhaled sharply from the glorious shock it dealt me. *God above, how that look brings memories to the surface, thou sterling witch.* "Don't talk like that, beloved. You've done more for me than I could ever tell you," she murmured, kissing my stubbled cheek. "You made me strong. You inspired me and gave me hope when I had nothing left of myself. So, please, don't be too harsh with the old ringmaster; I love him. Besides," kissing my other cheek and the tip of my nose, then snuggling back into the crook of my neck to kiss me there, she resumed, "we suit one another. I'll accept your darkness, your failures, and your wrongs, if you promise to accept mine."

I chuckled. She shuddered at the sound and feel of it, tucked in my lap at long last. Just as I'd "threatened" she'd be one day. "Promise me one thing," she whispered into my ear.

Now *I* was the one trembling. "Anything, Yassy."

She drew back to lance her stare deep into my eyes. "Be yourself."

I arched a quizzical brow. "I always am."

Her caustic smile filled me with boyish glee. "Not at all. Don't be the ringmaster performing for the masses. Don't be the isolated warlock who skulks about his attic, extracting superfluous texts in a vain quest for power. And above all, *never* be the raging, vengeful Dragon who wastes his last days in fire and ash, striving to annihilate an immortal forest demon." She paused to lovingly—*finally*—cup my face with real, warm, living hands. I sighed, closing my eyes from sheer bliss. "Don't you dare be any of those things, Sergio Erbanhue Vincenzo. Be with me, and *be yourself.* It is enough."

I was not a crier, as I need not assert, but there I went again. My lady comforted me until I made her laugh by using her hem to dry my blasted Draco tears, accidentally burning tiny holes in the fabric. Her laughter just about did me in. "Brace yourself, love," I warned her in a throaty whisper before my mouth devoured hers.

Snowflakes fluttered in through the shattered stained-glass window. The shards of a stern queen and a dragon glimmered on the floorboards, its subconscious prophecy fulfilled. The snow fell as elegantly as bits of ivory lace, with not a hint of pale blue to be seen.

Somehow, I had Yasmin on the floor with one hand pinning her delicate wrists above her head. Moaning with impatience, I unfastened her collar to kiss her flushed skin. The curves of her sharp collarbone were delicious, so I kissed them, too, ravenous for every inch of her. "Sergio..." my angel whispered, sighing beneath my warmth...

The sound of voices and approaching footsteps brought our passion to a halt. I flung myself off her, straightening my shirt and catching my breath. Yasmin sat up with a gasp and rearranged her rumpled skirt, which had somehow worked its way up her legs. *Wonder who did that,* my guilty face said, making her giggle again with that rare butterfly mirth of hers, a cascading melody that made me burn to pin her down again.

"Where is my Yassy?" Aislinn's merry voice called. "Where is my darling sister in Satan?"

"My lady!" We heard Osedis rejoice from below. Thank the gods, Aislinn was stalled a moment by the happy little devil, who was begging Aislinn to carry him to the attic.

With a charming, childlike squeal, Yasmin finished fastening her collar. She darted to the threshold, arms open wide to receive her friend. I leaned against the wall with a huff and crossed my arms, but my eyes twinkled with amusement. Aislinn was the only person on the face of the Earth who could interrupt without me cursing the interloper to oblivion and beyond.

I only hope this doesn't take too long. The fire in my veins required Yasmin's cooling influence... her touch, her sweet lips upon mine.

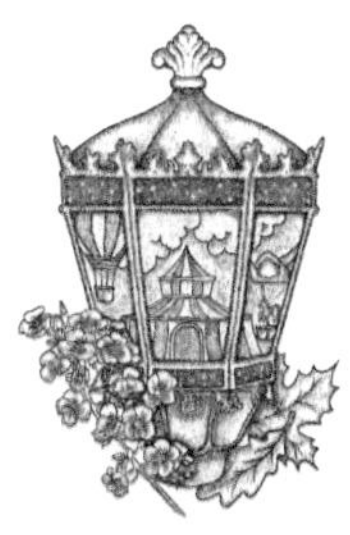
47

HOUSE VINCENZO PART 3

Yasmin

MY BEAUTIFUL AISLINN LOOKED like herself again. Still flushed from Sergio's passion, I rushed into her warm, golden arms with a laugh that echoed throughout the manor. She embraced me fervently and kissed me on the lips. On an impulse I couldn't explain, I kissed her back without one particle of doubt or shame. *Just this once, anyway.*

Once I withdrew, I kissed her forehead as well, standing on tiptoes to accomplish it. "Sergio rescued *both* of us? Dear, this is rather too good to be true. Pinch me, for surely I am dreaming!"

"Gladly." Aislinn obliged my whim. Giggling, we hugged again, exerting our best efforts not to cry. "And now to celebrate a Yule to crown all Yules," the Celt smiled. "Let's search this mansion top to bottom and see what else the ringmaster has to decorate with."

"Wonderful!"

An impish snort recalled us to Osedis's existence, leaning against the wall where Aislinn had just propped him. Unlike Sergio (who habitually forgot to be careful), she dropped the cane softly and made sure the cobra's face was pointed away from the wall so Osedis could see what was happening. "So, your tethering incantation worked," Osedis dryly remarked for Aislinn's benefit. Truthfully, there was no way to *prove* whether it had worked, or whether Rothadamas had ensured my restoration himself; but there was no need to crush Aislinn's pride by suggesting it. "I won't ask how it felt to wake up in a decade-old coffin, Yasmin, and you won't tell me." He wrinkled his pert little nose. "Dearest Lady Aislinn, do me the honor of carrying me far away from this bloody attic."

Aislinn laughingly obliged, cradling the cane in one arm with a faintly maternal pose. I heard Sergio stifle a snort. "I'm sorry, Osedis," Aislinn crooned. "Naturally, you wouldn't want to be anywhere near it." Lifting the cane, she kissed the bronze cobra on the head. He pretended to wince, but we all saw the glint in his slanted eyes. *He* is *rather cute,* I admitted to myself. *I wonder if he intends to stay in this form, even while he pretends to despise it?*

I beckoned to my ringmaster, who observed our reunion with amused forbearance. Hooking one arm through Sergio's and the other through Aislinn's, I practically skipped down the stairs, my feet light as feathers. We all chattered at once.

"Obliged to you, Aislinn," Sergio was saying. "If you hadn't trapped the demon in time—"

"Feel free to thank me with gifts. 'Tis the season, after all—"

"For shame, you Celtic sprite! You shan't abuse my Sergio just because he's rich now!"

"Oh, ho, ho! He's *your* Sergio, is he? And what about me?"

"I suppose we're obligated to adopt you—"

"I'll haunt you if you don't."

"We're already haunted, darling. Sergio! Don't pinch me. Keep your hands to yourself, if you please."

"Woman, I've waited over a decade to get my hands on you. If you think I've got an ounce more patience to spare, you're sorely mistaken."

"You'll horrify the staff! They'll quit."

"Not at all, my angel. They've walked in on me trying to summon spirits. At least flirtation is *normal*."

"Yassy, that makes the *sixth* Christmas tree. I'm beginning to suspect your ringmaster has a weakness for Christmas."

"No, not I," he protested. "My maids do."

"Liar!" I crowed.

"Impossible! My tongue isn't on fire. Actually, in a manner of speaking—"

"Sergio!"

"You liked it in the attic."

"We're not *in* the attic."

Aislinn groaned. "Just so you two are aware, the *only* way I'm going to tolerate being around your lovesick shenanigans is if you throw me a crumb or two in the interim. Feed me tasty treats, and you shan't hear a word of complaint."

"Oh, how naughty," Sergio purred—willfully misinterpreting her comment, as the infuriating man would. "Will you two kiss again, Yassy girl? I've no objection—"

"*Sergio!*"

And the weary walking stick concluded, "You're mad, the lot of you."

The cherry and black-oak paneling lent House Vincenzo a solemn opulence. Seasonal red, gold, and green velvet embellished the furniture. Sergio's dark red flames billowed in the fireplaces. And instead of classic

Christian baubles and imagery, pentagrams and Witch Knots sparkled from evergreen branches.

"It's as if I decorated it myself," I said, darting Sergio an impish look.

"You possessed me for months, ghost-witch. You practically *did* decorate it yourself."

A coy smile painted my lips. "I'll never let you forget it, sir."

He pulled me behind the grand room's tree to kiss me again.

Thus commenced the happiest season of my renewed life.

Sergio and I spoiled each other, living like royalty. Spiced hot chocolate, bow-wrapped truffles, sparkling wine, and home-baked treats flowed from the gothic kitchen. Music played at any and all hours (for Sergio knew I'd been deprived of it), and though Aislinn kept her cottage, she stayed with us so frequently that our neighbors concluded she'd moved in.

Such games we played! The three of us were as carefree as children. My Sergio's boisterous laughter and Aislinn's fae mirth rendered my heart so happy, there were times I thought it might burst. Osedis remained in cheerful spirits, too, plaguing or delighting Sergio as he took the notion, or gazing adoringly upon Aislinn as she recited winter fairy tales by candlelight.

But the best times were the quiet ones. I'd curl up on the rosy couch in the den, book in hand, eyes occasionally prying themselves from the intriguing pages to gaze into Sergio's garnet flames. He'd find me there. My ringmaster—for I shall always think of him so—stomped inside the cozy den, kicked off his boots, and snatched the novel from my hand, sitting down and pillowing my head in his lap as he read aloud in his rich, expressive voice. Then Aislinn would hear him and come, too. She'd curl up on the carpet near me and hold my hand, listening with a soft smile, her lovely eyes closed.

Once, while we were thus situated, the butler asked Sergio to come approve this or that project. Sergio folded a blanket beneath my head, kissing my brow. "I'll be back in a minute, beloved."

I could feel the stars sparkling in my eyes as I watched him leave, his muscular back and shoulders tempting me to run after him.

Aislinn's eyes opened as she lifted her head from the couch. "What is it?" she asked, for as my attention shifted to her face, my smile bore a touch of sadness.

"Crow's feet," I said, raising a finger to brush them in a loving gesture. "You didn't have them before."

She sighed, rubbing the corner of her eye with a brief, self-conscious motion. "All those beauty enchantments I cast on myself are gone. I haven't..."

Her sky-blue eyes welled with tears. She swallowed hard, forcing them back. "I haven't been able to cast a single spell. I'm not like Sergio; I don't carry the Craft in my bloodline."

"Neither do I, love," I gently reminded her. "And let me tell you something." I propped myself up on one elbow. "Your beauty is *natural* now, and I like it much better than that false porcelain preservation you cast on yourself."

She grinned, sitting up straight to tug my ashen hair. "You never did like my beauty charms, did you, you gray-haired hag?"

"How dare you!"

We tussled for a minute, giggling, until Aislinn pushed me back against the couch, proclaiming victory. "I want to stay with you forever," she smiled, nestling her glowing cheek against mine. "I... I know you love Sergio. You've adored him for half your life. After everything you've been through, you deserve all the happiness in the world with him. But do you think you could preserve a little corner of your heart for your Celtic sprite?"

"More than just a corner, darling!"

We embraced as Sergio returned to the den. He huffed, tossing himself next to me with a playful pout. "I see how it is. I leave for two seconds and you're fawning all over that Celtic fairy."

Beaming, I stroked his long hair. "I adore you both, beloved, but the shrine within my heart upholds your image, and yours alone. My dearest, devilish Dragon."

Sergio's mouth curved into a satisfied grin. He tucked me into the crook of his arm. "Bet she's not half as good a kisser as I am, either," he whispered against my hair.

"Sergio Vincenzo!" I flushed. Yet I secretly loved his jealousy, just as he had once loved to summon mine.

"About those beauty charms," Osedis was saying to Aislinn. "I might be of service to you, my lady."

My ringmaster proposed to me by the caravan that had once been my home. Eloquent and sincere as his speech was, he couldn't suppress a diabolical grin or two. I laughed helplessly through my joyous tears, for I knew what that look was for! That antique caravan was special, indeed, and Sergio had sent for it from across the sea to preserve our memories. He was thinking about all the insults, the arguments, the commandments and the teasing double talk... and about the time he kissed the top of my head as we sat on the narrow stairs together, baring our black souls without fear.

Sergio slipped the plain, white-gold band onto my pale finger.

After my emotional acceptance, he offered me his arm. We walked together as he smoked his pipe and discussed wedding plans. I took his cane and swung it lightly to and fro, content from my fingertips to my toes. Osedis grumbled but submitted to this treatment, aware that Sergio would not countenance interruptions.

"I want to get married right here," I decided. We stopped to bestow mutual gazes of pride upon House Vincenzo. "And I don't want to travel for our honeymoon, either. I'm happy right where we are."

To my surprise, Sergio hesitated. He drew a long, thoughtful pull at his fancy pipe before replying. "Believe me, Yassy, I feel the same, and it would be easier for Lillias and her man to attend... though explaining how you've come back from the dead is the toughest assignment of this entire endeavor! But..."

"She's got a level head, dear, and she remembers Roth—*him*—when she holds my diary. I'll give it to her again. Even if she remains confused, she'll accept your explanation once you show her your pyrocraft skills. As for her husband, he needn't know anything about my past. So why dost thou hesitate, my lord?" For everything was possible with Sergio beside me.

He smiled, his gloriously mismatched eyes aglow. The glow vanished as his parted lips dropped the name, "Rothadamas."

A thrill of unease trickled down my spine.

As long as none of us mentioned him or referenced Kheima in any way, it was surprisingly easy to forget him. To pretend Kheima didn't exist. To forget that there was no way to be eternally safe from him. Forcing him to regrow the Tree bought us time, but nothing more. It did not buy us protection.

Sergio slipped a comforting arm around my waist. "I think it's safe to suppose that he's moved on to bigger and better things. We're sly little fish to have escaped from his net, but at the end of the day, we're only three little fish in the sea." He puffed his pipe again, forehead creased in thought. "However, it might be a good idea to travel for the wedding and honeymoon. Maybe we ought to be elsewhere. He knows where we live, and he might try to... Well, he might try something on our special day."

Sergio didn't want to worry me with specifics. To his misfortune, my imagination was yet in excellent working order, so my mind played the scene: a horrifying demon crashing the wedding and stealing the bride. *And she was never seen again.*

I shuddered. Sergio's hand caressed my waist. "It's springtime, beloved. The new year has come and gone without him trying anything. As I said, chances are he's moved on from us, but safe is better than sorry when it comes to my long-awaited bride." He lifted my hand and kissed it.

I shook my head, lips pursing into a thin line. "I refuse to be intimidated. We belong in House Vincenzo; we shall be married in it. I've let fear rule my life *and* afterlife combined, and I shall have no more of it! So let us be brave, Sergio, and do precisely what we want to do."

Sergio bowed. "I hear and obey, my lady."

We recommenced our eager plans. Not once did I ever imagine myself *getting married*, so I cited only three absolutes: Roses, an ivory gown, and Aislinn as my cherished bridesmaid.

48

MINE

Sergio

RED MAPLE LEAVES BLESSED the roof of House Vincenzo.

I sprang down the stairs three at a time, singing at the top of my lungs. "Ouch! Damnation," I grumbled, careening to a stop to favor my pathetic knee. Lillias laughed at my boyish spirits. "Well, I pity dear Yassy and no mistake! You'll plague her life out." She straightened my tie, then patted my rogue hair into place.

Snorting out smoke, I inflated my chest. My daughter rolled her cinnamon eyes. "Explain yourself," I demanded.

Lillias checked my gloves next, well aware of my tendency to ruin them before the event had even begun. "I refer to your charming husbandly tendencies, including but not limited to marching around the house in muddy boots, humming and singing at the crack of dawn due to insomnia, and," leaning close to my neck and sniffing, wrinkling her dimpled nose, "Smelling like smoke and saffron the vast majority of the time."

"Yasmin likes it. She calls me the Dragon Emperor... sometimes. And if she can't chase me around to scold me for my muddy boots and my singing, how else is she going to amuse herself all day?" I chuckled, directing Lillias to hand me my cane. I'd have to place it aside for the ceremony itself, but I could lean on it until the last minute. My blasted knee throbbed. "She's spoiled rotten; she'll never have to see the inside of a kitchen again unless she wants to. Or sew a stitch, either."

"I'm sure she's thanking God for that," Lillias giggled, passing Osedis to me. "She hated sewing!" She kissed my cheek and hugged me, her soft tresses brushing my freshly-trimmed beard. "I know you'll be a good husband," she said, dropping her teasing tones. "The very best. I'm *so* happy for you both, Papa!"

"Thank you, Lillykins."

I squeezed her hand. She bestowed one last, glowing smile before scurrying back to Ulysses.

Heading for the chapel, I rolled my shoulders and flexed my hands. Osedis's rattling voice cracked my romantic rumination. "I must confess, I'm truly honored that you chose *me* as your best man," the little devil acknowledged, "despite the fact it's just between the four of us."

I grinned. "My best *devil*, you mean. It wouldn't do to present a cane as the best man, you understand. Yet no one deserves the honor more than you."

"... Thank you, Sergio." Osedis sniffled, unwilling emotion rising in his ruby eyes.

I grasped the handle gently, striding toward the chapel doors as they swung open for their master. *Yasmin Vincenzo, lady of the manor.* At long last... *long* last... She would be mine.

And I would devour every inch of her until she screamed my name.

49

LADY VINCENZO

Yasmin

Safely enclosed in the dressing room—a veritable bower of yellow hothouse roses—Aislinn helped me into my ivory dress.

I'd refused to wear a veil since I'd worn one in Kheima; for me, too many painful memories were associated with veils, including one memorable yet excruciating night when I witnessed the Fair of Phantoms for the first time, praying my ringmaster would not recognize me. No more veils for Yasmin Lange. Sergio would see my glowing, living face as I walked down the aisle to him. There would be nothing to remind us of our paranormal torment—no gothic crowns, no gray (besides my hair which could not be helped), and absolutely no thorns left on a single rose I carried.

However, I still loved the winter and the cold. 'Tis part of who I was—what my spirit would ever cling to. Whether listening to Sergio read aloud by firelight, or recalling his divine storytelling by the circus troupe's campfire, or tucking my arm a little more tightly through his as we navigated the circus tents, a sharp chill in the air still brought happy memories.

As I stared at myself in the full-length mirror, a brief memory of my Kheiman crown flashed a ghost of its horrid shape around my bare head. I blinked hard, turning away. When I looked back in the mirror, it was gone. *Don't think about him. Don't spare him a single solitary thought.*

Aislinn's warm hand grabbed mine. "You're cold!" She tenderly cupped my fingers between both her hands. "You've faced far more terrifying fates than marriage to a dragon shifter, darling. Don't tell me you have cold feet as well as cold hands?"

"Just cold hands," I reassured her. I kissed her cheek in thanks. "Might I have a moment?"

"Of course. Knock when you're ready."

Aislinn drifted out the door, breathtaking in her honey-hued dress overlain with a lace sheath. Despite the gentle aging in her face, she continued to make men and women alike stop in their tracks. An elegant aura of wisdom radiated from her countenance. *A woman who has indeed beheld other realms.* I smiled after her until the door closed. *I'm no matchmaker, but I'll make sure to introduce her to any compatible single women I meet.*

I turned back to the mirror and shivered. *Strange. I always get cold all over when Rothadamas is near... No, it's just nerves. Just nerves!*

Black static rippled over the mirror's surface.

No...

The demon's statuesque form slowly materialized.

No!

Jolting back, I tripped on my short train and fell on the carpet. I scrambled back from the mirror, choking on rising sobs. "No!"

His gem-encrusted wings sparkled in candelabra light. He lifted those long, white claws, motioning for silence. Utterly serene, his crystal-blue eyes and pale pupils lingered on my wedding dress. "Do not be afraid, Anmut," his cursedly flawless German echoed from the mirror. "I have not come to claim you."

Somehow, I believed him. Something about his eyes... I dried my tears, nodding for him to continue. Part of me despised how easily I cried compared to how I was before—part of me still confused emotional openness with weakness.

Silence fell as the forest demon absorbed my image, from my bare head to my satin slippers. I fumbled to my feet, casting the train out of my way. The wedding gown flowed around my body like water.

Dread had frozen my lungs. I had to remind myself to breathe. "Warum bist du gekommen?"[1] I dared to ask.

His pupils flickered to my wedding finger, bare—though not for much longer. "To see you, Anmut. To behold thee one last time before you belong to the Dragon."

Puzzled, I wanted to reply, but I couldn't think of a single intelligent remark. Rothadamas studied me as if to commit every inch of me to eternal memory. There was nothing hateful or possessive about his demeanor. It was *sad*. As my heart recognized the aching, detached, profound sadness... a loneliness I could certainly understand... I found my eyes were watering again.

For Rothadamas.

"I have made my decision," he intoned, touching his fingertips together. I clasped my arms, suppressing another deep shiver. "In acknowledgment

---

1. Why have you come?

of your matchless service at my right hand, I shall permit you a happy life with Sergio. I shall not impose upon your house, nor enslave Sergio, nor touch the lives of anyone else among your friends and family."

His dreadful voice suddenly sounded like music to my ears, resonant with thrumming, heavenly beauty. I caught my breath again—not from terror, but from awe.

"Aislinn is safe as well," the fallen angel pledged. I covered my mouth as I betrayed a sharp gasp. His sly, thin smile acknowledged my shock. "In exchange for this mercy, upon the moment of your death, your soul shall once again belong to me. Permanently. Upon his death, Sergio shall be mine as well." He paused to emphasize his point. "From this eternal life in Kheima, there shall be no escape."

My anger swallowed my fear as my hands curled into fists. "And if I decline to *ever* be yours again?"

"Then I'll take you here and now."

"Sergio rescued me once. He can do it again."

"Not with the new safeguards I have established," Rothadamas coolly replied, "and he'll find my regrown Tree admirably immune to Dracoblod fire. Alas, millennia of guardianship rendered me listless; your Dragon tested me. Henceforth, he shall find me unbreakable."

"Why?" I yelled, leaning close to the mirror to scream at his motionless face. "Why do you persecute us so, you damnable demon?" By God, I'd just shed *tears* for him, the hateful monster!

My rage demanded action. I snatched up a vase from the vanity, intent upon smashing the mirror and scattering his image beyond repair. He held up both hands to dissuade me, commanding, "Yasmin!"

He spoke my name. My *real* name.

I lowered the vase.

"*Danke.*"[2] He lowered his hands, too. His tranquil voice dropped to a near-whisper. And the forest demon said something that astonished me so much, I would spend the rest of my new life trying to discern fact from fiction.

Regardless of his true intentions, there was but one rational choice to make.

Aislinn stepped forward and took my bouquet. My hands shook as I placed them in Sergio's gloved palms. He waited until the priest began before leaning close and whispering, "Is everything all right, beloved?"

"Yes. I'm with you."

His grip on my hands tightened as he beamed down at me. "I'm glad you decided not to wear a veil."

"So am I."

Our vows passed in a blur. I removed his glove to adorn his tan, calloused hand with a gold ring. He removed my ivory glove and presented a diamond ring, its precious stones arranged to catch the light in sparkling clusters, like stars. "I told you not to do it," I fiercely whispered.

"Humbug," he whispered back. "I saw the way your eyes lit up when you saw it. You wanted it, so here it is."

The priest gave us a look. We fell guiltily silent, awaiting our turns to say the magic words.

I do.

---

2. Thank you.

The ceremony and the grand hall reception danced by uninterrupted. Our united social circle was small but dearly beloved, and we waltzed down the gothic halls with feet as light as air, rejoicing in our love and our freedom.

In spite of my smiles, a voracious question gnawed at my consciousness. Should I tell him? Or should I allow my husband to relish our life together without shouldering the same burden I carried?

The burden of our eternal fate.

50

No More Secrets

Sergio

THREE MONTHS POST-WEDDING, YASMIN and I settled into married life. A solid argument or two (or perhaps three, I didn't count) sufficed to bring us down from the newlywed high, and the *Dragon King* and *Beryl's Daughter* anchored in calmer waters. To be frank, I preferred it. After a tumultuous life of cursed circuses, demon wagers, and possession, the honest joys of a normal life with my Yassy were a welcome change.

Also... I wasn't getting any younger.

Yasmin was happy. Her gray eyes sparkled silver, her thin body flushed and filled out, and there was a spring in her step as she swept through the mansion with the house keys jingling from her proud châtelaine. Nevertheless, my wife silently lamented the loss of her magical prowess. She never realized it herself, but her dark Craft had surpassed Aislinn's in impact, accuracy, and range; it was only natural she would miss it. A few times, she pointed to an object she wanted, wordlessly commanding it to move and come to her—and when it didn't budge, she'd utter a short, pained laugh, lowering her hand as her face flushed.

While Aislinn openly mourned her loss, Yasmin privately bemoaned her own.

It was no surprise to me. I had expected Yasmin to "weep a little weep," then accept her normalcy, returning to cheerful spirits. However, something weighed her down. She'd start to tell me something, then shake her head and change the subject.

Endeavoring to strengthen my patience—which she frequently mentioned was in dire need of exercise—I waited for her to pour her heart out to me. Once six months had passed and that crease of worry on her forehead appeared to be permanent, I cradled her in my lap and demanded to know her secret.

"There's no secret, Sergio."

"Blows and botheration! You know something that I don't. Something that concerns you and makes you sad. What else should I call it but a damned secret?"

She exhaled a long sigh, rested her forehead against mine and closing her eyes. "All right. I'll be pulling a shadow over our lives, my love, and I hate to do it, but you have a right to know. An eternal right."

"Eternal right?" I lovingly chucked her under the chin. "You're so deliciously intense when you're unraveling your thoughts. Unravel your heart to me, beloved, and I'll help you untangle the snag, wherever it is."

"Thank you, husband."

"What else are husbands for, wife?"

She spoke slowly and evenly at first. Then her words poured faster, flooding my brain with a perplexing gush. Once she finished, she held both my hands and kissed my fingertips. "Was I right to tell you? Please don't be angry with me."

"I'm not angry," I grunted, gently removing her from my lap so I could pace the bedroom floor, hands clasped behind my back. "I'm confused. Pleasantly confused."

"*Pleasantly* confused, sir? Pray share whatever you find *pleasant* about it."

"Haven't you dissected what he said? 'Reject me and choose the way of fire. Accept me and choose the way of ice. Though both elements are painful, one destroys while the other preserves. Choose eternal life.'"

Yasmin tilted her pretty head. "I thought he meant that he would destroy our souls if we didn't accept his offer. Typical demonic manipulation. What on earth is pleasant about that?"

I ceased pacing. I bent over her, cupping her dear face between my hands. "Listen, darling. You were a witch. Not only that, but a demon's right-hand sorceress and later on, his queen. As for me, I'm not only a warlock, but a half-blood. An unlawful descendant of dragons."

In order to explain further, I nearly recited the legend of the first dragon and his human mate, but I resisted the temptation. As I mentioned before, not a story for the faint of heart—though my wife was anything but that. It was kinder to spare her the ugly story.

"Yes." She nodded. Her pupils locked onto my lips. She couldn't resist a quick kiss.

I grinned, lowering my hands. "Don't distract me, woman. As I was saying, unless we both suddenly conjure up a miraculous fund of saving faith—not likely, seeing as we're both quite fatalistic—we're banned from Heaven. Irrevocably barred from entering the pearly gates. Which means that without Rothadamas making his offer..." I waited for her to catch on.

Her silvery eyes flew open wide. "We go to Hell."

"Precisely. Hell. Excruciating fire, chains, nightmares, gnashing of teeth. The Second Death."

Yasmin's slow smile was delicious. "But since I accepted his offer—"

"We'll be in Kheima instead, which is no Heaven, of course. Yet it is the lesser of two evils. Rothadamas willing, we'll retain some measure of identity and agency. And we'll be together." I shrugged. "Besides, Kheima *is* beautiful, and not so dark since you co-reigned there. He even took fewer souls thanks to your influence on him. You might continue to soften him until enhancing the Garden becomes his sole objective, instead of soul-hunting from sheer boredom."

I stroked her hair as her forehead puckered with musing. "He was trying to shield me all this time," she murmured, emotion thick in her voice. "Shield *us*."

"Not the whole time, I wager. He's a demon. He squeezed every last drop of use out of you, didn't he?"

"Yes, that's true. He did." She twirled her thumbs, lashes aflutter with amazement. "But it makes me think. How many times was he punishing me because *he had no choice*? How many times did he treat me cruelly because he was bound to do so? What laws dictated and restricted his conduct, and continue to suppress his true desires? That entire time, I only ever thought of myself!"

"That doesn't change the fact that he used you until you went mad. I had to restore your sanity, tame the wild ghost. Don't blot out the black to paint it white, Yassy darling. He's gray at best. Dark gray."

"Yes, dear."

She folded her hands together and smiled up at me. I scooped her back up into my arms, cradling her and cooing loving nonsense into her ear. "You know I can't resist you when you pretend to be obedient."

"I don't know what you mean. I'm the most obedient wife this side of Kheima."

51

FIRST YULE OF MANY

Yasmin

I blinked, and I was celebrating my first Yule as Lady Vincenzo.

I stoked the fire in the grand room, smothering a twinge of envy as I contemplated Sergio's brilliant, enchanted red flames. Although I was certain he loved me without the Craft flowing through my veins, I missed it. Sometimes I still held out my hands and tried casting a spell from sheer habit. One time, I even walked straight into a wall, still expecting to float through it. I thought Sergio would die from his resulting fit of laughter.

But misery loves company, and at least I had that. Aislinn and I comforted each other through our mutual loss. "We're alive, we're healthy, and we're all together," Aislinn's rejoicing uplifted me. "Every moment we spend complaining is a moment we'll never get back."

How right she was.

Sergio's bloodlight embraced my ivory dress, braced with a scarlet girdle and a dragon pin. A cluster of holly bristled next to my châtelaine. I raised my head and smiled, brushing my lace-gloved hands together as I surveyed the mansion's main room.

House Vincenzo really ought to be called Castle Vincenzo. Its floor plan was gloriously open. The vaulted, beamed ceiling dazzled the eye with subtle touches of gem-cut colored glass, placed to cast a starlike glitter over the dark paneling. Sergio instructed his staff to switch out the colors according to the seasons. Red, green, and gold formed his Yuletide trinity.

Suspended from the center dangled a masterpiece of a chandelier. Five tiers of delicate gold horses in circus trappings trotted, cantered, or posed in slow revolution. They seemed alive in the dancing glow of candlelight.

To the left of the immense gothic fireplace glowered a matching gilt-patterned clock. Cut from dark-stained wood like the rest of the room, its face showed an arrangement of cauldrons (hour), potion bottles (minute), and the outstretched wand of a cloaked magician indicating the seconds. Four spellbooks decorated the borders—light green, gold, orange, and silver—of which one opened and the other three closed, according to the season. All custom made, I knew.

I teased Sergio for this extravagance, and he laughed me to scorn. "What use is a man's hard-earned fortune if he can't be extravagant, pray tell?" I supposed he had a point.

To the right of the fireplace preened our Yule tree. Aislinn and I made pagan ornaments and gleefully plastered them from star to tree skirt, scandalizing the majority of the Christian staff, no doubt.

Sergio didn't object to my pagan nonsense; in fact, he thrived in it, throwing himself headlong into my strange projects. How deliciously true to form! At long last, we were free to revel in our true selves. To that end, this darling husband of mine had the unmitigated gall to chase me into the empty Vincenzo chapel and do some vastly unholy things to me there.

My face burned at the memory: how he tore my corset and lifted me, placing me on the offering table. How his slitted pupils gleamed, his smoky breath whispered, and his scarlet scales flashed along his arms, so mirror-bright that I could see my awestruck face reflecting in them. In part-draco form he pinned my helpless, flushed body. Savage and domineering and insatiable, but murmuring the tenderest words all the while.

I yanked Memory back from her wicked recollections, biting my lip. My fingers brushed the ruddy imprints on my neck where his grasp had summoned whimpers and near-screams of pleasure. Not once in a lifetime of Sundays had I considered the ecstasy of violent intimate play... nor would I have thought myself the type to enjoy it. But from the first day he trained me as an aerialist, Sergio revealed hidden passions that burned undiscovered within me, begging for release. For *acceptance.*

And he accepted them all.

Drawing a deep breath, I redirected my attention to the grand room. Holiday furnishings, card and chess tables (with a circus-themed chess set gleaming with the haunts of former decimations), wine cubbies, cabinets specially for cakes and teatime sweets, bunches of holly and evergreen tucked in corners. Beneath a locked glass dome, my worn diary rejoiced in sweet repose; only Sergio and I knew where the key was. He liked to lean against the mantelpiece and watch his fire glow—vain man—and therefore preferred to keep my diary displayed there, though I didn't find it congenial.

Alas, I discovered that marriage was often about compromise, but I was learning to be a gracious wife. Sergio had made impressive strides toward becoming a model husband. Oh, he'd never "make it," of course—he was far too flawed—yet I loved his flaws more dearly than I'd love him all polished, smooth perfection. A perfect husband would bore and irritate me until I was all too glad to escape mortal life again.

That strain of thought reminded me of my final deal with Rothadamas. My other husband, in a manner of speaking. My *eternal* husband. Sometimes I caught myself wondering if he missed me. He didn't seem a demigod to me anymore, but a secretly pathetic forest angel with wings that did not work, and a queenly gothic crown perched upon the arm of an icy, empty throne. Waiting for its missing queen.

Anxiety stirred in my heart. I quashed it as it raised its ugly head. At times I was beset by worries of what nightmares eternity may hold… and yet, my last interaction with Rothadamas gave me hope. 'Twas a dim hope, but a tiny elfin light gleamed at the end of the tunnel. Sergio said that I had influenced Rothadamas for the better.

Did I, truly? I was so wrapped up in my own dark woes, I didn't pay much heed to the demon's softening. But when written out on plain paper, it did appear to ring true. Fewer children were taken when I took the crown, and I'd arranged chores for the Kheiman children, keeping them busy with useful home-bound tasks that kept their little cursed hands from working evil elsewhere. I encouraged the forest demon's interest in celebrating his realm by virtue of altars, serpent springs, ombre glaciers, and dark-ice cathedrals. The Tree itself sparkled with ornaments that danced among its forbidden fruit, at my suggestion.

And—most crucial of all—I taught our citizens to sing.

Musical instruments were banned in Kheima, as I knew to my sorrow; attempting to build my own harp had resulted in supernatural accidents that only an eternal curse could explain. But when the weary denizens of the winter forest lifted their voices in song, hope blossomed. It was timid and fragile as the snow that scattered over our specterous heads, but it was *hope.*

Perhaps beautifying a frigid hell seemed worthless to some and laughable to others... but those who laugh at the notion of hope in Hell shall be the last to receive it.

Wrapped in melancholy reverie, I missed Sergio's impending intrusion. Suddenly, his bulky arm was 'round my neck, and his hearty kiss smothered my coiffed locks. "Down, boy!" I exclaimed, patting my hair back in place. "It's the first time my hair has ever been shaped into the latest fashion, and here cometh the Dragon to set fire to it."

He laughed. I smiled, leaning back against him and touching his wrist. My husband kissed me again. His heterochromatic irises were filled with so much light, it was a wonder they didn't overflow with it. I imagined pure sunshine flowing down his cheeks and soaking his beard. "Do you like your new maid?" he asked, menacing my collarbone next. "She's under strict instructions to fatten you up, my good wife. You're still far too skinny."

I tilted my head back, settling it against his shoulder. A rare flash of mischief curved my coral lips. "I'm far too busy feasting on *you*, Master."

"Hmm." His shameless hand slipped from collarbone to waist, ensuring there was not a fraction of distance between us as he kissed me deeply.

Sergio's scarlet bliss chased my blues away. I wouldn't worry about the future anymore. Not now that I was his. No matter what eternity held for us, my Sergio was worth the price.

Once we separated, I nodded at his walking stick currently perched against the Yule tree. A red bow was tied around the serpent's neck. "What's Osedis all dressed up for?"

My husband's devilish smile invited me to kiss him again. "He's my gift to Aislinn, at his own request."

My face brightened as I gasped with delight. "Sergio! You're a darling!"

He snorted, waving my gratitude aside with pseudo-carelessness. "I haven't got any use for that blathering Noodle, and he won't shut up about being bonded to Aislinn to become the source of her Craft. Not that she'll be as powerful as she was before, but it's better than nothing."

"He doesn't wish to be released from the cane?" I asked, thoroughly astounded.

"Only if Aislinn does not wish to bond with him. I have a sneaking suspicion he needn't worry about that."

I kissed him yet again. A lifetime of kissing him would never be enough. *Good thing we have eternity.* "This is quite possibly the happiest Yule of my life."

"Of *our* lives, exasperating woman of mine."

Twenty Years Later

52

Autumn Comes to Kheima

Narrator

Yasmin opened her eyes in Kheima.

There were two things she noticed right away: She was holding someone's glowing hand, and that hand was Sergio's. "You're here," Yasmin smiled at her husband.

Sergio grinned boyishly, no longer in his sixties but returned to the strength of his prime. He wore soft, dark pants and shoes and a white collared shirt with the sleeves rolled up, showing off his plethora of tattoos. A burgundy cape lined with gold thread was carelessly hanging from one broad shoulder, only halfway on. "Of course I'm here, Yassy! I've been waiting for you."

At one glance, Yasmin absorbed that she, too, had been returned to her prime years, postmortem. She turned her attention to their eternal abode. The atmosphere remained chilly, but noticeably warmer than before. Crisp instead of frigid. Trickles of melting snow dared to peep from the black soil. The sky was iron gray instead of star-smocked black. A slip of sunlight even dared to touch the horizon, timid and tenuous.

Sunlight.

Yasmin blinked, uncertain if her specter eyes deceived her. "Sergio? I know we're dead, but where under earth *are* we?"

"Eden," her dragon shifter replied, his marvelous voice low and soft. He drew her closer to kiss her temple. "Welcome home."

Inhaling deeply, Yasmin rejoiced in the soothing change in the air. It felt more like autumn instead of winter. "It's different. It feels like... a glass of lemonade after a long day in the heat. Instead of ice in the dead of winter, forced down one's throat." She stretched, relaxed from her fingers to her toes.

Sergio nodded, quite accustomed to her morbid phraseology. "And there's something else. I've been tending it for you. Come with me!"

Grasping her wrist, he tugged her along after his massive strides just as he used to, fiery energy fully restored. Yasmin laughed and tripped over her skirt as she tumbled after him. "I see you missed me, husband."

His dashing eyes sparkled at he beamed over his shoulder. "More than you'll ever know, wife." His specter-form gleamed a subtle pale gold, contrasting yet complementing Yasmin's pale blue.

Sergio led her to the edge of the frozen waterfall—formerly one of Yasmin's precious haunts as the lonely Kheiman Queen—but the water no longer stared motionless in solid introspection. It flowed as a waterfall ought to flow into a dark, churning river. Still intimidating and mysterious, full of ice-cold secrecy and not a speck of life, but it was *flowing water*. "Wha—how—when?" Yasmin spluttered, dropping Sergio's glowing hand in her shock. "Did *you* do all this?"

"In a way," Sergio admitted, stroking his short beard. Tiny glints of red shone in its black-mahogany stubble. "I may have challenged Rothadamas to another wager or two."

Lady Vincenzo leveled a steely glare.

He held up his hands in self-defense. "What? I got bored! And I only lost once, but never fear! 'Twas a small price to pay in the face of eternity. Besides, it amuses both of us. It's better fun than chess!" He shrugged, standing akimbo. His cape draped over one arm. "Believe it or not, we're getting along well these days."

Yasmin sighed and shook her head, but her silvery eyes gleamed with pride. "Well, once upon a time, you did describe yourself as 'a devil in my own line.' You were right."

"Quite so!" Sergio flexed, summoning Yasmin's mirth anew. "He rolls his cursed eyes at my ideas ever and anon, but overall, I daresay we are friends. And you, Yassy..."

He snatched her up in his arms and kissed her hard. Once he finally released her, she pushed him away and giggled. "Is there anything else you wanted to show me, husband?"

"*Assolutamente!*" Seizing her hand again, he took her behind the waterfall to show a small, mossy cavern. Alight with sparkling frost, yet somehow abloom, there grew a dark-green rosebush fraught with blue roses, as blue as Sergio's right eye.

Speechless, Yasmin turned her baffled gaze from the sapphire petals to Sergio's beaming face, and back again. "Remind you of anything in particular, Yassy?" he asked, mockingly grave. She elbowed him. "How dare you!"

The cavern echoed his boisterous laughter. His wife flew at him, initiating a tussle as she upbraided him with bitter commentary. "It worked, didn't it, thou sterling witch?" the Dragon gleefully snorted. "Your little blue rose enchanted me for life. It was a slow-working, slow-acting love charm, but it worked. I'm yours till Second Death do us part... only, there won't be one for us."

He caught his wife by her flailing wrists and held her still, kissing her forehead. "Do you think you can be happy here with me, darling? Forest demon and all. 'Tis a strange fate, but I believe it suits us. We never fit in with the common lot, did we, Yassy girl?"

Yasmin leaned against his chest, listening to the rushing water and smelling the delicate perfume of the enchanted roses. She shook her head again, full to the brim with wonder. "If anyone can make accursed Eden Heaven instead of Hell, it's you, my beloved Sergio."

She relaxed into his warm embrace.

Beyond the glassy curtain of dark water, Rothadamas watched his immortal couple from afar.

A slow smile crossed his alabaster lips. He pointed one long, white forefinger at Yasmin.

A pastel-blue glimmer enveloped her, cloaking the demon's Schattengeist in a matching blue robe that swirled like living starlight. A new crown formed above her flowing locks, bright and whole, reminiscent of thorns but no longer made of them to inflict pain upon its wearer.

With a soft cry of wonder, Yasmin stepped away from Sergio. They spoke in low, surprised tones, then simultaneously glanced past the rush of water, pinpointing the forest demon with their stares.

Rothadamas nodded to Yasmin.

A fierce, triumphant joy embellished her immortal face. She pointed at the rosebush. Sliced by her renewed Craft, one rose was severed from the bush and dropped at her feet.

She knelt to pick it up. Holding it at her waist, Yasmin curtsied deeply to the fallen angel. He bowed his head in return. "Ihre erste Aufgabe kann warten. Willkommen zu Hause, Anmut."[1]

"Thank you, Rothadamas." A pause. "Warum?"[2]

The forest demon steepled his hands, a touch of mischief glinting in his pupils' icy flecks. "Der Fluch der Unsterblichkeit, meine Hexe."[3]

With that dubious statement, he vanished, leaving the witch and the warlock hand in hand, flushed and starry-eyed. For their adventures together were far from over.

They had just begun.

---

1. Your first task can wait. Welcome home, Anmut.

2. Why?

3. The curse of immortality, my witch.

THE END

The first love burns the brightest.

Acknowledgements

Profound gratitude to my beloved readers, especially my friends and family who supported my rash journey into the world of wordsmithery. Like Bilbo Baggins, I charged down the road to adventure with nary a stitch of preparation for the challenges ahead. There's so much left to learn! But thanks to your encouragement, I believed in my potential and forged my own path. Thus, Man Devil Press was born.

Bless you for supporting my mania, husband of mine. I hope to thank you properly by writing a bestseller that buys a cabin in the mountains. A bit far-fetched, perhaps, but if it never comes to fruition, then of course it's the thought that counts.

Affectionate appreciation to my editor and friend, Elise Nelson, whose guidance has been crucial for producing a professional book. I pray you don't despise my proclivity for characters who analyze their emotions half to death.

Special acknowledgement to V. B. Scott, my patient beta reader and a talented scribe who also thrives in classic prose. The possessed cane was his idea, so you can thank him for "Noodle." *Kanpai!*

And last but by no means least, my most humble regards to my sister-in-spirit, Charlotte Brontë. I mayn't have known thee in life, darling, but something in the soul of your writing connected with mine—your passion of restraint, your intimate exploration of the feminine psyche, and the shadows behind the light that is the female life. I've yet to feel so *at one* with another writer as I've felt with you… and I'm not entirely convinced that you didn't possess me while I wrote *The Witch and the Ringmaster*. May we meet in our own world below, with no bitterness in our illusions once deemed fair.